To the delightful Debbie

warmest

8-20-06

RENEGADE LIGHTNING

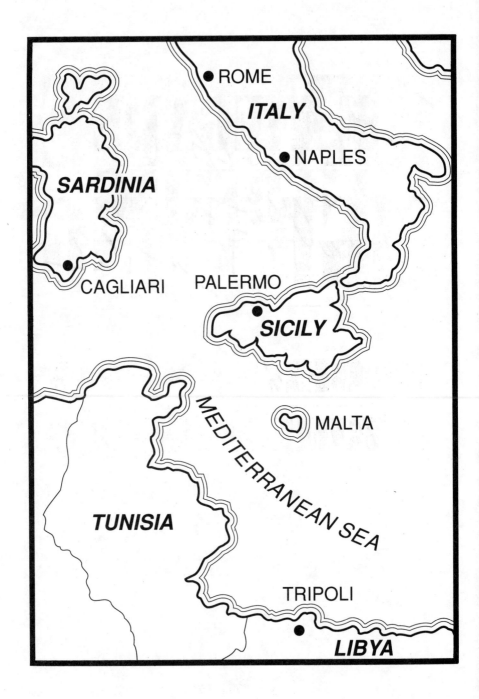

RENEGADE LIGHTNING

ROBERT SKIMIN
FERDIE PACHECO

LYFORD
Books

Although this novel is based on a true story, all characters are fictional and no actual person, living or dead, is depicted therein.

Published by Presidio Press
505 B San Marin Dr., Suite 300
Novato, CA 94945-1340

Library of Congress Cataloging-in-Publicaiton Data

Skimin, Robert.
    Renegade Lightning : a novel / Robert Skimin and Ferdie Pacheco.
      p.   cm.
    ISBN 0-89141-437-1
    I. Pacheco, Ferdie.   II. Title
PS3569.K49R46 1992   91-34462
813'.54—dc20   CIP

Typography by ProImage

Printed in the United States of America

To all of the intrepid flyers of World War II

ACKNOWLEDGMENTS

✤

To Betty and John MacGuire who have, with their own resources, created a remarkable war birds museum outside of El Paso, Texas. Called the War Eagles Museum, its ably staffed, mostly volunteer crew of pilots and mechanics keeps over twenty aged military aircraft flying. One of the full-time staff members, Guy Dority, was a member of the 97th Bomb Group, and this compelling museum is where Robert Skimin got his P-38 cockpit checkout. Thanks also to Dick Miller, John Turner, and Edmund Hicks (historian of the 97th Bomb Group). Two other museums were of assistance: the USAF Museum at Wright Patterson AFB and the San Diego Aerospace Museum.

RENEGADE LIGHTNING

PROLOGUE

✜

United States Air Force Museum, Wright Patterson AFB, Ohio

The man stood staring up at the nose of the B-17 heavy bomber. Olive drab on top with a gray belly, she was a G model. The famous Flying Fortress. The painting on the left side of her nose showed a reclining, pretty blonde in a bathing suit looking back over her left shoulder. *Shoo Shoo Shoo Baby* was lettered beside her. Just below, the twin .50s of the chin turret protruded. He counted the little bombs that had been painted above the blonde—twenty-two of them; this big-assed bird had flown twenty-two combat missions.

Suddenly the years fell away and he was in the left seat of a B-17 cockpit. It was 1943 again. There was turbulence from flak and he was having trouble keeping the big aircraft straight and level. The radio chatter was heavy and insistent: "Two 109s coming in at eight o'clock high!" "I got 'em!" "Focke Wulf at three o'clock low!" "B-17 spinning out at four o'clock." "Close it up! Close it up!" "One-oh-nine at ten o'clock high!" "I'm hit, skipper!"

"You ever fly one of these, mister?"

The man continued to stare at the bomber for a moment before looking down at the boy who had asked the question. He must be about ten, the same age as his youngest grandson, the man thought. The radio chatter from another time was gone. "Why, yes, as a matter of fact, I did."

1

The boy had a splash of freckles across his nose. His eyes widened. "Was it hard to fly?"

The man smiled. "Uh, at times. But it was a great airplane."

"What is a great airplane?"

The man looked up at *Shoo Shoo Shoo Baby* again and thought for a moment before he said, "I guess it's one that brings you home."

The boy's mother came up and said, "Billy, you quit bothering that man!"

Taking his hand, she led him away, protesting, "But Momma, he's a pilot!"

The man tore his eyes away from the Flying Fort and moved on. A small airplane caught his eye. A sleek fighter, it had black and white crosses on it. Glancing down at the sign that described the aircraft, he couldn't believe this was an Me-109, the dreaded German fighter that had made his life hell on so many occasions. No, it couldn't be this small! How many times had he seen one flashing in at his Fort? "Look out! One-oh-nine at five o'clock low!" "One-on-nine coming up behind!"

He heard some more radio chatter from the past as he stared at the famous little Messerschmitt. Actually it was a Bf-l09, but most of the American crew members called it an Me-109.

The Glenn Miller music drifted in: "String of Pearls." Truly memory lane today, he thought.

And speaking of memories, there it was, the P-38!

He tensed, then walked over and stared at the big, twin-engined fighter. It too was painted OD on top and gray on the bottom. It was an L model, but is was dolled up with shiny chrome spinners on the props. Beautiful, deadly airplane. . . . He clenched his fists as more radio chatter came out of the past, a P-38 coming at him with blazing guns. Those quad-.50s and the 20mm cannon flashing from its nose, dealing death, terror—

"Pennsylvania six, five, oh, oh, oh."

He took one more long look at the P-38 before turning away. Shaking off the bad memory and whistling under his breath with the Glenn Miller music, he briskly made his way to the information desk near the entrance. The crowd was picking up; he had been told that the museum could get pretty busy on a weekend. Reaching the desk, he asked, "Did the party I mentioned show up yet?"

"No, sir," the volunteer replied. "I still have your message."
"Good, tell him I'll be around the art gallery."
"Yes, sir."
It would be 1943 again.
"Pennsylvania six, five, oh, oh, oh."

CHAPTER 1

✜

Headquarters, Northwest African Strategic Air Force
Constantine, Algeria
June 1, 1943

Capt. Josh Rawlins settled into his seat in the briefing room and looked around at all the brass. All twelve of the U.S. Army Air Corps group commanders—ten full colonels and two lieutenant colonels—the four RAF Wellington Wing commanders, and a few group execs and staff officers were seated in the front rows. He was the lowest-ranking officer in the room. Upon leaving their group headquarters his CO, Col. Gideon Pillow, had merely said, "General Buell told me to bring you along." Pillow, thirty-three years old and a West Pointer, seldom came down from his throne to explain anything. Josh Rawlins considered him a fully qualified asshole.

"'TenSHUN!"

As the assembled officers snapped to their feet, Brig. Gen. Barney Buell strode into the conference room and turned to face them from the lectern. "Be seated, gentlemen," he said brusquely.

"As you know," the general began in a voice that sounded as though it was exploding from between two sheets of sandpaper, "this command has been losing an inordinate number of crippled bombers returning from missions over Sicily and Italy. The rumor has spread that some sort of a jinx is involved, and you know how deadly that kind of shit can be. It gets inside air crews like poison and cripples any organization.

"Now, we all know that aircraft go down. But we also know that our Forts, in particular, can fly with considerable damage, on less than four engines, and stay aloft for some time. Therefore, more of our wounded birds should be getting back."

He paused effectively before going on. "General Doolittle has given me the personal assignment of finding out why these aircraft are not returning, and I'm passing this requirement on to you people. I want every one of you to instruct your crew members to look at every logical possibility—no matter how bizarre—that could be a cause for this seeming phenomenon. It isn't just a run of bad luck—I don't believe in that shit." General Buell looked around the faces below him and abruptly asked, "Any questions?"

"What do you think is the cause, General?" the colonel commanding the 301st Bomb Group asked from his seat in the front row. His group had just the day before lost two stragglers that had looked as though they would have little trouble making it back.

Barney Buell's narrowed eyes hardened. "If I had a answer we wouldn't be here," he replied. He looked around again, and without another word as all the officers sprang to attention, strode from the room.

A murmur went through the room as everyone relaxed. Josh Rawlins raised an eyebrow at Colonel Pillow, but his group commander had already turned to say something to the CO of the 99th Group. At that moment Josh saw General Buell's aide-de-camp beckon to him from the back of the room and he headed in that direction. "The general wants to see you, Rawlins," the lieutenant said.

Josh nodded. Seldom did an aide ever use the word "sir" when addressing a captain. It was the nature of those self-important beasts. But it didn't bother him. While rank now and then offered some privilege, it wasn't a way of life to him. At twenty-four, he was not only one of the older pilots in the command, but had lived a busy life before entering the Army Air Corps. The son of a famous aviator, he had been a pilot since he was tall enough to see outside of a cockpit. It seemed as though he had known Barney Buell since he was too little even for that, ever since Buell had flown the mail with the old man. In fact, Barney Buell had always been sort of a make-believe uncle to him.

He followed the aide into the general's outer office, where Buell came out to greet him warmly. "How's my favorite young bomber pilot?" he said, wrapping his arm around Josh's shoulder. The profane forty-three-year-old brigadier was stocky, with gray already streaking his shock of short blond hair. The cold, hard eyes of the briefing room had softened.

"Okay, sir," Josh replied.

"Bring us a couple of cups of that shit you call coffee," Buell said to the aide. Inside his office he pointed to a chair by his desk. "Sit down and let's talk, Josh." Two flags hung limply behind his desk, Old Glory and a bright red flag with a brigadier's white star in its center. A model of a chunky little blue-and-white Gee Bee sat beside the general's nameplate on his desk. Buell had flown the dangerous racer in the 1934 National Air Races at Cleveland, one the few who had survived racing the mean little son of a bitch. Josh had flown one in 1939, but only long enough to make three difficult takeoffs and landings.

"What do you hear about this straggler problem?" Buell asked after some small talk and a couple of reminiscences about the elder Rawlins.

Josh shrugged. "Far as I know, we've only lost a couple of wounded birds in the 97th. And they could have gone down for a number of reasons."

"I know. But something is happening up there, I can feel it. Something abnormal."

Josh sipped his black coffee. "I'll keep my ears open."

The general nodded. "Everything else okay? Your boys getting fed well enough?"

Josh chuckled. "Uh-huh. Just like at the Waldorf."

"How many missions you got now?"

"Twenty-nine and counting."

"One of these days you'll be going home to sell bonds."

"I'm no salesman, but I won't mind soaking up a little bit of that San Antonio greenery. I don't give a damn if I never see another grain of this damned sand."

"With your fruit salad, you should be able to get reassigned wherever you wish. And I'll throw in my two bits."

Josh was one of the most highly decorated pilots in the command and the only captain with a Distinguished Service Cross. "I'd appreciate it, sir. Just make it Randolph for the duration." Randolph Field was the famous "West Point of the Air" at San Antonio.

Buell's phone rang. After a short conversation he got to his feet and stuck out his hand. "Gotta run. Come up and have supper with me some night, I might even pour you a good drink."

Josh tossed off a casual salute and thanked him. As he followed the general's thickset frame out of the office he thought back to his father. Jeremy Rawlins had enlisted in the Lafayette Escadrille as a pursuit pilot in the middle of the Great War, winding up with eleven kills. Electing to stay in the fledgling Army Air Service after the war, he was Buell's advanced flight instructor when the general went through flying cadets. Later, they flew the mail together for a time and struck up their extraordinary friendship. Jeremy exited the Army in 1929 via a hard punch to a colonel's jaw and became a barnstormer and racing pilot. A crash outside Dallas killed him in 1938. Josh had inherited his special touch with an airplane, that indefinable extra feel that separated a good pilot from a gifted pilot—the skill that permitted a Doolittle or a Buell to survive racing in the unforgiving Gee Bee while it killed others.

On the way back to Chateaudun du Rhumel, where the 97th Heavy Bomb Group was based, Colonel Pillow stared out the side of the jeep, deep in thought. Finally he asked, "What did the general have to say, Rawlins?"

"Oh, we just chatted about my father and some personal things, sir."

Pillow scowled. "Did you talk about the group?"

Josh was tempted to put him on and tell him that Buell had asked why group morale was bad, or something similar that would make the CO turn a little gray. But he decided against it. "No, sir, I just told him we were eating like guests at the Waldorf. He laughed."

Pillow looked at him closely. "You sure? I don't want him to get the idea that the men of the 97th are unhappy with their lot."

Josh kept from rolling his eyes and saying, Heaven forbid! They love living in the hot sand and smelling like camel dung. Instead, he stroked the CO. "Sir, he knows how air crews react to adversity. And he knows you run a good group."

"Did he say so? Did he say that?"

"Not exactly, but he implied it."

"Damn good." It was the West Pointer's favorite comment. He went back to his outside stare with a more relaxed look.

As the driver turned onto Rue Aoute Mohammed, Josh thought about the city. He had taken as many history courses as possible in his two and a half years of college, and always read whatever he could find about wherever he happened to be hanging his hat. An old French guide had given him the Cook's tour of Constantine the first time he'd been able to get into town on a pass.

Alexander Dumas had described the city in the nineteenth century as "an eagle's nest perched on the summit of a crag." Located two hundred miles east of Algiers and about fifty miles south of the Mediterranean, the city occupied the site of the old Punic town of Cirta Regia. It had been rebuilt by the Roman emperor Constantine in 313. Ruled by various Islamic dynasties, it was conquered by the Ottoman Turks in the sixteenth century and finally by the French in 1837. Now it was a city of over a quarter of a million, with the French influence prevailing. The main part of the city was built on a neck of land that dropped off sharply on one side to the plains below, while two other sides had sheer drops to a deep river gorge that was a hundred meters wide and a hundred and fifty deep.

For the most part, Josh thought Constantine was quite beautiful—if one overlooked the squalor in the native quarter. But again, that could have been due to his interest as a history buff in anything old that reached back to the past. It beat the hell out of their last station, Biskra, an isolated French field from which they'd fought in what was being called the Desert War, and had also battled some of the fiercest scorpions known to man.

On the edge of town an Arab riding a mournful burro tried unsuccessfully to sell Colonel Pillow a scrawny chicken when they were held up in traffic. Soon they picked their way onto the highway that led southwest to Chateaudun. Josh thought about General Buell's short but direct briefing. Could something or someone be up there in the sometimes violent sky picking on crippled bombers?

What? Enemy fighters?

Now that Rommel had been kicked out of Africa, enemy fighters, mostly German, clustered around important Italian targets. They came up to meet invading bombers, but their mission was defense, not chasing wounded B-17s or other aircraft out over the distant sea. This concern of Buell's was probably due to a freak of some kind. A coincidence of sorts. Josh didn't believe in superstition or bad luck any more than Buell did.

What troubled him was Joe Orosco, his best friend and bombardier.

Back in February, when they had crash-landed in the desert after a raid on Tunis, Joe had suffered a bullet wound that grazed his temple. According to the flight surgeon the wound had not been serious. But since then the bombardier had grown increasingly fearful of combat missions. Even on a couple of milk runs a week earlier, he had agonized. And just two days before, on a difficult raid over Naples, he had climbed out of their Fort looking ashen, his hands shaking so severely he hadn't even been able to light a cigarette.

Twenty miles later Colonel Pillow's driver turned the Jeep into the base at Chateaudun du Rhumel. The group commander's parting comment was, "If you hear anything relating to what the general said, Rawlins, I want you to come directly to me with it. Do you understand?"

"Yes, sir." Josh tossed off a salute and headed for his squadron area. The 414th Squadron was one of those units that seems to do things well and gets a reputation for being special. He decided to stop into the squadron commander's CP tent and let him in on the briefing in Constantine. Maj. Pat Cleburne, a slender history teacher from Cleveland, looked up from his desk as Josh said, "Can a flight commander get a cup of coffee around here?"

Major Cleburne grinned around some freckles and pointed to a folding metal chair. "Yeah, if you're done ass-kissing for the day. What did the brass have to say up at Bomber Command?"

Josh gave him a quick resume of the general's remarks.

"Hmmm," Cleburne said, stroking his chin. "What do they think, gremlins? When airplanes shoot at each other, some go down. Add flak, and it's a risky business, right?"

"Something like that." Josh took the cup of tired coffee that the squadron clerk handed him. "Anyway, you're forewarned. Pillow will probably make a big deal out of it."

Cleburne made a wry face. "The asshole."

"Is this a private party?"

Josh looked up to see Capt. Wilbur Scragg, the flight surgeon, leaning nonchalantly against a tent pole. "Yeah, it's reserved for superior beings like pilots."

"Shit," Scragg replied. "And I was just about to tell you I got that order of special medical alcohol in from Telergma. You know, that hundred-and-fifty-proof stuff that does magical things to fruit juice."

"You springing for cocktails?" Cleburne asked.

"Yeah," the doctor replied. "Five sharp tonight, in my tent."

"Glad you came in, Doc," Josh said. "Anything new on Joe Orosco?"

"Yeah, the Bomber Command flight surgeon bucked the request for reevaluation back, stating that there wasn't sufficient cause. He hinted that Orosco is malingering."

"Bullshit!" Josh snapped. "I've known him since primary and there isn't a malingering bone in that hot-headed Mexican's body."

Scragg shrugged. "What can I do?"

"You can ground him, that's what you can do!" Josh replied.

Major Cleburne interrupted, "Not with Bomber Command in the act, he can't."

"Then you ground him, Pat. It's your squadron."

"You know I can't do that."

Josh barely hung onto his temper as he headed for the door. "So my best friend cracks up and gets the looney ward. And in the meantime, he'll be so shaky he won't be able to hit *Sicily* with my goddamned bombs!"

The *Texas Bitch* was standing quietly in her chocks, like a thoroughbred mare being brushed by grooms. A Boeing B-17F, she had been Josh's aircraft since his last one had been shot down the previous February. They had named her that because not only was he from Texas, but so were Joe Orosco, the flight engineer, and one gunner. The painting on her fuselage near the nose was of a scantily clad, shapely blonde wearing cowboy boots and a Stetson.

Josh looked at her warmly as he strode up. The cowlings were up on two of the four engines where mechanics were busy working on them. And some patching work was going on where they had taken some flak two days earlier. The crew chief, Tech Sgt. Ambrose Tarbell, touched his cap brim with a screwdriver as he said, "Howdy, skipper. Heard you went up to straighten out the brass."

Josh smiled. "Yeah, they wanted to know whether we should authorize booze and women at squadron level, and I told them the men would prefer an extra chaplain's assistant."

Tarbell laughed.

"Is the bird okay?" Josh asked.

"She's sound. Had a hydraulic leak in the ball turret, but it's fixed. The rest is routine."

"Good."

"I heard there's a front coming through."

"Uh-huh. No mission until day after tomorrow. Say, Ambrose, just between us, have you heard any scuttlebutt about something strange happening in the air to stragglers?"

The noncom nodded his head. "Yes, sir, but it's just a murmur about the Guineas or Krauts having some kind of a secret weapon." He shrugged. "You know how those things go."

Josh spoke to a couple of the mechanics and then to one of the waist gunners, who was cleaning his .50 caliber machine gun. Then he walked over to the Raghead Ritz. The Raghead Ritz was a peaked-roof shack constructed from pieces of packing crates and welded pieces of corrugated sheet metal that served as a roof. Mosquito netting and some ill-fitting curtains that Josh had had made in Constantine covered the windows. On the south and east sides floppy panels dropped down to provide storm shutters. It wasn't painted, and would have looked even more grotesque if it had been.

The rest of the officer crew lived in pyramidal tents, but the Raghead Ritz was the proud home of its architects and builders, the four officers of the crew of the *Texas Bitch*. Four cots surrounded a folding table and four matching metal chairs. Outside, two washing racks— makeshift stands that held toilet articles and a hole in which to set a steel helmet—stood like flimsy sentries. As one's steel helmet served as one's daily wash bowl, this area was known as the "steel pot powder closet," or Pottstown for short. Josh's motorcycle stood off to one side, resting on its kickstand. It was a beat-up 250cc, four-cylinder Benelli that he and Joe had acquired back at Biskra. It apparently had been a courier vehicle in the Italian Army that had been left behind. A little bit of tinkering had brought it into full voice.

It was hot enough this late in the afternoon on the sunbaked plain where Chateaudun was located to weld one's brains to one's skull. But it was even hotter inside the Ritz. A small fan, operating from a line leading to a generator that also provided current for the overhead bulb, did little more than stir the heavy air. Josh wiped his brow with a handkerchief as he walked in.

The running gin game between his copilot, Walt Butler, and his navigator, Jimmy Bolivar, was in progress. But Jose Orosco, instead of kibitzing, was stretched out on his cot staring at the roof. As soon as Josh entered Joe swung his legs to the floor and asked, "Did you talk to them about me?" His eyes were wide, dark, too bright.

"No, I didn't get a chance, Joe. But I talked to Doc Scragg, and the news is bad. The Bomber Command flight surgeon turned you down."

Orosco's expression turned suddenly frantic. "But all I want to do is have enough time off to get hold of myself. You know that, Josh."

He jumped to his feet and grabbed Josh's arm as the other two lieu-tenants watched quietly. "You know I'm no coward, Josh. For Christ's sake, remember that time in London when I took on those four infan-try guys—or how about when I pulled that guy out of his burning turret over France?"

"It's okay, Joe," Josh replied softly. "You don't have to prove any-thing to me. Listen, the weather's going to keep us down tomorrow, so I got Cleburne to give our whole crew an overnight pass. You want to go in to town and drink up a little *vino?*"

Joe Orosco stared at him a moment, then slowly nodded his head. "Yeah, might be a good idea."

Josh turned to the other two officers. "You guys want to go in?"

"Naw," Butler replied. "I drank enough of that lousy shit last night to ruin my week."

"And he needs someone to play gin with," the navigator added. "If the cards keep running my way, I should have his whole paycheck by lights out."

Josh Rawlins was pretty much a loner. He cared for his crew, but he got close to only one of them: Jose Orosco. Although they hadn't known each other when they were young, they hailed from the same city, San Antonio. And they had gone all the way through flying school together. That is, all the way but graduation. Joe Orosco, the hotshot in their advanced class at Randolph, had buzzed his girlfriend's house out in Seguin on the last flight of his cadet program and had his AT-6's fin number reported. He might have gotten away with it, ex-cept that he kept the trainer on the deck and buzzed a few other things—four trucks, a girls' school, and a freight train. He was suspended im-mediately and boarded out of the program soon after. Bombardiers' school was his next stop. Against all odds, he was assigned to the 414th Squadron of the 97th Bomb Group (Heavy) as soon as he graduated. The moment Josh heard about it he talked the squadron CO into making Orosco Josh's bombardier. And he was good; he could put those eggs in a cracker barrel from thirty thousand feet.

Now he was shot.

They sat in the bar of the grand old Hotel Cirta and sipped red wine. The grandest of the city's major hotels, the Cirta was located at 1 avenue Achour Rachmani, right on the edge of the Place des Martyrs. For some reason the room was relatively empty, considering it was so soon after payday. Perhaps the fighter pilots who frequented this particular bar had some kind of heavy training mission in the morning. Reminiscing was the name of the game to keep Joe's mind off his problem. That and having the little Mexican nurse from the station hospital with them. Joe had met her when he got his last X-ray a month earlier. Her name was Hermelinda, but Joe called her Linda. From Los Angeles. Second lieutenant. Pretty.

"Remember the night they didn't want to let me into the Anachono Room at the Gunter Hotel?" Joe asked.

Josh grinned at Hermelinda. "Yeah, the Emil Coleman band was playing. He was a regular there. They didn't want to let any wetbacks in."

"So this damned Anglo here, he says to the head waiter in that quiet voice of his, 'He comes in, or I call my father, General Rawlins, and have this place put off limits for discriminating against a soon-to-be U.S. Army Air Corps officer.' And you know what, the guy just stared into Josh's dark eyes for what must have been a whole minute before he shrugged and took us to a table."

Hermelinda smiled at Josh. "I didn't know your father was a general."

"He never got above captain!" Joe chortled.

They all laughed, and then Hermelinda looked at her watch. "Oops, I have to be in by ten."

Josh watched them depart. San Antonio had other memories for him as well. Burying two parents. School at Trinity, the River Walk, lots of flying. There had been a few pretty girls, but nothing special. They always got sticky, wanted too much of him. Then he got on with the airline and quit school. Who the hell needed a bachelor's degree in the cockpit? Oh, sure, Doolittle was supposed to have a doctorate in aeronautical engineering, but he wasn't human anyway. A god.

He poured another glass of wine from the bottle as a woman in a low-cut red dress came brazenly up to the table and asked him something in French. When he shook his head, she asked, "Do you want some company, *mon Capitaine?*"

Josh had never been with a whore, and wasn't interested in starting. "I'm waiting for a friend," he replied.

She stroked his cheek. "But I will take you to my place, and the charge for a whole hour is only five dollar."

He shook his head. "Sorry."

The woman couldn't be much over thirty. She pouted. "I don't do this often, *Capitaine*. But so many of you boys are lonely, and I have no food."

"Yeah, things are bad."

The lady shrugged. "Ah, well, for you, *Capitaine*—since you are so handsome and so blond—I will make an exception. Ten dollar for all night, and I will provide some wine."

Josh shook his head. "I told you, my friend will be here soon."

The woman in red tossed her head. *"Au revoir,* then."

He watched her well-formed buttocks as she walked away, and wondered why he was so particular.

They climbed off the motorcycle at shortly after midnight. But before going into the Raghead Ritz, Joe suddenly grabbed Josh's arm. The bright moonlight outlined the anguish on the bombardier's face. "Josh," he said in a voice brittle with pain, "Ground me. I can't take another mission. I'll crack right up there in the airplane, right in front of the whole crew."

Josh looked into the dark shadows of his friend's eyes and patted his hand, as he would a child's. "I can't ground you, old buddy," he said softly. "You know that."

"Just tell them I'm too sick to fly."

"We've already tried that. You know you have to go on sick call and Doc Scragg's hands are tied as well."

"Try it," Joe pleaded.

"I'm sorry, Joe." Josh was afraid his friend would get on his knees. The sight of his torment was terrible.

"Then I have no choice. I'll refuse to fly and they can court-martial me."

A lone dog, one of the mascots, barked in the distance. The only sound in the silent desert.

Josh blew out a deep breath. "A first lieutenant with a Silver Star for heroism can't do that, Joe. Besides, it'll reflect back on me." Maybe that tack would work.

"How could it?"

"I'm your aircraft commander. Your cowardice . . ." He let the word hang there for a moment. "Your cowardice would indicate that I lack the leadership quality to command a crew."

Joe's dark eyes widened. "No, it wouldn't be that at all. You're just trying to talk me out of it. Well, I'll tell you for sure. I'm finished up there."

Josh played his trump card. "I need you, Joe. I don't want some green replacement bombardier after having had the best. Tell you what, fly one more mission. It could be a piece of cake, as the Brits say. Might give you your confidence back. If it doesn't work out, I'll go over everybody's head and talk to Buell."

Joe wavered. "I don't know. I tell you, I nearly get sick when I think of crawling back into that Plexiglas nose."

"Give it one more shot."

"You promise you'll go to the general?"

"On my word."

Slowly, as the moon slipped behind a small cloud, Jose Orosco nodded his dark head.

CHAPTER 2

✛

The *Texas Bitch* was a good airplane. A B-17F, she was the replacement Josh had received for the bomber he had brought to North Africa and lost. At times he thought she was a better airplane. Josh concurred with all the pilots who said the seventeen, or Flying Fortress, was an airplane driver's machine—a pretty strong accolade. Officially she was a four-engine, long-range heavy bomber, but she was more. Many who flew her thought she had a soul. She was a huge beauty in the air, sometimes referred to as "the big-assed bird" because of her high and wide tail section. And she even seemed to think she was a bird, so much did she try to keep flying after being brutalized in one way or another. There was a story of one that was all shot up that flew herself back to England and landed in a pasture without anyone aboard.

There were dozens of stories about the B-17's prowess: it flew superbly and fought almost miraculously at times. One pilot had summed it up for the rest of the B-17 flyers: "This is an airplane you can trust." But she was also mortal, and men who flew enemy fighters or fired flak guns could sometimes find her vulnerabilities.

Josh pressed the mike button on the control column's wheel. "Everybody awake?" The rogers came back from each of the seven gun positions. "Okay, the coast of Sicily's coming up, so let's stay alert." He nodded to the copilot, Walt Butler. Being the low flight of the low squadron was the hottest position in the group formation. There wasn't another Fort between them and the naked sky. And that bothered Josh. When he promised Joe Orosco a piece of cake on this next flight, he'd had no idea where they'd put the *Texas Bitch*.

He pushed the mike button again. "Pilot to bombardier. Everything okay down in front, Joe?"

Orosco's voice was strained as he replied, "Roger."

There was nothing else from the nose, none of the old banter that Joe used to offer to keep the crew loose. Josh could only guess what agony must be going through his friend's tormented head.

The target was the Palermo railyards, not a long mission, but one that could get hairy. Since the Germans had pulled out of North Africa many of the Luftwaffe fighter squadrons were concentrated on the north and west sides of Sicily. Palermo was located on the north coast of the big island, sixty miles from its westernmost tip. Weather at the target was supposed to be broken to scattered clouds at nine thousand feet, the residue of the front that had grounded the Strategic Air Force the day before.

It was clear and smooth above the clouds at twenty-seven thousand feet. The sky was a darker blue, the sun a bright observer casting its reflections in the cold air. Above, Cleburne led the squadron's other flight in two Vs of three Forts each. And above him the other three squadrons of the group completed the combat box in a vertical wedge formation. The Forts, with their OD camouflaged tops and gray bellies, reminded Josh of huge sharks plying a becalmed sea that would soon turn violent. He looked off to his left; the nearest one was staggered back, fifty-odd feet off his wing.

He glanced at his watch: 0711. They'd been en route fifty-eight minutes. He could make out the land mass through thin clouds now. Switching to the flight channel, he said, "Okay, Big Blue, Spaghetti Land is coming up, so stay loose." He didn't have to say any more. Each one of the five aircraft in his flight was manned by a veteran crew.

Within seconds Maj. Pat Cleburne's voice came in over the squadron channel. "Okay, lads, I suspect our little Kraut friends will be coming up to say good morning shortly. On your toes, now."

Sometimes the intercepting fighters came out to meet them well before they made landfall. On this morning's mission the 97th had friendly fighter support in the form of a squadron of the twin-tailed P-38 Lightnings from the 14th Fighter Group. But they were flying high cover, so Josh hadn't seen them.

The minutes passed and Sicily loomed larger. Suddenly Charlie Burns in the ball turret on the belly shouted, "One-oh-nines six o'clock low! 'Bout eight of 'em I think. No, ten—twelve. Closing fast!"

Chatter over the air alerted the P-38s, and they swooped down to intercept the intruders. "One-oh-nine five o'clock!" the tail gunner shouted.

Josh heard firing and chatter as a Messerschmitt closed and flashed by, and another came back, head-on, into the *Texas Bitch*'s vulnerability. Josh felt a jolt as something hit the aircraft. "All right," he said calmly to the rest of the flight. Between gunner reports of enemy aircraft, he added, "Stay loose and let's keep our intervals on the money. Our little friends'll chase away the bad guys momentarily."

He looked off to his left wing. The inboard engine was trailing a little smoke. Checking the gauges, he saw that the number one engine's oil gauge was acting up. The damn thing was losing oil!

The acrid smell of rapidly firing machine guns permeated the aircraft as transmissions crackled in his earphones: "Em E at one o'clock high!" "He's trailing smoke—I got him!" "Watch that bastard at three o'clock!" "Flight of two at five o'clock high!" A flaming B-17 with part of a wing missing fell out of the sky in front of their squadron.

Then, just as the remaining Messerschmitts dropped away, a violent black burst of smoke with a bright yellow center exploded just below and ahead of the *Bitch*. It was followed by another and another, each one rocking the aircraft. They were now approaching Palermo and it could only get hotter. Josh's mind went to Orosco. "Pilot to bombardier. You ready to nail those railyards, Joe?"

Once more the reply was a curt, "Roger."

Josh jerked off his earphones and leaned over to the copilot, shouting, "You take it, Walt. I want to go down and check on Joe."

The copilot nodded and Josh slipped out of his straps. Moments later he stood behind the bombardier, who was straining over the Norden bombsight. He watched as Joe put his hand over his eyes and then shook his head like a shaggy dog. He wanted to reach out and touch his friend's shoulder, but he didn't want to startle him. Orosco took over control of the aircraft for the bomb run and Josh could see his hand shaking as he reached for a knob. All at once, Joe looked up and stared at him as if he'd been caught doing something wrong.

Josh smiled and nodded his head. Pulling an earphone a little bit away from the bombardier's ear, he shouted, "I just wanted you to know I know what you're going through and I care!"

Joe's eyes were hard black, blinking. He nodded slowly.

Josh gave him a thumbs-up and climbed back toward the cockpit. He had just gotten buckled back into his seat when the copilot said, "I had to feather number one." He looked out his left window and saw the propeller slowly windmilling. The flak was heavier but far enough below that they were missing it. Just at that moment an explosion jolted the Fort.

Instantly Orosco shouted over the intercom, "I can't do it, Josh, I can't!"

"Dump the eggs!" Josh snapped, taking the wheel even though they were on automatic pilot.

"I can't move my hands!" Joe's voice was frantic.

"Jimmy!" Josh radioed the navigator. "Toggle those bombs for Joe!"

"Rog, skip!"

Josh waited the several long seconds it took for Jimmy Bolivar to unhook and get to the bombardier's position. The controls were heavy and the aircraft seemed to yaw.

Bolivar's voice came through, "Bombs away, skip."

Josh hurriedly took the big Fort off autopilot and worked the elevator trim as he brought it under control. "Who knows what was hit?" he barked over the intercom.

Tech Sgt. Darrell Dickson's reply came from the top turret. "A flak blast got the front of the right horizontal stabilizer, skip. Big hole."

"You all right, Harry?" Josh asked the tail turret gunner.

There was no answer. Josh repeated the question. Still no answer. He called the senior waist gunner. "Ellis, can you go back and check Harry?"

"Rog, skipper," the sergeant replied.

Josh called the squadron leader and outlined his damage. "'Fraid I'm gonna have to fall out of formation and make my way back by myself," he said. Cleburne rogered back and wished him luck. Back on intercom, Josh called the waist again. "Ellis, you back yet?"

Moments later the sergeant replied in a halting voice, "Roger, skipper. Uh, God, he's . . . God, Harry's dead, Captain. Looks like some of that shrapnel that hit the stabilizer got him."

Josh blinked. Dead? Harry Johnson had been with the crew since shortly after they arrived in England. Nineteen years old. A farm boy from Nebraska. Now he sat dead, strapped into the hemmed-in barrel of a machine gun turret. Damn! He cleared his throat. "Anybody else hit?"

"Yeah, Cap'n. I got it in the thigh." It was Charlie Burns in the ball turret on the belly.

"You need help?"

"I think I'm okay until it's time to land. Then you'd better send someone down to help."

"Okay, take it easy, Charlie." Josh called the flight engineer, "Darrell, take a break and go check out Burns."

Shortly the tech sergeant called back, "He's jammed into the turret, skipper. Definitely stuck there until we land and cut him out."

Shit! Josh asked if there were any more casualties. None. After Dickson described the stabilizer damage in more detail he said, "Okay, fellas, we're going to nurse this bird home, so keep your eyes open for visitors and do all those little things you do to get ready for a swimming party."

By using most of the rudder trim he was able to compensate for the drag on the damaged stabilizer and maintain the return course Bolivar gave him, one that swung them north to escape any return flak. With the torn tail surface and the dead engine, the airspeed indicator fluctuated between 135 and 140, twenty or more miles per hour less than normal indicated cruise, after he levelled out at eleven thousand. Eleven was low enough to get along without oxygen if necessary, but high enough to have a glide factor if anything else went wrong. And it was much warmer down at this altitude. He pulled off his oxygen mask and blew out a deep breath.

His mind went back to Orosco. He had forgotten all about his friend. "Joe, you okay?"

There was no answer.

"Joe, do you read?"

Still no answer. Jimmy Bolivar said, "I'll check on him, skipper."

Moments later the navigator appeared at the back of the cockpit and spoke into Josh's ear, "He's in some kind of shock, Josh. Just sitting there staring at nothing. Stiff, like he's frozen."

Josh frowned, then told the copilot to take over again. Getting out of his seat once more, he went back down to the nose section. Joe Orosco was exactly as the navigator had described him, bent over at his station but stiff as a board. His dark eyes stared at the bombsight, ap-

parently unseeing. His cheekbones were sweaty. Josh pulled his earphone aside and said, "It's okay, Joe. It's all over. We're heading home
on three good fans with plenty of fuel. This big-assed bird is going to
take us back to some good booze and a nice long rest for you, pardner.
Yeah, I'll get the general himself to ground you. Probably send you
home to old San Antone to a hero's welcome, then give you a nice
ground school class to teach for the duration. You'll probably screw
yourself crazy with all those horny Mexican girls."

Orosco didn't move.

"I heard about this kind of thing, Joe," Josh persisted, putting his
hand on the bombardier's shoulder. "I guess you're off somewhere,
fighting some demons of your own. When you're ready to come back,
you will. Now, old buddy, I have to get back up there and play pilot
for about another hour and a half, then we'll be home. Just let it all
out and remember one thing—you're in old Josh's safe hands."

Moments later, after giving a few words of encouragement to Charlie
Burns in the ball turret, he returned to the cockpit, where the navigator provided him with a new, direct course to Constantine.

Fifteen minutes later, Josh was surprised to hear, "Hello, big buddy,
this is Brubaker Two-five on Baker channel. Over."

Josh depressed the mike button. "Aircraft calling Broadway Four-
one say again."

The voice seemed to have a Boston accent. "This is Brubaker Two-
five, big buddy. I'm a lonely Lightning about two angels above you
in the sun. Looks like you got a sick fan. Would you like a little company the rest of the way home?"

A P-38! Josh grinned at Walt Butler. "Yeah, Lonely Lightning, you
can fly shotgun, if you wish. I'll tell my watchdogs to hold off, so come
on in and see us."

"Rog, big buddy, be there in a couple of minutes."

Josh looked around the sky as he told his gunners to hold their fire
when the P-38 arrived. Shortly he spotted the shape of a twin-engined
fighter descending rapidly, and moments later the dull blue-gray Lockheed
Lighting throttled back and pulled up just off his left wing. The pilot
waved cheerfully.

"Hi, big buddy. What's the other guy look like?"

Josh smiled at the old reference to a fist fight. "Kicked the shit out
of him," he replied. "What are you doing here?"

"Had a fan quit on me also, but by the time I got it started again, everyone was gone. Where you heading, Constantine?"

"Roger. You from Boston?"

"Yeah, the Scully Square kid. Can't ever seem to get rid of that accent. What about you?"

"Texas. What outfit you from, the 14th?"

"Yeah. You got wounded aboard?"

"Roger."

"Looks like your tail section got hit pretty bad. Tell you what, I'll pull in close and take a good look at it. You sure your gunners all know I'm a friend?"

"That's what I told them." Josh watched as the P-38 pulled up a shade and slowed as it banked over the top and behind the *Bitch*. No more than a second later the Fort shuddered, and he saw a flash as the number three engine exploded. Slamming in full left rudder as the *Bitch* tried to roll into its good engines, he immediately pulled all of the throttles back and lowered the nose.

"The son of a bitch is shooting at us!" Dickson screamed over the intercom from the top turret.

Jerking his head around, Josh saw tracers lace into the wing. "What the hell are you doing, Brubaker Two-five?" he shouted over Baker channel.

The answer was another 20mm cannon shell exploding into the prop of the number three engine. A moment later the Lightning pilot radioed, *"Mi dispiace, amico mio. Questa è la guerra."*

"Get him!" Josh shouted to his gunners. He heard more explosions as the *Bitch* continued to stagger. "Where is he, Dickson?"

No answer.

Another explosion! Then Josh remembered: a Lightning had four .50s and a 20mm cannon in the nose.

"Skip! Number four's on fire!" Walter Butler shouted.

Josh leaned around him and looked. Sure as hell! At that moment he looked up and saw the P-38 levelling off straight ahead of him for a frontal attack. The fighter's nose was blazing as it grew large in a hurry. The son of a bitch! He slammed the wheel forward, throwing everything that was loose into the air and putting the *Bitch* into a spiralling dive to the right. "Pilot to crew!" he barked into his mike. "Prepare to ditch, prepare to ditch!"

God, Burns was trapped in the ball turret!

He looked at the rate-of-climb indicator as its needle approached a thousand feet per minute of descent. He had to slow it down and hope the bastard would just let them go on in without another attack. Quickly, he ran through the ditching procedures in his head.

Christ! Was Joe still frozen in his trance in the nose?

"Joe, you all right?"

Just as he thought, no reply. God!

"Jimmy!" he snapped at the navigator. "Is Joe okay?"

There was no reply.

"Pilot to navigator," Josh said sharply.

No answer.

"He must've gotten hit on that last pass, skip," Walt Butler said from the right seat.

Josh glanced down at the dark sea that was getting close in a terrible hurry. There wasn't time to do anything about the two officers below, not a goddamned thing. Oh, Joe, damn you, come out of it and get out of there! He blew out a deep breath. Stay cool! "Darrell, do you read me?"

"Roger, skip."

"Just like we practiced it, right? Parachutes and heavy clothing off, boots off. Life rafts ready to be inflated the second we stop. You know what to do. You're the boss back there. Okay?"

Dickson was a rock. "I'll take care of everything, skip."

"And see if there's anything you can do for Burns."

"Roger." It was unsaid: if he wasn't killed by the impact of a belly landing in the water, Burns, stuck in that turret under water, would surely perish very quickly from drowning.

"Charlie, do you read me?" Josh asked the ball turret gunner.

"Yes, sir?"

"Maybe the force of impact will jar you loose, so be ready to get out of there at once. The waist doors are open, so you can swim out through them. Okay?" It was a farce, but he had to say *something*!

Charlie Burns's voice was quite calm. "Roger, but I'm not going to make it, am I?"

"You never know, old buddy." It was a goddamned lie, but one never knew. Josh threw a hurried glance around the sky—apparently that bastard in the P-38 had decided not to waste any more ammo. There was no sign of him.

He had Walt take the controls long enough to get his boots off.

The unwinding altimeter showed them going rapidly through three thousand feet. He eased back on the control column and lessened the degree of bank. The wind should be from the west. He had never ditched before, but the book said to land crosswind, between crests of waves, to keep from nosing over. Didn't need any kind of a landing pattern; just line up and keep enough airspeed to keep from stalling out until it was time to skip the *Bitch* into the water. Through one thousand. Now he could see tiny white crests on the waves, moving east to west. He felt sweat running down his back. "Pilot to crew," he said into the mike. "All right, everybody in the right position for bracing? Good. As soon as we stop in the water, hop to it. You all know what you're supposed to do. See you shortly. Good luck!"

He told the radio operator to radio a final S.O.S.

Seven hundred feet, six hundred. Full flaps. Hold her tight. If she shakes, lower the nose. Steady, steady, between those waves . . .

"Brace, you guys!"

The tail of the *Bitch* ticked the water just as he pulled the nose up slightly. Then it all happened at once, the sudden jolt, the water spraying high, and the immediate, eyeball-pulling force, as the big aircraft decelerated and skidded to a stop.

Instantly Josh unhooked his straps and was out of his seat. "I'm going down to the nose!" he barked at the copilot as he headed below. One look at Jimmy Bolivar's bloody head hanging over his shoulder told him the navigator was dead. Moving instantly to the bombsight, he found Joe Orosco, still frozen, staring unseeing off into some distant place known only to his troubled mind. "Joe!" he shouted. "We have to get out of here!"

The water was already beginning to come into the compartment. *"Joe!"*

His friend still didn't respond.

Unbuckling Joe's harness, he took his friend's arm and pulled him from the seat. "C'mon, Joe, for Christ's sake, you've got to get out of here!" But it was no use. With a heave he got the bombardier over his shoulder and managed to get back to where Walt Butler could give him a hand. After another minute of struggling they joined the surviving crew members on the left wing. Roy Roper, one of the waist gunners, was missing.

They got Orosco into the inflated raft that was resting on the wing flaps. Walt Butler, the radio operator, and the other waist gunner joined him and cast off, rowing away into the choppy surf. Just as Tech Sergeant Dickson got the other life raft inflated Josh heard the sound of two Allison engines. Jerking his head around to the south, he saw the P-38 levelling off just above the water a half mile away. It was coming straight at them! Suddenly its nose flashed into a sunburst of fire as tracers streamed at them. He heard the screams as the shells tore into the men in the life raft. He swore he could see the enemy pilot's dark features as the P-38 flashed overhead. Dickson was down in the water, blood streaming from his mouth.

What was left of the raft was going down in a huge, roiling bubble of scarlet. An arm swung out of the water, a foot, the glimpse of a face—Joe's face. Josh stood there, frozen, staring at what had been the remainder of his crew. Bloody bubbles. Slowly he turned as the Lightning peeled off for another run. Jerking his .45 pistol from its holster, he screamed, "You murdering son of a bitch!" Jerking the trigger, he futilely emptied the magazine at the oncoming fighter.

But this time the nose of the blue-gray Lightning was quiet. A couple of hundred yards away the pilot waggled his wings and quickly passed overhead without firing a round. As the plane climbed away to the south Josh watched it with burning eyes that could barely see. Through gritted teeth he rasped, "I'll get you, you son of a bitch. No matter what it takes, I'll kill you!"

CHAPTER 3

✛

USAAF Station Hospital
Constantine, Algeria

Josh stirred from his restless nap as he heard the nurse say, "Here comes the general now." His hospital bed was half cranked up in a sitting position, so it was no problem to reach over to get his water glass. Although they had had an IV in him, he was still thirsty from the two days in the life raft.

"Josh, my boy, how are you?"

He looked up to see Brig. Gen. Barney Buell at the foot of his bed. The doctor who was treating him was at the general's elbow, a nurse behind him. He shrugged. "Compared to what?"

General Buell's smile was quick, efficient. "The doctor here tells me that you're in pretty good shape, and that he might be able to discharge you in a few days."

Josh glared at the doctor. "I'm ready now."

"What's your hurry?"

"The son of a bitch killed my whole crew, that's the hurry."

Barney Buell moved close. "Who killed your crew, Josh?"

"Oh, that's right. You don't know, do you?"

"Will you start at whatever your beginning is?"

"I solved your goddamned riddle about the stragglers, General."

Buell's eyes narrowed. "What do you mean?"

Josh had been fighting the memories of his dead crew since that moment on the wing of the sinking *Bitch* when the enemy P-38 had flown away. Now he stared at the wall behind the general. Joe Orosco's face, surrounded by bloodstained foam, came back to him. It had haunted him throughout the time in the rubber raft, aboard the PBY Catalina that had finally picked him up at sea, and during his fitful three days in the hospital.

"Well?"

Josh blinked, coming back to the moment. "It's a son of a bitch from Boston flying one of our P-38s. A yellow-bellied Italian murdering bastard!" Haltingly, fighting off the pain its recall caused him, he related the whole incident to the general.

When he finished, Buell said quietly, "And you say he said something in Italian. How do you know it was Italian?"

"I've been studying the army phrase book. I think he said something about being sorry—that it was the way of war. Hell, I don't know, General—he was shooting my goddamned airplane out from under me!"

Buell stroked his chin. "That's an interesting scenario. You sure about the accent?"

"General, I spent six months in Boston one time, and I can spot that accent anywhere."

"Can you pinpoint where he jumped you?"

"About fifteen or twenty minutes northwest of Palermo over the water, I think. My navigator could—" No, Jimmy Bolivar was dead too. "They're all dead," he murmured absently.

"What about markings? You remember any of them?"

"Not offhand. It was painted that washed out blue-gray. Had white markings on the booms near the engines."

"Think hard, Josh, the numbers will pinpoint the group and squadron."

Josh shook his head, trying to picture the P-38 as it flew alongside. An E! "It had an E something, yeah, E5 something, I think."

"The 14th was flying cover that day and their ID letters are ES dash and a numerical designator. Could your E5 have been ES?"

"Quite possibly. I had a sick airplane on my hands and I wasn't paying attention."

"I'll check it out." General Buell turned to the doctor. "When do you think Captain Rawlins will be well enough to discharge?"

The physician glanced at Josh's chart. "I'd like to keep him under observation for a couple more days, General. If nothing shows up I can put him on convalescent leave or nonflying duty for awhile."

Josh grabbed Buell's arm. "Goddamnit, Barney, get me out of here now. I vowed I'm going to get that son of a bitch, and I can't do it in here!"

The stocky general's voice was calm. "When you're fully recovered we'll talk about it. In the meantime, if you come up with anything else about the P-38 or its pilot, let me know immediately. Okay?"

Josh shrugged. "What can I say?"

Buell touched his arm. "I'm so sorry about your crew, son."

Josh just nodded. As he watched his father's old friend depart, his eyes took on what the famous combat artist, Tom Lea, had captured as "the thousand-yard stare." He saw Joe standing with hard, unseeing eyes over that bombsight, lost, off in some distant place beyond the impending doom. Beyond the safe hands of his best friend, his pilot. That's what he had told Joe: "You're in old Josh's safe hands." Safe, shit! Yeah, just one more mission, Joe, a piece of cake. A fucking piece of cake.

He thought back to the time at Randolph, when as cadets they were each supposed to be doing basic flight maneuvers solo in their own sectors. They had plotted to meet with their T-6s at that bridge over the San Antonio River out by Schertz and sneak in some follow-the-leader. Flying under that bridge had been the first stunt of several they had gotten away with that day. And that night, downtown in the Cork Room, they'd made their drunken pact to someday come back and fly under that meaningless bridge again, someday when the war was over and they were the two most famous pilots in the Army.

Yeah, Joe, a piece of cake.

If he hadn't tried to play God, Joe Orosco would be alive. The Mexican might be in some hot water, but not dead!

What was that phrase? "I do nothing upon myself, and yet am mine own executioner." John Dunn, no, Donne. "Any man's death diminishes me. . . ."

Charlie Burns—how long had that boy lived in his ball turret, how many seconds before the warm Mediterranean filled his plexiglass coffin while he choked for air? Another of my charges, another who trusted me.

Any man's death diminishes me. . . .

Josh turned to his pillow and sobbed.

An hour later a soft voice stirred him. "I just found out you were here, Josh." It was Hermelinda Prospero, the pretty little nurse from Los Angeles, Joe's girlfriend. She was in her starched white uniform.

The gold bar on her right collar caught a reflection from the window that flashed in his eye.

He shook the grogginess out of his head. He'd thought of her, knowing he'd have to tell her, but he'd put it off. He hadn't been up to it, he told himself. But that was a goddamned cop-out too. "Uh, yeah, Linda. Yeah, I was just about to have someone find you. I've been, well, I just haven't gotten around to it."

Her black eyes were wide. "It's about José, isn't it?"

He nodded, not wanting to look into her fear, but unable to pull away.

Her voice was soft in the quiet cubicle. "Is he dead?"

He nodded again. "Yes, I lost my whole crew."

She didn't even blink. "He should never have gone, not even on one more mission. He was shot, Josh, at the end of his rubber band."

"Don't you think I know that?" he replied angrily. "I made him go! Big, smart-assed psychologist here, using his leadership. I talked him into giving it one more go. And now he's dead."

Hermelinda Prospero exhaled a deep breath. "Can you tell me about it? Did he break?"

He should give her some brave lie, but he couldn't. He needed to lay it out, confess, flail himself. He started with Joe's taciturnity in the aircraft, then told of his freezing, omitting nothing, ending with, "So you see, if I'd just gone to the group CO and pounded on his desk, Joe would be here right now." He looked into those wounded dark eyes. "I killed him, Linda. I killed my best friend."

"No," she whispered. "He was already dead. Remember, he was the big man on the Mexican campus. He wore his massive pride as proudly as he wore his Silver Star. The day José Orosco had to admit to himself that he was finished in combat he was a dead man. And when he had to beg to be grounded, it was like putting a pistol to his head." She touched his hand. "No, Josh, the war killed Joe long before that mission—the war and his hot Mexican blood that demanded too much."

Josh shook his head. "No. Nice try, Linda, but I'm not buying it. I made him go on that last mission. I told him I'd go to the general if it didn't work out, and I killed him."

Her eyes were brimming. "Don't do it to yourself, Josh."

He took her hand. "I'm sorry, Linda, so sorry I'd steal an airplane and dive it into the man who shot us down if I could find him. But I don't even know who he is. Please forgive me for taking away someone dear to you."

She held her head high as she turned and walked away.

* * *

Josh was all set to walk out of the hospital when he discovered that the air evac people hadn't forwarded his flight suit from Tunis. They had flown him to Constantine in hospital pajamas and a bathrobe. He did get to keep his water-soaked wallet, but that was all; he had no other uniform, not even shoes. And the medics were real horses' asses about letting patients near a uniform. He bribed a corpsman to get a message down to the 97th at Chateaudun, to Tech Sgt. Ambrose Tarbell, his crew chief on the *Bitch*. He had no idea what new assignment they might have given the crusty old maintenance chief. Ambrose Tarbell was one of those old regular army types who could never manage to keep that sixth stripe on their sleeves for very long. Sometimes it was nip and tuck to keep any stripes on. They'd probably given him and his mechanics another Fort, maybe a new one now that his airplane and crew were gone. The message was short and sweet: There's a fresh uniform hanging by my cot. And break into my locker and get some underwear and socks, plus shaving kit. Also need shoes and cap. Get them to me in a box here at the hospital ASAP.

At seven-twenty that night Tech Sgt. Ambrose Tarbell, sober and turned out more smartly in his Class A uniform than Josh had ever seen him, arrived on Ward 12 with a box marked Red Cross. After a short conversation in which Tarbell told him the maintenance crew from the *Bitch* was in limbo pending the return of its captain, the old mechanic tucked in his beer belly and departed.

Pulling the drapes shut on his cubicle, Josh quickly got dressed in the khaki uniform. He felt a little weak at first, but pushed it away. Hell, he'd just had a couple of days off on a little rubber yacht. No reason to be weak. Next time, he'd pick one with food and water in it. He watched through the crack in the curtain until he saw the nurse go by on her way to the other end of the ward. Pulling his service cap low over his forehead, he sauntered out of the cubicle and hurried past the nurses' station and out of the ward.

Fifteen minutes later Josh entered the bar of the Hotel Cirta. The room was crowded and boisterous. Smoke hung heavily in the air as at least three dozen flying officers and a number of local European women filled the tables and booths. Two fans, stirring lazily from the high ceiling, did nothing to cool the place. As usual, the Cirta bar had enough fighter pilots in it to start a massive dogfight.

And that was his target tonight: an Italian fighter pilot from Boston.

He looked around for black hair and eyes, settling on one slender lieutenant who was telling a flying story to three others. He watched the ritual: both hands acting as wings as the storyteller reenacted a combat, no doubt embellished considerably by repeated tellings. Josh bought a bottle of local beer and moved closer, listening carefully and watching the fighter pilot intently.

But the lieutenant had a Southern accent. And someone called him by a French name.

Shit!

Josh moved on, searching another group, then another. Finally he spotted a captain he knew to be Italian. The fighter pilot was standing beside a booth, talking to an attractive young blonde woman who spoke English with a French accent. Josh moved close and felt goose bumps on his skin when the captain said something in the unmistakable soft accents of someone native to the Boston area.

"Excuse me, Captain," Josh said, brusquely interrupting. "Are you with the 14th Fighter Group?"

The pilot swung his dark eyes away from the Frenchwoman and replied, "Yeah, why?"

"Were you on the raid to Palermo four days ago?"

The captain shrugged. "Yeah, as a matter of fact I was. You writing a book or something?"

Josh moved right into his face. They were both just under six feet tall, so their gazes locked at the same level. "Some son of a bitch in a P-38 with ES markings shot my wounded Fort down after I had to fall out of formation . . . some *Italian* son of a bitch with a *Boston* accent."

The fighter pilot's eyes narrowed as he took up the gauntlet. He bit off the words, "You think it was me, asshole?"

"Could be. I'm asking."

"Just what are you asking?"

"Were you with your formation throughout the mission?"

"No, actually, I lost an engine and had to make it back by myself."

A handful of other fighter pilots had been drawn by their words and now surrounded them. The room grew quieter. A couple of bomber lieutenants from the 414th, Josh's squadron, sauntered over.

Josh balled up his fists. "And while you were on the way, I don't suppose you shot down a crippled B-17 just for kicks, did you?"

The fighter pilot's eyes turned to slits. But before he could reply, a bulky lieutenant pushed between them and glared into Josh's angry face. "Do you know who you're talking to, asshole? This is Sal Leneo, the leading ace in the 14th. He also happens to be my flight leader, so why don't you get off this shit and go find a hole to crawl in."

Josh's look was bleak. "Get lost, junior."

"Yeah," Leneo said, "His bitch is with me. Now why would I want to shoot down a Fort? Tell me, Captain."

But the lieutenant, flushed with alcohol, had to keep interfering. "We save these candy-assed bomber pilots' tails every day, and they come in here and mouth off like—"

Josh's roundhouse right caught him flush in the mouth. His left rammed into the lieutenant's stomach. Pushing him aside, Josh swung at Leneo, catching him on the cheek. The fighter pilot jabbed back, hitting Josh in the forehead. With a roar Josh barrelled into him, knocking him over a table to the floor. A 414th bombardier took a swing at another fighter pilot, and the brawl was on. Josh and Leneo rolled over and over until they pulled apart and started swinging at each other again, pumping blows like two flailing featherweights. One of Josh's punches hit home and Leneo went down. At that moment the troublesome lieutenant hit Josh in the forehead, knocking him to his knees. He got up slowly and went after the fighter pilot. Blood trickled from his mouth, but all he could see was Joe Orosco's face in the water, and he just kept swinging.

The MPs arrived moments later, blowing their whistles and waving their sticks. One, a sergeant, got knocked down, and it was another couple of minutes before they got things under control. The last struggle ended when an MP put a throat lock on Josh with his nightstick.

Josh looked up from the holding cell at the military police station. His watch showed 0010. "C'mon, Cap'n," the MP sergeant said, "Your CO is here." Josh picked up his cap and stopped at the small mirror on the wall just outside the cell. His left eye was swollen half shut and already discolored. There was a purplish welt on his forehead and another on his right cheek. His upper lip was swollen and the knuckles on both hands were skinned. His blond hair was matted with some blood over his left eye. He raised an eyebrow; he was a goddamned mess.

Following the NCO out of the holding area and into a large room with a wooden table and some chairs, he saw Pat Cleburne standing with another figure under a lone incandescent light bulb. It was Col. Gideon Pillow and he was livid. "That will be all, Sergeant," he said coldly. As the door closed, he looked at Josh and said, "I simply cannot believe what I've been told, Captain Rawlins. The duty officer here has informed me that you are AWOL from the station hospital, that you accused a leading ace of the 14th Fighter Group of shooting your aircraft down—and that you started a common brawl in the top hotel in Constantine. Am I back where I should be at this time of the night having a bad dream, or is this nonsense possible?"

Before Josh could reply the group commander added, "And he also stated that you involved three other members of the 97th in this brawl. Is this true, Captain Rawlins?"

It hurt to talk. Josh replied thickly, "I didn't involve anyone except that fighter pilot from Boston, Colonel. And I wanted some straight answers out of him."

Colonel Pillow paced a few steps with his hands behind his back. "What in the living hell are you doing out of your hospital bed? You're supposed to be recovering from your ordeal at sea!"

"I'm recovered."

"Recovered, *sir*!" Pillow reminded him.

"I'm recovered, *sir*! But I'm not recovered from losing my crew to the guns of a traitorous Italian-spouting P-38 pilot with a Boston accent!"

"Do you think starting a brawl in the Hotel Cirta is the answer to that?" Colonel Pillow leaned into his battered face. "Do you, Captain?"

Josh said nothing.

"Major Cleburne told me about your oral report. Are you sure it was an American P-38?"

Josh gritted his teeth. "The son of a bitch was within a hundred feet of me at one point."

"And he spoke good English?"

"He *pahked* his *cah*," Josh replied caustically.

"It doesn't make sense."

Josh's control snapped. "I don't give a fuck if it makes sense or not! I lost an airplane and a fine crew of men that included my best friend, so don't you give me any shit about sense!"

"Take it easy, Josh," Pat Cleburne warned.

The blood drained out of Colonel Pillow's face. "I could have you court-martialed for what you just said, Rawlins. But in view of the stress you're under, I'm going to wait and see what my course of action will be. I'm having you delivered back to the hospital under armed escort. You will remain there until you are officially discharged as a patient, and then you will report directly to your squadron commander at Chateaudun, where you will be placed under house arrest until further notice." Pillow leaned close, obviously getting some pleasure from displaying such ultimate authority. "And that is a direct order, witnessed by Major Cleburne. Do you understand, Captain Rawlins?"

Behind the colonel's back, Pat Cleburne nodded for him to agree.

Josh fought his anger, replying, "Yes, sir, I understand, *sir!*"

"Very well." Pillow nodded to Cleburne. "Now let's round up those other troublemakers of yours and try to salvage a little sleep out of tonight."

Josh had to wait until the seven-to-eleven shift came on duty at the hospital to get a message to Hermelinda Prospero. His contusions and cuts had been treated by the surgical OD when the MPs brought him back to the ward, and the hospital commander had dropped by at shortly after eight to lecture him about going AWOL. Now, at 0840, Lieutenant Prospero poked her pretty head into his cubicle. In her starched white uniform she didn't show any signs of her loss. When she saw him, she gasped. "What hit you?"

He told her briefly about the previous night's adventure.

"Oh, Josh," she said, troubled. "Why couldn't you wait? I know Joe's death is eating at you, but you can't change it. Why get yourself in all kinds of trouble?"

"It's something I have to do. You don't look any the worse for wear, considering that he was your boyfriend."

Her eyes hardened. "That's not fair. Just because I don't wear my grief on my sleeve doesn't mean it isn't there. I just happen to think it's better to work and *do* something than to sit around and mourn."

"I thought all Mexicans liked to grieve."

Her voice was flat, "Don't pull that crap on me."

He reached out to touch her hand. "Okay, I'm sorry. That was stupid. Look, I can't sit here in this medical trap for another week. The bastard who's flying that P-38 is going to shoot down others. We've got to find out who he is."

She held his gaze. "You sure it isn't your own distorted sense of guilt that's driving you?"

"No, I'm not," he replied honestly. "But I still have to get at it."

"What do you want me to do?"

"Get my uniform out of wherever these bastards hide them. Medical holding supply or whatever."

"How can I do that?"

"You're an officer. Just tell whatever enlisted man who's in charge that you're picking the uniform up on the orders of the head nurse. Whatever. Some little corporal isn't going to argue with you—you're on their team. We patients are the enemy."

"I could get in trouble."

"Yeah, you could." Josh found a smile. "But if the question ever comes up, I'll tell 'em I had another uniform. Linda, other lives could be at stake."

She frowned, nodded her head. "All right, I'll try."

"Good girl. I'll buy you the best meal in town when this is over."

"At the rate you're going, I'll never collect."

CHAPTER 4

✣

Tech Sgt. Ambrose Tarbell had left Josh's motorcycle at the Hotel Cirta as requested. Josh picked it up shortly before noon and drove on out to Chateaudun, parking it near the maintenance line of the 14th Fighter Group. Casually strolling down the line of parked P-38s as if he belonged there, he finally reached the 48th Squadron. Wearing his cap low and hiding behind his sunglasses, only his puffy lip and a small bandage on his cheek indicated that he'd been in a fracas the night before. Going up to a P-38 that had its cowlings up, he spoke to a staff sergeant who was working on the left engine. "Howdy, Sarge, can you tell me which one of these birds the squadron ace flies?"

The crew chief grinned. "If you mean Capt. Sal Leneo, you're looking at it, sir."

Josh looked at the numbers on the side of the cockpit pod: ES-37. "All your birds have ES numbers on them?"

"Yeah, we started with thirty-one through sixty, or something like that. Course we don't have 'em all now."

Looking closer, Josh saw the pilot's name on the fuselage, along with twelve little swastikas, one for each kill. No Italians, only Germans—the harder ones to shoot down. Seeing those badges of Leneo's exceptional combat record, Josh suddenly felt unsure of himself. Why would a top ace shoot down any B-17? Didn't make sense. The pilot would have to be completely crazy. Still, there was one more point to check. "Nice airplane," he said. "I fly Forts myself. Always wanted to fly one of these."

"Yeah, the pilots love 'em."

"How about these Allison engines? Are they pretty reliable, Sarge?"

The mechanic shrugged as he looked back over his shoulder. "Usually, but this rascal quit on the captain a few days ago. Fuel pump went bad."

"That wouldn't have been on the Palermo raid, would it?" Leneo had said he lost an engine.

"Matter of fact, it was."

Josh nodded his head slightly. There went that theory. "You don't happen to know where I can find your pilot, do you?" he asked.

"Yes, sir, he's over at the squadron orderly room."

Josh thanked him and walked away. He owed a certain captain from Boston a hell of a big apology.

But he also had a hell of an idea!

An hour later he rode into Constantine and parked the motorcycle near Strategic Air Force headquarters. Entering Barney Buell's outer office, he told the aide he wanted to see the general. The lieutenant looked him over rather disdainfully as he asked, "What for?"

Josh's eyes were cold. "Just tell him I want to see him, Lieutenant. I haven't got time to fuck around with you."

The aide sniffed and disappeared into Buell's office. He was back out immediately. "The general will see you now, Captain."

He shut the door as he went inside and saluted. "I've got to talk to you, sir," he said, standing in front of Buell's desk.

"You're damned right you do, Captain," Barney Buell said abruptly. He held up an MP report. "What's this bullshit about you going AWOL and starting a brawl in the goddamned Cirta last night? And what the hell are you doing out of the hospital now?"

"I was all fucked up last night, General. I just had to do something besides lie on my ass in that hospital, but I made a mistake." He explained the Sal Leneo story, including his visit to the 14th earlier. "So I made my apology and left the good captain with my tail between my legs. Now I'm here to tell you about my theory."

Buell's eyes were still cool. "It had better be good."

"Would you think I'm crazy if I thought the Italians might have one of our P-38s—a perfectly flyable one? One that the 14th lost? Now, General, I don't know how the hell they could have found a pilot with a Boston accent, but I suppose it's possible. Okay, suppose that's the story. This bastard could be lying in wait to jump our crippled birds on the way back from any raid he wanted to shadow."

The general nodded his head. "That's a pretty good deduction. In fact, it's the same idea I started pursuing this morning." He handed Josh a sheet of paper. "These are the P-38s that have been lost since the 14th arrived here and began escorting missions over Italian territory—Sicily, Sardinia, and the mainland. Some are marked as 'known shot down.' The others are just missing. I had squadron commanders query their pilots to see if any of these could have gone down unscathed, from mechanical failure. There are two possibilities: they are ES-41 and ES-53."

Josh felt his pulse quicken as he looked at the numbers. "It must be one of those two."

"Right. Now we have to find out where it's operating from." General Buell got up from his desk and opened the door. "Billy," he said to his aide, "Get Major Sabatini for me."

Coming back to his chair, he said, "I called an army friend this morning and had him pull some strings to have an OSS officer assigned to me on temporary duty. He has experience behind the lines in Italy and is fluent in the language. I think he might be able to help us."

Moments later a heavyset, swarthy man, wearing sloppy khakis and unshined Corcoran jump boots ambled into the office and tossed off a casual salute. He had large dark eyes under heavy black eyebrows, and wore a bushy black mustache. The black hair was almost gone on the top of his head. His collar sported a gold major's leaf and the crossed rifles infantry insignia. Over his left shirt pocket the red, white, and blue Silver Star ribbon with two oak leaf clusters was pinned crookedly under his parachute wings. His name was Rudolfo Sabatini.

After the introductions, Buell told them to be seated and had Josh go through his story.

Rudolfo Sabatini listened carefully, finally asking in a pronounced New York accent, "You're sure he said something in Italian?"

"Positive. Sounded like *'Mi dispiace, amigo. Something la guerra.'* I thought he was apologizing and blaming it on the war."

Sabatini nodded his head. "Yeah, sounds like it. You speak much Italian?"

"No, just phrase book minimum."

"And the airplane looked like any other P-38 with those markings?"

"Far as I could tell."

"You said it was a dull, washed-out blue-gray. Aren't some of these planes camouflage or OD in color?"

General Buell answered, "The 14th had its aircraft repainted late in the spring."

Sabatini raised an eyebrow. "If we pinpoint the date, we'll know that the Italians couldn't have gotten one before a certain day. It may be a factor."

Josh noticed that the major never used "sir" when he addressed the general. He answered more of the New Yorker's questions until finally Sabatini shrugged at Buell. "I think we ought to set up a drop for me in Sicily."

"You mean you'll parachute in?" Josh asked.

Sabatini nodded. "Only way I know to find out who this bastard is and where he's operating from."

Josh turned to Buell. "I want to go too."

The general shook his head. "You're a pilot, Josh, not an intelligence agent."

"I don't care. This bastard killed my crew. He's mine."

"Look, sonny," Sabatini said with a easy smile, "you stick to your airplanes and stay out of my way, and I'll take care of it."

Josh's expression hardened. "My name is Rawlins, Major. Don't give me any of that 'sonny' shit."

"All right," Buell said sharply. "We have a problem to solve and we don't need any of this bullshit. I want the two of you to spend some time together in the next twenty-four hours, so you'll have to start getting along."

Josh eyed Sabatini warily as the major shrugged. "What about my hospital problem?" he asked Buell.

"You go back there and let that doctor check you over, and I'll take care of the AWOL thing. To keep their medical egos happy, you'll be placed on extended convalescent leave, but you'll be working directly for me. My aide will fix you up with quarters here."

"My group commander wants to fry my ass."

"Your group commander will do exactly as I tell him to. Any more questions at this point?" Buell frowned. "And, Josh—if you get in any more trouble, your ass is in the wind."

Major Rudy Sabatini had to weigh at least two-twenty, but he didn't look flabby. In fact, he exuded power. Dark, bull-necked, confident, he looked as if he should be wearing stars. One thing was for sure, Josh decided as he watched him dance with a redheaded nurse, he was light on his feet. They were in the bar of the Grand Hotel, a French hostelry in which none of the furnishings looked as if they had been replaced since Napoleon. But the Grand was popular with headquarters officers because they didn't have to put up with the arrogance of the often troublesome young fighter pilots and also because the nurses came there to unwind. A trio of Europeans was playing American music. At the moment they were doing a credible job on a jazz number, "Boogie Woogie."

"I see you're with Sabatini," a major said at Josh's elbow.

Josh looked around in surprise. "More or less."

"You a big buddy of his?"

"Not exactly." Josh looked at the speaker, a dark-haired man in his thirties wearing judge advocate general's corps insignia on his collar. He was what was called a JAG officer, a military lawyer.

"Known him long?"

"Just since this afternoon. Why? Who're you, Major?"

The JAG officer stuck out his hand. "I'm Jim Fellini, a former assistant district attorney, Borough of Manhattan, City of New York."

Josh shook his hand and introduced himself. "What's your big interest in Sabatini?"

"I spent four years of my life trying to put him behind bars."

"Oh?"

"You don't really know who he is, do you?"

"No, not really."

"He was *consiglière* to Vito Genovese before the mobster ran off to Italy. Sabatini was a big man, lotsa influence. He volunteered for OSS to beat an income tax rap the Feds pinned on him. Rumor has it he's the most decorated Mafia type in the service."

"You don't say." Josh sipped his drink, regarding Sabatini in a new light. "He ever kill anybody?"

"I'm sure he has, at least in the war. And he probably had a hand in some murders in civilian life, at least from an advisory end. His nickname in the mob is Rudy Lotions, supposedly for his smoothness in influencing policy and moderating troubles."

"Who was Vito Genovese?"

"Another poor Italian immigrant who came to New York to make his way in life. He became Lucky Luciano's number two man in the twenties and set up the murder of the old boss of bosses, Joe Masseria, in thirty-one. After that, he and Luciano formed the national crime syndicate. In thirty-four he had an underling who was trying to blackmail him killed. But this murder didn't go away. When Tom Dewey, my old boss as Manhattan district attorney, turned up the heat on New York's racket bosses, Genovese decided to skip. He had prepared a nest back in his native Naples when he visited Italy a few years earlier, and supposedly had plenty of money in Swiss bank accounts."

Major Fellini sipped from his beer. "Rumor has it that Luciano and Meyer Lansky, the Jewish don, gave him two million in cash, which he took with him in a suitcase."

"You mean he just slipped out of the country?"

The lawyer laughed. "Hell, no. He left with an entourage that included some limos, a few bodyguards, and a retinue of servants. The word on the street was that Rudy Lotions greased it with Dewey and with Italian customs, but it was never verified."

"Did Sabatini go to Naples with him?"

"Yeah, but he was back in New York within a couple of months. He had a beautiful young wife in a nice house in Jersey, and some close connections to organized gambling."

Josh looked back at where the smiling Sabatini was still dancing with the nurse. "Is he still married?"

"I don't know."

"What happened to this Vito Genovese?"

"Again, I don't know for sure. Supposedly he ingratiated himself with Mussolini by contributing a big sum of money and became part of his inner circle. He's said to have quite a mansion in Naples."

The music stopped and Sabatini came back to the bar to join Josh. Seeing the JAG officer, he snorted, "Well, if it isn't my old bosom pal, Fellini. How are you, Jimmy boy—still chasing me?"

Fellini shrugged. "With people like Hitler and Mussolini in the game, you're small fry, Rudy."

Sabatini flashed his wide grin. "I never was anything but small fry, Jimmy boy. You know that."

"The war'll be over one of these days, you know, and the law will begin to grind again. You'll get yours."

The OSS officer grinned again. "I don't know what you're talking about. Hell, I may just stay in the army, or go to work for the FBI or something. You just never know." He turned to Josh. "This lawyer type tell you we grew up together? Yeah, same neighborhood. C'mon, drinks're on me, even though I promised my sainted mother I'd never sink to consorting with a lawyer."

Fellini shook his head. "Gotta go, Rudy. Got a date at the casino. I'm surprised you're not over there, you know, with your interest in gambling."

Sabatini laughed, a rich deep production that came from way down inside his big body. "Only when I'm doing the dealing."

As they each sipped from a fresh beer Josh asked, "What's your plan for Sicily?"

The big man shrugged. "I parachute in outside of Palermo and make my way to the don of dons. He's head of the Mafia, the Man. I met him once before the war."

"When you were with Genovese?"

"Ah, I see Fellini's been giving you a history lesson. Yes, in thirty-seven."

"Then what?"

"Then I use my inside pull to find out about our renegade Lightning and its pilot."

"Would the Sicilian mob know about such things?"

"Ha! They can find out anything."

"What if they don't want to play ball? Maybe things have changed with the war."

Sabatini shook his head. "Wars are only passing phases to the Friends. Customs and rituals are eternal."

"Didn't I read somewhere that Mussolini did away with the criminal organization on Sicily? What was it called, *Mafen* or something like that?"

"*Mafia* was an old term sixty or seventy years ago, but it isn't used. In a society where no one talks to the government or the police, why have a name? As far as Mussolini goes, he sent a strongarm guy to Sicily to cut the balls off the dons—the power guys—but most of the ones he put out of business were the little guys."

"I definitely want to go along."

"No way, flyboy. It could get tricky even for me. There's no way I could take a chance on bringing in an outsider. Besides, you'd only get in my way."

Josh's gray eyes darkened as they bored into the Italian's black gaze. "Major, there's one big difference between us. With you it's another ho-hum mission where you can get a medal for seeing some of your old gangster buddies. But I'm the one who lost a whole crew, including my best friend. I'm the one who had to watch that murdering bastard gun down what was left of them. And by God, I'm going to get him for it!"

Sabatini pursed his lips. "I understand, Rawlins, but the answer is definitely 'no.' Now, I gotta go trot that redheaded nurse off to the sack before she gets outta the mood."

As the New Yorker walked away, Lt. Hermelinda Prospero tugged at Josh's sleeve. "Buy a poor little working girl a drink?"

Josh blew out a deep breath and pushed his irritation with Sabatini aside. "Yeah, sure, Linda. I didn't expect to see you out like this, I mean, well, so soon after Joe's death and all."

She was lovely in a suntan uniform, open at the throat, a female officer's cap pulled low over her lustrous black hair. She frowned. "I can't seem to get it through your thick head, Josh Rawlins, that life goes on. I'm terribly sad that he's dead, but he wasn't everything in the world to me. You want to wear a black band on your arm the rest of your life, fine. Not me."

She turned to go, but Josh caught her arm. "I'm sorry. After all, you did stick your neck out to get my clothes. You get any static about it?"

"No, they're so screwed up the war'll be over before they figure it out. I'll have a glass of the hotel's best *vino,* flyboy. And then you can tell me what you were doing with that handsome, sinister-looking major."

"I had to see you before you got tied up this morning, sir." Josh said as Barney Buell came striding into his office at 0715 the next morning.

The general told him to take a chair and get on with it.

He decided to fire his whole volley before Buell could turn him down. "I want to go along with Major Sabatini on the mission into Sicily. There are many ways I could be of value. Something could come up involving flying, the aircraft itself. Who knows, if we get real lucky, we might even find that P-38. I could—"

"No."

Josh blinked. "You didn't hear me out, General."

"The answer is 'no,' Josh. You're not a goddamned behind-the-lines type, you're a bomber pilot. And you've just gone through a hell of a trauma. Christ, you'd still be in bed if the medics had their way."

"I'm back to full speed. Didn't I kick the shit out of a couple of fighter pilots the other night?"

Barney Buell had to smile as he shook his head. He had been in his share of fights when he was younger, more than the average officer ever even heard about. He just hadn't gotten caught. "I'll buy that, but there's one primary reason why you can't go: the officer in charge of the mission doesn't want you along. He says you'd just endanger the whole thing."

Josh leaned forward, trying to control his anger. "That Italian pilot killed *my* men, General!"

"That could be the precise reason why you would be a problem on the mission."

"Who's making the call, you or that mobster from New York?"

Barney Buell's eyes narrowed. "I am! You are not parachuting into Sicily or anywhere else! You will pass on any further information you may recall to Major Sabatini, and that will be the limit of your participation until he returns. Do I make myself clear, Captain?"

Josh jumped to his feet and saluted. "Yes, sir!"

"Then get the hell out of here and see if you can do something constructive for a change!"

Josh parked the Benelli motorcycle outside the 64th Troop Carrier Group's operations tent and went inside. He had talked a sergeant back in General Buell's headquarters into telling him that Sabatini's flight had been assigned to the 51st Troop Carrier Wing, where it had been passed down to the 64th. Going up to the blackboard that listed the day's scheduled missions, he saw one that read "C-47 #3641, 16th Sqdn, Pilot: l/Lt Bltner, Depart: 2010, Time enroute: 6 hrs." Under Destination, it read: CLASSIFIED, and under Remarks it read Low Level Parachute Drop."

Six hours flying time would get a C-47 to Sicily and back with an adequate reserve, and it was the only classified mission, so he knew it had to be the one. Pilot: Bltner. There could only be one Lieutenant Bltner with a missing vowel in the whole Army Air Corps, and they had gone to flight school together!

He rode over to the squadron area and found Lt. Billy Bltner playing gin in his tent with another C-47 pilot. They hadn't seen each other since graduating from cadets and getting their wings. Bltner jumped to his feet, grinning and sticking out his hand. From Mississippi, his drawl was thick. "Well, I'll be double damned, old buddy. I heard you were around here somewhere. Flying Forts, right?" He looked down at the dark blue ribbon trimmed in thin red stripes below Josh's wings. "DSC, huh? That's only the second one I've ever seen up close. Down here in troop carrier, we're lucky to get a theater ribbon. Oh, I guess you can get an Air Medal if you *die*." He introduced the other gin player and an additional pilot who was kibitzing. Like Bltner, they were wearing khaki shorts and T-shirts in the heat.

Bltner broke out a bottle of wine and opened it. After a serving from jam glasses, he asked, "How's that buddy of yours, that Mexican you used to raise hell with? Washed out right at the end. What is his name?"

"Joe Orosco."

"Ever see him again?"

"Yes," Josh replied quietly. "He was killed the other day." He told them about the P-38 and asked, "Have you been briefed on your mission tonight, Billy?"

"Yeah, an hour ago."

"You dropping an OSS major near Palermo?"

"Sure am."

"Can you get me a chute?"

"Why? You aren't going to do something stupid like jump out of a perfectly good airplane, are you, Josh?"

"I plan on it—if you'll let me stow away in the crew compartment. That major'll have my ass if he sees me too soon. I'd greatly appreciate it, but it could get you a little heat."

"Shit, what can they do to a lowly first john in a troop carrier squadron? I'll even bring you a coffee cup."

CHAPTER 5

✥

Sabatini got up from the gooney bird's bucket seat and lit a cigarette. They had been in the air well over an hour and the dark coast of Sicily loomed in the distance. Looking out into the bright night, he regarded the big moon and its reflection on the water a hundred feet below. They were staying low, "on the deck" as the pilots described it, to escape any electronic detection device the enemy might have working. Intelligence had reported a direction finder on Mount Erice, the first peak of any consequence inland from the northeast corner of the big island. Sabatini noticed the banking motion of the C-47 as the pilot turned it to parallel the coast and elude Capo San Vito where it jutted out into the sea.

He inhaled deeply on the Lucky Strike and thought about the upcoming jump. The excitement, the dread, began to settle in. It was hard to explain, this prejump tension that always seemed to grab him. The C-47 door reminded him of the thirty-four-foot tower back at Benning, where he had gone through jump school. He had had more damned trouble getting out of that practice tower, in fact he had almost busted out right there. But he had managed to get his big ass out enough times in a passable manner to get through that phase. He sometimes wished he had flunked out because the fact was, he simply didn't like to make parachute jumps.

Shortly he would be falling back to the land of his forefathers, back to a part of his real life. This army thing was all right; actually, he enjoyed a lot of it because he thrived on danger and they practically let him write his own ticket in the OSS. But there were important matters to be taken care of on that backward island with its superstitions and passions, where protest against the governing class had long been a mode of life. Cicero had written, "a nation of acute and suspicious genius, born to controversy." But that was too simple; Sicily was far too complex for such simple reduction.

He thought of the "men of respect," one of the terms applied to the gangs that lawlessly, or sometimes aided by the law, actually held such influence that they ran the island, usually by fear. But it was more than that, it was a way of life. He had tried to tell young Rawlins that there was no such thing as a mafia, but that was only a term. There was a loosely threaded society of *cosche*, the gangs, that had taken the silent rule of Sicily through an intricate form of extortion that was hard to define. It was everywhere, and touched priests as well as killers.

He ground out the Lucky Strike in half a C ration can.

There was a proverb, *A liggi e pri ricca, la furca e pri lu poveru, la giustizia pri li fissa.* It meant, "the law is for the rich, the gallows for the poor, and justice for the fools." As long as he understood such a philosophy, he would be successful in Sicily. There was so much to be done, and only a part of it was this P-38 problem. He looked back at the nearby land mass and easily picked out Capo San Vito in the moonlight.

The crew chief, who was standing on the far side of the door, motioned to him. "Ten minutes, sir!" he said loudly.

Sabatini went back to his bucket seat and picked up his pack. Fastening it to his harness, he mentally went over its contents: some concentrated food, clothes for a ten-day stay, a small URC radio to contact the pickup people, one of those tiny round compasses that you could stick up your ass, plenty of Italian lira, ammo for his .45 pistol, a bottle of champagne, a lace head covering that he'd picked up in Constantine, a compact first aid kit, and incidentals. He checked the reserve chute on his chest and tugged the flat Sicilian peasant cap low over his eyes. Moving to the doorway, he hooked the static line on the overhead cable and jerked it to make sure it was securely fastened. It was his lifeline. He felt the plane bank to the right and knew the pilot was heading in over the Golfo di Castellammare, the large bay west of Palermo. Once more he felt the tension build.

A figure moved toward him from the cockpit.

"Nice night for a jump, huh, Major?" Josh Rawlins said casually.

He covered his surprise. The flyboy was wearing parachutes. "What the hell are you doing here?"

"I'm about to visit sunny Sicily. Know any good beer joints?"

"You're as close to Sicily as you're gonna get, flyboy."

"I hear it's just one short step."

"You'll spend the rest of the war in Leavenworth if you even get close to that door."

"Might beat the shit out of a flak wreath. No, I'm coming along, Major. I don't trust you."

Sabatini reached for the .45 on his hip. "I'm giving you a direct order— stay in this fucking airplane, Rawlins."

"Don't bother. There's no one to stop me from following you out that door, so you might as well save your breath."

The large Pratt & Whitney engines changed their pitch as the gooney bird began to climb slightly. Drop altitude was a low six hundred feet to reduce the chance of the jumpers being seen. Simultaneously, the small red light over the door came on, warning that the drop zone was coming up. Sabatini glared in its scarlet glow, then shrugged and swung into the door. No more time for argument. Josh hooked up his static line and watched the top of the door.

The pressure rose to a crescendo as Sabatini stared at the red light and the dark bulb beside it. He glanced down; it didn't look right. Suddenly the green light flashed! Get out! Without a moment's hesitation, he sprang up and out. He counted, "One thousand, two thou—" *Whap!* the chute opened with a vicious jolt. He looked around in the silver moonlight. Trees. It didn't look right. It was silent except for the light drone of the gooney's engines as it dived away from Sicily. Silent and eerie. Glancing back and above, he saw another dark form against the moon. That damned flyboy.

The ground was coming up fast, a goddamned tall tree. He hauled on the parachute risers to slip away, but to no avail. At the last second he covered his face with his arms. With a loud crack he smashed into the limbs, jarring his way to an abrupt stop. A severe jolt of pain shot up from his right foot. He tried to move but the cords were wrapped tightly around his arms. He couldn't even reach his knife to cut himself loose. Son of a bitch! He struggled furiously, but it was no use. Vito Genovese's powerful *consiglière* was hopelessly ensnarled in a goddamned oak tree twenty feet over Sicily!

A pinpoint of light. Couldn't be a Kraut.

"Hey!" he whispered loudly. "Up here!"

Rawlins replied, "What're you doing up there?"

"Playing tiddlywinks, asshole. Cut me loose!"

"Won't you fall and break your ass?"

Sabatini gritted his teeth at the pain. "No, I know what to do. Hurry, before someone figures out they've got company!"

Josh worked his way up the big oak, finally climbing out on a limb to reach him. In short order he cut enough of the parachute cords to free Sabatini's right arm. As he took the knife and slashed at the remainder of his bindings, Josh asked, "Now what?"

Sabatini pulled the handle on his reserve and spilled it out. It tumbled almost to the ground. He then unsnapped his pack from the harness and connected it to his belt. Next he slammed his fist into the quick release on his main chute harness, releasing the straps, and painfully worked his way hand over hand down the parachute to the ground. Crawling painfully over to a rock, he sat up against it, wiped the sweat from his face, and lit a Lucky Strike.

Josh waited up. "You okay?"

"Naw, I think I might have busted an ankle or something."

"Let me see." Josh knelt beside the extended right foot and looked at it. "You think you can stand it if I unlace this shoe?"

"Yeah, I have to." He gritted his teeth as Josh loosened it.

"I don't see any bones sticking out. Could be a sprain. Once back at Kelly, one of the cadets in my flight ground-looped a Stearman and the same thing happened. Broke a small bone in his foot."

"Fuck Kelly and Stearmans! Get me something so I can walk!"

Josh shrugged and went to a small tree. Shortly he had a crude splint trimmed and tied to the inside of Sabatini's ankle with parachute cord. "Okay, lean on me," he said, holding out his hand.

Sabatini pulled himself to his good foot and carefully tried the injured one. It hurt like Hell! He looked around. "I think that goddamned pilot dumped us in the wrong fucking place."

Josh nodded. "I do too. I thought we jumped a hair early."

* * *

They had jumped early all right, over a half mile early. With Josh providing his shoulder as a crutch, they moved out across the field to the east. Stumping along slowly over the rocky, silvery landscape by vineyards and olive groves, they looked for a landmark they could recognize. The ankle was swelling badly, but Sabatini was afraid to take morphine for fear that he might lose his mental edge. And he would have to be sharp for a while yet. After twenty-five minutes of their painful trek they finally dropped down for a sweaty rest on the edge of an orange grove. Sabatini had just sucked down the second deep drag from a Lucky when he heard a tiny sound. He stiffened, his hand creeping to his .45, but a strong grip caught his arm and he felt the razor sharp edge of a knife at his throat.

"Say something in Sicilian," a deep voice said in Italian.

Sabatini looked over to where another man in a dark suit was holding a sawed-off shotgun in Josh's face. He drew in a deep breath and said in his best Sicilian dialect, "My name is Sabatini, Major Sabatini. We are friends of Don Nizzi Calgogeri."

"Why we? We were supposed to meet one fish who drops from an aeroplane. What's the password?" The man with the knife was burly, with a large, drooping black mustache and eyes that glittered in the moonlight.

"Joe DiMaggio."

"Okay, Yankee Stadium. Why the hell didn't you come in where you were supposed to?"

"It's a long story." Sabatini watched the other men release Josh. "Who are you?"

"I am Salvatore Scagnelli, Don Nizzi's right arm, his general. Who is this other fellow?"

"He flies the big American birds that drop the eggs and he has a strong vendetta. He came against my will, but helped me when I injured this damned foot."

Salvatore Scagnelli gestured to his strongest man to help. "We are late. Gregory, here, will help you to our car."

"Good morning, Captain."

Josh rolled over and shook himself awake at the slightly accented English. A handsome young man with expressive black eyes and a wide grin that flashed over exceptionally white teeth stood beside his bed.

He was tall and slender, and sported the fuzz of a nurtured mustache over his seemingly constant grin.

"Ah," he said pleasantly, "I'm so glad to meet you, sir. I am Bernardo Calgogeri, the son of Don Nizzi, your host."

Josh swung his legs out of bed and stuck out his hand. "Glad to meet you. Call me Josh." He looked at his watch. He'd gotten five hours sleep. Glancing out the open window, he saw his room was on the second floor of the old stone castle, high enough up that it could discourage a jump. Rays of the warm sun were working their way inside. The smell was fresh and pleasant.

"I once lived in New York," Bernardo said proudly. "My father sent me there five years ago when I was fourteen. I stayed two years."

"That's good," Josh replied, going to the large white porcelain bowl on the wash stand. "You speak English very well."

"Oh, sometimes I make little mistakes. I no practice much, you know. You speak Italian?"

Josh wiped his face with a light towel. "No, just a few phrases."

"My father has told me to be your escort. I am to stick to you like, like—"

"Glue. That's good. I want to find an airplane." Instinctively trusting the young Sicilian, he told him briefly about the P-38. "Do you think your father will let me roam around looking for it?" he asked.

Bernardo scowled momentarily. "Perhaps. I'll ask him. I've laid out some better clothes for you. Where did you find those cheap rags you were wearing?"

"In Constantine. I didn't have much time and I didn't really know what a Sicilian man wears."

The wide grin. "I've been in Constantine." He pretended to spit. "Frenchmen and Arabs. No wonder."

"You've travelled quite a bit, haven't you?"

"Yes. And to Paris, and London—and Rome, of course."

Josh picked up the loose-fitting white shirt. "I suppose you know the island pretty well. Do you know where any military airfields are located?"

"Some. What will you do if you find this Lightning flyer?"

Slowly Josh drew his forefinger across his throat.

Bernardo nodded. "That's something any Sicilian understands. Come, we must have some breakfast." He grinned. "I told the cook how to fix you some fresh scrambled eggs. You like?"

Josh grinned back. "Yeah, if memory serves me right."

*   *   *

Don Nizzi Gaetano Calgogeri lived in an old Norman castle that stood on a bluff overlooking the town of Mistano, several kilometers from Palermo. It was a gray stone structure of several stories, complete with battlements and even a moat, although the drawbridge had been replaced a few centuries earlier. His father had been an ambitious *gabelloto*, an overseer and collector of rents for the absentee landlord of the large estate that belonged to the castle. Such was the elder Calgogeri's power that he "convinced" the landlord that it was better to sell him the castle and a fair portion of his land at a "comfortable" price than it was to put up with destruction from "vandals and bandits." When the father was shot to death in 1913, the young Nizzi assumed the leadership of his Friends and began restoring the old, rundown castle. He renamed it Castello Carmelo.

This ostentatious residence was but one of several of Don Nizzi's departures from the outwardly common way of life manifested by most Sicilian dons.

As Sabatini waited for an audience with the don, he stared out a window to the bright flowers in the sunlit garden below. It had apparently been the castle's courtyard in days of yore. He liked the feeling of power the old structure emitted and thought about how nice it would be to have something like this in Jersey or out on Long Island after the war. But that made him think of his own house, and Teresa. He pushed the unhappy thought away.

He was about to be Rudy Lotions again, the silver-tongued *consiglière* whom his boss, Vito, had once described as a man who could patch things up between God and the devil. And there was much to discuss with the don. He'd been here once before, in 1937, after Vito had settled in Naples, so he should feel at ease. But he wasn't. Something akin to that tension he felt before a jump crept over him. Maybe it was the stakes he was about to play for, maybe it was a touch of fear about dealing with the strongest don on the island, a man whose connections reached to Rome, to New York, to Chicago, and God only knew where else, a man whom even Mussolini had skirted and now accepted money from. He, Rudy Lotions, had set that up back in 1937, or at least the opening through Vito. In the States he would be called the *capo di tuti capi*, the boss of all bosses. He—

The huge, gold-knobbed door opened and a woman's voice said, "Good morning, Signore Sabatini. The don will see you now." It was the don's wife, a handsome, buxom woman with bright teeth and a blaze of white that ran through her straight black hair to a bun at the back of her head. Her demeanor was cool. She was another of the don's departures from the norm, since the average Sicilian don's wife knew nothing of his business. Signora Isabella Zerilli Calgogeri, the well-educated daughter of a wealthy Messina merchant, was Don Nizzi's *consiglièra*!

He greeted her and followed her into the huge, dark bedroom, limping on a pair of crutches that were too short. High, wine-colored velvet drapes guarded the room from the sun. He made out a huge four-poster bed with side curtains. Like in *Henry VIII* with Charles Laughton, he thought. For some reason the dark room reminded him of going to that movie one afternoon in Manhattan. It had been some little theater near Times Square and he had sat right on top of a couple making love. An uncomfortable moment. He hoped this wouldn't be an uncomfortable moment with the don.

Signora Calgogeri opened a door off to the right and sunlight burst into the dark room. Inside was a huge bathroom with a black and white checkerboard marble floor. A large open window admitted the sun and the pleasant scent he thought might be orange blossoms. At the far side, from a round white marble tub that was nearly large enough to be a pool, a tan, lined face with a neatly trimmed white mustache beamed at him. "Welcome to my home, Major Sabatini," Don Nizzi Gaetano Calgogeri said warmly in a deep, melodious voice. He laid aside the book he had been reading and extended his hand.

Sabatini quickly tried to kneel and nearly fell as he lowered his head, saying, "I kiss your hand, my Don." He was surprised at the size of the don's large hand as he kissed it.

The don's other hand touched the thinning bald spot on the top of his head. "In Sicily," he said, "you don't see so many bald men, but I could have been one. Once, when I was your age, I went out for a walk with no hat and got caught in the rain. Suddenly I felt some cold drops hit my head in the same place as you are getting bald, and I said 'Nizzi, this is how it starts!' So I went right home and ask my sainted mother why I should be like this when the rest of my family, and especially my handsome father, have such strong, beautiful hair."

The old man leaned forward as he lowered his voice in a confidential tone. "My sainted mother took me to my father's barber and told him to shave my whole head and for me to rub the best virgin olive oil from our groves into it four times a day. I did this for six months and look!" He turned his head so his thick, full stand of white hair could be seen from all angles. "Never again did I have this problem. Enough! I give you this secret gift as a welcome to my humble house. Now tell me, how is your beautiful wife?"

Sabatini tried to control the flush that he felt flooding his face. Why did he have to ask about her? Had he heard? He managed, "She's fine, my Don, just fine."

Pointing to an overstuffed chair close to the tub, Don Nizzi said, "Sit there and be comfortable. I'm sorry about your injury. My doctor will take care of you later." Signora Isabella Calgogeri moved quietly to another nearby chair.

Sabatini pushed away the uncomfortable thought of Teresa and brought himself under control. He recognized the smooth way the don had taken pains to set him at ease. He would like to slide into the business at hand, but to do so without his host initiating the change in conversation would be impolite. He waited, trying not to think of his painful foot as Don Nizzi slowly got to his feet in the pool and gestured to his wife for a towel. He was fatter than one would have guessed, cherubic in fact, maybe like what Santa Claus would look like in the nude. Sabatini averted his eyes, looking at the edge of the black tub and murmuring, "I've never seen white marble like that."

"The finest marble in the world. My father had it brought here from the quarries of Carrara, in the Apennines. Did you know that some of the finest of Michaelangelo's sculptures are made of Carrara marble?"

"It's beautiful," Sabatini said as the don stood before him, arms outstretched as in crucifixion, while his wife briskly rubbed him down with the huge towel.

"My father had an eye for beauty as well as power. Do you remember that he was the most important *gabelloto* in this part of Sicily? He thought of himself as one of the old mafiosi, and a protector of the people. Ah, the people—I still give them protection and in return they offer me their fealty." Isabella helped him into his underwear. Abruptly, he changed the subject. "Are you here only on army business, *Consiglière?*"

Sabatini leaped softly into the breach. "No, my Don, that is only the momentary part. Some of these days Mussolini will be carrion and

Hitler will be hung by the balls with the Torah up his ass. Then we can make great strides in our business."

The don's wife fixed gold cuff links in his monogrammed white silk shirt and helped him into his trousers. As he shrugged into the suspenders, he said, "Do you know, *Consiglière,* that I have never bathed myself, not once since I was born. First my sainted mother did it, and now my beloved wife. A few times when they weren't available, a trusted servant. They have always shaved me as well. No barber to make a planned slip with his razor for me, oh no." He patted his wife's shoulder as she tied his trademark white necktie. Again he spoke abruptly, "Now, Major, tell me why you are here."

Sabatini began softly, "Like your 'men of respect,' I, too, am loyal, my Don. Soon, after the mighty Allied armada crushes Italy, my Don Vito will want to return to America. One way is for him to come here and work with the American Army. Then he will need your help. But sooner than that, the U.S. Army will need your help. I know you've been approached by our intelligence agents, and that you sit on the fence." This was bold talk and Sabatini watched the don's eyes carefully, looking for any sign that would tell him he'd gone too far.

He went on, now confident on his turf as a negotiator, "Your people can disrupt the rear areas of the German and Italian Army units following the invasion and create major problems as they retreat toward the toe of Italy. But more importantly, you can help our army set up an operational government. I know that the 'men of respect' have always controlled parts of the government; now you can put your people exactly where you want them. The long-range payoffs can be staggering."

The don stepped into the crushed white velvet jacket with its fresh red lapel rose. "Yes, I have been thinking about the possibilities both here and with you in America. It could be interesting. I'll think on what you've said, my nephew."

"And I'm here for another matter, as well, my Don. This is more urgent at the moment."

"And it is?"

"The Italians or the Germans have a captured American fighter airplane. It looks like two crucifixes welded together. It has two powerful motors and the pilot sits in between them like a pea in a pod. They are flying it and shooting down our bombers. We think an Italian is the pilot, and we would like to find out who he is and where he is flying from."

"Is that why the young American is with you?"

"Yes, my Don, he has a vendetta against this pilot. I apologize for bringing him unannounced. He—"

Don Nizzi waved his hand. "I like Americans." He pursed his lips thoughtfully. "Regarding this stolen two-motored aeroplane, I will have my people start asking questions. And now let's go down to the garden for a fine breakfast. You know what they say about Sicilians, we would rather eat than make love."

CHAPTER 6

✥

Josh looked up from his Italian phrase book as Bernardo Calgogeri walked into his room. "My father has given permission for you to look for the airplane," he said with his ever present grin.

"Good!" Josh replied. "When can we get started?"

"We may leave in a few minutes, if you wish. As soon as Leopoldo is ready."

"Leopoldo?"

"*Si*, father doesn't believe I can protect you by myself. Leopoldo is one of his most experienced bodyguards and is also a most good driver of a car."

Josh frowned. "I don't want a whole army with me."

Bernardo shrugged. "We have no choice."

"Unless we get lucky, this could take a few days."

"If we remain overnight somewhere, I must telephone."

"Okay, tell me some more about Leopoldo."

"He, too, lived in New York for a time. He speaks pretty good English, considering the short time he was there, although not so good as mine. If he were a cowboy gunfighter like Tom Mix in your American cinema, he would have many notches on his gun handle."

Josh smiled at the metaphor. He had two extra magazines of shells for the Colt .45 automatic that was stuck in his belt under the dark suit coat Bernardo had given him. But while the pistol gave him a certain amount of security, after those rounds were gone, his arsenal was shot. Besides, the .45 wouldn't be of much value if he got into a real tight position. But as he said, he didn't want an army along—too many people would attract too much attention. On the other hand, supposing something happened to Bernardo? He could never get by on his limited Italian, even with the half-assed cover story he'd cooked up in case he had to fend for himself: he had taken a year of German in high school, so he would fake his way through as a downed German pilot, tired of the war. His cover story while he was with Bernardo was that he was a mute relative from Trieste. Leopoldo, with the notches on his gun, huh? Well, if one had to have someone riding shotgun, literally, it might as well be someone who knew how to kill.

The car was a black 1938 Fiat sedan.

Leopoldo Civitella was stocky and looked as though he was in his late forties. He had a bushy black mustache that hid his upper lip and black eyes that seemed to be narrowed all the time. He exuded animal strength and smoked incessantly. His English was heavily accented. As he was apparently far more devoted to the don than to Bernardo, his conversation was guarded. He wore a flat black cap tugged low over his forehead and carried a *lupara*, the popular sawed-off shotgun.

Josh had decided to try the international airport of Palermo first, because military aircraft flew from there and because it wasn't too far from Castello Carmelo.

When they topped the rise that overlooked Palermo, Bernardo told Leopoldo to pull the Fiat to the side of the road and stop. He was ready to play guide. "You told me you like history, Captain Rawlins. You are about to enter the ancient capital of our great island, a great port that the Phoenicians founded in the sixth century before Christ." His voice was a bit singsong, as if he had learned this spiel by rote. "It has been occupied by the Carthaginians, the Romans, the Normans, the Spaniards, and the Italians, among others. The Arabs left their mark in some of its buildings and Moslem flavor. You will easily detect the Greek columns in some of the government structures.

"What you're about to see is a—how do you say it—fascinating mix of oriental bazaar and modern commerce, of the past and the present. Over a half million people live down there, including some of the sharpest traders, most persistent beggars, and best pickpockets in the world."

As Leopoldo slowly drove down into the city Josh saw that it was located in what looked like a huge amphitheater that had been created by an ancient volcano. High limestone hills guarded its three inland sides like ancient sentries, while the dazzling blue Mediterranean lapped the shore to the east. There wasn't a cloud in the clear azure sky to filter or block the brilliant blanket of sunshine that found its way into all but the narrowest of winding alleys. In fact, Josh decided, with its bright, sometimes garishly colored houses, it was the most sparkling city he'd seen in this part of the world. The narrow, winding streets were a throwback to the Arabs, and were jammed with noisy people: vendors, women in black shawls, children darting in and out as they played, here and there a barking mongrel, soldiers and sailors, both Italian and German, and the *carabinieri*, the Italian National Police, who seemed to patrol every other corner.

There were a few small cars, bicycles, now and then an old motorcycle, and everywhere carts. There were carts drawn by mules, carts drawn by donkeys, and small carts drawn by people. Most of them were vividly painted and often decorated with well-drawn historical murals.

And more noise.

"Why are there so many young and healthy-looking men in the *carabinieri*? Josh asked as they worked their way down a short hill.

"Ha!" Leopoldo spat out. "Because it's easier to be a pompous prick in the *carabinieri* than to get shot in the army." Like all Sicilian men and particularly mafiosi, he was contemptuous of the police.

Twice Josh noticed remarkably beautiful young women, but didn't comment. There was too much he didn't know about the mores of these people; he didn't want to offend them in any way. He saw one bombed-out building, then another. He had forgotten that this was an enemy city that was a target for Allied bombers, that he had bombed its railyards himself. "Looks like they don't know a war is on," he said quietly. "Apparently our bombers haven't come here today."

"My father said they don't want to cause too much damage because the Americans want to be our friends after the invasion," Bernardo replied. "Remember, we are *Sicilians*, not Italians. We didn't start this war."

"That makes sense to me," Josh agreed. He cast a wary eye to the sky. That would be all he needed, to get caught in an air raid, possibly even by the 97th, and get his ass shot up.

"You must remember, being a Sicilian means something special!" Bernardo persisted.

Suddenly, as Leopoldo stopped for traffic, Josh's eyes locked on an officer wearing the uniform of the Regia Aeronautica, the Italian Air Force. He was standing on a street corner, not ten feet away, waiting to cross. Tall, swarthy, with several ribbons on his left breast below his gold wings, a combat pilot! Josh continued to stare at him. The eyes were dark, narrowed against the shimmering sunlight, alert like a hawk's, like a fighter pilot's. It seemed as though every nerve in his body tensed. It could be him, could be. His hand went to the butt of the .45. He could blow his murdering head off right here! He tried to remember the Italian insignia of rank—yes, three narrow gold bars topped by a diamond on the sleeve emblem—this bastard was a captain. He sucked in a deep breath and slowly blew it out. Let it go, he told himself; there were probably thousands of combat pilots in the Regia Aeronautica.

The captain's features burned into his memory. Now he had a model to fix on, an image in a gray-blue uniform adorned with the trappings of his conquests and the eyes of a hunter—of a killer.

Bernardo interrupted him, "We are turning on the Via Vittorio Emanuele, one of two great roads that cut through this mess."

"Good," Josh replied, tearing his eyes off the Italian pilot and jerking himself back to reality. "How long will it take us to get to the airport?"

Leopoldo grunted an answer, "Forty minutes."

"Yes," Bernardo added with a broad grin, "and you'd better start thinking like a mute. You can hear, which will explain any expression you make a mistake and show, but you don't have to talk. Okay, *Capitano*?"

Salvatore Scagnelli squinted out through the satin side curtains that had been installed to shield the back seat occupants of Don Nizzi's black Bugatti. "There was a time when this was the only car that could go anywhere on the island without being stopped. No Sicilian policeman or bastard *carabiniere* would dare halt it. Even the Germans have been told not to stop it, but now, with so many of them jammed onto Sicily from Africa, things are bad. The respect has slipped. It'll be so good when those bastards are gone."

Sabatini had his curtains pulled back so he could see the town. A funeral procession with the flower-covered casket being carried awkwardly by some black-suited pallbearers crossed in front of them, forcing the driver of the Bugatti to utter an oath and stop. More black-garbed mourners followed the casket. They looked like peasants. "Don Nizzi told me at breakfast that no one lives in the country anymore," he said.

"No, the people moved to the towns many years ago. Safer, no bandits. They go out in the mornings to work the fields, and come back at night."

"How much does a field hand make these days?"

"Less than an American dollar a day."

The New Yorker's eyes narrowed. "Can't you 'men of respect' change that? I would think since you are protecting both the employer and the worker, and there are many more workers than employers, that you could make more money if the workers were better paid."

Salvatore shook his dark head. "You are an American. Leave such things to us who know about them, *Consiglière*."

Sabatini nodded his head. Such problems were none of his affair. It was just that he liked to figure out how any racket could be better managed. And he always wanted the poor people to be better off. It went back to his own childhood on the East Side, when his mother had a hard time making do on his father's meager pay from the docks. With four kids to feed and clothe, it had never been easy. He had even chipped in most of the pennies he earned selling newspapers. Later, when he met Vito and started doing odd jobs for the young numbers runner, he earned more to take home. By the time he was twenty he was driving for Vito and offering advice. Those were the days when Vito first got thick with Lucky Luciano. As Vito grew in the mob, so did he. Soon, after Vito and the others knocked off the Boss of Bosses, he became the youngest *consiglière* in New York. That was when he bought the big house in Jersey and put his widowed mother in it. And his new wife, the beautiful Teresa.

He still felt the pain when she slipped into his thoughts. He blocked her out, saying, "This is one hell of a car, Salvatore."

"The don wanted a Bugatti Royale, their grandest limousine, but the car had such a wide wheelbase it couldn't navigate many of the mountain roads or the narrow streets in the towns."

"I've never seen anything like it in New York, except maybe Father Divine's big Dusenberg limo, the one that had a throne in the back seat."

"A throne? Who has a throne in an automobile? A king? A politician?"

"He's a jigaboo preacher. Goes on the radio. Makes a mint hustling his own people."

"A man of God. Too bad."

"Well, Salvatore, didn't the don tell me he has a brother-in-law who is a priest in Messina who 'does little things for him?' And I've heard there have been a bishop or two—"

Salvatore frowned as he turned from the window. "That's different. We represent the people, we're their guardians."

Sabatini smiled to himself. Yeah, sure.

The big Bugatti's Michelins ground on the gravel as the driver stopped in front of a small clinic. Before the New Yorker could get his painful foot out of the limo a beaming little man in shining eyeglasses and a white smock came running out to assist him. "I'm Doctor Vizzinni," he said in heavily accented English. "Since you are a privileged guest of my don, I want to treat you personally." He put his arm around Sabatini's shoulder and helped him inside the white building.

The X-ray machine was so antiquated Sabatini wanted to ask if it was the one invented by that guy Röntgen back before the turn of the century. The fawning little doctor made a big show of the procedure, twisting and turning his ankle for at least twenty different shots. Most of them weren't clear enough, so he had to go through the painful process again. Finally the decision was pronounced with a broad smile: "You are most fortunate, sir. I thought you had broken your fibula, but I can't even find a thin little crack. You have a sprain, which I will wrap with a special bandage that you can take off when you bathe. And I must insist that you stay in bed for a week. If you must get up, always use the crutches. Do you understand?"

Sabatini nodded. Well, it was better than a broken ankle. "How long before I'll be able to walk on it?"

Dr. Vizzinni gave him the age-old shrug of the medicine sage. "Maybe ten days, maybe several weeks."

The Palermo International Airport at Punta Ráisi had been thoroughly hammered by Allied bombers, but a number of obsolete prewar aircraft, mostly civilian, sat around the more remote parts of the field. Extensive damage to the buildings was obvious. Due to the flatness of the terrain, they couldn't see much of what remained in the way of military planes. Watching two fighters take off in formation to the west, Josh thought they were Macchi C-202s, but he couldn't be sure. They looked enough like Messerschmitt Bf-109s, even when they were shooting at you in the air, that you almost had to see their markings to know for sure. As it was still only a little after noon, Leopoldo recommended they try to get information at an inn that bordered the airdrome. "It's called the Eagles' Nest," he said, "And always when I've been in it

there have been flying soldiers bragging and talking about their aeroplanes."

They parked the Fiat in front of the Eagles' Nest. Leopoldo hid his
lupara under the front seat and checked the two pistols he wore in leather
holsters under his coat. Watching, Josh decided that his bodyguard was
a truly dedicated professional and wondered how many other weapons he might have stashed somewhere on his powerful body. They went
inside.

The dining room, which also doubled as a *taverna*, was dark because there were no windows. Oil paintings of various sizes in ornate
frames covered the walls, and an attractive young waitress smiled as
Bernardo selected a small table near the wall. Nearby, at another table,
two Italian pilots sat drinking wine. Josh caught himself bristling at
the sight of them but kept himself under control. They looked quite
young and wore only one ribbon below their gold wings. Their insignia announced that they were second lieutenants. Josh sensed at once
that neither could be his man. No, the one he sought would be experienced, probably an ace, one of some maturity and depth, even a romantic.
His last words over the radio came back: *"Mi dispiace, amico mio.
Questa è la guerra."*

He was also a ruthless killer.

They ordered a bottle of local red wine from a waitress with saucy
brown eyes and a promising figure. After sipping for a few minutes
Leopoldo lit a fresh cigarette and got to his feet. Going to the other
table, he said, "Excuse me, gentlemen, but my stupid nephew over there
is having an argument with me. Will you please tell him the truth?"

One of the officers glanced over at Bernardo, then said, "About what?"

"He insists that an American pursuit aeroplane with two long motors that is painted gray and blue flies from this airfield. It takes off
and comes back to stay until it flies again. It's, uh—"

"Based here."

"Yes, that would be the word."

"No, I don't know anything about such a plane, but we are new
replacements from Naples. We just arrived yesterday to fly the Macchi
202s."

Leopoldo threw up his hands in a gesture of despair. "Damn, now
I'll have to keep listening to his nonsense. Well, thanks anyway."

Shortly after the bodyguard returned to the table the two pilots left.
But within a couple of minutes three young enlisted men wearing the
insignia of aircraftmen came in and took a table. They ordered pasta

and a bottle of wine from the attractive waitress with the bold eyes. As soon as she delivered the bottle and filled their glasses Josh nodded to Bernardo. In a loud voice the don's son said, "I know I've seen that airplane taking off here. I'll bet you three hundred lira—no, five hundred lira!"

"That's a bet!" Leopoldo said darkly.

Bernardo got up from the table and walked over to the aircraftmen. "Hey, would you fellows do me a favor? My stubborn uncle over there won't believe me when I tell him that an American airplane has been flying in and out of our airport here. And we've made a bet. It's a fighter plane with two big engines, sort of gray with the American markings still on it. You've seen it, haven't you?"

The taller of the three, a corporal wearing two red stripes, nodded his head. "Yes, you're right."

"Will you speak up? I want to make sure he hears you."

The corporal raised his voice. "Yes, there was an American fighter flying from this field. It is what they call a P-38. But I don't know much about it. They always kept it in a revetment by the edge of the field, away from the main hangars."

Bernardo scowled. "You said it *was* flying here. Is it gone?"

"Yes, for several days now."

"Do you know where it went?"

"I think to Trapani, but I'm not sure." His two companions both shrugged in agreement.

Josh had to clench his fists to look passive and keep from shouting, who was the pilot?

Bernardo was right behind him with a wide grin. "Who would be flying such a plane, one of our test pilots?"

"I don't know. I never saw him."

"Did you hear if he ever shot at other American planes. Ha, I'll bet that would be fun!"

The corporal shrugged. "Don't know."

Bernardo thanked them and told the waitress to bring them another bottle of wine. Returning to his own table, he slapped Leopoldo on the back and said, "Pay up old man. And the next time, don't be so quick to call me a liar!"

Trapani. Josh knew right where that city was; he'd flown a mission there to bomb ships anchored in its harbor.

*   *   *

Thirty-five minutes after leaving the Eagles' Nest, Leopoldo slowed for a traffic holdup. Minutes later they crept up to a roadblock manned by several Germans and a sergeant of the *carabinieri*. "Where are you going and what is your business?" a pimply-faced German corporal asked in badly accented Italian.

Leopoldo gave him a cold look through the open window, then wiggled his finger at the sergeant. "Hey, *carabiniere*," he said loudly. "Come here."

The federal policeman obviously didn't like being summoned in such a peremptory fashion, but something in the driver's tone made him obey. "Yes?" he asked politely.

Leopoldo held up his papers. "I am chief bodyguard to the son of Don Nizzi Calgogeri, who is seated in the back. Now tell this German pup to wave us through before we are held up any longer."

The *carabiniere* sergeant stepped back and touch his forehead in a salute. "Yes, Signore Civitella." He spoke briefly to the German corporal, who quickly waved them through.

Josh smiled as they drove on. "You're pretty good, Leopoldo. How would you like to come back to Constantine with me when this is over and be my head gunner? Christ, we could end the war in nothing flat."

A touch of pride flitted through Leopoldo's eyes, but he shielded it by lighting a fresh cigarette. He murmured, "I can serve only one master."

Stopping the Fiat in the saddle of a limestone crest near Mount Erice two hours later, Leopoldo pointed down toward the sea and said, "There is Trapani, *Capitano*."

Josh looked around. The view was magnificent. Stretching to the southwest, the great expanse of Sicily greeted him. And beyond that the sea, now more green than ultramarine, seemed to run to infinity. Below his feet lay the port and the white buildings of the city where it stretched out on a scimitar-shaped promontory that helped form its harbor. Some eight or nine miles to the south, identifiable by its new concrete runway, was the airfield. He squinted, as if he might pick out the form of a captive Lightning waiting to be freed.

Workmen were busy digging a hole in the stone face of Mount Erice. Bernardo pointed to it and said, "They're building an air raid shelter. The Germans have a bunch of their fighters around here someplace."

As if in confirmation, a flight of five Messerschmitt Bf-109s roared around the peak and headed for the Trapani airfield. Falling into trail, looking like tiny dark seagulls, they peeled off in a fighter approach and landed. Josh felt his breath quicken, wondering if there might be a way to destroy some of them on the ground. He looked back at Mount Erice, saying, "I don't think they know our invasion will make shelters unnecessary before they get that big pile of dirt hauled away."

They drove down the curving road into the old city and stopped at a *taverna*. But this time they weren't as fortunate; there were no soldiers or anyone in uniform, for that matter. Of the few patrons, no one knew anything about the goings on at the air base south of town. They drove on, stopping at a small hotel that had a sign out front that read "Bar." Inside, they again drank local wine, hoping someone would come in with information. While they played the waiting game Josh dropped his role as a mute and quietly plied both the friendly Bernardo and the taciturn Leopoldo with questions. After a second glass of wine the bodyguard loosened up bit, and Josh was surprised to find that he had a droll sense of humor, that he could actually be quite entertaining. Josh asked about those who are called mafiosi, but they reacted as if a curtain had suddenly been drawn. While Leopoldo lit a cigarette and looked stern, Bernardo said quietly, "My friend, do not ask about such things. There are parts of life here in Sicily that are not like anywhere else in the world. Perhaps sometime, the major—Sabatini—can explain. But even he will never know everything." He shrugged. "He isn't a real Sicilian."

Josh nodded. The message couldn't be clearer. He would keep to safe ground the rest of his stay.

They waited another forty minutes, in which Leopoldo asked the old waiter if he had heard anything about their phantom P-38. But he drew a total blank. It was now after six o'clock and no one from the airfield had come into the place. They drove to the fenced-in airfield and up a winding side road to where they could look down on it. Several anti-aircraft gun positions were easy to spot. Josh thought they were the dreaded German 88s. Apparently there had been some kind of an air raid that day because one of the main hangars was destroyed and wisps of smoke still drifted up from its charred remains. There were fewer old aircraft than at Palermo, but they could see revetments where fighters were parked. Again, he couldn't tell for sure if they were 109s or Macchis. But he knew for sure at least five 109s had checked in for the night. The air war over Sicily, he reminded himself, was fought along civilized lines: only in the daytime did the flying gladiators meet in major combat. A handful of assorted Italian bombers were parked around the field, but he guessed they were grounded for one reason or another. The Italians hadn't done any serious bombing in some time. And there were at least a couple of dozen burned wrecks, the result of strafing or the good eyes of some Allied bombardiers.

But nothing that looked like a P-38.

They stopped at another inn, the Orchid, and went inside its *taverna*. A handful of boisterous German pilots occupied a table some fifteen feet from where they sat. They wore shorts and caps that were stained and faded enough to have seen Africa. Josh decided to go back into his mute role in case one of them spoke English or Italian. He watched them carefully, noting the signs of the experienced and battle-weary in their actions—talking too loud, chain-smoking, eyes darting about, drinking fast. One wore what he thought was the Knight's Cross, Hitler's equivalent of the famous Blue Max of World War I.

Their waitress was a slender brunette in her early twenties. Her eyes were quite large and coal-black, sensitive. She smiled at Josh when Bernardo ordered, and said in Italian, "You are not from here are you?"

He slowly shook his head.

"Where do you come from?"

Josh spread his hands, then pointed to his mouth and shook his head.

"He's a mute," Bernardo said.

She immediately raised her hands and began to swiftly flutter them in sign language.

He blinked. What the hell was he supposed to do now?

She repeated whatever it was that she had conveyed.

"Don't you understand?" she asked, watching his eyes. "I just told you I had to learn to speak this way because my sister is a mute."

Josh shook his head again.

"You're no mute," she said flatly.

Bernardo broke in, improvising, "My cousin was hurt in the war last year. He hasn't had time to learn the sign method."

She looked at him suspiciously. Quickly he handed her one of the cards Bernardo had filled out for him in case just this sort of a bind arose: "I am Pepi. What is your name?"

She waited a moment before replying, "Corina. My mother owns this inn. Where is your home, Pepi?"

He understood the question and wrote "Trieste," fearing that she might say, "Oh, I used to live there." Then he'd really be screwed. But she didn't. Instead she gave them menus and went for a bottle of wine. When she poured Josh's glass she looked deeply into his eyes and asked, "What did you do in the war, Pepi?"

"He was a bomber pilot, flew Piaggio P-108s, the big four-engined birds," Bernardo offered.

She gave Josh one more look, then turned to business. "You're in luck in regard to food. We have some excellent inky squid that I bought just today from our local black market fishmonger."

Leopoldo looked up from his menu with a frown. "A little expensive, isn't it?"

She shrugged. "Isn't everything?"

They all decided on the squid. Still, there were no airmen other than the Germans in the place. "Maybe the Italians don't come because the Germans are here," Bernardo said at length. He got to his feet. "I'll get us some rooms here so we have a place to sleep later."

Shortly after he returned to the table, Corina served them. Placing Josh's plate in front of him, she gave him another long look with those large dark eyes. The food looked appealing. The squid was accompanied by a red salad covered with the pure first pressing of local olive oil, spaghetti topped with a spicy tomato sauce, and a big bowl of huge olives. Josh began to eat in zesty silence.

Later, over a steaming cup of black espresso, he looked up as one of the German pilots, a sergeant with a beefy red face and scraggly light blond mustache, lurched toward them.

"Hey!" the aviator said loudly in heavily accented Italian, "How come you healthy young men aren't in uniform?" He had a dangerous glint in his eye.

Leopoldo gave the interloper a hard look. "One is a wounded veteran. The younger one is the son of Don Nizzi Calgogeri. Do you know who he is?"

"No, and I don't give a shit. I just want to know why we have to fight your damned war, go up there and get our asses shot at every day, and you just eat like fat Sicilian pigs."

The look on Leopoldo's face was frightening. Slowly, he pulled a big .45 revolver from under his coat and jabbed it against the pilot's genitals. His voice was harsh, "Don Nizzi is the most important man in Sicily, you piece of German donkey shit. Now you go back to your table like a good little boy, or I'll send you back like a good little girl. Move!"

The German looked down at the revolver and blanched. He glared at Leopoldo for several seconds, then turned and lurched back to his friends. "We'd better get out of here before there's trouble," Bernardo said.

Corina, who had been watching from the bar, hurried up with their check. "Yes, I think it best you leave," she said, eyeing the Germans. "Sign this and I'll put it on your room bill."

CHAPTER 7

✛

The light gray formal dining salon of Castello Carmelo was high-ceilinged and richly decorated, with a massive oil painting of the castle on one wall. The painting was guarded by burnished bookend suits of armor that were either authentic or expensive reproductions. Colorfully carved coats of arms embellished another wall. But a third wall broke from the theme of the huge room to allow French doors that were now open, admitting the sweet scents of the garden's flowers to mingle with those of the spicy meal that had just been consumed. They also admitted the last burnt-orange rays of the sun as it began to settle behind the western hills.

Sabatini twisted uncomfortably in the wheelchair Isabella Calgogeri had produced following his return from the doctor's clinic. There was no way he was going to stay in bed all the time, and the wheelchair gave his sore armpits a break from the crutches. He sipped his brandy and bit off a small piece from an anisette stick. A servant had laid out a tuxedo for him and, surprisingly, it had fit his large bulk quite well.

Like nearly everything at Castello Carmelo, dinner was not a normal Sicilian endeavor.

Across from him, near the head of the long banquet table, Isabella Calgogeri quietly sipped her espresso. Since taking him into the don's bathroom that morning she hadn't spoken two dozen words to him.

The silent *consiglièra,* he thought. She was fully secure in the exalted role her don had designated. Possibly the only woman advisor to a major don in all of Italy. A heady position for one not so sure of herself as this handsome woman. As if to prove her right to sit beside Don Nizzi's throne, she was wearing purple this evening, a long satin dress with a plunging neckline that revealed much of her ample cleavage. A triple strand of exquisite pearls contrasted with her smooth olive skin. He wondered how old she might be. Without the blaze of white running through her tightly bound black hair she could be forty. But the don had told him they had been married for over thirty years.

On his left, sitting in a tall, carved walnut chair, Don Nizzi lit a long cigar and blew out a bluish, almost perfect smoke ring. The don had dressed for dinner—or rather his wife had dressed him—in a white dinner jacket with a black tie. With a smile he said, "And now for the news you have waited for, *Consiglière.* My people have brought me the information you seek about the pilot, and it has a few surprises for both you and me. There is a proverb that many have claimed, but it belongs to Machiavelli: 'Revenge is a sweet plate, but especially when eaten cold.' "

Sabatini waited quietly, somewhat taken aback by the pleasure in the don's bright black eyes and the allusion to revenge.

"Your aviator is Franco Adamo, a major in the Regia Aeronautica. He has many medals because he is an ace, I believe they call it, with forty-one enemy planes shot down to his credit. These include many in the Spanish war, where he flew a Fiat. Now he flies your P-38. Supposedly Mussolini himself authorized the use of this American aeroplane to shoot down its cousins."

Sabatini nodded his head in gratitude. "Thank you, my Don. I had no idea your people could move so quickly. I thought it might take days."

One of Don Nizzi's thick black eyebrows arched as he smiled again. "And now the good part, *Consiglière.* Do you remember when Enrico Basila was fingered in Boston in 1935 and sent to prison for murder?"

"Yes, he was Vincenzo Coli's underboss."

"Precisely. Do you know who fingered him?"

"I think it was a junior *capo* by the name of Accurso, or something like that."

"Francis Accurso, to be exact. In America they called him Frank."

"Right. Seems to me he disappeared. I assumed somebody nailed him."

Don Nizzi grinned. "As a government informant, he went underground with Hoover's protection program and they sent him back to Italy, along with his wife and son. To Florence. There, with a new name, money, and a deal with Mussolini's secret police to protect him, he began a new life."

The don laughed harshly.

"Fools! They forgot that Vincenzo Coli was a member of my *cosca*, that *I* had to avenge the rat's break in *omertà* as much as Coli did. Accurso, using his new name, was now on my turf, so to speak. By working with our Friends in Florence and bribing some of those black-shirted Fascist peacocks, we soon found our traitor."

The old man looked at his wife and laughed again. "We caught him one night leaving a cafe. We let him die slowly, painfully, and we cut off his balls and put them in his mouth before we delivered him to his doorstep."

Sabatini nodded. The old way of branding an informer. "What about the rest of his family?" Vengeance seldom stopped with just the perpetrator—the whole family could be included.

"The wife and boy had fled, and for once we couldn't locate them. And then the war with Spain began and our vendetta against Accurso faded. Now, thanks to you, it has suddenly been brought back to light. The pup of Francis Accurso, the dog of a traitor, will now be taken care of."

"I don't understand, my Don."

Don Nizzi paused for effect, slowly saying, "The name Accurso took when he returned to Florence was Adamo."

Sabatini let out a low whistle. "And Maj. Franco Adamo is his son."

The don's eyes glowed as he smiled and slowly nodded his head. "The very man who is flying your aeroplane is the one who must be put to death to wipe our slate clean."

"Then you kill him and that will take care of that."

Now the don's crafty smile was evil. "No, that would be too simple. And besides, he's a big hero. No, I have a much more Sicilian way. You Americans will kill him for us, but he will know why."

"Where is he?"

"Flitting around from airfield to airfield, but we'll find him."

Sabatini lit a Lucky and blew out a cloud of smoke. It was absolutely beautiful.

Josh turned restlessly in the comfortable bed. It was warm, even though he was sleeping only in his undershorts. He had slept well for over an hour, but the day's events rushing through his head had broken his slumber. He couldn't escape the phantom plane and its pilot. They'd gone on to four other places near the airfield, playing their "bet between Leopoldo and Bernardo" scene. But while several airmen and civilians had seen the Lightning, no one knew anything about it. He got up and looked out the open window at the big moon. The courtyard behind the inn was bathed in its silvery glow, a placid study in inky shadow and varying shades of gray. He thought of his first night solo at a field outside of San Antonio. He was about thirteen but already tall enough to reach everything and still see. The moon had been at about this same stage of its passage and his father had nixed the idea of using flarepots on the deserted runway. He had said calmly, "Josh, you learn to land without lights, you'll always be better off when you *have* to land without them." He had gone up with his dad and shot three good landings before he was on his own. When he pulled back the throttle on that first solo approach, it had been so quiet, so alone with the big moon. He'd—

"Hello, Pepi."

Startled, he turned to see Corina, the waitress, closing the door to the small room. She came to him and touched his cheek. "I had a *fidanzato*, a—how do you say—fiancé, who was killed in North Africa," she said softly in accented English. "He was blond like you." She was wearing a thin negligee and smelled faintly of orange blossoms.

Why was she speaking English? He gave her a quizzical look.

"I know you are not Italian. I watched you eat. But I knew before that. You are British or American, I can tell."

He remained silent.

She touched his cheek again, running her forefinger over his lips. "It's all right. You can speak English. I hate the war and the sooner the Americans come and drive out the German pigs and their Italian lackeys the sooner Sicilians can break away from Rome and govern themselves."

Could he trust her?

"I don't know why you are here, but it isn't just for our squid. And I don't care." She leaned up, brushing his lips with hers. "I've wanted you since you walked into the *taverna*."

Somehow he'd known she'd come.

He'd read it in her eyes. And it excited him.

He kissed her, meeting her curious tongue. As she came into his arms her firm small breasts pushed against his bare chest through the thin negligee. The kiss quickly became more vigorous. She moved up to him, gyrating slowly, pushing against his quickly growing erection. Breaking the kiss, her mouth moved down his throat to the top of his chest before returning to his mouth. He held her tight, matching the movements of her versatile tongue, his hand sliding down her back over the swell of her buttocks and stroking them.

Their kisses became more fervid.

Now she was up high, one leg around his hip, riding her clitoris against his full-grown erection. Slipping her hands inside his shorts, she stroked the cheeks of his backside. His mouth found a breast, an erect nipple. "Oh, God," she moaned, pulling him to the bed.

In a moment she guided his erection inside and gyrated against him. She climaxed almost instantly, crying out, pausing, then slowly moving with him, building to his pace, murmuring words of love to her lost fiancé, wrapping her legs around his buttocks. . . .

Finally, after they were both spent, she sat up on the bed and looked into his moonlit face on the pillow. "Now will you talk to me in English?" she said softly.

"Yes, I'm sorry I was so guarded." He stroked her shoulder gently. "What I'm doing is dangerous."

"I guessed that."

"May I ask you a question?"

"Certainly."

"Have you ever heard of a captured American airplane flying from here?"

Her answer was immediate. "Of course. It is what you call a fighter aeroplane, right?"

"Yes, we call it a P-38."

She shrugged. "The pilot comes here at times."

Josh felt himself stiffen. "You've seen him?"

"Yes, I've served him. He likes a light white wine and lamb when we have it."

Josh knew his face must have paled. His mouth was dry. "Can you tell me what he looks like?"

"Certainly. Do I look blind?" She smiled. "Or mute?"

"Tell me!"

"He is about so tall as you. Dark hair, with flashing brown eyes and pretty white teeth. He has a strong jaw with a—what do you call it—dimple in the middle of his chin. He seems very sad at times and drinks too much wine. I think he is a major—I don't know the ranks so good."

Josh gripped her arm. "When did you see him last?"

"He was here yesterday afternoon. But he said he was leaving."

"Did he say where he was going?"

"Yes." She frowned down at his hand. "You're hurting me."

He blew out a deep breath, relaxing his grip. "I'm sorry. Where?"

"To Sardinia. A place called Elmas."

Elmas was the Italian air base near the largest southern city of the island of Sardinia, Cagliari. He had bombed it just two weeks earlier! "When did he say he was going?"

"This morning. He said he'd be there for some time, shooting down enemy planes."

God, Elmas! He had to get there! How? His mind raced. Sardinia was a long way off, probably well over two hundred miles. No way to fly. Could he go back and talk the general into letting him bomb the shit out of the place? No way. Buell was waiting to slap him in irons.

Her hand touched his cheek. "Am I to lose you now, as well?"

He shrugged. There was no way he could tell her how it was, no way she could understand about his murdered crew, a dead Mexican boy from San Antonio—or could he? Quickly, he explained about losing the *Texas Bitch*, and as he did so the hatred for this Italian killer resurfaced and made his mouth taste stale. When he finished, he looked away and said quietly, "I don't expect you to understand."

"Ha!" she snorted. "I am Sicilian! Both my father and my brother are dead from a vendetta!"

He nodded his head. He was sorry, but all he could think about was the killer pilot. Suddenly he asked, "Do you know his name?"

"Yes, it's Franco Adamo."

Franco Adamo! Now he had a name!

She dropped down beside him, putting her head on his shoulder. "And now," she said softly, "can you hold me for a few hours?"

Corina was gone when Josh awoke at six. He dressed hurriedly and went down the hall to Bernardo's room. After a couple of taps on the door the sleepy young Sicilian opened it. Quickly, Josh related what Corina had told him about Adamo.

Bernardo's grin was fully awake. "Aha, I knew she had eyes for you. Was she a good lay?"

"Let's talk about Adamo," Josh replied. "How can I get to Sardinia?"

"I don't know. Let's ask Leopoldo."

"Ask Leopoldo what?" the frowning bodyguard said from the doorway of the next room.

Josh explained quickly, then asked, "Can we get a boat of some kind?"

Leopoldo shrugged. "Possibly, but we would need permission from the don. Sardinia is a long way."

Josh scowled. He was going to Cagliari one way or another, if he had to swim. "The don has already given his permission for me to go where I wish, right?"

"But he meant in Sicily."

"How do you know what he meant?"

The bodyguard's jaw came out. "I know what he would say if I let his son go running off on some crazy trip to Sardinia. If something happened to Bernardo, he would cut my head off!"

Bernardo turned on him angrily. "You make me sound like a little boy! Do I have to remind you, Leopoldo Civitella, that I killed my first man when I was twelve? Or that my father has entrusted me with several important jobs?"

Leopoldo shook his head, but Josh could see he didn't want a struggle with the don's son.

"Or do I have to remind you that some day I will be the don?"

"No. I just think—"

"You can think when we get back. Now we have to find a boat that will get us to Cagliari."

The *Gaia* was a twenty-nine-foot-long fishing boat that had been built for a Palermo smuggler in the late twenties. It could sleep eight and had a tiny galley in its cabin. It was powered by twin inboard 250-horsepower diesel engines and carried enough fuel to get them to Sardinia and back easily. The current owner, a Friend of the don's, did enough fishing to look legitimate, but his real business was still smuggling and moving high-priced black market goods around. Purposely, to avoid any look of prosperity, the *Gaia's* paint was peeling and she was a rundown-looking craft. But her engines gleamed and her hull was as clean as a freshly scrubbed kettle. Her captain was the owner, Giuseppe Madeo, a stocky man in his middle fifties with a deeply etched face and a black beard sprinkled with salt-colored bristles. The beard was the bushiest Josh had ever seen; it reached nearly to the captain's eyes and seemed to burst out of his face in tiny curls.

Capt. Giuseppe Madeo was pleased to do a favor for the don's son, and reminded Bernardo of that several times in a deep, raspy voice. After leaving the Fiat in a safe garage Leopoldo joined them on the boat and they debarked from an old wooden wharf on the north side of Trapani's scimitar shape at shortly after ten A.M. The *Gaia* could easily cruise at twenty-five knots, meaning they would arrive in the vicinity of Cagliari by eight o'clock that evening. The captain also spoke English.

There was one other crewman, a nondescript little fellow named Topo— mouse. He handled the wheel after they cleared the local coast and picked up a west-northwest heading. It was another clear, hot day, but the relative wind allowed some comfort outside the cabin.

"When are you Americans going to invade Italy?" the captain asked.

"They haven't told me," Josh replied with a smile.

"Do you think it will be Sicily?"

"I really don't know, but I would think so. Good place to get a big toehold before going into the boot. And I think there are some good beaches for landings."

The stocky Giuseppe Madeo stroked his heavy beard. "Yes, I believe so too. I can't wait."

"He expects to make a lot of money," Bernardo said from where he sat at the stern.

The captain shrugged. "Don't we all? The American Army will bring many riches. And when there are riches, an enterprising sea captain can find ways to make a comfortable living."

"Ha," Bernardo laughed. "An enterprising sea captain can make a fortune!"

They had been at sea for shortly over two hours when a shout went up from Topo. *"Aeroplano!"*

Josh immediately snapped out of his doze and searched the bright sky. An aircraft was coming down from eleven o'clock some distance away.

"The flag!" Captain Madeo shouted, running to the stubby mast on the stern and hauling in the Italian flag. In moments he had run up the tricolor of France, and none too soon, for the aircraft was already approaching. As it circled overhead at about four hundred feet, Josh stared. It was a P-38 with ES markings, a 48th Fighter Squadron Lightning! He couldn't make out the number. 41 and 53 were the magic combinations. He felt his skin prickle as the fighter swung out in a wide circle to come in for a low pass. Was the pilot going to *shoot* at them?

Everyone's eyes were fixed on the twin-engined plane as it levelled out and came in head-on. But in a moment Josh saw that the P-38's path would be to the starboard side of the *Gaia*. His eyes locked on that peapod canopy, picking out a leather-helmeted head and goggles just as the Lightning roared by. Its number was ES-24, so it couldn't be Adamo. Now they had to worry about whether the pilot wanted some strafing practice or not. He couldn't have missed the French tricolor.

The P-38 climbed to about seven hundred feet in another arc and bore down on them once more. Josh strained to see if the telltale flashes would come out of the nose, the announcement of incoming lead. But he saw nothing. Moments later the Lightning flashed by again, this time pulling up in a victory roll and climbing on out to the east.

Josh let out a deep breath and shook his head in relief as he caught Captain Madeo's eye. Even the cool Leopoldo Civitella pulled out a handkerchief and wiped his brow. Bernardo grinned rather foolishly and said, "I knew all along he wouldn't shoot." That broke the tension and everyone smiled.

But seeing the P-38 only whetted Josh's appetite to get to Sardinia. He had a date with a murderer.

CHAPTER 8

❖

Maj. Franco Adamo kept his eyes on the number two engine's oil pressure gauge. It had fluctuated for the last twenty minutes, even dropping at times toward zero. He hoped it was just a seal, something that Diego could manufacture. The 12-cylinder, 1,425-horsepower, liquid-cooled Allison engines weren't easy to jury rig. The trouble with having an enemy aircraft such as the Lightning was that there were no replacement parts. If something went out it had to be supplanted by a part that was made by hand or from a somewhat similar part that could be modified. Either way, it didn't make for safe or long-term operation. But what was long-term about the remainder of this war anyway?

All he wanted to do was survive until it was over.

But how long would that be? From what he'd seen, the Allies were putting together an enormous effort to make the invasion. And with the tired equipment the Axis pilots had to use these days, the air would belong nearly unchallenged to the Allies once they put all of their air power into the sky. It was bad enough right now.

A glance at the oil gauge showed it hitting zero more often. He looked out at the number two engine and saw a shiny black coat of oil streaming back on its nacelle. Just hang in there for another minute! He called the tower: "Elmas, this is Outlaw One, for immediate landing. Over."

"Do you have an emergency, Outlaw One?"

"Yes, I'm about to lose an engine."

"One, you are cleared runway 26, winds are 251 at eleven knots. Over."

"Roger."

Another glimpse of the oil gauge was disconcerting, so he decided not to look at it again. He'd just stay ready to take immediate action to counteract the loss of the engine if it suddenly cut out on him. He lowered the landing gear and then the flaps as he lined up on runway 26 and pulled the throttles back. No problem now. He was high enough that he could glide the big fighter in if he lost all his power.

The Lightning skipped as it touched down lightly. Instantly Franco cut the fuel and switches to the number two engine. Two minutes later he taxied up to the revetment near the end of the runway that was the P-38's home when it was at Elmas. Sergeant Diego held up his hands in the signal to stop as Franco chopped the power to the other engine. Franco pushed the canopy back. Another mission, another enemy bomber shot down. Five more unknown faces frozen in death in the depths of the sea, shot down by a predator they trusted. He unstrapped himself and stared at the instrument panel, barely hearing the faint sound of the gyros running down.

As he swung a leg over the side Diego asked, "Get anything?"

"One B-25."

"Forty-six."

Franco nodded. He hated the numbers game. At one time it had been the most important part of his flying career. Now it was hollow, mocking. "Number two's got a bad oil leak," he said quietly as he stood on the ground and pulled out a silver flask. He undid the little cap and tipped it back, letting the fiery brandy go straight down his throat.

"I see it," the master mechanic replied.

The sun was still high, working its way down to the west. He went into the revetment and got out of the parachute and inflatable vest, hanging them on their respective hooks along with his leather helmet. It was cooler inside the sandbags. He sat down at a small field desk and pulled out an after-action report. Scribbling quickly, he made the proper notations, ending with: "Solo B-25 bomber destroyed; no survivors," and signed it.

Going back to the aircraft, he said, "Send word to my quarters when you find out if you can fix that engine."

"I'll fix it," Diego replied confidently.

Franco went to the rear of the revetment, where a small Fiat sat in the hot sun. It was dented and needed a new paint job. Diego had offered to fix it up and make it look like new, but he had refused. A shiny car would merely cast off reflections that a bored Allied bombardier might think was an interesting target to toggle his bombs on. As long as it ran and had petrol, it served its purpose.

He drove to the underground operations center and found his boss, Lt. Col. Fillipo Canepa, angrily staring at a letter in his small office. Canepa was in his early thirties and had been one of Italy's first aces in the Spanish war. Short and skinny, quite dark in the skin, he chain-smoked nervously. His black eyes always seemed to be darting around, as if he were airborne and waiting to be jumped by enemy fighters. He had simply seen too much aerial combat before suffering the wound that cost him his left foot and grounded him.

Franco hadn't cared for Canepa when they had served together in Spain, and he disliked working for him now. Because the P-38 mission was so special—it was supervised directly by the senior Regia Aeronautica aide to Mussolini—Canepa knew Il Duce had a personal interest in what happened, and he fretted constantly. Dubbed "Operation Outlaw," the mission had been conceived when a P-38 pilot from the 14th Fighter Group had lost both engines returning from a long-range mission to Italy. The pilot had been able to land at an auxiliary airfield on Sardinia, but for some reason had been unable to destroy or cripple the aircraft before being captured. The P-38 had suffered damage to the fuel lines of both engines—an extremely rare event—but was otherwise undamaged. Once these lines were repaired and the fighter plane had been successfully test flown, Fillipo Canepa had conceived the idea of using it to boldly join up with Allied aircraft and shoot them down. Not only would the plan create enemy losses, it would also produce a major morale problem.

The request went all the way to Mussolini and he, personally, made the decision to proceed. In fact, it was rumored, Il Duce had rubbed his hands in glee at the prospect.

Canepa slapped the letter into his palm. "The cowards are already planning on losing," he said heatedly. "Read this!" He handed the letter to Franco, who scanned it quickly. It was classified most secret and outlined a plan whereby, in the event of collapse of the government following an Allied invasion, loyal members of the Regia Aeronautica would continue to fight with the Germans.

Franco shook his head slowly. The moment this great debacle of a war was ended by any legitimate government of Italy would be the same moment he would lay down his sword forever.

"What do you think of that shit?" Canepa asked.

Franco had to be careful with his jittery boss. The man was not only a rabid Fascist, he was a fanatical nationalist. "I think a patriot should fight for his cause as long as it exists," he replied carefully.

Canepa's eyes narrowed as he considered the remark. Finally he nodded his head. "That's well stated, Adamo. With your permission, I'll use that thought in my response to this treason. Now, how did your last mission go?"

"I shot down a B-25 about fifty miles out toward Palermo."

The crippled ace frowned. "Just one for the day isn't very good, Adamo. I'm not pleased and certainly Il Duce will not be happy."

Franco had flown two missions and had spent over five hours in the air. He shrugged, choking back an angry retort. No sense in struggling with the asshole again. "There simply weren't any more stragglers in my sector," he replied matter-of-factly.

Canepa lit another cigarette and blew out the smoke. His left hand clenched into a fist. "You simply must bring me better results!"

Franco decided to let him have it. "We may have a major engine problem. Oil was leaking out of number two as if it had a hole big enough to jump through."

The colonel stared at him as if he'd slapped him. "What happened, did you firewall it for an extended period? What's wrong with you, Adamo—you know better than that!"

Franco wanted to reach over, grab him by the lapels, and tell him to shove the whole thing. This Lightning mission was all the bastard had left in the world, at least in his very limited world, and he was totally unhinged by it. But again he controlled his words, "No, I didn't hurt it. Aircraft engines have ways of acting up. You know that."

Canepa reached for his cap and cane. "I'm going down there right now!"

"If it can be fixed, Diego will have it flyable by morning. Why harass him?"

The colonel's eyes narrowed. His tone was icy, "You just take care of the flying, Adamo, and you had better start getting some more kills, or—"

Franco couldn't hold it back any longer, "Or what? You got somebody else to fly these goddamned sneak missions? Good, I'll head for the beach. My swimming has suffered too much lately, anyway."

Canepa's voice was shrill, "I'll have you assigned to one of those suicide squadrons!"

Franco slowly shook his head and stepped away.

"Don't you dare walk away from me!"

Franco turned. "What are you going to do, court-martial me? How would you explain *that* to Il Duce?"

Maj. Franco Adamo's quarters were in a one-story barracks that was removed several hundred yards from the bomb-damaged buildings and hangars. So far its remoteness had helped it escape even a wandering Allied bomb. He had a large corner room facing west with a limited view of the sea and usually a fresh breeze. But it was still quite warm this particular evening because the hot sirocco from Africa had arrived to torment the Cagliarians. He took the jacket of his dress uniform from its hanger and donned it. Looking in the mirror, he saw that all of the insignia seemed to be in place. He had a temporary batman, and didn't trust the young man to get things right. There had been a time when he would have been pleased to wear the dress uniform and display his awards. Now they were mere baubles to him, the jewelry of what someone had once called God's greatest game. A game that had become so repugnant to him that he had to blot it out constantly.

Above his several war medals were his decorations: the blue-with-red-striped Medaglia al Valore Aeronautica, Oro, or gold award, his nation's top award for valor; the blue-and-white Croce di Guerra al Valore Militare with sword; the Spanisch Kreuz in gold and diamonds with its Nazi swastika in the center that the Germans had awarded him, and two Spanish decorations. Above them he wore his gold pilot's wings. The heavily starched collar of the dress shirt felt uncomfortable; he was used to wearing an open collar and shorts when he wasn't in flying clothes.

The occasion was a reception for several high-ranking dignitaries. Count Galeazzo Ciano and his wife, Edda, were visiting, as was Generalmajor Adolf Galland, commander of the Luftwaffe Fighter Arm. The general, who was in the Mediterranean to restore morale and efficiency among his battered fighter wings, had been visiting the squadrons on Sicily and was spending one night here in Sardinia's capital before flying back to Rome. As his visit coincided with that of the Cianos, a reception had hurriedly been put together and all RA officers above the rank of captain had been ordered to attend. The soiree was being held in the Regina Margherita, the dowager queen of Cagliari hotels.

Franco sipped from his wine glass as he turned from the mirror. He could just ignore the performance, but he thought it might be interesting to see Galland again. The years fell away, and it was 1938 in Vitoria, Spain. He had been sent on detached duty to the Luftwaffe's Condor Legion to fly the Messerschmitt Bf-l09 fighter plane. It was two weeks after he shot down two Ratas in one day that the commander of the Condor Legion decided to give him a goodwill medal, the Spanisch Kreuz. Oberleutnant Adolf Galland, then commanding a ground support fighter squadron, had been part of the ceremony, and they had gotten a little drunk together afterward. The tall, black-mustached Galland, who wore his peaked hat at a jaunty angle, had shot up in rank when the big war had started, becoming the youngest general in the Luftwaffe at age thirty.

Yes, maybe seeing the German would create a sliver of interest in his otherwise empty, vacuous life.

Like nearly everything else, the Regina Margherita had suffered with the war. Once the jewel of the city's hotels, the old lady was shabby around the edges and reminded Franco of an aged duchess wearing poorly applied makeup, a crooked tiara, and an out-of-style gown that sported both torn places and patches that couldn't be hidden. The reception was in the main ballroom, where the capital's society had used the occasion to turn out and pretend that its current lifestyle wasn't in for a change the day a fleet of Allied ships appeared on the horizon. The governor and his wife were there, along with other high-ranking politicians. Evening dress and bright gowns mixed with colorful bemedalled uniforms of all the services under the brightness of the room's huge chandelier. Early summer flowers added their fragrance and alluring colors to that of the many Sardinian beauties sporting their finest jewelry.

White-gloved waiters carried silver trays filled with glasses of fine wine that had been carefully hoarded in some deep cellar, far from possible enemy bombs. And the hotel's still proud chef had prepared an abundant selection of delicacies from the sea. As Franco sipped from a glass and nibbled on a piece of pickled sardine, he thought all wars should be fought near coastlines, where the friendly sea would always keep the inhabitants from starving.

An attractive woman in her early thirties withdrew from a nearby cluster of talkers and walked up to him. "Aren't you Maj. Franco Adamo?" she asked with an easy smile.

He nodded his head over his glass.

"I'm Baroness Ricardi," she said, holding out a hand enclosed in a pale blue glove.

He kissed it, saying nothing, as he looked into her confident eyes. They were pale green, like his Sella's, and they startled him momentarily.

"I recognized you from the newspaper photograph. But you are even more handsome in person. My husband was in the RA."

He nodded his head again. The goddamned newspaper story; here he was on a secret mission and the local paper had splashed a big article in the previous day's edition about a leading RA ace being assigned to Elmas.

"He was a colonel." A look of sadness touched her eyes momentarily. "But he was killed in a crash over a year ago."

"I'm sorry," he mumured. She was quite attractive and wore the low-cut blue silk gown well.

She sipped from her glass, looking at him contemplatively. "I've only recently come out of mourning. One gets lonely, you know."

He guessed that she had probably made up for being alone in a hurry. "Yes, I suppose," he replied.

"Do you know what loneliness is, Major?" she persisted.

"Doesn't everyone?" He glanced a few yards away to where Galland was talking to a handful of flying officers. "If you'll excuse me, Baroness, I have to speak with the general," he said, turning away.

She caught his sleeve. "Can we carry on our conversation later?"

"Not if I get to him first," Edda Ciano said with a bright smile as she stopped in front of them. She held out her hand to be kissed. "Hello, Franco, darling. I heard you might be here."

He smiled as he bent over the hand and told the daughter of Benito Mussolini how lovely she was. Right after his return from Spain as the RA's current hero he'd been assigned as the count's special aide and pilot for a brief period. At that time he'd become closely acquainted with the auburn-haired contessa, close enough for her to offer her charms when he once flew her down to Sicily for some kind of political visit.

It was now nearly five years later, and at forty-two she was still a handsome woman.

Edda Ciano had apparently met the baroness already. "This is the best-looking pilot in the RA," she said with a shrug. "But like the god Mars, he remains coolly aloof from the wiles of lowly earthling women."

"I had just begun to notice," Baroness Ricardi replied pleasantly.

"I'm afraid I must steal him from you," the countess said, linking her arm in his and drawing him away. Stopping near a huge potted plant that needed some time in the fresh salt air, she said, "How are you, darling? I mean *really* how are you? I heard you were flying some kind of special missions. Galeazzo told me that father is gloating about it."

"It's supposed to be classified."

"Are you all right?"

He shrugged. "Just tired of it all."

"Yes, some frightful things are happening in Rome."

"I've heard rumors that the monarchy will support an armistice when the Allies arrive."

The countess frowned. "I don't even want to think about it. Have you heard from your beautiful wife, darling?"

"No, far as I know she's still in Egypt with her work. At least I hope so."

"Do you miss her terribly?"

He shrugged. "After four years the wound ceases to fester."

She touched his cheek, saying softly, "Any time you want some solace, you know where my open arms are."

He found a smile. "Thanks, Countess. The thought is provocative."

She laughed. "Now don't let that Ricardi witch get her hooks in you. I saw the gleam in her eye."

He shrugged. "She's just a lonely widow."

Edda Ciano snorted. "Ha! She was probably the same way last night, until she met a handsome pilot."

"I have to see General Galland."

"And I have to get back to my husband's charmed circle. Remember, darling, my shoulder is available."

As the Countess Edda Ciano walked away he admired her tall figure and wondered if that American gangster, Genovese, was still keeping her and her husband in drugs. Vito Genovese, the New York partner of Lucky Luciano—he'd heard the talk about them on several occasions back in Boston. Particularly after he started driving for his father, before his father suddenly uprooted the family and moved back to Naples. Boston—it seemed a million miles away and a hundred years ago. He wondered if he'd ever get back.

Adolf Galland was as handsome as ever in his gray dress uniform. Dangling from his collar was the Knight's Cross with Oak Leaves, Swords and Diamonds, which he had been awarded by Hitler after his seventieth kill. Overall, he had more than a hundred aerial victories. When he spotted Franco approaching he stuck out his hand and said with a grin, "I guess there aren't many of us old Bf-109*b* pilots around anymore, right, Adamo?"

"Not many, General." The last he heard, the 109 was up to a k-model, a vastly advanced machine from the old b they had flown in Spain.

"Just today, I heard an interesting little story about you and a special fighter plane."

Franco shrugged. "Big secret."

Galland broke away from the others, all at once an enthusiastic young fighter pilot again. "Tell me about it. How does this *gabelschwanziger Teufel,* this fork-tailed devil, fly?"

They each grabbed a fresh glass of wine from a passing waiter as Franco replied, "It's a pilot's airplane. Feels good, solid, like a fast, light bomber. But it'll get up to five thousand feet in less than two minutes and you ought to see that awesome firepower. God, when those four fifty-calibers converge in front of you, you can blow just about anything out of the sky. Add the twenty millimeter cannon and it's incredible. And it's fast. Course, you gotta fly the machine. A sloppy pilot wouldn't last very long in it."

Galland's eyes were gleaming. "How does it compare to your latest Macchi?"

"The Macchi better not challenge one on even footing."

"And our latest Focke Wulf?"

"I don't know, General, I haven't flown one. All I can tell you is this—don't let a P-38 pilot line up his sights on you."

Galland nodded, sobering. "And our Fuehrer wants my tired pilots to go head to head with everything in the air."

Franco shrugged. It was the same in the RA. Quietly, he asked, "Will your fighter pilots hold out until the end, or will you pull them back to Italy for the big fight?"

The general shook his head. "I'll be damned if I'll see them slaughtered over Sicily. But unfortunately, I don't have the final say. And between us, Adamo, Goering will do anything Hitler demands."

Franco sighed, then raised his glass. "Which brings us to the present. *Prost, Herr General!*"

Galland also raised his glass, *"Brindisi, Signore Maggiore!"*

Just as Galland broke off to join the governor Lt. Col. Fillipo Canepa caught Franco's attention and beckoned to him. "What was that all about?" he asked suspiciously.

"We were just talking about flying," Franco replied casually.

"Did you discuss the Lightning mission?"

"Seems as though he knew all about it."

"He couldn't. My security has been too tight."

Franco shrugged, saying nothing.

"Maybe he heard about it from Air Staff. That's it, probably got to him when he came through Rome." Canepa's eyes took on a far away look. "I wonder if Hitler knows about it. You know, I might even get a German medal before this is over."

Franco was beginning to feel the wine. He touched his chest. "Here, you want mine?"

The scowl instantly erased the colonel's pleased expression. "Don't be such an ass, Adamo. This mission is important to the Reich."

"Yeah, well, I hope you get a dozen medals out of it."

"Oh, there you are!" Baroness Ricardi said at Franco's elbow. "I was afraid you'd departed."

Suddenly, talking to an attractive woman with a plunging neckline was far more appealing than carrying on an asinine conversation with an asshole like Canepa. Besides, he was entertaining interesting thoughts about knocking the fool on his ass. He took her by the elbow and steered her away. "No, the colonel and I were just talking about the price of metal."

Her first name was Angelina and her black hair was done in a floppy bob. She was from one of the old families of Sardinia and had married her husband, the baron, when she was twenty-one. After another glass of wine she said, "Do you have a car, Major?"

"Yes, an old RA Fiat. Why?"

"I'm living in my country house out by Poetto. How would you like to drive me home while it's still daylight? I have some wonderful brandy I've been hoarding for a special occasion."

He didn't know whether it was the wine or the fact that she was actually quite pleasant, but he didn't resent her at all anymore. In fact, he wanted to get away from this stuffy reception and this was as good an excuse as any. But the mention of a good brandy was what really did it. "Sounds fine to me, angel-girl," he replied in English.

Quickly, she replied in quite good English, "I attended Wellesley for two years. Where did you get that Boston accent?"

"From a short-wave radio."

She laughed. "And you got all those medals at the grocery store."

They drove from the middle of the city toward the Margine Rosso—Red Bluff—where the long Poetto beach ran off for six miles to Sella del Diavolo. About midway, Angelina Ricardi told him to turn up a narrow road that led past an ancient ruin to a partially hidden old house overlooking the sea. A slightly faded white, the two-story structure was bathed in the long reddish rays of the setting sun.

Inside, family portraits adorned the walls of the main salon. The place was typically old tradition with worn edges. "I gave the servants a night off," she explained as she went to a richly carved mahogany cabinet and withdrew a bottle of Remy Martin Cognac. Unscrewing the cork, she poured two snifters half full and handed one to him. They touched glasses. "To life," she said.

"I'm not sure I know what that is," he replied soberly.

She led him to a more comfortable room and pointed to a sofa. "I have an idea," she said. "Back at Wellesley they initiated me into the art of drinking with what they called a French 75. Of course I got very drunk the first time, but anyway I just happen to have some fair Champagne in my little wine cellar. So if you'll wait a minute, I'll get it."

He watched her glide away over the top of his glass and decided her rear end looked quite good in that blue silk dress. He turned his attention back to the Remy Martin. Excellent. Tonight he would wipe away the war in style, blot it out with a touch of class. He hadn't had brandy this good in ages.

She brought the Champagne in a bucket, just as if they were in a restaurant, and poured the bubbly wine over what was left of his Cognac. "Try that," she said with a smile, as she poured her own.

"Excellent," he said after a sip. Again they toasted, and he noticed that she drank fully a third of hers at once. A lady after his own heart, he thought. "*Santé*," he said, raising his glass.

She turned on a wind-up Victrola and played a Paul Whiteman record. Closing her eyes, she danced slowly by herself in front of him for several moments before stopping to mix herself another French 75. "I really loved my husband," she said. "He was several years older, but he was such a fine person. It was terrible for me the first few weeks."

"How did he die?"

"He flew in the last war, and had his own aeroplane. When Il Duce began his Ethiopian campaign my Rollo accepted a colonel's commission. He died in the crash of a transport." Her words caught, "He wasn't even the pilot."

Franco looked away. He shouldn't have asked. In fact, he didn't care one iota. He'd lost too many close friends to let the death of a stranger inflict any kind of pain on him.

"Have you ever been married?" she asked.

He told her about Sella, briefly.

"You haven't seen her in over four years?"

He helped himself to the Cognac and topped it with more champagne. "No." He switched the subject. "Quite a sunset." Getting to his feet, he walked to the open French doors and looked at the deep scarlet reflection of the top of the dying sun sinking below the mirrored surface of the distant water. "One can almost forget." He drank deeply and felt the powerful liquid quickly work its way down.

She came to stand beside him, the crimson glow washing over her. "One *can* forget," she said quietly. "I do it every night."

He nodded his head, staring off into the past where the faceless ones sometimes called out to him. "The shadows that are out there make it difficult."

"Do you have many women?" she asked softly.

"No."

"Like the countess said, you can probably have what you want."

He turned abruptly. "*This* is what I want," he said, holding up his glass and draining it. "A woman is momentary, and when the passion is past, the shadows return."

She went back to the sofa, and drew her legs up beside her. Lighting a cigarette, she said, "I can only sleep about four hours when I drink myself out of it. Then I wake up, wide-eyed, and the sadness returns."

He nodded his head again and mixed himself another drink. He knew he was getting drunk because that wonderful state of not giving a single damn about anything was settling over him. He watched as she went to the Victrola and turned the Paul Whiteman record over. It played

"Begin the Beguine." Returning to the sofa, she leaned down and brushed his lips with hers. "Could I talk you into a dance?"

"Why not?" he murmured, taking her into his arms. They moved slowly, their bodies melting together, their feet practically still. Her hand found his neck, moving slowly to his ear and stroking it. He felt the arousal as her lips came up to touch his.

CHAPTER 9

✤

Rudy Sabatini savored a deep puff from his fine after-dinner cigar as he leaned back in a comfortable chair and listened to Don Nizzi expand on the difficulties Mussolini had visited on the Friends in the '30s. His ankle was better, thanks probably to both the hot soaks and the fact that he'd stayed off it completely. The spicy ointment that the cook had provided may also have been of some value. At any rate, he thought he might be able to walk on it much sooner than the doctor had anticipated. He sipped from the monogrammed brandy glass as the don leaned forward from his nearby chair of red velvet and spoke earnestly. "There is something I must discuss, *Consiglière*. Yesterday when you spoke of the future after the war, I'm afraid I was playing Sicilian with you. Now I must be more candid. I already have big plans for my American connections, but first my friends and I must deal with the problem here in Sicily."

He puffed on his cigar as he paused.

"Separatism has long been a popular subject in Sicily. This whole terrible adventure with Mussolini and his Fascist pigs has merely added emphasis to the fact that Sicily simply does not belong as part of the Italian commonwealth. We never *have* been Italians and we never *will be* Italians. There are several other possibilities, the primary one being that we become an independent state and govern ourselves."

As the don paused again, this time to sip from his brandy glass, Sabatini murmured, "I would think that would be most desirable."

"No," the don replied. "My friends and I think being a new state in the union of the United States of America would be the most desirable. Most Sicilians have a fondness for your country and your people. It's possible, since Sicily is so far from Washington, that we could be loosely governed, with most of the control being here. Personally, thinking of business, I can't imagine anything more profitable."

He looked over at his wife, who was sitting quietly as usual in a nearby overstuffed chair. "I foresee, in the next quarter of a century, vast opportunities for profit in the world. While they can be planned from here, many of these possibilities must be put into effect in the riches of America. An apparatus that reaches well inside your government must be constructed, my friend. And our being a state will make everything so much easier."

Sabatini's mind raced ahead. Sicily a forty-ninth state? Members of Congress on the payroll of the Friends? Laws favorable to the mob's business? Open gambling throughout the country? If Vito came back their organization could become all-powerful. No limits to where Rudy Lotions could go.

"So you see, I am more than willing to cooperate with the American Army when it arrives, but I want you to make sure that your generals know that I have done so."

Sabatini nodded his head. "That'll be no problem. I'll write a report tonight that will outline your desire to help. It'll be part of a larger report when I get back to Africa, my Don."

The don got out of his chair and walked to the window. After a moment he looked back and said, "There is much to be done, and we have to pick our new friends carefully. Being able to walk on water may not even be enough." He looked directly into Sabatini's black eyes. "I think you—with or without your Don Vito—can be one of our best friends in America."

Sabatini held his gaze as he waited.

"But there will be tests, and I have one for you. Have you ever killed a woman, Major?"

Sabatini looked quickly at the impassive Isabella Calgogeri, but her eyes were as hard as her husband's. "No," he replied, thinking at once about his Teresa.

"*Could* you kill a woman?" the don persisted.

The New Yorker took his time, trying to decipher what his motive might be. "Yes," he said, "if it were necessary. In war, one must look at the objective and do whatever is necessary."

The don nodded his head. "Good. I have a request."

"Name it, my Don."

"I have learned that Major Franco Adamo is now located at Elmas aerodrome by Cagliari, Sardinia. As I told you yesterday, he is the responsibility of you Americans now. But he has a wife."

Sabatini waited.

"Normally we would stop after killing the traitor and his immediate family, but since the man's wife died naturally, and since we wish to announce to the world that the Friends will never brook treachery, Franco Adamo's wife must die as well." Don Nizzi sipped again from his brandy snifter and glanced at his wife. "She is an Italian Jew, an archaeologist working with the British in Egypt."

Sabatini held his breath.

"You, *Consiglière,* will find her and kill her."

The *Gaia* sidled up to the wharf in Cagliari's lagoon and Topo quickly jumped ashore to wrap a line around a piling. Josh watched through a porthole from the cabin in case, by some chance, any unfriendly eyes might be observing their arrival. Although the sun had fallen below the horizon and only a dark, cherry-colored memory of it remained, it was still light enough for him to see the old buildings that formed the waterfront. There were many other boats docked nearby, but most of them were small, of the two-man fishing variety. The captain had decided it would be best for them to stay at a small hotel where he knew the proprietress, a widow of a Friend of the Friends. Topo would stay on board and guard the boat.

They gathered up their meager belongings and followed him as he led them up a short hill to where a sign that read *El Cinghiale* hung in front of an old three-story structure. The Boar was aptly named. From the small lobby one stepped directly into its dark *taverna,* where a number of stuffed and tusked heads stared back from their positions on the wall. Several men in seagoing clothes looked up from their glasses in curiosity, then went back to their conversations. The room smelled of old tobacco.

"Giuseppe!" a buxom woman in her forties with wild black hair shouted when she spotted Captain Madeo.

"Elfida!" he shouted back, catching her in his arms as she came running around the end of the bar.

They kissed zestfully and she threw her head back and laughed. "You devil, you haven't been here in months!"

"Do you have rooms for my friends here?"

"Of course, my Captain." She quickly glanced from Leopoldo Civitella to Bernardo to Josh.

"This is Don Nizzi Calgogeri's son," Madeo said softly.

Elfida's eyes lit up as she smiled at the young man, and Josh realized at once the far reach of the don's power. "I have two fine rooms for you gentlemen," she said with a broad smile. "And I must feed you the finest dinner in all of Sardinia. It will start with a delightful *antipasto di mare*, then a *burrida*, a zesty stew that my great grandmother first cooked. And then a fine lobster with a salmon spaghetti that is so good it will make you hate your mother!"

Madeo patted her on her buttocks. "You're as beautiful as ever."

Elfida beamed. "Ha! You don't come to see me often enough to know. Why all the way from Sicily now?"

"We're here to catch a big fish—a flying fish."

"You must tell me about it later."

Josh gathered that the captain would not be sleeping in their rooms. But that was none of his business. All he wanted to do was learn how to find his way around Elmas so he could get on with things.

As they drank the strong coffee after the big meal Elfida had fixed, Giuseppe Madeo finally asked about Josh's plan. They were at a large table in the back of the room, away from any other patrons. Josh glanced up at their hovering proprietress, his caution showing in his expression. Quickly the captain said, "Don't worry for one moment about our beautiful hostess. This establishment is owned by Don Nizzi and our lovely Elfida manages it for him."

Elfida smiled, nodding her head. "If I can help with what you came for, just ask. In any case, my lips are sealed and elephants couldn't pry them apart."

Bernardo quickly translated, adding, "She might be of value."

Josh nodded. "Ask her if she knows anything about Elmas."

Bernardo switched to Italian and complied.

"Yes, I have been there to a dance with the sergeants several times."

As soon as Bernardo translated, Josh asked, "Is there a fence around the base and do you know where the officers live?"

Yes, the base was surrounded by high barbed wire, and yes, she thought she knew where some of the officers lived, a one-story building apart from the main hangars and such.

Josh nodded again. The following day was a Wednesday; could she use one of her contacts to find out for sure, possibly even to find out if Maj. Franco Adamo lived on the base, and if he was presently there?

Her dark eyes flashed. "Yes, there is a sergeant-major who has tried to get in my bed for months. I'll send word to him that I want to see him and he'll come running and panting." Bernardo translated again.

"Good!" Josh said. Turning to Civitella, he said, "Leopoldo, can you get on the base as some kind of a laborer or something?"

The bodyguard nodded his head, then asked Elfida, who told him she would have a Friend of the Friends take care of it in the morning.

"But I still don't know your plan, my friend," Captain Madeo said.

Josh sipped the liqueur as he looked at the expectant expressions on their faces. "Nothing has changed. I have a vendetta against Adamo. Once he is dead, I want to steal the airplane and fly it back to North Africa. Simple as that."

The dawn's peach reflections on the thin clouds cast a soft glow on the room as Franco Adamo swung his legs over the side of the bed. He blinked, trying to get oriented. His head complained, and he pressed the heel of his palm between his eyebrows. Looking back at the sleeping form on the other side of the canopied bed, he put it together. Goddamned French 75s. Naked, he got to his feet and went to the bathroom. When he returned, Angelina Ricardi was sitting up smoking a cigarette. He said nothing as he reached for his undershorts.

"You're as pretty as you were last night," she said casually.

"My head isn't pretty."

"There's some lesser brandy in that decanter on the night stand."

"No, I'll suffer until I get to my aircraft. Oxygen does the job."

"I remember my husband telling me that."

She continued to watch as he dressed quickly. Finally she asked, "Did I help you forget for awhile?"

"Yes." He didn't tell her it was only for a short while. Inserting his cuff links, he thought about how strange he'd look in his dress uniform at this time of the morning. But he didn't give a damn, so why even waste the time thinking about it?

"Will I see you again?" she asked softly from the bed.

The guilt was there, eating at him. "I don't know," he replied. "In spite of what you may think, I'm pretty much of a hermit. And, even though I haven't seen her in some time, I do love my wife very much."

"We could keep it casual."

He finished with his tie and turned from the mirror. Even disheveled, she looked good. Slowly he shook his head. "No, I don't think it could ever be casual. Neither of us are that kind. And you'd only get hurt in the end. No, I haven't got room for any kind of a relationship until this goddamned bestial war is over, and then I have a marvelous wife to find."

She got up from the bed silently, poured herself some brandy, and sipped it. She smiled ruefully as she came to him in her thin nightgown. "Suppose I don't care if it won't last?"

"No, it's no good. I shouldn't have come here last night."

Suddenly she sobered. "Oh, stop it! Don't get sanctimonious with me. You wanted to get drunk and go to bed with me, and you did. We needed each other and now it's the morning after. If you want to go off to your stupid war and punish yourself, do so. But don't do it in front of me!" She stomped off to the bathroom.

Arriving at his Elmas quarters twenty minutes later, Franco found a note from Diego: "The aeroplane is flyable." Good! he told himself. Now he could go kill some more people. Actually, he was glad for the chance to fly; it would get him away from earthly complications for a while. He showered quickly and got into the fresh uniform his batman had laid out. How incongruous, he thought. Here a major modern nation was getting close to losing a monstrous, devastating war, and he still had a servant preparing his clothes for wear.

He stopped by the underground base operations and went down the hall to Canepa's office. The colonel was already at his desk, although Franco couldn't imagine what he could possibly have to do—unless it was that stupid thing about fighting on if the government crumbled. He tossed off a salute to keep Canepa happy and asked "Anything special today, sir?"

The crippled ace looked bored. "No, just get better results with the Lightning than you did yesterday."

Franco disguised the mockery. "I'll have the eyes of a hawk."

His next stop was the weather office. Except for a few high scattered clouds, the whole area was clear with unlimited visibility. There was a chance of some late afternoon thunderstorm activity, with attendant turbulence. The whole morning and early afternoon should provide excellent hunting conditions.

In base operations, the duty officer told him they expected more of what they had been getting day in and day out: heavy raids from enemy bombers, plus possible strafing from fighters and light bombers. The Italian fighters that still remained at Elmas, as well as the two squadrons of Germans, would be airborne to meet the Allied aircraft once their ETA was determined. The direction finder on the highest hill west of the city was back in operation, so the advance warning should be good.

Franco was to refuel at the small auxiliary field over to the east by San Vito and use it as an emergency field should he need it.

Finally he parked the Fiat behind the sandbag revetment that held the Lightning. It was covered by a tan, black, and green camouflage net that not only made it practically invisible from the air but diluted some of the early morning sun. Sergeant Diego and the leading aircraftsman corporal who was his assistant were doing some fine-tuning on the number one engine. The P-38 looked big inside the enclosure of sandbags, in fact, like two long, blue-gray sharks carrying an elongated egg between them. Its white squadron numbers stood out: ES-41. "I got your note," Franco said. "Thanks. Everything else okay?"

Diego nodded his head. "She's ready to go." He dropped down from the wing and pulled a portable oxygen bottle out of a cabinet. Without a word, he handed its attached mask to Franco, who took it, held it to his face, and inhaled deeply several times.

"Thanks," Franco said, feeling better after several deep inhalations.

"Coffee's ready."

A smile touched Franco's lips. "You know, Sergeant, some day this war will be over and I won't know how the hell to get along without you."

Sergeant Diego was possibly the finest aircraftsman in the RA, and in Franco's opinion definitely the best engine mechanic he'd ever met. It seemed that Diego could hear that added decibel no other human could distinguish in a properly tuned engine. He had been in Franco's squadron in Spain and twice they'd served together in this war. Small and wiry, almost effeminate, he was nevertheless as strong as a mule. And intensely proud. Now he said, "I had to make a part for the oil pump in that number two engine, and I don't know how long it will last, Major. It's a spring that can give you a few hours or many. I can't guarantee it."

Franco nodded. "This bird has two engines, so I'll get home."

Diego shrugged. "I just thought you should know."

The sandbag revetment was Diego's temporary home. He had a cot inside the sandbag walls in the far corner under one of the tail booms. His assistant, Corporal Mazzei, slept there as well. He also kept a small icebox filled with cheese, meats that he bought on the black market, and bottles of a good Cagliari beer. The only time they went to the underground barracks was when they had to use the latrine.

The bags were brown, piled in a double wall to a height of three feet above the highest part of the aircraft. The exterior of the revetment had camouflage netting draped over it as well. It would take a direct hit to reach the Lightning, which they had dubbed *Outlaw*. The name painted on the left side of the cockpit nose when they acquired the aircraft had been *Mary Ann*, apparently after the American pilot's girlfriend. But Diego had painted it out and had an artist letter *Outlaw* in its place. Not a single one of the enemy pilots with whom he had been in close contact in the air had questioned him about the name. But then, he usually pulled up on the left side of the enemy bombers, so they wouldn't see it.

Franco took another long pull from the oxygen bottle, then sipped from the coffee cup Corporal Mazzei handed him. It was what the Germans called *ersatz*—artificial—but one got used to it. He looked at his watch: it was only two minutes after seven, well before they could normally expect the first raid. He picked up the field telephone to check it. When Operations answered, he asked, "Any reports on our visitors yet?"

"No, but they should be airborne soon. We'll call you as soon as we know."

He hung up and tore a piece of dark bread from the loaf that Diego kept by his icebox. Spreading some jam on it, he casually began to eat. This was the part that preyed on some fighter pilots, this waiting, knowing the enemy is coming, knowing you had to go up there, possibly to your death, just sitting and waiting for the loud jangle of a phone that will jar your nerves and send you running to your airplane. His case was different; he was the hunter and didn't have to throw himself into deadly bomber formations. He would take off and fly off the beaten path to a place where he could lie in wait for stragglers. Like a bloody highwayman. Although age was no factor in getting the presortie jitters, he was a very old man in the game. His biological age was twenty-six, but his fighter pilot age was somewhere around three hundred.

He had been at it somewhere—Spain, North Africa, or in Italian airspace—since finishing his tactical flight training in 1937. He had been shot down three times and had escaped serious injury each time; twice he had made an adequate crash landing and once he had parachuted. The little squint lines around his eyes were the marks of a flyer who had seen almost everything the sky could offer. By the law of averages for a fighter pilot, his number had long been up. But he had quit worrying about such things in North Africa. All that bothered him now were the faceless shadows that came to him in the still of the night.

If there was one particular thing Franco didn't like about the P-38 it was its lousy heater. At twenty-seven thousand feet, where he had been lurking for the past twenty minutes, the temperature was probably about five degrees below zero Fahrenheit. The airplane didn't have an outside temperature gauge, but it didn't matter: it was cold! He reached for the cabin heat control up by the right window and worked it up and down in its slide, leaving it in the full on position. But it didn't do any good. He rubbed his gloved hands together and wiggled his toes. What he needed was an electrically heated flight suit.

And a bottle of good Scotch.

And a two-year leave in some exotic place like the Caribbean. Yes, Bermuda, that sounded nice and warm. Good rum, he'd heard.

He really liked the comfortable cockpit though. It was large for a fighter, and with the engines several feet away it afforded excellent visibility. And he was just an inch under six feet tall.

He caught a reflection. Below and to the right, heading due south, he saw a single speck moving west. He eased the Lightning around to intercept, keeping the sun at his back. Slowly he began to pick out details: the aircraft was several thousand feet below him, a twin-engined bomber, maybe a B-25. No, it had a single tail. He eased back on the throttle to lose altitude. It looked like a Martin B-26. No, it was more like a Vickers Wellington. Yes, now he could make out the roundels on the top of the wings—yellow, blue, white, probably a center of red. Yes, an RAF Wellington out of North Africa. Now he could see that its right engine was trailing smoke and a huge chunk of its right elevator was missing.

Victim number one had wandered into his web.

He looked at his reference card and cranked in a radio frequency that should work. Pushing the mike button on the left side of the control wheel he said, "Hello, big Brit brother. This is a little Yank friend in a Lightning. Like some company on the way home?"

"Why, good morning, little Yank," the pilot of the Wimpy radioed back immediately. "Yes, I think that would be a splendid idea. Sorry I can't pass over a spot of tea, but I seem to have my hands full at the moment."

"Yes, looks like someone's been picking on you."

"Right. Ran into an uncommonly uncivil one-oh-nine back there over Cagliari."

Franco throttled back to match the lumbering Wellington's low speed and pulled in close on the Wimpy's side. He waved at the other pilot. "Looks that way. Do you have any wounded?"

"Yes, seems my tail gunner may be in bad shape."

"Want me to take a close look?"

"Would you be so kind?"

"Roger." It was all so incredibly easy. He throttled back a shade more and fell behind the tail of the bomber. But only for a moment. Banking off to the left, he turned back so he could fire directly into the Wimpy's remaining good engine and its cockpit as well. His left forefinger froze momentarily on the gun trigger. They are the enemy! he shouted to himself, and mashed the firing mechanism. The four .50s and the 20mm cannon had been rigged so the same button fired all of them at once. The Lightning bucked slightly under the savage firepower that was suddenly unleashed from its nose. Diego had set the guns so they converged at a shorter range than normal. Now Franco watched the tracer rounds tear into the Wellington's Rolls Royce Merlin engine. Just as he pulled close, black smoke streamed from it. He hauled back on the wheel and pulled up to miss the staggering bomber, then came around for another run.

"What the bloody hell are you doing, Yank?" the British pilot screamed over the radio.

Franco didn't even want to answer. He again squeezed the firing button and watched the tracers converge on the Wimpy's cockpit. The last he saw as he pulled the fighter up over the reeling bomber was twisted metal and shattered windscreen. And all he heard was a choking final transmission from the British pilot: "You . . . bastard!"

The Wimpy was now in a shallow, skidding dive, as the pilot tried to effect some evasive action. One more time Franco poured his rounds into the bomber, this time shattering the high tail section. By the time he released the firing button it was all over. The bomber fell over on one wing and suddenly snapped into a spin. Following it toward the blue sea below, he watched for white parachutes to blossom, but there were none. Several moments later, with a big white splash, the Wellington crashed into the sea and cartwheeled once. Breaking in half, it sank within a minute.

He blew out a deep breath as he watched the sea close calmly over the grave of six brave young Englishmen.

The taste in his mouth wasn't pleasant.

He had been aloft for nearly three hours on the second sortie when he decided he'd had enough. The sky—he liked to refer to it as "the violent sky"—had yielded a second victim for his guns, this time a crippled B-17. Its markings had told him it was from the 97th Bomb Group at Constantine. There had been four survivors, and he had merely flown low over their rubber dinghy to salute them. No more strafing—not since that time a week or more earlier when he'd gunned down the crew of a ditched Flying Fort only to spare the life of its last survivor, a brave man who stood up on the wing of his dying airplane and shot back at him with a peashooter.

When Operation Outlaw was ready to begin, Fillipo Canepa had told him, "No survivors." When he'd questioned that edict, Canepa had shown him an order from Mussolini himself, stating that there would be no survivors to report the existence of a killer P-38 in enemy hands.

But since he had spared the B-17 man, surely the word had gotten out and there was no need to slaughter any more helpless men. That was his decision and no one in Elmas or Rome would know the difference. At least that grotesque part of this repulsive mission was ended for him. And he was convinced the Americans knew about him, at least those out of Constantine, because one pilot had been suspicious and had asked him a strange question about the 1941 World Series. But he hadn't even bothered to reply; he'd just shot the aircraft down.

He looked at the instrument panel clock: 1422. Twenty-two minutes after two in the afternoon. He had called Control and had been told that the raids were apparently over for the day. The docks and fuel tanks at Cagliari had been hit hard. He had been able to see the billowing black smoke from the fuel tanks at Cagliari a long way off, so he knew the city's docks had been hit again. The Elmas airfield had taken another pasting, but the crews were already hard at work repairing the bomb craters in the runway. A hard-packed dirt emergency runway was in operation on a heading of 240.

He was about fifteen miles south of the field when he noticed that the coolant gauge for the number one engine was acting up. It was quite high. He quickly checked that engine's oil temperature gauge and saw that it, too, was high. Jerking around to look at the Prestone Cooler on the inboard side of the left boom, he saw that it was glistening from streaks of fluid. The damned coolant was leaking! His eyes darted back to the gauges. Now number one's coolant temp was going out the top! God, couldn't he land anymore without a problem?

Without coolant that engine would heat up and blow in short order. He didn't hesitate a moment. He feathered the engine, slamming in hard left rudder to compensate and make the aircraft fly straight and level on one engine. Single-engine operation in this rascal took good pilotage. Entering the traffic pattern, he declared an emergency and was cleared number one to land.

The needle on the coolant gauge was clear off the top of the scale as he slowed his landing roll and taxied off the active. Quickly, he turned back for another look at the egg-shaped Prestone Cooler. Now fluid was all over it. He raised the canopy and heard a clanging noise in that direction. Something had apparently torn loose. Heading for the revetment, he shrugged. Another problem for Diego to solve.

Leopoldo Civitella had watched the twin-engine fighter's approach with what appeared to be casual interest from where he was working with a construction crew repairing a bomb crater in the middle of the main runway. He stuck the shovel in the ground and put his foot on it as he wiped the sweat off his forehead with a handkerchief. He kept the Lightning in sight as it taxied off to the south, the propeller on its left engine standing still. It continued on to what looked like some kind of a shelter a quarter of a mile away.

Turning to the man beside him, he asked, "Wasn't that an American plane?"

The laborer replied, "I think so, but I don't know about such things."

"That place where he's going, what is it?"

"It's a sandbag place, like a garage."

"Does that plane always stay there?"

"I've never seen it go any other place."

Leopoldo nodded. The Friends' connection had worked it so he reported to work on the ground repair crew at ten that morning, but two air raids had kept them in the shelter. Wary of attracting attention, he hadn't asked any questions about the P-38. Now he had seen it, and it was no longer a ghost.

"It's the coolant line to the Prestone radiator," the master mechanic said from his ladder by the boom. "Whoever fixed it some time ago made a bad solder where it attaches to the radiator, and it came loose. Apparently when you lowered the gear the wind made it bang around. The hoses and the radiator are torn up."

"Which means?" Franco asked.

"It means that until we can get another radiator this airplane can't fly."

"You can't fix it?"

"No, sir."

"What do we do about it?"

"I heard this morning that there's a P-38 that crashed up by Nuoro. The man who told me was a crew chief who has a girl up there. He said the plane was in pretty good shape and that we might get some parts from it. Maybe one of the four Prestone radiators will be intact."

"You talking about going up there to take a look at it?"

"I'd like to, Major."

"How long will it take?"

"Depends on how hard it is to get to. And I'd like to have enough time to cannibalize everything of value. Two, three days, maybe four."

"I suppose I'll have to check with Canepa."

"You could probably use a few days off, Major."

"Yeah, maybe."

Lt. Col. Fillipo Canepa was pleased that Franco had two kills for the day. But his smile turned sour when he heard about the coolant problem. "I thought your Diego was supposed to be the best. Why can't he fix it?"

"The radiator is shot, like I told you," Franco replied. He told the colonel about the proposed trip to the wrecked Lightning near Nuoro.

"How long will it take?"

"Could be up to a week, depending on how much trouble it is to get to the crash site. And as long as he's there, he might as well get everything that's usable. He'll take a truck."

The crippled pilot slammed a fist down on his desk. "No week! I want him back here and I want that Lightning flyable in no more than four days, do you hear, Adamo?"

Franco shrugged. He'd stretched it to a week so Canepa wouldn't get upset over three or four days. "I'll inform him."

"You going with him?"

"No, I'd just get in the way. He'd have to play the officer-sergeant game, and that would just slow him down. If you have no objection, Colonel, I want to take that few days of leave that I'm long overdue."

Canepa lit another cigarette while he made up his mind. "Yes, well I suppose if you take it here in the Cagliari area, and check in with me every day. . . ."

"No problem if the telephones work."

"All right. Let my sergeant know where you'll be staying."

"Right."

Franco was halfway out the door when the colonel said, "Oh, by the way, this came for you about an hour ago by special courier from Rome." He handed Franco an envelope.

There was no return address on it. Opening it, Franco read its short message, then read it again, his jaw setting and his eyes narrowing. Its words were hand-printed in harsh black letters:

FRANCO ADAMO ACCURSO: IT WILL SOON BE TIME FOR YOU TO PAY FOR YOUR FATHER'S TREACHERY WITH YOUR LIFE. SINCE IT HAS TAKEN SO LONG, YOUR WIFE MUST PAY AS WELL.

CHAPTER 10

✥

Josh Rawlins sipped from a glass of red wine as he listened to Leopoldo relate what he had learned that day at Elmas. "Did you get near the revetment?" he asked when the bodyguard finished.

"No. Not even close."

Josh had a map of the base spread out on the table they were occupying in the corner of the Boar restaurant. "Show me where it is on the map."

Leopoldo squinted at the map, trying to get oriented. Finally he touched a place with his index finger. "Here, this is about where it is."

Josh carefully drew a square at that point and marked it "Revet."

He looked up at the bright-eyed Elfida. "What did you learn from your amorous sergeant-major today?"

Bernardo translated.

The proprietress smiled. "I learned mostly that he's still hot for me, but also that some of the senior officers live in that separate building we discussed. I couldn't come right out and ask him about Major Adamo without creating some suspicion."

Josh put another square on the map and marked it "Off. Qtrs." Turning to Bernardo, "And what did you find out, my friend?"

Don Nizzi's son smiled. The Friends had given him a bogus pass to clean windows on what was left of the base's buildings. "The RA's security is pretty lax, except around the places like this revetment where they keep the airplane, and their headquarters, the fuel dump, and such. I talked to a man who's been cleaning buildings around there for years and he told me a little about that sandbag place. There are two mechanics who stay there most of the time. The pilot comes early in the morning and flies, often until mid-afternoon, then the mechanics work on the plane."

Josh nodded his head. "Now, what about Adamo? Could you learn anything about his movements?"

"Yes, I saw him. I was washing windows in that senior officers' house and I talked to a couple of the batmen, the soldiers who act as servants. I told one of them I had heard that the famous ace, Franco Adamo, was living there. And he pointed out his room. There were too many people there for me to try and get into it, but later, when I was washing a window by the entrance, this pilot came in. He answered Adamo's description, so I watched where he went and it was straight to the corner room that was supposed to be his. I know it was him!"

Josh's eyes were bright. "What did he do?"

"After a little, I went down and started washing his windows from the outside. I could see in pretty good. He drank quite a bit in a hurry. Seemed like he was staring at some photographs. I should have just killed him for you."

"No, he's mine." Josh scowled at the map. It would be difficult to pull it off in the dark, particularly getting out with the airplane. He could memorize the taxiways leading to a runway, but there wouldn't be any lights at all. And he'd flown a Lightning only once. It had been in England, when Barney Buell had thought it would be a good idea if some of the bomber pilots and some of the fighter jocks exchanged seats for familiarization, sort of an "understand the other guy's picture" type of thing. He'd gotten about an hour's flying time in the aircraft.

All he needed now to get airborne was to remember what switches to use to get fuel and juice to start the engines. The rest—the radio stuff, engine synch, cruise speeds, and the lot—he could figure out once he was upstairs. As soon as he neared the North African coast he would have to call in and identify himself. He already had the final scene worked out: once he killed Adamo he'd rip off the killer's pilot wings and take them along. When he landed back at Constantine he would go directly to Buell's office carrying the Lightning's Form 1—its maintenance record—and toss it, along with Adamo's wings, on the general's desk. That would damn well take care of the whole thing!

"Later, I talked to Adamo's batman again," Bernardo added. "Seems he's a loner and stays in nearly every night. Apparently he doesn't eat much, just drinks. The batman is new and doesn't know him very well. But he brings him three bottles of red wine every day. Now and then some cold lamb when he can find it on the black market."

Josh was satisfied. "He could be pulled out of here any day now and start hopping around like he was in Sicily. So it had better be tonight." He looked hard at the map. "Here's what I want to do. . . ."

They rode up to the Elmas main gate, a two-lane entry and exit, at 8:20 P.M., three nondescript men on worn bicycles with lunch pails holding hard bread, fruit, and wine strapped to their backs. Josh was warm as he pedalled along, but he was thankful that the hot sirocco had diminished. Under his Sicilian clothes he was wearing a khaki uniform shirt complete with wings and ribbons, and regulation shorts. He wanted this bastard to know exactly who and what he was when he killed him. He'd packed them along from Chateaudun just for this purpose. He'd even had Elfida iron the wrinkles out of them. He wondered if this apparent symbolism was a result of the Sicilian mysticism he'd been exposed to in the last couple of days. He didn't give a damn—nine dead men deserved a bit of ritual.

Bernardo and Leopoldo rode in front of him. He was once more the mute from Trieste in the event anyone questioned him. All three were armed with German machine pistols and extra magazines of ammunition in their pockets. The passes the Friends had arranged to get them on Elmas stated that they were working for a special night construction team.

A bored RA corporal at the main entrance to the airfield looked casually at the passes. "I don't know why they even bother fixing anything," he said nonchalantly as he handed the papers back. "The bastards just come back and drop their eggs on us the next day, right?" He waved them through.

They rode directly to the officers quarters and parked their bicycles in its rear. Now Adamo had to be there, Josh told himself, feeling the tension mount. How long had it been since this murdering Italian had slaughtered his crew and his best friend? He'd lost track of time—eleven days? He nodded to Bernardo, who would lead the way. Leopoldo would stand guard over the bicycles unless for some reason there was trouble inside. Quickly Josh stripped off the outer layer of clothes and tugged an army overseas cap low over his forehead. His lunch pail was just large enough to hold the machine pistol.

He and Bernardo carefully edged around to the front of the building, where he hid behind a bush while the young Sicilian boldly walked inside. Moments later, after getting a signal, he hurried through the door. Without a word the don's son led him silently down the hallway to Adamo's room. Josh quickly withdrew his pistol from the lunch pail and pasted himself to the wall. Making sure the safety was off, he took in a deep breath and gradually let it out. It was time. He nodded at Bernardo, who softly tapped on the door.

No answer.

Another tap, louder this time. Still no answer. Damn! Josh thought, his breath coming in short bursts, *where was he*? Could he be asleep? Bernardo tapped again, then pulled out a thin metal lock pick. In less than a minute he had the door open. Josh burst into the room with his pistol at the ready.

No one was there.

Josh hurried to the attached bathroom, then to the large closet. No one. Son of a bitch!

"What do you want to do?" Bernardo whispered.

Josh couldn't believe the man wasn't there. He had to be! "Maybe he just went somewhere for a short time. You told me he seldom goes out. Maybe he's someplace else in the building, or out for a walk." He squelched his bitter disappointment. He'd been all ready to kill a man who'd hounded his dreams incessantly, shoot him until the pistol was empty. And now he'd been cheated. He went to the desk and looked down at a photo. It was of a dark-haired man, a woman, and a youth. The man was quite handsome; the woman reminded him of the don's wife, except that her expression was softer. The youth, who appeared to be about sixteen or so, looked much like the older man. He turned the brownish photo over. The inscription in English read, "Father, Mother, and myself. Boston, 1934." Josh stared at the young man; it was undoubtedly Franco Adamo. It was also the first time he had been able to put a face to his enemy. Boston? Adamo had probably lived there, so what he had said in the air that day had been true. What else could the photo disclose?

As Bernardo quietly closed the door to a thin crack, keeping his eyes on the hallway, Josh looked at the other photograph. It was of a lovely young woman with her arm around the woman from the other photo. The writing on the back announced: "Momma and Sella, Rome, 1939."

An empty wine bottle was tipped over on the desk.

Josh waved his pistol at the door. "Go see if his neighbors are home, and if anyone knows where he might be." The disappointment left a sour taste in his mouth.

Bernardo nodded his head and slipped outside.

Josh went back to the closet and found Franco's dress uniform, complete with his medals, hanging on a rod with some other uniforms. He ripped off the gold pilot's wings and stuck them in his pocket. Going back to the desk, he looked up at a bookshelf and was surprised to see two Hemingway novels: *A Farewell to Arms* and *Green Hills of Africa*. Steinbeck's *The Grapes of Wrath* was there as well. Somehow that seemed totally incongruous to him; what the hell was an Italian doing with Hemingway and Steinbeck? Another photograph of the young woman in the photo on the desk hung in a frame on the wall. This one was professional and showed her holding a pith helmet in front of an Egyptian pyramid. She was very lovely. Must be Sella. Adamo's wife? Girlfriend?

He heard a voice, some low conversation in Italian.

Shortly Bernardo slipped back into the room. He looked downcast. "Bad luck, Captain. Our bird has flown. I just talked to a colonel who said Major Adamo just went on leave this evening. He thought Adamo was off to Naples and would be gone for at least two weeks."

"Naples?" Son of a bitch! Must've just missed him! Naples seemed a million miles away.

"What now?" the young Sicilian asked.

Josh swore again and dropped into an easy chair. "How could I miss him this closely?"

"The plane's still here."

"But I want *him!*"

"You can get him another time. Maybe after your invasion. My father will keep close track of him, you know you can count on that."

Josh's mind raced ahead, blotting out his disappointment. He couldn't hang around Cagliari for two weeks. He was already AWOL at both Chateaudun and Constantine. Besides, Adamo could easily come back in a fortnight, pack a fresh shaving kit, and go off to fly from somewhere else for a month or so. Son of a bitch!

"Or we could go on back to Sicily."

No, the plane that was shooting down innocent American airmen was here, right over there in a revetment. The least he could do was steal the P-38 back, which would at least end the treacherous preying on friendly aircraft. Yes, that's what he had to do. He could get Adamo some other time, but now he had to be practical. "No," he said quietly. "I have to get the airplane out of here."

But before he left the lair of his enemy he had to make some kind of a statement. Withdrawing the extra magazine of 7.63 shells he carried in his pocket, he extracted a single round and set it up in the middle of Adamo's desk. Almost as an afterthought, he pulled his dog tags over his head and removed the one on the short chain. He leaned the dog tag up against the bullet and walked grimly from the room.

They rode up close to the revetment on their bicycles and stopped. Josh pulled the civilian shirt collar up to make sure it hid his uniform, as an armed guard in an RA uniform challenged them. He couldn't have been over sixteen. "Halt!" he shouted, stepping around the side of the sandbags.

Bernardo went into his story with a wide grin. "We were working tonight and were told that this thing holds a captured American aeroplane. We just want to take a peek at it."

The guard glared at them. "No one is allowed near it."

"Oh, come on," Bernardo pleaded. "Just one little peek won't hurt anything. We won't touch it."

"My orders—"

"Hell, orders are always stupid. You know that. We have some good wine with us, too. Why don't you have a taste while we peek inside, then we'll ride along."

The guard eyed the bottle Leopoldo held up in the fading light. "Well, I suppose one look won't hurt anything."

All four of them went inside the revetment, where Leopoldo handed the boy the bottle. Josh stopped and stared. There in the semidarkness, looking larger and more forbidding than it could possibly be, was the blue-gray P-38. His eyes went to the left boom, where the white letters ES-41 stared back at him. They'd been right on the money back in Constantine! And now it was time to repossess it. He felt his pulse quicken. Turning to Bernardo, he said in English, "I think it's time to tie our friend up."

The young guard lowered the bottle and looked at him quizzically. At that moment Leopoldo stuck his machine pistol in the boy's face. In Italian he snarled, "On the ground quickly or I'll blow your stupid brains out!"

As the bodyguard quickly bound and gagged the soldier, Josh and Bernardo pulled the camouflage netting up from the front of the revetment. Removing the chocks, they manhandled the fighter out of its shelter. They would have to hurry! As it was common practice to top off the fuel tanks after an aircraft landed, Josh assumed they were full; he'd check them shortly. He quickly walked around the Lightning, looking for control locks and removing a cover the Italians had put on the Pitot tube. The gear looked all right. That was about all he knew how to do in the way of a preflight inspection. He had to hurry. There was no time to worry about a parachute. The little ladder was at the rear of the cockpit. He turned to his friends and stuck out his hand. First Leopoldo shook it and then Bernardo. "Goodbye, my friends. See you after the war. I promise."

Quickly they picked up their bicycles and pedalled off. Josh hurriedly pulled off the civilian clothes and climbed the ladder to the wing. Looking into the open but dark cockpit, he withdrew his thin little flashlight and turned it on. A final glance at his disappearing friends told him everything was going right. His plan called for him to give them five minutes before he cranked up the engines. Crawling down into the padded seat, he figured it would take him that long to *find* everything. He turned on the switches to his right front and saw the gauges jump. He had juice. Finding the fuel gauges, he saw they indicated "full." Throttle levers, mixture, props, primer, fuel selectors, ignition switches. Yeah, he'd be all right.

He looked at his watch. His friends should be nearing the main gate shortly. He pushed the primer up and down and moved the mixture controls full forward. Closing and cracking the throttles, he decided he would start the right engine first. Making sure he had the parking brake set, he turned on the ignition switch and hit the starter button. The big three-bladed propeller began to turn, coughed, caught, died, turned, coughed again, and started. It idled fine. Good!

He began the same procedure on the left engine, but when he hit the starter button nothing happened. What the hell? He rechecked the fuel selector handle, ran the mixture control back and forward again, flicked the battery switch up and down, and turned the ignition switch off and back on. But when he pushed the left engine starter absolutely nothing turned. He looked out in the dim remaining light at the left engine and back down the boom. That was when he saw the red cover on the cooler pod. Snapping around to the right engine, he saw no such cover on that cooler. Why in hell hadn't he noticed it when he made his walk around? What the hell was wrong? Apparently the juice to the left engine was disconnected. Christ! He'd have to get out and see if he could figure it out! Son of a bitch! Shaking his head and trying to shake off the sinking feeling that was pouring over him, he drew back the mixture control on the right engine and shut it down.

Quickly he pulled himself out of the cockpit. But just as he dropped down from the ladder a harsh voice barked in Italian, "Put your hands behind your head or I'll shoot!"

Turning, he saw an open truck ten feet away. It held three men in uniform who were pointing guns at him. The one in front jumped out and aimed a machine gun at his stomach.

As the two Sicilians rode their bicycles up a short grade just outside of the main gate, Bernardo stopped and turned to watch the Lightning take off. But what he saw alarmed him. "Look!" he said sharply, pointing to the revetment location. There was just enough light to make out some kind of a truck with its headlights casting bright beams near the glint of the fighter. The aircraft wasn't moving. "Something's wrong!"

"I knew we should have waited until he left," Leopoldo muttered. "Let's go back!"

Leopoldo caught the young man's arm. "We can't."

"Maybe we can ambush them."

"This isn't a cowboy movie, Bernardo."

"What could have happened?"

"Maybe the guard was changing or something. Maybe someone in the tower saw the aeroplane being pulled out. Who knows?"

Don Nizzi's son watched in anguish as the vehicle by the revetment turned and headed toward the base headquarters area. He knew they had his American friend.

"Now *we* have a problem," Leopoldo said angrily. "That guard can identify us."

The military police interrogation room was a dirty white, 12x12 room with a table and chairs in the middle and a single shaded incandescent light hanging from the ceiling. Josh was seated in the middle of the table, in the center of the upside-down funnel of light. Behind him stood two burly guards, while across from him a bull-necked captain stood behind a chair that held his interrogator. The man questioning him was a balding major with a bushy black mustache. His brows were equally bushy and black over deeply recessed dark eyes. He had introduced himself as Major Lionetti earlier. "Let's start over, Captain," he said patiently in English. "Where did you come from?"

Josh sighed, reciting his name, rank and serial number for the umpteenth time. "Rawlins, captain, 01688586."

"I'm trying to be patient, Captain Rawlins, but it isn't easy. We have methods that are far more persuasive, but I'm the queasy type. So why don't you just start telling us where you came from, where you were going to take the American aeroplane, and how you got into Elmas."

"Rawlins, Joshua E., captain, 01688586."

Major Lionetti nodded to one of the guards. Josh was jerked to his feet and held while one of the guards threw a murderous punch into his kidney area. Three more smashing punches followed, causing so much pain that Josh had to cry out in spite of himself.

"Now, let's try again, Captain Rawlins," Major Lionetti said in an oily tone. "You'll talk in the end, no matter what you think, so you might as well make it easy on yourself. How did you know about the aeroplane?"

Spittle ran out of the side of Josh's mouth as he mumbled, "Rawlins, captain, 01688586."

"Have you ever experienced the match game?" the major asked. "That's when we stick matches under your nails, head first, and light the other end."

Josh just stared at the table.

"Or we could move directly to the electric wire on the balls game. That's when we shoot an electric charge into your testicles." Lionetti grinned. "Everyone talks then, Captain Rawlins. After a few of those incredibly terrifying jolts, they tell us anything we want to know."

Josh ignored him.

"Do you know what will happen after a few more heavy blows to the kidneys, Captain Rawlins? You will begin to piss blood. You may even suffer permanent kidney damage. If that doesn't kill you, it'll make you suffer the rest of your life." The major nodded once more at the guards, who dragged him out of the chair and again smashed two vicious punches into his lower back.

"That's enough!"

Major Lionetti turned at the sound of Lt. Col. Fillipo Canepa's voice.

Canepa limped to the table and stared down from the darkness. "So you are the one who wants to steal my pretty P-38," he said softly in accented English. "I know why. You think it belongs to your air force." He sighed. "But you see it doesn't. Under the rules of war, when enemy equipment is acquired in an honorable manner, the one who captures or finds it owns it. Since one of your generous pilots saw fit to land it at one of our airfields, the aeroplane was simply impounded. Then, seeing as it could benefit our war effort, we decided to use our new aeroplane."

He smiled thinly. "So now you are a thief who wants to steal it from us. Why, Captain Rawlins?"

Josh found a small smile in answer.

"Oh, I know," Canepa went on. "You are playing the Geneva Convention game, and I respect you for it. I also respect your bravery in coming here. But you see, we know you had friends. The guard told us he thought they were Sicilian by their accents. Now, you know we can't have a bunch of Sicilian traitors running around committing treason, don't you?"

This time Josh's reply was a blank look.

The colonel's look hardened. "But we can get to that later. What I want to know is how you found the aircraft here. Did your intelligence know it was here, or did you find it yourself?"

Josh spoke firmly, "Rawlins, captain, 01688586."

"Did your Sicilian friends know it was here?"

No answer.

"Did your Sicilian friends find it out from Sardinian collaborators?"

Silence.

"From Regia Aeronautica personnel?"

Josh said nothing.

Canepa nodded his head, watching Josh's eyes for several seconds. Turning to Major Lionetti, he said, "Come with me," and headed for the door. Outside the room, he said, "I don't want him tortured. No more beating. Put him in solitary confinement and don't feed him. Just water. I'll be back in the morning to talk to him again."

The major shook his head. "I disagree, Colonel. Let me drag it out of him. By morning I'll have your information."

"No," Canepa said softly. "I don't think so. That one is strong, I can see it in his eyes. And that blue ribbon with the tiny red stripes he's wearing is the Americans' Distinguished Service Cross. Captains don't get it for idle talk. Do as I say, Major."

Lionetti shrugged. "As you wish, sir."

CHAPTER 11

✛

Captain Giuseppe Madeo pulled the *Gaia* into the harbor at Trapani at twenty minutes to five the next morning. The decision to come back hadn't taken long the night before. As soon as Bernardo and Leopoldo reached the Boar and told the captain what had happened, they all agreed that they couldn't do anything about Josh's capture. Even to think about trying to rescue him could bring on the wrath of the don. It was one thing to help the American captain, but quite another to fight with the RA. Besides, the don hadn't given them permission even to be in Sardinia. No, even the impulsive Bernardo thought they should get back and report to his father.

As Topo fastened a line to Madeo's dock the captain handed the don's son a card. "Here's my telephone number. I'll stand by for twenty-four hours. If I can be of any assistance to my don, please call me at once."

Bernardo thanked him. "I'll tell my father how very helpful you've been, Captain. I'm sure he'll find a way to repay you."

Madeo shook his healthy beard vigorously. "I am forever in his debt. Tell him only that Capt. Giuseppe Madeo kisses his hand."

Bernardo stuck out his hand. "I will do so."

The younger Calgogeri and Leopoldo debarked and hurried away. They had to get the Fiat out of the garage where they had left it and hurry on to Castella Carmelo.

*   *   *

It was nearly eight o'clock when Bernardo told his father what had happened since their departure from the castle. The don sat in the huge bed, still wearing his light blue silk pajamas, sipping from a small cup of black coffee. Off to one side Isabella Zerilli Calgogeri listened impassively, while on the other side Rudy Sabatini payed much closer attention. Finally, Bernardo summed his tale up with, "And that's how it is, Father. The captain is probably a prisoner at Elmas."

The don's eyes narrowed. He didn't like being up this early, and he particularly didn't like dealing with unpleasantness at this hour. "You should have asked permission to go to Sardinia," he said with a dark frown.

"Captain Rawlins insisted we go while his information was hot."

"Does Captain Rawlins run this island?" Don Nizzi asked coldly.

"No, Father."

"You were given permission to scout around the local air bases to try and find the aeroplane, not go on a cruise."

Bernardo avoided the wrath in his father's eyes by looking downcast.

"And then you allow our guest to be captured. This speaks very poorly of my house."

"Yes, Father," Bernardo said softly.

"And now we have a major problem on our hands. I must apologize profusely to our other guest."

Sabatini put his coffee cup on the end table. "No need, my Don. The captain is headstrong and his judgement is influenced by the overpowering hate of his vendetta." Sabatini's calm was the Rudy Lotions part of him in action. Internally he was boiling. That goddamned Rawlins had gone too far, traipsing off to Sardinia like that. Now the bastard was rotting in some dungeon, maybe having his fingernails pulled out, possibly spilling his guts. No, somehow he didn't think they would make him talk. At least not right away. And they wouldn't be in too big a hurry. Or would they? He had no idea what was going on with this Franco Adamo and that damned fighter plane, or how frantic the Italian High Command might be—

"What do you wish for me to do, *Consiglière?*"

Sabatini frowned. It was almost impossible to keep hiding his anger at Rawlins. The B-17 pilot was like a crazed street fighter—throwing all caution to the wind. Charging off like that. What the hell did he think he was, some kind of a commando? An OSS type? Still, he had to hand it to the kid. Gutsy play. No wonder he had a DSC, probably earned it, too. Yeah, they'd probably make it pretty rough on him, maybe even kill him in the end—

"Major Sabatini?"

Everyone was looking at him. He blew out a deep breath. "I need him, my Don," he said slowly, making up his mind. "He's a vital cog to everything we've discussed. I want to go get him."

"But your foot—"

"I've been getting around with a cane all afternoon. It'll be all right. Besides, maybe I can kill Adamo myself."

The don nodded his full head of white hair. "How can I help?"

"I'll need some men. Not too many. Transport to Cagliari, escape transport. Weapons. The usual."

"Done."

The *Gaia* was sitting quietly by the pier in Palermo harbor at two o'clock that afternoon when the Fiat pulled up and disgorged its occupants. Bernardo had convinced his father that he was essential to the mission, that he needed to go along as the son of Don Nizzi Calgogeri to rectify any shame he may have brought on their name. He stepped aboard to a warm welcome from Captain Madeo. Leopoldo Civitella took Sabatini's elbow as he assisted the major in the big step down to the deck of the fishing boat. Sabatini held back a wince as his ankle complained. Just walking wasn't a major problem with the cane, but he wouldn't be able to use it in Sardinia. Too slow. The ankle was tightly bound; he would loosen the bandage during the sea voyage over to the other big island, and it should be no problem in the operation; he wouldn't let it be. He shook the effusive Madeo's hand and nodded to Topo, who was at the wheel.

He had decided to use only the ones who had been with Rawlins in Sardinia. He didn't need a damned regiment to rescue one man, and he hoped this wasn't the type of operation that called for a pitched battle. He had pulled off a major rescue a few weeks earlier, getting a captured intelligence colonel out of Corsica. Surely he could outsmart a bunch of RA security types.

He liked Captain Madeo on sight. The guy oozed confidence. And experience told him Civitella was probably a rock. But the kid, Bernardo, was an unknown, probably too eager to make up for what looked like a gaffe with Rawlins. Have to keep an eye on him.

After Topo stowed his gear below, Sabatini sat near the stern and

looked around the harbor as Madeo cranked up the engines and swung
the boat out into the deep water. It was a beautiful day, the blue waters
filled with white sails as if it were some idyllic Sunday in a land of
peace. But further inspection disproved such a thought. There had been
two air raids that morning and smoke still drifted skyward from the
center of the dock area. And a small freighter's stern stuck out of the
watery grave it had settled into after a five-hundred-pounder did its
job.

But Sabatini didn't want to think about the big war.

He liked the surge of power the *Gaia*'s engines gave the vessel. He'd
always been fascinated by boats back in New York. In fact, when he
was about eleven or so he used to go down to the East River and sit
by the hour, just watching them go by and pretending that he was the
captain of a fast destroyer looking for a U-boat that had snuck in through
the harbor. Even now he enjoyed pretending to be this boat's captain.

He closed his eyes; he wasn't the captain of the *Gaia* now, he was
the flotilla commander. . . .

Lt. Col. Fillipo Canepa sighed and lit another cigarette. Leaning forward,
close to Josh's face, he blew out a cloud of bluish smoke. "I have kept
Major Lionetti away from you, you know."

Josh's stolid expression didn't change. His face was utterly blank
in the harsh light of the incandescent lamp in the same dark interrogation room.

Canepa went on, "I feel like I know you. I guess it's because we're
both pilots, as if we belong to the same elite club. Lionetti wouldn't
understand that. He's gross, lacks our sensitivity. It's rumored that he
was a police sergeant in Rome, and that over a hundred prisoners have
died at his hands. Of course, they probably died from the torture . . . did
you notice his eyes? You can see it, the sadism that makes a prick like
him tick. He probably masturbates after a particularly brutal beating."

Josh tried to look through the colonel and not listen. He had once
done some crop spraying out in Arizona and had gotten to know a young
Apache from up by the Salt River. His name was Edgar Perryman, and
he had actually lived on the edge of the famous old army post, Fort
Apache. In exchange for an airplane ride Perryman had given him a
lesson in what he called "Fuck your enemy." It was an old Apache mental
game in which you pretended you were somewhere else, totally detached. "Pick a place like a small desert island with some warm sand

and a single gently waving palm tree. The sun is shining warmly and all you see is that tree moving ever so slowly, in the warm sand, moving ever so slowly, slowly, in the warm, sunny sand, ever so slowly and gently in the warm sunshine in the warm, warm sand." He had tried it on a couple of occasions when he had a headache or couldn't sleep, and had actually made it work. But he had never used it with severe pain or anguish before. But some part of it had helped, because he had already endured some pretty tough pain from Lionetti. But it didn't matter—regardless of what they did to him, and whether it worked or not, he wasn't going to give them *shit*.

"There's no sense in getting permanently maimed or killed."

Josh could see that palm tree swaying ever so gently over the face of Franco Adamo.

"How did your commanders know the P-38 was here?"

"Rawlins, captain, 01688586."

Sabatini lit a Lucky Strike and looked at his watch. It was shortly after six. Forty minutes earlier Topo had served some sardines in a tart but tasty oil, with olives, dark bread, and a good red wine. Dates had made a fine dessert. He had been over the maps with Bernardo and Leopoldo, both the one of Cagliari and the one of Elmas, and felt some familiarity with the layout he would be facing. They'd even practiced some shooting from the stern. Both of the Sicilians were pretty good with their Mauser machine pistols.

He preferred a Smith & Wesson .38 revolver. It wouldn't jam on him and had enough punch to make anyone stop and think. He also had a sound suppressor for it—what the amateurs called a silencer. Funny thing about the use of that word: silence was an ultimate, not something that lessened the sound intensity. Ha! Who would ever have thought a tough kid like him would ever grow up and think about ultimate words?

Reflecting about growing up took him back to the old house, but that quickly led to memories of Teresa, and he didn't want any part of that.

He pictured Milton Hall, a pleasant memory. . . .

It wasn't too long after Pearl Harbor when the FBI agent had made him the offer. At least he thought the man was an FBI agent; he had government identification. It seems a lot of effort had been expended by the Feds in regard to his income and the tax he hadn't paid. The old Capone shit. And they had enough on him to put him away for a few years, they said. But the agent had stated that there was a way out. "Wild Bill" Donovan, the old World War I hero from the Fighting 69th, was setting up a small, new group of guys with special qualifications to operate behind enemy lines. If Rudy Lotions would volunteer for this elite organization and serve honorably, the government would conveniently lose its file on him, for good.

It not only made sense, but it sounded challenging. And he'd been itching to get in the war anyway. After all, it was his country that was fighting! Due to his age and background, they offered him captain's bars. They didn't even bother with any kind of basic training, just a short orientation about the Army—how to wear a uniform, how to salute, who to "sir," and all that crap—and then it was off to jump school at Fort Benning. After earning his parachute wings, the next stop was southern England, a magnificent country estate called Milton Hall, near Peterborough.

That is where they had taught him everything an OSS—Office of Strategic Services—agent needed to know. At least they taught him what they thought he needed to know: radio, hand-to-hand combat, weapons familiarization, marksmanship, explosives, and a language brush-up. Those British commandos and intelligence types had been very thorough.

His first mission had been into northern Italy, where he had managed to raise a lot of hell with a handful of Italian partisans. He had had a lot of fun and been lucky. When he came out after three months the brass gave him a Silver Star and a Purple Heart for getting shot up a little. Then they dropped him into the southwest corner of France, just north of Nice. The mission was to coordinate French underground activities with Italian partisans across the border. He had some more fun there, eliminating a number of senior Nazis, and when he came out they hung another Silver Star on him. And made him a major. Then there was that mission into Corsica.

And here he was, about to risk his ass for a stubborn damned pilot. Dumb.

But in addition to getting Rawlins's ass out, he had another motive. It involved the assignment the don had given him. Adamo's wife in Egypt. Rawlins could help him on that. He had a plan working. He settled back and closed his eyes. A little more rest before getting to Sardinia wouldn't hurt anything.

*　　*　　*

Franco Adamo sat in the wet sand watching the white bubbles of the warm seawater slip away from his toes. It was so clear and so simple; just sit still and let the water come in and go out as the small waves broke on the soft sand of the beach. The water bore no malice, it was just curious. It had no war, no enemies, no vendettas. He tipped the two-liter wine bottle back and took a big swig. It was a local wine. He didn't recall its name and it didn't matter. He wasn't one to make a big thing about wines. One drank the right color with certain foods, and one drank to feel better. Or to forget. Or to just drink. The almighty grape was god, and its preservation was what man should be working for, not these stupid power-struggle idiocies.

Another petered-out remnant of a wave slid up past his feet, around his buttocks, reached its furthest millimeter, and once more crept past him and back to its origin. The sand glistened momentarily in its wake, reflecting the burnt orange of the low, dying sun.

Why couldn't life be as simple as a curious little sheet of bubbly water running in and out? He squinted into the sun, guessing at how long it would take to slip behind the nearby cliff. Five minutes; no, more. Seven. What did it matter, his watch was back in the room of the small hotel in Pula. Who needed a watch in limbo? Limbo: that place or that space, that vacuum where nothing mattered, where one turned everything off and communed only with the grape god.

He got to his knees and then to his feet, taking another huge swig and ignoring the little rivulets that streamed from the corners of his mouth. Holding the wine bottle high into the now-reddening sun, as a priest holds the chalice during Mass, he shouted, "Hail Mary, fallen from grace. Drink to *our* god!"

His once-white swimming trunks were red with spilled wine, and his handsome face hadn't seen a razor since he came back to the base from that goddamned baroness's place the morning before. He had driven the twenty-five miles down to Santa Margherita di Pula from Cagliari the afternoon before. It was pristine here on this secluded beach in this quiet inlet, not fouled by the putrescent assholes who made war or even those who followed in their wake.

He'd had no intention of calling in and reporting to Canepa's sergeant during these four days. They were his, owed to him, to do whatever he wished with them. To wash away the evil in any way he desired, with the wine god, in the bubbly, curious little ripples of the sea, if he wanted. He had even told another colonel that he was going to Naples, which would wreak terrible little disasters in Canepa's twisted mind if he heard about it.

On the cliff above, a simple shepherd boy watched his flock along with his noisy black-and-white sheepdog. That was love, that was reality. No vendetta there, no beautiful wife being threatened by ogres who lived in the past and ruled by fear, who killed for some obscene code.

The harsh, ominous words came back to him: SINCE IT HAS TAKEN SO LONG, YOUR WIFE MUST PAY AS WELL. How could these bastards come out from under their rock after all these years? They'd killed his father—wasn't an eye for an eye enough? No, he knew better. That was why his mother had gone into the convent to work as a lowly kitchen maid until she died of a broken heart two years later, to hide. Fear, that was the name of the game.

It was also why he'd changed his name and enlisted in the Regia Aeronautica shortly after his father's murder. Although in his case it wasn't exactly fear, it was logic. They were bigger than he was. Then the wars and all, his status as a hero, closeness to the Mussolini family. Even if they had known he was the son of Frank Accurso they couldn't come after him.

Why now? Was it because the war was about to end in Sicily and they wanted to reestablish themselves? Reestablish their rule through fear?

How could they get to her in Egypt, assuming she was still there? Surely the British had some form of security. The Friends of Friends just couldn't terrorize people in a place like Egypt. Besides, she might not even be there any longer. No, she could be in England. Maybe she had even found another man, possibly even divorced him in absentia, or something like that.

No, it was just one of their evil ruses, a ploy to make him sweat.

Well, he wouldn't let them.

He tilted the wine container back and drank deeply again.

CHAPTER 12

❖

Sabatini liked the Boar; it was a perfect safe house. Enough people came and went that they could escape notice. After all, an inn, a popular little inn in the busy capital of Sardinia, catered to strangers. And being part of the don's empire, it should certainly be secure as far as its help was concerned. He also liked the food. And he liked the voluptuous Elfida. He thought she was right out of an Italian movie: long, frizzy black hair, flashing brown eyes that spoke a language he knew so well, a ready smile, a décolletage that revealed much of its charms when she bent over, and generous, suggestive hips. He could spend the rest of the war eating her fine dishes and warming her bed.

But he had a mission.

The man Leopoldo brought to him at 9:50 the next morning was a janitor at the base *prigione*, the stockade or jail. His name was Cordobi and he was a middle-aged Sicilian who had moved to Cagliari just before the war. His cousin in Palermo was a Friend of the Friends. It was his day off, but he had been at the *prigione* the day before. Yes, he had seen a special prisoner they had captured the preceding night. He had been cleaning a hallway right outside the cell where they had put him in the isolation block. And he had gotten a good look at him. Blond American. Looked like they might have beaten him. He limped like the ones whose kidneys had been clubbed. They put him in a cell no larger than four by four. Just some water, no food. Not even a pot; once he had relieved himself, he would have to sit or stand in it.

Twice while he worked in that block during the day they had taken this American out, hauled him off to one of the interrogation rooms where screams could sometimes be heard from stubborn prisoners.

"But this American prisoner, he didn't scream," he said, shaking his head. "He seemed a cool one."

They were in a back room of the inn, and Sabatini had the map of Elmas on the wall. "Show me where the jail is," he said to the janitor.

"There," he said, pointing to a corner where two streets formed an intersection. "Its upper level is dug in and covered by sandbags. The lower floor is totally underground. That's where the cells and interrogation rooms are."

"Can you help me draw a map of the structure?" Sabatini asked, turning back the cover of a large tablet and handing him a pencil.

"Yes, but I'm not much of an artist."

Cordobi slowly drew rectangles, erasing a line here and there and making changes as he explained which room was which. When he finished, Sabatini turned to another blank page. "All right, now draw the lower level, starting from the stairwell and specifically showing the location of the American's solitary cell."

Within five minutes the janitor had provided a fairly legible floor plan of the lower level. Sabatini nodded his approval. "Are there any steel bars to pass through from the stairs to the American's cell?"

"Yes, two times."

"How do they open?"

"With keys. The duty sergeant keeps them."

They went on, with Sabatini asking the man everything he could think of. Finally he turned to the others and smiled. "Gentlemen, I think we all need to ride our bicycles to Elmas and make a little reconnaissance. How soon can you have my identity card, Bernardo?"

"The man said he would have it ready by noon. Can you ride a bicycle?"

"Certainly. My ankle is almost healed. But we'll need a car for the raid. Josh may not be able to walk."

"Our man will get us a sedan."

Sabatini rubbed his chin. It was coming together. And they'd need some uniforms. . . .

*   *   *

It was shortly after ten that night when a Regia Aeronautica staff car pulled up to the main gate of Elmas. The driver, a young corporal with an engaging grin, showed his identification to the guard and said, "Colonel Ruffini wishes to go directly to the duty officer." He tilted his head toward the back seat. "We've driven all the way from Sassari tonight."

The guard leaned down and looked into the back seat, where he saw an RA colonel and a fierce-looking major sitting on his left. He snapped to attention and saluted smartly, then waved the driver through the gate.

"Very good," Sabatini, garbed in the RA colonel's uniform, said. Looking warily around as Bernardo drove toward base headquarters, he added, "I think you'll make a hell of an OSS agent."

Bernardo grinned over his shoulder. "Hear that, Leopoldo?"

The bodyguard didn't reply. He was too busy sweeping the darkened area for any sign of trouble as the don's son turned the sedan toward the one-story building that housed Maj. Franco Adamo.

Sabatini checked his Smith & Wesson one more time, making sure the suppressor was firmly in place. He had decided to go after Josh just after full darkness fell and the moon came up. He'd like to wait another day to double-check the routines of the military police operation at the base jail, but he couldn't take a chance on what they might do to or with Josh. It was quite conceivable that they could decide to kill him or turn up the wattage on whatever torture they might be inflicting on him. Or they could evacuate him, possibly to Rome, for interrogation. Any number of reasons might exist for rushing the timetable.

Stopping in front of the officers' quarters, Sabatini quickly got out of the back seat and went inside. Although there was no light in Adamo's room, the major could still be there. It was a long shot because of the report that the pilot had gone to Naples, but Sabatini was a thorough man. He tapped lightly on Adamo's door, then more loudly. No answer. He quickly picked the lock and opened the door, his .38 levelled in his right hand. But no one was in the large room. He knew instinctively that there was no need to search it. Moments later he returned to the back seat of the staff car and murmured, "No one home."

Bernardo put the car in gear and they headed out toward the revetment that held the P-38. Sabatini wanted to take the quick shot that the fighter plane might be lightly guarded and they could get to it. If so, he'd plant a timed charge that would destroy it just about the time he planned to be leaving the base. But before they were within two hundred yards he could see the bright floodlights around the revetment. An armored scout car blocked the entrance to the revetment. The New Yorker told Bernardo to stop. If they had gone to that much trouble to safeguard the fighter plane the revetment area would be infested with guards. It would take a whole platoon to destroy that aircraft.

The second part of his plan was thwarted.

But his primary mission was to get Josh Rawlins, and it was time to zero in on that. "Let's go to jail," he said firmly, feeling the excitement he always felt when danger was imminent.

They pulled up directly in front of the jail bunker and Bernardo jumped out of the driver's seat to open the door for the two officers in the rear. A military police guard with a submachine gun strapped across his shoulder stepped out of the shadow of the bunker's entrance. "What's this?" he asked. Seeing the rank of the two officers, he hurriedly saluted.

Leopoldo quickly held out his bogus ID card. "I am Major Trono," he said brusquely. "Colonel Ruffini and I have come from Sassari tonight to interrogate the American prisoner. Will you please notify your duty officer?"

The military policeman stood at attention. "We have no duty officer, sir. There is a duty sergeant."

"Take us to him."

Sabatini watched with an air of detached arrogance. It was agreed that he would do no unnecessary talking because of his American accent. They were led inside a blackout curtain to a small, brightly lit antechamber that led to a row of steel bars. The guard said loudly, "Spagnuolo! Open up, we have important visitors!"

Another military policeman, a burly corporal, came out of a room to the right, just inside the bars, and yawned. He had obviously been asleep. "What important visitors?" He quickly saw Sabatini's rank and said, "Sorry, sir."

Leopoldo held out his ID again, saying curtly, "Please take us to your duty sergeant."

The corporal pulled out a ring of keys, found the right one, and unlocked the door of bars. "Wait here, please, sirs," he said obsequiously, then ran down the hall to another office.

Moments later, a fat, balding sergeant puffed out saying, "Sirs, I am Sergeant Parri. What may I do for you?"

"We are here to interrogate the American prisoner," Leopoldo said briskly. "And we've driven all the way from Sassari, so we'd like to get started as soon as possible."

The sergeant blinked his little round eyes. "I was told of no such interrogation, Major."

"Rome told us they would call ahead late this afternoon."

"I came on at five, sir. I was told nothing, and there isn't anything in writing."

Sabatini frowned as he looked at his wristwatch.

So did Leopoldo. The bodyguard scowled. "I don't want to waste any time, but if you insist, Sergeant, you can put in a call to Rome."

Little beads of sweat stood out on Parri's brow. "I don't think that's necessary, sir."

"Or call your commander. I'll talk to him."

"Major Lionetti is away from the base tonight, and so is Colonel Canepa."

Leopoldo turned to Sabatini and shrugged. "That damned Canepa didn't get the message or he'd be here." Looking back at the sergeant, he growled, "Then you'd better get busy on that telephone trying to raise someone in Rome."

Sergeant Parri held up both hands in protest. "No, sir. I'll take you to the prisoner. You know his name, of course."

"Yes—Capt. Joshua Rawlins."

The sergeant nodded to the corporal, who selected another key and unlocked the entrance to the second row of bars. He then led the way down a row of cells, some of which were occupied by curious prisoners, to a heavy wooden door. Inside, four more wooden doors greeted them. Once more the corporal selected a key; he opened the first one on the right. Sabatini tensed, his hand going to the handle of the Smith & Wesson inside his jacket. Now he had to hope Rawlins hadn't been so badly beaten that he didn't have his wits about him. This was it, the most dangerous moment, the thrill that made him love this job. He drew in a deep breath.

"Outside, *Capitano!*" Sergeant Parri barked.

Moments passed before Josh Rawlins stepped blinking from the narrow cell. Both of his eyes were puffed and swollen nearly shut and there was a heavy splash of dried blood on his uniform shirt. His trousers were stained and there was a foul smell about him. He limped, but managed to draw himself erect as he looked first at Leopoldo, then Sabatini. He showed no sign of recognition.

Leopoldo spoke to him in English, "We are from Regia Aeronautica headquarters in Rome, Captain. We wish to talk to you."

When Josh did not reply, the bogus major nodded to the sergeant, who led them back down the hallway past the other cells toward the same interrogation room where the heaviest beating had taken place earlier that evening.

They were nearly there when they heard an angry voice coming from the entry room to the bunker. "What do you mean two officers from Rome are here? Get that damned corporal and let me in!"

Alertly, Josh barked, "That's Canepa, an asshole colonel!"

Hearing the English, Parri whirled in surprise. But the silencer of Sabatini's muted .38 jammed into his stomach. "Take us out of here!" the New Yorker snapped in Italian.

Leopoldo covered the corporal with his Mauser and ordered him to open the inside door of bars. As they went through and moved toward the outer row of bars, Canepa blinked in amazement for a second before shrieking, "Who are you people?" Turning to the military policeman beside him, he shouted, "Sound the alarm. Call out the guard!"

Sabatini's .38 slug caught him in the chest.

His second one spun the military policeman around, dropping him.

"Open that door!" Leopoldo snapped.

The bug-eyed corporal jumped, shakily finding the key and inserting it just as another military policeman came out of the hallway. Sabatini shot the newcomer instantly and turned to the fat sergeant. Parri's eyes were wide, his face very white, like old paper. Sabatini squeezed the trigger again as Leopoldo rammed a knife into the corporal.

Bernardo waved them to the door. "It's clear out here! Hurry!"

"Can you run?" Sabatini asked Josh.

"I don't think so."

Sabatini wrapped his arm around him and practically carried him as they rushed past the bodies of Canepa and the guard, then burst through the bunker entrance and hurried to the open doors of the waiting automobile. Without making the tires squeal, Bernardo sped toward the main gate. Slowing as they approached the closed barrier, the don's son drew his Mauser. But the same guard was there as when they had entered, and he cheerfully raised the gate and waved them through.

They hurtled off into the night toward the waiting *Gaia*.

"Get aboard the boat," Sabatini ordered quietly.

"But I haven't finished it!"

"You *can't* finish the son of a bitch!"

"He'll be back and I'll get him!" Josh shouted.

Sabatini shook his head. "Yeah, sure. You're just gonna walk back in there with another phony pass and a lunch box and Adamo's gonna be waiting on the front steps for you. Let me tell you something, sonny. When he gets back and finds out you were trying to steal his airplane, he's gonna pack up and go bye-bye in that bird."

"Not necessarily."

"C'mon. They're not going to take a chance on us getting near that plane. Tell you what, my friend. I'll make a bet with you. We go back to Algeria and you set up a raid on Elmas. You fly lead, or whatever you call it, and you come in low. You know where that revetment is, so you come in as low as you want and you and your buddies plaster it, put a fucking hole fifty feet deep where they've got it parked. And if your photo boys can show me one single piece of a P-38, I'll give you two hundred bucks. If I'm wrong you pay me a hundred. Okay?"

Josh turned to look at the dock, then back to the waiting Captain Madeo. Bernardo and Leopoldo were watching him. His face hurt, his kidneys were terribly painful where they'd kicked and prodded him, and he was sure he would lose a tooth or two. But he'd live. He just hated to give up now, even though what Sabatini said was undoubtedly true.

He hadn't killed the son of a bitch.

But he'd touched him, taken his pilot's wings.

No, it hadn't been a total loss; unless he missed his guess, Adamo was a man of some feel for intrigue. He flashed back to the day the bastard shot the *Bitch* down, and saw again the blue-gray Lightning diving toward him, its nose quiet. A couple of hundred yards away, the pilot waggled his wings and quickly passed overhead without firing a round.

The man who spouted a philosophical phrase about war and had spared his life, the man who was now his mortal enemy, that man was one who would take up the gauntlet when he found that he was being hunted.

He looked at Sabatini and slowly nodded his head. They could go.

But this thing between him and Adamo was far from over.

CHAPTER 13

✛

Franco Adamo knocked on the front door of the two-story house near Poetto. He was wearing an old pair of uniform shorts and an unbuttoned short-sleeved civilian shirt. He had nothing but sandals on his feet and he hadn't shaved in three days. In his hand he held a two-liter jug of cheap local white wine.

He knocked again.

It was shortly after 6:00 P.M., and she was probably off to some inane social function, he guessed.

He knocked once more, waited, and was about to go when the door opened. Baroness Angelina Ricardi's bright smile was guarded. "Well, if it isn't my sanctimonious friend. I thought you said—"

"Don't make me pay for changing my mind," he said, cutting her off. "I have been drinking alone for three days and have cleansed my soul of all of the lesser purgatorial crap." He held up the wine jug. "I thought you might like to get in on some of the major guilt."

She looked at him skeptically.

He made a sweeping bow. "Baroness, I request the pleasure of your hospitality and your company. If you know of some nearby low-class restaurant that will accept my informal attire, I will even take you out to eat."

She shook her head, chuckling, "Come in, Major, before someone sees you."

He fished the corkscrew from his pocket on the way in and stopped in the vestibule to put the wine jug on an antique table.

She shook her head again. "Give that to me and I'll open it."

"Impossible," he replied, twisting the screw into the cork. "This is my party."

"May I at least provide some glasses?"

"If you insist."

"May we go into the parlor?"

"Said the spider to the fly. Of course."

The cork came out and Franco tipped the jug back to take a long swig. "Yes," he said, nodding his head to an imaginary waiter. "It'll do quite well, waiter, even though I don't think this was a vintage year."

She took the jug and filled glasses for each of them in the parlor. Sitting opposite from where he slouched on the small sofa, she sipped and regarded him quietly. Finally she asked, "Have you really been drinking for three days? What happened to the war?"

"I divorced it."

"When does the remarriage commence?"

"I may never go back."

"Yes, you will. What's the occasion?"

He told her briefly about the Lightning and its engine trouble, then poured himself another glass of the white wine. It was a warm night and she was wearing a sleeveless, low-cut blouse and white shorts. "You've got nice legs," he said, "for a Wellesley girl."

"Thanks. I think I'll decline your dinner invitation. When was the last time you ate?"

"Doesn't matter. In fact, you're quite lovely for a Wellesley girl."

"May I fix you something? I think you mumbled something the other night about liking lamb. I just happen to have some cold lamb that I can serve with some bread."

"No." He got up abruptly and came to her, pulling her to her feet and into his arms. Kissing her roughly, his hands slid down her back to her buttocks.

She pulled away, turning her face, her dark eyes blazing. "No! A few mornings ago, you played the righteous married man caught up in a terrible war and told me you didn't want to hurt me. Then you walked out on me like I was the village whore begging you to come back to her bed. Now you come in here, looking like the wrath of God, half-drunk, and paw me like you own me. Sorry, Major, wrong number." Breaking away, she went around the chair and looked back at him. Her tone was even, "If you want to drink with me in a polite manner, that's fine. If you want to make love, that may be possible. But if this whole episode is some final act of a three-day orgy of self-pity, I pass."

He blinked, looking into her eyes for several moments. Finally he wiped his mouth and said, "I shouldn't have done that. You're right, I shouldn't even have come here. Let me take my jug and get out." He reached for the wine container on the low table.

"You don't have to leave," she said quietly.

He blew out a deep breath and slumped back onto the sofa. "I don't want to. But I was an ass."

"I agree. Now, why don't you just sit there while I get that lamb? Will you do that?"

"No, no food. Don't go away." He looked at her beseechingly. "Just sit here and talk to me. I won't touch you, I promise."

She shook her floppy black bob and sat beside him on the edge of the sofa, facing him. After a few moments she asked, "Have you been in touch with civilization, or just your private hells?"

"Why? Did the world do something sensible?"

"No, there was a raid on Elmas."

His eyebrows shot up. "What kind of a raid?"

"They didn't exactly say, but they implied that it was an American commando raid to rescue a prisoner. I've got the newspaper account here." She went to a table and picked up a newspaper. Handing it to him, she added, "They don't tell us much, you know."

He took the Cagliari paper and read, KILLERS CRASH ELMAS STOCKADE. The text stated: "A team of skilled specialists broke into the Elmas stockade last night and kidnapped a prisoner. Several military policemen and one of the Regia Aeronautica's older aces were killed when the assailants forced their way into the base prison. As the prisoner they kidnapped was an American officer, it is believed the killers were Americans or British. The dead officer is Lt. Col. Fillipo Canepa, a pilot with twenty-three victories and several medals who bravely tried to stop the raiders. Maj. Sergi Lionetti, base provost marshal, has stated that they know who the killers are, and will have them in custody within twenty-four hours."

Canepa dead?

He didn't like the bastard, but *dead*?

"Wasn't that colonel you introduced me to at the reception the other night named Canepa?" Angelina asked.

Franco nodded. "That was him." American officer prisoner? What was Canepa doing there? What the hell was going on?

"Was he a friend of yours?"

"Not exactly."

"Does it have anything to do with you?"

"I don't know. Canepa was my boss."

Her fingers gently touched his scowl. "I'm sorry."

He pulled himself to his feet. "I think I'd better check in and see what's going on."

It was her turn to raise an eyebrow. "In your condition? What can you do tonight?"

"I don't know."

"Why don't you eat something, then let me give you a good hot bath? You can stay here tonight and go in refreshed in the morning."

He looked into her lovely dark eyes. Tempting. That was why he'd come here wasn't it, to go to bed with her again? But something was telling him this thing, this raid and Canepa's killing, had something to do with him. "No, I'd better get back."

"I can make you some strong tea to sober you up."

He shook his head. "I'm all right." He reached out and touched her cheek. "This is probably for the best anyway."

Moments later he turned to wave to her as he opened the door to the Fiat.

For some implausible reason she reminded him of Sella.

After shaving and showering, Franco brushed his teeth vigorously and put on a khaki uniform. It was 8:25 when he reached Major Lionetti's quarters. The bull-necked military police officer greeted him coolly.

"I've been out of touch on leave," Franco said, entering the major's suite. "I just heard. Can you tell me about it?"

Lionetti shrugged. "He was an American pilot trying to steal your fighter plane. I'm convinced he was working in concert with some kind of a large organization. Canepa was stupid. He thought gentle persuasion would work. It didn't."

Franco didn't like this bastard; he was like too many of Mussolini's thugs. He even looked like the Duce with his shaved head and jutting jaw. "I suppose you beat him," he commented casually.

A tiny smile touched the corners of Lionetti's mouth. "Let's say that he'll remember his stay."

"But he didn't talk?"

"Nothing. I would have broken him today, though."

"What was his name?"

"Captain Joshua Rawlins."

Franco rolled the name around, saying it three times to himself. "Doesn't mean anything to me. How did Canepa get killed?"

"Shot though the throat. Died instantly, I was told."

All at once Franco felt sorry for the crippled pilot. A terribly unhappy man who had already been dealt a terrible blow by being crippled. Shame.

Another face to roam around back there in the haze.

He arrived at the revetment a few minutes later. In spite of the normal blackout policy floodlights blazed all around the sandbags. A guard challenged him as he drove up. Crawling out of the Fiat, he told the young man that he had been on leave and didn't know the password. He held out his identification. Another guard came up, pointing his submachine gun, acting important. But at that moment a familiar voice from the edge of the revetment barked, "Leave him be, you idiots, he's my major." It was Sergeant Diego, his crew chief.

Inside the revetment, Franco looked up at the P-38. The cowling was closed on the left engine and the cooler pod looked normal.

"It's fixed," Diego said matter-of-factly. "And I have some good parts that I salvaged."

"Can I fly it tomorrow?"

"Of course."

"They may want us out of here. You heard about the American?"

Diego nodded his head.

"Better take the rest of the night off and tell your girlfriend goodbye."

"Any idea where we'd go, Major?"

"Could be anywhere."

Franco's next stop was Canepa's office. He looked through the papers on the colonel's desk, finding nothing except a telegram dated that day, which read: CONTACT MAJOR ADAMO AND HAVE HIM REPORT IN PERSON TO THIS HEADQUARTERS AS SOON AS HE RETURNS FROM LEAVE. He reread the wire. No other orders. He would get a

Macchi and fly over to RA headquarters in Rome in the morning. He couldn't take the Lightning; it was still an enemy plane and he didn't want to take a chance on some trigger-happy types jumping him when he reached the mainland.

He looked through Canepa's desk drawers for no particular reason before leaving. Nothing more he could do; let the base commander and his chaplain handle it all. He picked up the phone and called Base Operations. "Is there a Macchi I can fly to Rome tomorrow?" he asked. "To RA headquarters?"

"Yes, Major. Departure time?"

"Make it 0600."

"It will be ready, Major Adamo."

He stood and pursed his lips. A picture of a pretty woman in a floppy hat smiled back from a frame on the desk. Some photos of different airplanes Canepa had flown decorated the walls of the office. Some medals, framed, a picture of Il Duce decorating him. The colonel's dress sword. Canepa, another man who had tasted the joys and fears of innumerable combats in the cockpit of a fighter plane, had passed on. He hadn't cared for him, but in this moment they were as old friends. Momentarily, he let a flash of sadness through his armor.

And then he closed the door.

Men died.

He hurried on to his quarters and poured himself a glass of red wine. Drinking over half of it at once, he went to his Victrola and wound it. Absently, he picked a record, "Stardust," by Benny Goodman. As its melody drifted over him, he went to his desk and sat down.

"I wonder why I spend each lonely night . . ."

A small metal shape in the center of the desk caught his eye. It was leaning up against a bullet.

He picked it up. It had rounded edges and small stamped letters. Looking at it closely, he saw a P and an A, some numbers, 01688586, and a name: Joshua Rawlins. *Joshua Rawlins!* That was the name of the captured American pilot! Capt. Joshua Rawlins had been here, right here in his quarters, right here at his desk!

He had left this identification tag to say so!

He drew in a deep breath.

There was something terribly personal about this. It was one thing for an American pilot to find out about the P-38 and try to steal it.

But to come here to his room, to leave such a loaded message as this ID tag and a bullet . . . that was *intimate*.

He knew at once: this Rawlins had sworn to kill him.

Something strangely, intriguingly personal had begun.

And he knew as surely as he knew his own name that the day would come when he would meet this man in mortal combat.

CHAPTER 14

✛

Josh watched quietly as Sabatini lit another Lucky Strike. The sudden glow of the flame from his Zippo broke the darkness, even though he cupped his hands around it. The *Gaia* rocked lightly as it sat quietly in the water. Giuseppe Madeo had the boat's running lights burning as a signal. "What are you going to do after the invasion?" Josh asked the unusually quiet Bernardo Calgogeri.

The don's son shrugged, his generous grin evident in the light of the slim moon. "I think there will be many opportunities."

"Doing what?"

"Making money. With thousands of American soldiers having many things to sell and lots of money, the black market will be big."

Josh nodded his head. "And a smart young man who speaks good English will have a field day."

"Field day?"

"A big time of it."

"Oh, it will all be carefully worked out. My father has been planning for some time."

Josh looked at the New Yorker. "You going to have your fingers in that pot, Sabatini?"

His answer was a grin and a small cloud of smoke. "I kiss the don's hands."

"What about your old boss, Genovese? Who's ass will he be kissing when Mussolini gets his?"

Sabatini frowned. "Don't you worry about him, sonny. He made his bones when you were still in short pants." He looked at the luminous dial of his watch. "Hey, Captain, you sure you got this tub in the right place?"

"*Perfetto.*"

As if to emphasize his reply, the dark gray prow of a submarine kicked off white foam as it broke the calm water seventy-five yards off the *Gaia's* starboard bow. In moments it was stopped on the surface, its conning tower opening. Quickly a signal light challenged them. And just as quickly Captain Madeo signalled back with his own light.

An American voice barked at them through a megaphone. "Approach and tell our passengers to be ready for the rubber raft."

"Roger!" Sabatini replied loudly.

Moments later Madeo had them alongside the sub, twenty feet away. A small raft with two sailors aboard slid over the undersea vessel's side and quickly made its way to the Sicilian boat.

The submarine was the *Threadfin,* a *Gato*-class vessel with ten torpedo tubes. It could make nine knots underwater or twenty on the surface. It looked dark and menacing in the black water.

The two Americans quickly shook hands with the Sicilians and were soon in the rubber raft. Josh looked back at the *Gaia* as they pulled away and waved, wondering if he would have to come back someday to fulfill his destiny.

"Now you do as I tell you, sonny."

"I don't want to go near that damned hospital," Josh replied.

"You want that iron-assed general to lock you up for the duration?"

"He wouldn't do that."

"Oh no? You were already up to your ass in trouble and then he gave you a direct order not to go to Sicily. So you've actually been AWOL all this time. You expect him to pin another medal on you?" Sabatini shook his head. "Wise up and listen to me."

"What then?"

"By the time you get out I'll have a new plan worked out."

Josh sipped the strong Navy coffee. The *Threadfin* was ploughing along on the surface, making good time before daylight, and they were in the wardroom alone. "What's your plan?"

"I haven't got it worked out yet."

"Give me a hint." Sabatini had saved his ass and he greatly appreciated the fact, but he still didn't trust the man.

The New Yorker grinned. "You just lie there and heal up a little bit, because I want you in top shape for the next phase of our 'Get Adamo' operation."

"I didn't know you were going any further."

Sabatini looked at him in mock dismay. "I've grown too fond of you to quit now."

"Tell me."

"All right. While you're being coddled by those nurses, think about the Pyramids."

Franco Adamo had made it over to Rome in just under fifty minutes. He had kept the Macchi C.205V on the deck for the early part of the flight to avoid any early Allied visitors. Flying this late-model Macchi was like driving a long-nosed hornet after his last few weeks in the stubby pod of the P-38. But it had hummed along smoothly and gotten him to his destination, the capital of Italy and once the capital of the world.

Now he was looking into the dark eyes of a lieutenant general who had once been his squadron commander in Spain. General Manzella was the deputy chief of staff for operations for fighters, and the officer who reported directly to Mussolini about the covert Operation Outlaw. He had also been Canepa's boss since the scheme's inception.

"I'm sorry about Canepa," the general sighed. "Tragic man. Without worrying Il Duce about how the colonel was killed, or even mentioning the presence of the American pilot at Elmas, I spoke to him about the future of Operation Outlaw. He wants it to continue, Adamo, and he wants you to be the officer in charge. It gives him personal satisfaction to know that we can create even a small amount of havoc with the enemy air effort in such a manner."

General Manzella sighed again. "In his illness, Adamo, you are providing him with a ray of sunlight, a small source of pride, if you will."

Franco raised an eyebrow. "Shooting down trusting aircrews under false colors? He gets pride out of *that*?"

Manzella's dark brows jammed together. "Don't criticize our commander-in-chief, Major. He has the weight of Italy on his unwell shoulders. And you know how arrogant the Germans have been lately."

Franco nodded his head, saying quietly, "My apologies, sir."

"In fact, you have all the more reason to be supportive of his desires, Adamo. At his personal direction, I have something for you." The general reached inside the middle drawer of his huge mahogany desk and withdrew a pair of blue-gray shoulder boards. Each one held a gold-embroidered crown, a wreath, and two small stars.

They were the rank of a lieutenant colonel.

Manzella went on, "Your date of rank will be today." He went to the door and opened it. A major and an RA photographer entered the office.

Moments later, as the promotion order was being read, Franco felt as though he were in some kind of a strange vacuum. Lieutenant colonel—an exalted rank for a Boston boy who was the son of a gangster. There was a time when he would have felt extremely proud of being selected for this rank.

But not now.

Not with all the death and deceit that had piled up in his path. Not when it meant that he had gone one step higher in the Fascist lie; not when it meant that he had to continue filling his hall of ghosts.

"Congratulations, Colonel!" the general said with a broad smile as he finished fastening the second new shoulder board in place. "Il Duce told me to tell you of his personal pleasure in directing your promotion. And I'd like to add that you've come a long way from being that raw young pilot who reported into my squadron in Spain." He shook Franco's hand and embraced him as a flashbulb erupted.

Benito Mussolini had moved into the Villa Torlonia shortly after his ascent to power in 1922. A forty-room mansion, it was a substantial structure of vulgar neoclassical design. It had elaborate carving around its roof line and thick pillars at one end. Surrounded by a large garden, it gave the appearance of being in a small park. The twenty acres of grounds contained a tennis court and a riding track that Il Duce used often when his failing health permitted. Its tasteless interior hadn't been improved over the years as he added the often vapid and sometimes ostentatious gifts a head of state acquired.

Newly promoted Lt. Col. Franco Adamo sat on a chair in the garden, just outside the back of the house, sipping an American bourbon and listening to Edda Ciano.

"Oh, Franco, darling, I'm so pleased with your promotion. I wish Father had told me so I could have been there to represent him." She crossed her lovely legs in the chair across from him and smiled. "Just think, darling, I knew you when you were a young lieutenant just back from the heathen war in Spain. Oh, you were so pretty then."

A smile touched his lips. "And now I'm old, tired, and cynical."

"Ha! You are just reaching the prime of manhood."

He smiled again. "Forever the huntress, aren't you, Countess?"

"Call me Edda, darling. Why the formality?" She sipped from a highball of contraband Jack Daniels, her large, dark eyes holding his.

He was once more impressed by how much they were like her father's. "Habit, I guess," he replied.

"How long will you be here in Rome, my pretty one?"

"I'm flying back to Sardinia in the morning."

Her bold eyes didn't waver. "Pity. Galeazzo is in Germany, meeting with Ribbentrop again, and I'm bored. Serving as a nurse on the Russian Front was no fun, you know."

"Yes, I heard you were there. Did you actually get into the gore?"

"They wanted to treat me like Il Duce's daughter, but I insisted on being in the heat of it. But let's not talk about that. As I said, I'm bored."

"And you want me to be an amusement?"

She recrossed her lovely legs, replying softly, "I want you to be whatever you want to be, darling. As I told you many years ago, my fires can easily be unbanked and they can erupt in flames with the right stoker."

Franco smiled as he shook his head. "I'm tempted. But the reason I've come to you isn't quite in keeping with passion."

Edda Mussolini Ciano shrugged. "Very well. How can I help you, darling?"

Franco leaned forward, his manner suddenly intent. "It's about Sella. I received a warning from the Friends—you know, the gangster types. I told you years ago about how and why they killed my father."

She pursed her lips. "Yes, I remember. But my father stamped them out in Sicily years ago. They don't exist."

"Wrong." He handed her the telegram.

She read it quickly:

FRANCO ADAMO ACCURSO: IT WILL SOON BE TIME FOR YOU TO PAY FOR YOUR FATHER'S TREACHERY WITH YOUR LIFE. SINCE IT HAS TAKEN SO LONG, YOUR WIFE MUST PAY AS WELL.

"Hmmm, and you believe this is serious?" she asked.

Franco nodded his head slowly. "I believe it. They used my real name, Accurso."

"Is it possible that they know where your wife is?"

"They found me after all these years, didn't they?"

Her large eyes were wide. "But surely they wouldn't dare come after you, not with your position and fame."

"They know the war can't last too much longer, Edda, and they want to make me sweat. But that's no problem. I have ghosts that frighten me more."

"What do you want from me?"

"Ask your husband if we have agents in Egypt who can protect her."

"He may not be back from Germany for some time."

"Can you ask your father?"

"Maybe. When he comes back to the city."

"When will that be?"

"Next week, but I can't promise anything. I really know nothing about his intelligence network."

"Ask him if there is a way for me to go there."

She lit a cigarette. "How could you stop them?"

"I don't know. Maybe I could bring her back here."

She blew out a cloud of smoke, handing him the telegram. "If they can send you this, they can find her here as well."

Suddenly he lost his control. "Damn it! At least I'd have her with me! This ignorance, this goddamned not knowing, is what is tearing me apart!"

She touched his hand gently. "When I was young my father taught me how to control my fear and revulsion. He made me hold a frog in my hand. And it worked. My dear, Franco, I don't have a frog to give you, just the idea. You can think about holding one when this troubles you."

He sipped from the Jack Daniels. "I'll try it. Will you get word to me when you've talked to either of them?"

"At once." Edda got to her feet and picked up the whiskey bottle. "Now let's have another drink before we think about dinner."

He nodded his head. "I'll take mine without soda, and strong."

"Good," she replied with a bright smile. "We have your promotion to celebrate, and after we've done that for a while, we can think about more pleasant possibilities."

He found a brief smile.

She never gave up.

CHAPTER 15

✛

They put Josh in exactly the same bed on the same officers' ward as when he came back from being shot down in the *Texas Bitch*. Two doctors asked questions and poked around his body. They had him X-rayed and then asked him more questions. Neither of them had ever seen a man who had been tortured before, and he felt as though he were a new toy for them. One was young, blond, skinny, and obviously from the South. The older doctor was a balding Jewish man in his mid-thirties, who mentioned being from Chicago.

Viewing the last X-rays, the ones of his spine and kidney areas, the younger doctor said, "Incredibly, nothing is broken. Not even a hairline fracture anywhere. From what you tell us, Captain, you're a lucky man."

Josh still had pain in his lower back area and there were also traces of blood in his urine, but he was glad to hear that nothing was broken. He just nodded his head in response.

They had flown into Chateaudun du Rhumel on a medical evac C-47 from Tunis. And as soon as the gooney bird's propellers had stopped turning Sabatini had gone outside to round up an ambulance to take Josh directly to the hospital in Constantine. "No group commander, no squadron leader for you," he had said. "You're a badly injured hero,

Josh, my boy, and we're not going to let anyone but the general himself get his hooks into you."

"I think the discomfort and the urine problem will go away if we keep pouring water into you," the second doctor said. "An IV will help. We'll give you something for the pain, as well."

"How long will I be in here?" Josh asked.

"Depends," the younger doctor replied. "If all goes well, maybe several days. Could be as much as a few weeks."

"I can't afford more than a few days."

The older doctor, Heintzelman, raised an eyebrow. "Why—are you going to win the war single-handed?"

"No, Doc, I've got things to do."

"What, go back to Sardinia so they can finish the job? C'mon, Captain, count your blessings." He fiddled with his stethoscope.

"He doesn't know how!" Gen. Barney Buell barked as he came up to the bed with Sabatini in his wake. He scowled down at Josh. "Do you, Captain?"

Josh shrugged. "Good afternoon, General."

"Good afternoon, my ass! What do you think this is, the goddamned social hour? You think the bloody tea dance starts in a few minutes?"

Josh just watched Barney Buell's angry eyes.

The general's hands balled up at his sides. "You disobeyed a direct order from me, Captain." His dark brown eyes were narrowed. "You went AWOL. In fact, I could probably stretch it to desertion. And then you fucked up government property by getting yourself hurt! I ought to have you pulled off this ward and put into a prison ward. That's right, in a goddamned cell!" The stocky general turned to the medical officers. "Beat it, I'll talk to you guys later."

The two doctors looked at each other with raised eyebrows and quickly walked away.

Buell continued to glare at Josh as Sabatini looked on. "Just what the hell did you think you were doing when you got on the C-47, Rawlins? You could have fucked up the whole mission for Sabatini! But that isn't the major issue. You went against my direct order, and for that you could spend time in Leavenworth!"

Josh still said nothing as the general's eyes bored into his.

"All right, Captain Rawlins, now you tell me just what the hell I should do. I can send you down to your squadron and let that asshole group commander of yours court-martial you. Or since you were on detached duty with me, I can court-martial you, or I can give you an Article 15 and fine your ass. Tell me, what should I do?"

Josh decided to play tough. "None of the above, General. I found our goddamned Boston/Italian pilot. I touched the bastard's personal things and stole his fucking wings from his dress uniform. And I almost stole back that goddamned P-38—all by being aggressive. Isn't that what you want in a young officer?" His frown then faded into a boyish grin.

For a moment it looked as though Barney Buell was going to explode, and then slowly the color receded from his flushed face. He shook his head. "You asshole, Josh. How could you dare pull that aggressive young officer shit on me? And then lie there and grin as if you stole all the chestnuts."

"That's the way it is, sir. Going into Sicily with the major was no big deal. And we have to look at the end result. We know who the bastard is. And as soon as these quacks let me out of here, I'll go after him."

Buell stuck out his forefinger. "You aren't going anywhere! You are confined to this goddamned bed. You'll have to sign out to go to the shithouse! Do you understand?"

"But I think you should listen to—"

"I'm not listening to anything! Come along, Sabatini." The general spun on his heel and strode away.

As he followed Buell, the New Yorker grinned back over his shoulder and gave Josh a thumbs-up.

"We gotta figure an angle to get to Egypt," Sabatini said as he strode up to Josh's bed thirty minutes later.

"Yeah," Josh replied, "I remember your little riddle about the Pyramids. You want to explain it now?"

The New Yorker dropped into a chair beside the bed. "It's Adamo's wife. Her name is Sella and she's an archaeologist. She's working on a British dig in Egypt."

"How'd you find that out?"

"The don. Seems as though she's from an old Naples Jewish family. Got out of the country before Hitler's soap factory program could take hold in Italy."

"What good is she to us?"

Sabatini shrugged. He'd grown to like the aggressive Josh, but the job he faced—the assignment Don Nizzi had given him—left no room for any kind of confidence. Considering the way he hated Adamo, Josh would probably be totally indifferent to the killing of Sella Adamo. But one couldn't take any chances. "What else we got to work with?" he replied. "Adamo's still flying from somewhere in those Italian islands and we can't do anything about it yet. Why not go after her? Who knows, maybe she'll be the key to some kind of a plan."

"Get me out of this hospital and I'll try anything."

"No more AWOL shit, Rawlins. I think you've pushed your luck about as far as it'll go on that."

Josh frowned. "You know, I've been thinking. There's a guy—he's out on pass right now—but there's a guy who just came in from England a couple of weeks ago. Came down with dysentery and they stuck him in here. Anyway, he told me about a special airplane they've got back there in the Eighth Air Force. It's a B-17 that's all beefed up with extra armor plate and firepower. It's got about twice as many machine guns as the regular F model Fort. They're using it for escort duty, and they call it the YB-40."

"So?"

"Supposing I could talk Barney into getting us one of those?"

"What are you gonna do, send Adamo your gauntlet so he can meet you at dawn?"

"No, I haven't got that part worked out yet. Why don't you use that gangster mind of yours and come up with an idea?"

Sabatini shrugged. "I'll think about it."

"Hello, Josh. I heard you were back." It was just after the orderly took away Josh's supper tray, and First Lt. Hermelinda Prospero was standing beside the bed. Her olive skin and bright black hair were a sharp contrast to her starched white duty uniform. Her large dark eyes were concerned as she asked, "What did you do to yourself this time?"

He shook his head. "Actually I was over there in Sardinia and I heard that the nurses back here were putting out. So I drank some bad *vino* on purpose, just so I could get in on it."

"Don't give me that. I heard Dr. Heintzelman talking about you getting tortured." Her eyes widened. "Is it bad?"

"I'll live. How are you doing?"

She nodded her head. "Fine. Was it dreadful, Josh?"

"No, I laughed the whole time."

"Be serious. I think it's terrible. How'd it happen?"

He shrugged. "I got caught trying to steal back the P-38. Just plain got nailed. And then they wanted me to share all of my little private thoughts with them. When I told them I didn't want to play, they pounded on me. Like I said, I'll live."

"How'd you find the airplane?"

He gave her a thumbnail rundown of his journey to Sicily and Sardinia, then abruptly switched to the thoughts that had been plaguing him ever since he returned to the Constantine hospital. "Are you able to get him out of your head?" he asked quietly.

"Who, Joe? Yes, I've even had a few other dates since you disappeared. You know how it is."

Josh frowned. "It hasn't even been a month yet."

Linda shook her pretty head. "How many times do I have to tell you, flyboy? He was fun and maybe we might have found something together if he'd lived. But he was a runaway freight, destruction bent."

"He couldn't help it."

"I know, but that doesn't change anything."

"I almost got the bastard that shot us down, Linda."

"And you almost got killed."

"Did you ever hear the phrase, 'Any man's death diminishes me?' "

"I think so. Maybe you used it in your self-flagellation."

"Well, I got diminished down to almost nothing until I jumped into Sicily. But tracking that killer gave me new life. Then I almost got to him." He held up two fingers. "I had his wings right *there*, Linda!"

She watched him quietly for a few moments, then asked softly, "So what's next? Is there another chapter in this vendetta that seems to be consuming you?"

He relaxed, found a smile. "Yes, but I'm not being consumed. I'm even trying to figure out how a starched white uniform can hide so much of your terrific figure."

It was her turn to smile. "Maybe there's hope yet."

They took Josh off the intravenous fluids three days later. At shortly before 1500—three in the afternoon—Gen. Barney Buell once more led the bulky Sabatini up to Josh's bed. Buell, as usual, was brusque. "Major Sabatini tells me you've got some kind of a plan to get this Adamo."

Josh looked up from his book. "Yes, sir."

The general pulled out a pack of Chesterfields and offered them around before lighting one. "Okay, fire away."

Josh told him about the YB-40.

"Yeah," Buell replied, "I read a report about it. So what does a YB-40 have to do with a goddamned Guinea flying a P-38?"

Josh had been fooling with ideas for two days. "I figure if I can get that son of a bitch to come in close, with all those guns with heavy loads we can nail him."

"And how do you propose to get him in close, send him an invitation to a tea party?"

"I haven't worked that out yet. Do you think you can get us one of those planes, General?"

"Maybe. I can probably sell Doolittle on it. Actually, we ought to have one here anyway. See how it works and all." Buell was holding his chin, looking thoughtful.

"Can I get a special crew for it?"

"What makes you think I'm going to let you fly it? You're still under hospital arrest."

Josh grinned. "Because I'm not only the best Flying Fort pilot you've got, but I'm an aggressive young officer. Remember?"

Buell shook his head. "I oughta let you rot here, but you're right. Okay, I'll see what Doolittle says, and if he okays the idea I'll contact the boys up in England."

"I've got it!" Sabatini exclaimed, snapping his fingers. "I don't know why I didn't think of it before. It's a natural!" The general and Josh both watched him as he continued excitedly, "While you're getting us one of those YB-40s, General, Josh and I go over to Cairo and find this broad, this Adamo's wife, Sella. Then we get some of her clothes off and take some pictures of her. We bring the pictures back and have a good artist paint a big picture of her on the gunship. Then Josh finds Adamo up there somewhere in the sky, and when Adamo see that picture, he'll shit!"

Josh's eyes lit up. "Yeah, and when I talk to him on the fighter frequency, I'll tell him she's the greatest piece of ass in Egypt, a real slut. That'll get him in close!"

"Yeah!" Sabatini added, "You can tell him she takes on whole crews at a time. He'll lose his fucking marbles!"

Barney Buell slowly nodded his head. His narrowed eyes relaxed.

"Yeah, I like it. Tell me more about Adamo's wife. How do you get next to her?"

Sabatini grinned. "I'll work something out with the Brits. She's supposed to be working on a British dig somewhere. While Josh continues to recuperate, I'll hop on down to Cairo and talk to British intelligence."

"No need," Buell said. "We can get everything through the British staff here. After I talk to Doolittle, I'll set something up."

The British intelligence officer visiting from GHQ Cairo was Wing Commander Harry Macgruder, a Royal Air Force pilot who had been grounded after receiving a crippling wound during the Battle of Britain. A tall, balding man with a big pipe constantly in his mouth, Macgruder looked the epitome of a stuffy staff officer, but Sabatini had already discovered that he had a ready wit. General Buell had given Josh permission to leave the hospital to meet with the wing commander.

"I did my time in Hurricanes," the Britisher said, "before they let me get into a Spit. The Hurricane was a highly underrated machine, you see, and never got its bloody due. The Spit could never take the same beating, but it flies like a dream." He smiled. "But then, I'm rambling on, aren't I?"

Sabatini smiled. "Captain Rawlins, here, may understand all this flying talk, but it's all Greek to me. I'd just as soon get down to business and talk about Egypt, if you don't mind, sir."

Macgruder sipped from his lukewarm tea. "Quite. The lady's name is Sella Adamo, *Doctor* Sella Adamo, I believe. She has a doctorate in archaeology from Oxford. 1938."

"Yeah, that's her," the New Yorker replied.

Josh sipped his tea, saying nothing. This was Sabatini's show.

The wing commander looked at some more notes. "She's a member of Dr. Justin C. Cunningham's team, which is working a dig in the Valley of the Kings. More specifically, the dig is involved with the tomb of King Tutankhamen. She has been with Cunningham's team since early 1940. Her status is a bit odd. Though she's an enemy alien, she has never been treated as one who is interned, while technically speaking, she should be. She has never in any way given us reason to believe she's involved in the war effort, either overtly or covertly. We do know that her husband is one of Italy's top aces. She is also a Jewess and her parents are dead."

"Will Dr. Cunningham cooperate?" Sabatini asked.

Macgruder raised an eyebrow. "He can be a bit stuffy, I'm told. However, as long as Dr. Adamo isn't harmed, I'm sure he'll see things our way. When do you plan on going down there?"

Sabatini shrugged. "Soon as Captain Rawlins can be released from the hospital."

The next day Josh got permission to go out to Chateaudun. Although he still had some pain in his lower back, he was feeling much better. He stopped in to see General Buell first and was told that General Doolittle had requested the loan of a YB-40 from England, but that it could take as much as two weeks to get it. Buell had lost his anger, much as a vexed parent might with a favorite child. He had also given Josh permission to do some unofficial recruiting for a crew, as well as a staff car to get him to the air base and back to the hospital, where the doctors wanted to keep him under observation.

It was a scorching 12:40 when he arrived at the 414th Squadron orderly room. After telling the driver to go get something to eat, Josh went inside the pyramidal tent and found Pat Cleburne sitting at his GI desk frowning at some papers. Josh tossed off a casual salute. "Afternoon, Pat."

The major looked up, feigning confusion. "Who are you? You look like someone who's supposed to fly an airplane in this squadron, but it's been so long I can't remember." He got to his feet and stuck out his hand with a grin. "I heard you were back after some weird adventure with the Italian Gestapo. Right?"

"Something like that."

"You back for duty?"

"No, I'm still a patient."

"When are you returning?"

"Don't know." Josh told him about the YB-40.

The former Cleveland school teacher raised an eyebrow. "Pillow will shit when he finds out. He told me to have charges ready for the moment you return. He wants your ass court-martialed so badly he wets the bed."

"Fuck him. He'll have to go through Buell."

"I told him that, but you know what an asshole he is."

"I'll get out before he spots me."

"You know about this?" Cleburne held up a citation request form. "It has to be initiated here, since you're still a member of this command. Buell's giving you a Silver Star for going into Sicily and Sardinia as a volunteer." The squadron commander laughed. "Pillow's gonna have the double shits when he sees this and has to recommend approval."

Josh shook his head. "I don't give a damn about that medal."

"Don't knock it. It could get you home sooner. They need heroes to sell war bonds, I heard."

"What have you got Ambrose Tarbell, my old crew chief, doing?"

"I damn near took a stripe from him for getting rip-roaring drunk the other day. He's got a new airplane, skippered by a replacement pilot named Burnside. Why?"

"I may want him to crew my YB-40 when it arrives."

"Pillow will have another violent bowel movement if you take anybody out of the 97th."

Josh grinned. "So they send him home with diarrhea and we win the war. He's too smart a West Pointer to buck Buell. It would only be a short stretch of temporary duty."

"Orders are orders."

"Does Doc Scragg have any of that killer alcohol around?"

"I think so. Want to go see?"

Josh nodded his head. He wanted a stiff drink before visiting the Ritz.

Josh knew the little homemade shack known as the Raghead Ritz was unoccupied because his personal effects were still in it. He entered tentatively, fully aware of the ghosts that lingered there. The four cots surrounding the table and the four chairs greeted him silently as he looked around. Only his cot had bedding on it. And only his foot locker and the clothes hanging behind the cot indicated that anyone inhabited the place. It was insufferably hot. He pulled out his handkerchief and wiped the sweat from his brow.

Turning on the little fan, he stared at the table.

He could almost hear the banter from his copilot, Walt Butler, and Jimmy Bolivar, the navigator, as they played nonstop gin.

Now they were both dead. They and all of his enlisted crew members.

He turned to Joe Orosco's cot. It stared back at him in silent accusation. You told him he was safe in your hands. One more mission and you'd go to the general. Yeah, safe in your hands, a fucking piece of cake.

His eyes filled.

How was I to know, Joe? God, how was I to know that son of a bitch would sneak up on us and kill you? How, Joe?

He sat on the edge of his cot and saw José Orosco's merry eyes back in the Gunter Hotel bar. Joe had just picked up two pretty Mexican girls on the street and steered them into the bar. "Here," he said with that bright grin of his. "Here is the handsome gringo I told you about. He has just returned from a secret mission into the South Pacific and he hasn't even talked to a girl in over a year. They're going to give him a big medal and make a colonel out of him. Girls, may I present Joshua Rawlins, the finest pilot in the Army Air Corps. . . ."

A piece of cake, Joe. Give your confidence back.

He was back in the cockpit of the *Texas Bitch* on that last flight. Jimmy Bolivar was speaking into his ear. "Joe's in some kind of shock, Josh. Just sitting there staring at nothing. Stiff, like he's frozen." He got out of his seat and made his way down into the nose section. And Joe was exactly as the navigator had described him, bent over at his station, but stiff as a board, his dark eyes staring at the bombsight, unseeing, sweating. He pulled Joe's earphone aside and said, "It's okay, Joe. It's all over. We're heading home on three good fans with plenty of fuel. This big-assed bird is going to take us back to some good booze and a nice long rest for you, pardner. Yeah, I'll get the general himself. . . ."

It was the last thing he ever said to José Orosco.

His eyes filled again as he balled his fists. "I'll get the bastard, Joe, I'll get him," he said through clenched teeth.

After putting some of his things in an overnight bag Josh made his way to the glaring, almost sizzling, flight line. A corporal directed him to the third B-17 of the 414th. Tech Sgt. Ambrose Tarbell was up on a wing helping a mechanic work on the number two engine. He looked up when Josh hailed him, squinting into the sun. Quickly climbing down, he grinned when he walked over. "Howdy, Cap'n, where you been?"

"Eating spaghetti," Josh replied. "C'mon, I want to talk to you."

They moved under the shade of the wing as Josh told him about the incoming YB-40 and how they were going to use it. Tarbell wiped the sweat from his flushed face and leaned against the big tire. He had a Mississippi twang and a gap where one of his front teeth had been knocked out in a brawl. He listened noncommittally, nodding his head now and then.

"So I want you to recruit the best mechanics you can find, Ambrose. This YB-40 will be in the air as much as we can keep it there. And I want you to find out who the best portrait and cheesecake artist in North Africa is. I'll need him to paint a particular woman on that gunship when it arrives."

Tarbell nodded his head. "There's a guy over in the 301st who's a regular Rembrandt, I hear."

"And, Ambrose—"

"Yeah, Cap'n?"

"I'm going to need one hell of a good crew. You got a flight engineer in mind?"

The crew chief frowned. "Yeah, there's a skinny little runt over in the 99th that I been gettin' drunk with for a few years. He can fix almost anything. Make a hell of a line crew chief, but he likes to fly. Name's Gregg, David M. He was still a tech sergeant last Saturday."

"Has he got balls?"

"I saw him take on three rednecks down in Montgomery one night. He's got a Silver Star and a couple of Purple Hearts."

"Tell him to come see me in my shack at 1330 tomorrow afternoon."

"Right. You know when this bird's coming in?"

"Inside of two weeks, I hope."

Josh could raid his own squadron for the officers he needed, but he didn't want to get Pat Cleburne any more involved than he already was. He went directly to General Buell. "Sir, I don't know how tough it's going to be to push this gunship around the sky. It'd be kinda nice to have some experienced officers on board. Oh, I know, they're all busy down in their squadrons, but maybe there are a few good ones that are sort of unattached. You know what I mean."

Barney Buell tossed a sheet of paper at him. "That goddamned Adamo got two more of our airplanes today. He sidled into a P-38 squadron formation, and before they knew what he was doing he flamed two of them."

"The bastard!" Josh spat out.

"He's clever. Seldom repeats himself. Except he never shoots survivors anymore."

"I'm going to get him!"

"I'm thinking about strapping this latest-model Lightning to my own ass and going after him."

"He's too smart to play that game, General. Besides, he knows I'm coming after him. The die is cast. How about the crew that brings the YB-40 in from England? Maybe I could kidnap some of its officers."

"No, Eighth Air Force will want them back."

"How about keeping one of the pilots for me? A couple of weeks of detached service for one bomber jock won't cripple the war effort up there."

Buell frowned. "Yeah, I think I can handle that."

"When're you going to get me out of the hospital, General?"

"That doc, Heintzelman, said he'd give you a physical tomorrow morning. If you pass, he'll release you. But he doesn't like it."

Josh shrugged. "Adamo doesn't care what our doctors don't like."

For the first time since his return, Josh saw Barney Buell smile.

First Lt. Hermelinda Prospero could pass for twenty. Actually, she was twenty-five. Her eyes were large and such a dark brown that they appeared to be black in anything but sunlight. Her olive skin was like soft, unblemished satin and her nearly perfect teeth often flashed in bright contrast. She wore her lustrous black hair short, not bowing to style or the long effect that made for Spanish buns at the back of the head. Since age fourteen she had had the fully developed figure of a well-proportioned, grown woman. And ever since the age of twelve she had fought off the sexual advances of pawing boys in the barrio. Her father owned a small grocery store in East L.A., and since she was a rare only child the pinch of poverty had evaded the Prospero household, or actually "storehold," because they lived in a small but comfortable apartment over the establishment. She had been a cheerleader in high school and had been runner-up for homecoming queen in her senior year. She had gone through the usual three-year nursing program, but at Rockford Memorial Hospital in Illinois rather than in Los Angeles, to get her cherished RN. It had been a matter of getting away from the barrio completely, learning what life was like outside the restrictive world and pressures of Mexican America.

Hermelinda Prospero had applied for active duty as an army nurse on December 8, 1941, the day after the Japanese attack on Pearl Harbor.

Now, as she walked into the bar of the Grand Hotel, the old, tarnished French hostelry, she felt good. She had the next day off and she was meeting the appealing major from New York who had gone to Sicily with Josh. Frankly, she would rather be meeting Josh, but if that flyboy had a romantic thought in his head it was well guarded. He was too busy treating her like a grieving lover who should be wearing a black veil. Sabatini had asked her for the date that afternoon. She smiled to herself as she entered the darkened bar; he had all the makings of an exciting man.

Rudy Sabatini got up from his bar stool to meet her, a broad grin on his dark face. "Ah, the lovely Linda," he said, openly admiring her. "If every young woman looked as good as you do in a tan uniform, no one would go off to fight."

She knew it was flattery, but she liked it.

He gave her his bar stool. "I came a little early, but all the tables were already taken." He grinned as he stood close and put his arm around her. "Besides, this is much cosier." He ordered her a glass of white wine.

The bar was full and noisier than usual, partly because some air crew officers had invaded the place. The three-piece European band was playing a bit louder than normal to overcome the competition. Two slowly turning fans hopelessly tried to move the smoke-filled air around. She saw two or three nurses she knew and a few male officers. One was an orthopedic surgeon whom she had dated a few times, until he had gotten too demanding in the "doctor-nurse" game.

She had just taken a second sip from her wine when a voice said, "Well, well, Rudy Lotions. What are you doing back here?"

The OSS officer turned and smiled. "Well, well, yourself. I see you're still fighting the war at a safe distance, Fellini." He introduced Hermelinda. "Honey, this is Jim Fellini, a hard-fighting JAG officer who has tried to put me in jail for a long time. I stole one of his marbles when we were little kids growing up in the same neighborhood, and he's been convinced that I'm a crook ever since."

Fellini smiled. "I've admired you each time I've seen you, Linda. And Sabatini, here, is lying. *I* stole *his* marble, but saw the error of my ways. He has never seen the error of his corrupt ways."

Sabatini laughed. "Now, now, James. Linda is my date and I'll never even get to hold her hand if you keep telling her such fables. C'mon, I'll buy you a drink."

Fellini shook his head. "No, I'm still particular about who I drink with." The former assistant district attorney smiled at Linda. "Keep your hand on your watch and purse, Lieutenant."

"Does he mean any of that?" she asked as the lawyer moved away.

Sabatini chuckled. "Every single word. But forget him. C'mon, let's dance to this."

The song was "Begin the Beguine," and as she took the first dance step she knew she was in the arms of a superb dancer. So smooth, assured. And she knew; she had been on every ballroom floor in L.A. Soon the little floor was so crowded all they could do was keep the beat in one place. The combo shifted into "Sentimental Journey," and she asked, "Did Major Fellini call you Rudy Lotions?"

"It's a nickname I picked up back in New York a few years ago. You see, I was a *consiglière* to a business organization. That means I had to be able to smooth things over and unruffle feathers at times. You know, negotiate. Since I'm pretty good at that, they tacked 'Lotions' onto my first name."

She smiled. She'd have to be careful of this strong, persuasive, appealing man.

It was an hour and twenty minutes later when she and Sabatini returned from the dance floor to find Josh glaring at them. He was sipping from a beer bottle. "Hi," Hermelinda said. "Did they give you a pass or are you up to your old tricks?"

"Pass. The general says they're going to spring me tomorrow if I pass a physical."

"Then you oughta be home resting, sonny," Sabatini said.

"Are you two together?"

"Yeah, why?"

Josh looked down at her and back to Sabatini. "I just don't think you're each other's type."

The New Yorker laughed. "Why? She girl, me boy."

Josh's eyes narrowed. "She's also Joe Orosco's girl friend. You know, my best friend who's dead."

Hermelinda tensed. "Cut it out, Josh."

"You know he just wants to play around with you, don't you?"

She returned his angry look. "So? Is that any of your business?"

"Yeah," Sabatini added, putting his hand on Josh's shoulder. "Take it easy."

Josh flung the arm away. "She's off limits, Sabatini."

Linda's dark eyes blazed. "Who the hell do you think you are, Josh Rawlins? I'm not off limits to anyone I want to be with!"

Sabatini grinned. "Look, sonny, I think you're a little off base here. We're just having some fun dancing, that's all. Why don't you let me buy you a drink and you can dance with Linda too. No sense in getting upset over nothing."

"No dice. I'm going to leave."

"I think that's a good idea!" Hermelinda said sharply.

Josh inhaled deeply and blew it out. "Yeah. See you." He spun on his heel and strode from the room.

"Sorry about that," Sabatini said. "I guess he's under a lot of strain. Those people in Sardinia worked him over pretty hard, you know."

Hermelinda watched him disappear. "I know."

"Let me get you some more wine."

"No, I don't think so, Rudy."

"Dance? They're playing 'Somebody Else is Taking My Place.' "

"No, I think I want to go home, Rudy. The chief nurse has a ten o'clock curfew on our quarters."

"We could go to mine. No curfew there."

She shook her head slowly, looking into his eyes. "No, I don't think I want to play that game."

Sabatini shrugged. "Then I'll take you home."

Dr. Heintzelman pronounced Josh fit to fly at 1030 the next morning. After clearing the hospital Josh reported to General Buell, and was told he would be going to Egypt with Sabatini the next morning. He would remain on temporary duty, keeping his assignment in the 414th. Minutes later he stopped by the small PX in the headquarters building and ran directly into Hermelinda Prospero. Feeling awkward about his conduct in the Grand Hotel bar the night before, and still a bit peeved that she had been with Sabatini, he said hello coolly.

"Well, if it isn't my guardian angel," she replied, just as coolly.

"I suppose I should have kept my mouth shut last night."

"Yes, you should have."

"It's just that—"

"I know, you still see me as the tearful loved one. Why don't you drop it, Josh. Just forget all about Joe and me, and particularly me!"

"Now, don't be like that," he said lamely. "It's just that I know Sabatini, and I know what he's after. And, well, I—"

"And just what is it that he's after that none of these other guys are after? Tell me, Josh."

"You know what I mean."

"What about you? I believe the term is 'getting laid.' Don't you ever get laid?"

"I didn't know you could be so crude," he replied lamely.

"Crude? Who am I, your little sister in the convent?"

"No, I just feel that you can do better than fooling around with a gangster like Sabatini."

"Go to hell, Josh Rawlins!" Hermelinda Prospero spun around and stomped away.

Tech Sgt. David Gregg *was* a runt. No more than five-four, he couldn't weigh over a hundred and twenty. The bill of his sweat-stained khaki baseball cap was turned up, his flight suit was dark and wet at the armpits. Probably in his early thirties, another regular. He had a pale blond mustache and a receding chin. But his light green eyes didn't waver as he took the glass of wine Josh offered him in the heat of the Raghead Ritz. Josh pointed to one of the chairs. "Relax, Sergeant."

"Just as soon stand, Captain," he replied in what sounded like a Chicago accent.

"Ambrose tell you what I'm looking for?"

"Yeah, you're getting in some kind of a fucked-up Fort?"

"Right. YB-40. A gunship. F model with lots of armor plate and sixteen heavy machine guns."

Gregg's expression remained blank. "Sounds like a tub of shit."

Josh shrugged. "I don't think we'll be doing barrel rolls in it."

"And you want a crew?"

"Yes. I understand you can fix about anything. That's good. No telling what we'll run into up there, maintenance-wise. But the rest of the men, well, I want the best fucking gunners in North Africa. There's a P-38 running around up there with a murderous Guinea pilot in it, and I want to blow him out of the sky."

Tech Sgt. David Gregg nodded his head. "I heard about your vendetta."

"You want in?"

The flight engineer shrugged. "Why not? Break up the routine a little."

"You know any good gunners?"

"A few. I'll ask around. There's a pair of Indian twins over in the 301st. I heard they can shoot the eye out of a sea gull at a thousand yards."

"Sounds like a good start."

"This job got priority, Captain?"

"I can pull anybody I want. It's General Buell's private show."

A small grin revealed a gaping hole in Gregg's front teeth. "Yeah, but it's *your* vendetta. Some day I'll tell you about the trouble I had back on the South Side with some wops when I was a kid."

"I'm going to Egypt tomorrow and may not be back for several days."

"Can I ask what's in Egypt, Captain?"

"Yeah, our model."

CHAPTER 16

✛

The staff car Wing Comdr. Macgruder sent for them was a small black
Austin sedan. And Josh quickly learned why, as the driver, an army
sergeant, tried to work his way through the incredible crush of humanity
and vehicles in downtown Cairo. They had flown down from Constantine
in a gooney bird, the very same one that had dropped them into Sicily. Josh's old classmate, Bltner, had again been the pilot. Sabatini wiped
the sweat off his brow with an already moist handkerchief as he said,
"This is worse than the Bronx when the Yankees won the series."

The sergeant nodded his head. "Nothing like bloody downtown Cairo,
sor," he agreed in a cockney accent.

Josh took in the welter of people, animals, and vehicles. Uniforms
were everywhere: mostly British, sprinkled with Indian, Australian, New
Zealand, Greek, Yugoslav, Polish, Palestinian, and now and then American.
Peddlers ware all over, hawking everything imaginable. Cripples and
other beggars worked their wiles, from women with fly-encrusted babies
to an armless man juggling with his bare feet.

The slow-moving conveyances reminded Josh of a junkyard back
home, except that the cars were running. There were a couple of bro-
ken-down Model A Fords and a wheezing 1933 Buick that looked like
a windowless elephant shaking in its tracks. One Morris taxi with a
flat tire looked as though it hadn't been washed once in its long life.

A dusty Mercedes had no headlights or windshield wipers. The slow, verminous streetcars were jammed, with passengers clinging precariously to any handhold they could get or sitting cross-legged on the roof. The ancient buses were just as crammed. Impeding the motor vehicles were the mule- and donkey-carts, and the gharries drawn by scrawny horses ready for the stew pot. Bored camels, unruly sheep, raucous goats, barking dogs, and here and there a monkey gave the whole teeming tide a zoolike flavor. Wide-belted policemen wearing everpresent sunglasses seemed impervious to it all. The Egyptian men greeted one another exuberantly, swinging their right arms outward until their hands met in a loud clap, then shaking hands at length while grasping each other's shoulders with their left hands and speaking excitedly. Many of the older women still wore the traditional black veil and robe, while slender young women smiled in their bright cotton dresses and ornate jewelry.

Josh couldn't remember ever hearing a place as noisy. Arab music blared from cheap radios playing full blast from cafés. Vendors shouted their wares at the top of their lungs. Horns blared, streetcar drivers rang their bells continuously, and to make sure they had their say, cart and camel drivers screamed their parts of the chorus. A donkey brayed loudly almost in his ear.

"Like I said, sor, there ain't no place like downtown Cairo," the driver repeated.

They met Wing Comdr. Harry Macgruder at GHQ in an airy office with a slow-moving overhead fan. He offered them tea, which both accepted, more out of politeness than to drink anything warm on such a hot day. The RAF officer got right down to business. "Dr. Cunningham has been informed that a highly decorated American officer on convalescent leave is coming to his dig site outside of Luxor to gather information for an article he is preparing for an American newspaper. He has been further requested to cooperate fully in any logical manner, and to include Dr. Sella Adamo in that regard."

"Excellent!" Sabatini replied enthusiastically.

"Do you have any background in Egyptology, Captain?" Macgruder asked Josh.

"No, sir."

The wing commander extracted a small brown book from his desk drawer. "This is an account written by Howard Carter entitled *The Tomb* *of Tut*Ankh*Amen Discovered by the Late Earl of Carnarvon and Howard Carter.* It was published first in 1923, but this is the 1933 printing. I would suggest that you read this, or at least part of it, before you fly down to the Valley of the Kings. Since Howard Carter is the authority on King Tut's tomb, it will give you valuable background information."

Josh thumbed through the first few pages. "Thanks, I'll try to finish it by morning."

"No need. The Lysander that's taking you down there isn't set up until the following morning. Gives you another day."

"I'll lock myself in my room and absorb it. I'm a history buff anyway."

"Good. These people you'll be meeting are very knowledgeable and highly experienced archaeologists. Cunningham worked with Carter on the project before he died four years ago."

Josh nodded in understanding.

Macgruder went on, "You must be circumspect with them. It will be far better for you to simply state your ignorance—or minimal knowledge—than to try any kind of a bluff. If you have any trouble with Dr. Cunningham or anyone else, do not try to resolve it. Contact me immediately. All right?"

"Yes, sir."

Sabatini flashed his big grin. "What about the other arrangements, Wing Commander?"

"Those that involve you? They are progressing, Major."

Acquiring females had never been a problem for Rudy Sabatini. There was something about his somewhat sinister dark strength that attracted many of them. His large, dark eyes offered a challenge and advertised his passion. His baldness just seemed to confirm his virility. Now, as he looked with open admiration at the WAF lieutenant standing at the bar with a British army nurse, he smiled and nodded his head. She had glanced over the shoulder of her companion twice, giving him a passing look. The third time, he caught and held her gaze for a couple of moments. She was tall, perhaps an inch or so taller than he. And she had a rather plain face with that British peaches-and-cream complexion. The two women had arrived at the Anglo-Egyptian Union and were sipping their first drink. However, a handful of RAF officers had quickly surrounded them, including a group captain who seemed to have a special relationship with the WAF officer. At least his expression and the way he casually touched her arm a couple of times indicated as much.

Oh, well, one couldn't win them all, Sabatini concluded.

He watched as the Egyptian bartender made what he guessed was a martini and then ordered one of the same. "Just let the vemouth breathe on it," he instructed. One thing about the Brits, he thought, they always kept their priorities in a war: one had to have his gin and whiskey, no matter what. No ice, but who cared?

The army officer beside him nodded his head in greeting. Royal Engineers with three pips on his shoulder, a captain.

Sabatini didn't waste any time. "What does one do for entertainment around this town?" he asked directly.

"What kind of entertainment you looking for?"

The New Yorker grinned. "The kind that wears nylons when she can get them and fills them well."

The captain was in his early thirties and had a thin, neatly trimmed mustache. "They're around." He glanced at his wristwatch. "In fact, I'm going to have one more drink and then go on to less civilized haunts. You're welcome to join me, Major. That is, if you'll tell me what an American Army officer with all those Silver Stars is doing in Cairo."

Sabatini winked at him. "I told you, looking for girls."

The captain stuck out his hand. "Name's Hooker—Joe."

Sabatini grinned again as he introduced himself. "Perfect. Did you know that we had a Union general by that name during our Civil War? Yeah, and he always had a bunch of girls following his army. They called 'em camp followers and also Hooker's girls. The name stuck and eventually it became a moniker for girls of the night. Yeah, Joe Hooker, I'm definitely with you."

Thirty minutes later they arrived at the Royal Opus, a large nightclub operated by a retired sergeant-major named Tom Fauntleroy. "He started as a sapper," Capt. Joe Hooker said. "Came to Cairo in 1927 and started getting his fingers into the pie. By the time he reached retirement, he'd already had this place going for three years. Popular hangout for our officers and their chippies. Has the greatest dancer in Egypt here, little vixen by the name of Nefertiti."

"Wasn't there a queen by that name?"

Hooker grinned. "Right, but I doubt she could do what this one can!"

They stood in line for about fifteen minutes behind—just as Hooker had said—several British officers with Cairo girls. Finally a ramrod-stiff man in a dinner jacket and a bristling Guards mustache came up to them and spoke warmly to Hooker. "Come along, Captain, I have a spot for you."

He led them to a small table under a palm tree that grew through the roof just off the stage. He shook hands with Sabatini and introduced himself as Tom Fauntleroy. "I taught this young blighter how to salute when he was a subaltern," he said with a touch of a smile.

"Not so," Hooker replied. "He was too busy taking his money to the bank to think about duty."

Fauntleroy snapped to, stamping his foot and rendering a brisk salute. "It's hurtin' my feelings you are, Captain. I was the most hardworking sergeant-major in the Royal Engineers, I was."

Hooker shook his head with a smile. "Do we still have to drink that cheap champagne of yours, or can we get a little decent gin? The major's here on a special mission for the Queen and he has a tender stomach."

Tom Fauntleroy raised an eyebrow. "We can't have the other customers see you getting any special treatment, but I just happen to have some very fine gin in a champagne bottle, I do."

After watching a musical review with some pretty though not overly talented dancers, and a comic who did a cockney humor routine, several of the customers began to clap their hands and clamor for Nefertiti. Sabatini sipped from his third glass of warm gin and tonic. "She must be something," he said, thinking back to a time in a Manhattan supper club, an intimate place up in the eighties. The lights had gone out and all at once, as a tiny spotlight came on, a slinky singer in a low-cut black dress had appeared. She had skin like satin, honey hair, and eyes as green as seaweed. Her voice was low, sultry, as she softly began to sing "Deep Purple." He remembered those thin straps that held up her dress. But mostly he recalled those remarkable eyes and her full lips as she seemed to sing directly to him. He had sat there staring, hardly breathing, riveted to his chair. Her name was Teresa, and he had fallen in love in the first stanza, so hopelessly and completely that he had been unable even to applaud when she finished her act. Teresa.

She became *his* Teresa.

The fanfare from the small orchestra broke his memory trip.

Moments later, following a drum roll, the house lights dimmed and a spotlight followed a whirling dervish figure to the center of the stage. Amidst a sea of reflections cast from the star's sequined halter and extensive jewelry, she threw herself to a kneeling position, head down. Softly the music slowed as Nefertiti sensuously rose to her feet and began gradually to gyrate her belly.

A tiny jewel cast bright reflections from her moving navel.

Even Sabatini drew in a sharp breath. Sheer, baggy trousers revealed her shapely hips and legs as the rhythm quickened and her hands began to caress the rest of her trembling, shaking body. Her long, expressive fingers found her moving, shapely breasts, pausing long enough to fondle her nipples before moving down past her lively stomach to her pelvic area. Sabatini knew she wore nothing under the translucent trousers and was aroused by the thought. Her face, framed in the wildness of unrestrained black hair, was beautiful, with high cheekbones, full black brows, and teeth so white they flashed against her brown skin when she opened her mouth to moan in sexual frenzy. The tempo increased even more. Her eyes were closed, her head shaking over her breasts, hair disheveled, seeming to set off blue sparks in the spotlight.

There wasn't a sound from the spellbound audience.

She whirled, moving close to Sabatini, her belly now pulsating wildly, and then was once more back in the center of the stage. Again her expressive hands caressed her now-glistening body as her tongue ran around her lips and her moans grew louder. Head back and eyes fully closed, she slid slowly to her knees, one hand stroking her breast, the other her pelvic area. With one final shriek she threw her head forward to her knees and the music suddenly stopped.

The spotlight softened and went out.

A crash of applause and shouts of approval followed. After several moments Nefertiti slowly rose to her feet and glided from the stage.

Sabatini turned to Hooker, raising an eyebrow and letting out a low whistle. "Quite an act," he said huskily. As applause diminished he lit a Lucky Strike. "Well, now that you've got me primed, what's the next act?"

The Royal Engineer captain smiled. "Only an experienced guide such as me can lead you to the true pleasures of this great city of sin. We're off to the Old City."

"All of us need to forget at times," Captain Hooker said as he knocked on the heavy wooden door. "It's good for the soul."

While far from being thick-tongued or staggering, both officers could feel the effect of their many drinks. They were in the Birka, the off-limits old part of the city where few people held a moral approach to life and simple existence was paramount. Sin had been a part of the Birka under many sultans and pashas long before the British Empire dreamed of sticking its long fingers into Egypt. "You know," Hooker went on, "a character in the *Arabian Nights* said, 'He who hath not seen Cairo hath not seen the world. Her soil is gold; her Nile is a marvel; her women are like the black-eyed virgins of Paradise . . . she is the Mother of the World.' "

"I'm ready for one of those black-eyed virgins of Paradise," Sabatini replied.

A woman of uncertain age, wearing long gold earrings and bracelets nearly to her elbows, opened the door and smiled at them. "Ahhh, Madame Faruk," the engineer said with a broad smile as he swept off his hat and bowed deeply. "It's such a pleasure to see you again. May I introduce Major Sabatini? He is here on a special mission for the president of the United States and I have told him of the healing powers of your magnificent establishment."

The woman's face broke into a brief smile. "Yes, Captain Hook, you are both most welcome." She held out her hand as they entered.

"Five quid," Hooker had told him earlier, "for the visit, and one for the old girl at the door. "It's a bit stiff, old man, but it keeps out the riff-raff." Sabatini forked over six pounds of the British money he had acquired earlier.

They were led into a high-ceilinged room that reminded him of an old-fashioned hotel lobby. The furniture was early Ritz with a frayed edge showing here and there. A pair of huge ceiling fans turned lazily in the dim light of a large crystal chandelier. A faded mural of the Pyramids filled one wall. On the opposite wall velvet draperies guarded several alcoves, some of which were closed. Madame Faruk pointed to two pillows close to the alcoves and said in her accented English, "You will be attended immediately."

Both of them sat on the pillows and looked around at the handful of other customers and the girls with them. Three fat Egyptians who Sabatini guessed to be quite wealthy had pretty girls over in a corner. Laughter echoed from their spirited conversation. A man Sabatini thought was a European officer in mufti came out of an alcove with a scantily clad girl on his arm.

Within moments a lovely girl of about eighteen came to them and handed Sabatini a blackened narghile, a pipe in which the smoke is drawn through water before being inhaled. He shrugged at Hooker and sucked hard on the stem, drawing the smoke deeply inside and holding it several moments before exhaling.

"You ever smoke hashish before, Rudy?" the British officer asked.

"Once." Sabatini drew in another deep drag of the smoke and handed the narghile to Hooker. He began to feel lethargic, relaxed, as the intoxicating drug mixed with the alcohol in his blood stream.

Hooker exhaled and inhaled deeply again. "Ah," he said with a smile. "It's far better than confession to cleanse the soul."

The girl who had given them the pipe brought another girl for Hooker, then sat cross-legged in front of Sabatini. She had very large black eyes and a pretty smile. "I am Victoria," she said softly. "Named for the Queen."

Her transparent pants reminded Sabatini of Nefertiti and aroused him. "And I am King Henry the Eighth," he said with his big grin.

Joe Hooker handed him the pipe and said dreamily, "I'm off to partake of this lass's beauty before my cleansed soul goes clear into bloody dreamland. Whistle when you're ready to depart, will you old chap?"

Sabatini watched the other girl's behind as they moved away, then turned back to Victoria. He reached out and touched her cheek. It was soft like a child's, the color of light chocolate. She kissed his hand and pulled him to his feet. Leading him to the nearest alcove, she drew him to the pillowed floor. After closing the heavy curtain she kneeled before him and removed her halter. Her breasts were full, with large aureoles around the nipples. He leaned forward and kissed one. It was all so pleasant; absolutely nothing mattered. He was beginning to float. She undid his belt and slowly pulled off his trousers, her experienced hand quickly finding his semierect penis and fondling it. As soon as he had a full erection she slipped out of her baggy pants and climbed on top of him. He entered her, sighing and letting the hashish transport him to wherever it wished.

The tramline from Cairo to Giza that was completed in 1900 had made the beautiful new hotel that stood at the foot of the Pyramids a serious rival to the famous Shepheard's in entertaining the rich and powerful. Now, forty-three years later, the Mena House was a British officers' billet. However, its lavish neoclassical decor and excellent service made it difficult for one to remember the war. Josh returned to the hotel after taking a late walk and being impressed by the Pyramids. They seemed so close and powerful in the moonlight. He had done some of his homework and knew now that they were known by the names of their builders: Khufu, or Cheops, the Greek version of the name; Kafre, who also built the Sphinx; and Menkaure.

Now, in the comfort of his room, he was reading the book Wing Commander Macgruder had given him. By an English archaeologist named Howard Carter, it was the story of the discovery of the tomb of King Tutankhamen, or King Tut, as a fascinated world had grown to know that ruler of ancient Egypt. He read, enthralled by the suspense Carter had experienced in finally finding the burial place and the history it divulged.

Finally, around three in the morning, he went to the window and looked once more at the Pyramids. They seemed to float together like huge ghosts in the distance. Yet they seemed close, overpowering, blue-gray in the darkness. He felt enriched by what he had read. Although he was a self-proclaimed history buff he had never been interested in Egypt. Now, being in this land of a great ancient civilization that had left magnificent tributes, he felt awe and a stimulation that could only lead to increased interest when he reached his destination. He even thought about the possibility of becoming an archaeologist when this damned fool war was over.

But first he had to find a man and kill him.

And before that he had to meet the man's wife and lie to her.

Then he thought of Joe Orosco and nothing else mattered but the killing.

He hoped his scheme would work.

CHAPTER 17

✠

"What you should do, Captain, is go down to Abu Simbel in Nubia and see the Temple of Ramses II," Sergeant Pilot Dennis said over the intercom from the front seat. "That bloody pharaoh built himself a temple that has statues of him in four stages of his life—sixty-four feet tall!"

"I doubt that I'll have time," Josh replied, "but I'll keep it in mind."

"You know those Egyptians back then seldom lived past forty, and they were small. I heard old Ramses II lived to be about ninety, had dozens of wives, hundreds of children, and was king for sixty-some years."

"Interesting," Josh replied through the mike. This Dennis was a veritable tour guide, as well as a competent pilot. They were zooming along a thousand feet above the Nile in a Westland Lysander III, a rather high-powered two-place observation airplane that had short-field capability but could still get out and exceed two hundred m.p.h. Its nickname was the Lizzie. This particular Lizzie belonged to an RAF squadron that had delivered a number of Allied intelligence agents deep into enemy territory before being transferred down to Egypt. They had been scheduled to leave early, but an engine problem had held them up to a 1500 departure. It was now nearing 1700.

Josh wiped the sweat from his forehead with a soggy handkerchief. Even with the windows open the Lizzie was a hotbox in the peak heat of the Egyptian afternoon.

"The sheer arrogance of some of those pharaohs was bloody obscene," Dennis went on. "Do you know that some of those blocks in the pyramids weigh *tons*? How many slaves do you think died building the wretched things?"

"I read that much of the labor was hired. Aren't we about to Luxor?"

"Coming up directly. Below that bend in the river off to our left."

Josh checked the map. It was about three hundred and twenty air miles from Cairo to Luxor, once the great capital of Upper and Lower Egypt when the city was known as Thebes.

"You'll be able to see the Temple of Karnak just a few clicks north of Luxor. Now that's a bloody famous one."

"How close is this air strip to Cunningham's camp?"

"Oh, I'd guess four or five miles."

Josh continued to look down. The Nile Valley was wide now, but most of its lush greenery lay to the east of the river. It looked as though the desert began about two or three miles to the west. He guessed that the famous Valley of the Kings was in those strangely pink hills that rose from the mounds at the edge of the desert like pastel fortresses. The slate-blue Nile, turning to a deeper blue in other places, was now yellowish, as if a heavy rain had stirred up its bottom. He had read the night before that a man named Herodotus had said that "Egypt is the gift of the Nile," and that someone else had said that "the Nile was the *ka* of Egypt"—its soul.

Dennis throttled back on the big Bristol Mercury XXX engine and began a shallow descent. "There, you can see old Queen Hatshepsut's temple, that big building set in that bowl against those purple mountains. See it?"

"Yeah." Josh felt the excitement taking over. He was going to touch not just the past, but thousands of years of the past!

A few minutes later, Dennis came in low over the air strip, a flat piece of ground where the sand met the vegetation of the valley. It was packed sand, only about the width of a stateside two-lane highway. A frayed windsock showed a slight crosswind from the right. The sergeant climbed a couple of hundred feet and came around for a landing to the southwest. Dennis brought the monoplane in deftly, lowering a wing slightly to the crosswind and skipping lightly on the right main gear. Moments later the Lysander's big propeller slowed to idle and Josh crawled out with his B-4 bag. With a thumbs-up and a casual thank you salute, he said goodbye to Dennis. Holding onto his service cap to keep from losing it in the prop wash, he watched the big two-seater roar down the runway in the opposite direction and lift off.

He looked around, wondering how long he'd have to wait in this oppressive heat. His question was answered at once, as an ancient Land Rover came bouncing down from a mound of sand dunes. As it drew closer he saw a man in a pith helmet standing up in the passenger side energetically waving a red bandanna. He waved back.

The Land Rover skidded to a halt not three feet from him and the man with the bandanna hurriedly climbed down with extended hand. He was about fifty, with deep wrinkles around eyes that smiled through round, steel-rimmed glasses. He wore a scraggly salt-and-pepper beard. "I'm Winfield S. Hancock, Doctor Cunningham's assistant and secretary," he said exuberantly. "Welcome to the land of dead pharaohs."

Josh shook hands and introduced himself.

"And this is Hassan," Hancock said pointing at the driver, a dark-skinned man wearing a jaunty red fez and a broad, toothy grin. "He's our man Friday. In fact, he's so resourceful, life is almost bearable up there in the valley."

"You stay there, rather than in the city?"

"Yes, much of the time. Our particular team seems to work better away from the distractions of a town like Luxor. Our accommodations are close to the Tut and Ramses VI tombs in the Valley of the Tombs of the Kings, most commonly known as the Valley of the Kings. Not frivolous, but adequate." Winfield S. Hancock grinned. "We do not, however, have an officers club."

Josh smiled. He was glad to see a touch of humor. He hadn't known what to expect, but he had convinced himself these archaeology types would be staid at the best. He climbed in the back of the Land Rover and in minutes they were heading up through the boulder-strewn foothills. The Valley of the Kings, Josh mused. The sheer romance of the name was intriguing. He had read that over thirty of Egypt's greatest rulers had been buried there. Soon, as they continued heading northwest, the road began to ascend a rocky defile that skirted a towering pinkish cliff facing east.

"This is known as Deir el-Bahri," Hancock said over the strain of the engine. "You won't find a more dried-out, hot, unpleasant, and remote place of great historical note anywhere else in the world."

They drove on until Hassan stopped the vehicle on top of a low rise. "There," Hancock said, pointing down to where the road joined some kind of a settlement. "The high entrance is to the tomb of Ramses VI and close by is that of Tutankhamen. The war has decidedly cut down on the flow of visitors, which is fine by us."

They descended to an area of huts and a few trucks. A handful of pyramidal tents added to the settlement. A couple of native workers were the only human beings outside in the boiling sun. "That tent on the right is our guest quarters," Hancock said. "That's where you'll be staying. Since we have electricity, you will at least have a fan to cool you. The largest mud hut belongs to Dr. Cunningham. We'll be dining there tonight at eight. Cocktails at seven."

"Can I get some kind of a shower?"

"Yes. Hassan will show you our bath house."

"I hope we're not dressing. I left my dinner jacket in Cairo," Josh said with a smile.

"Hardly. If you have a change of uniform, just give it to Hassan and he'll have it pressed and ready for you in plenty of time. By the way, can you tell me briefly the scope of your interview so I can pass it on to Dr. Cunningham?"

"Yes, I want to center it around Dr. Adamo if possible. I thought someone had explained that."

"I believe there was something to that effect."

"Yes, it's an interesting approach—enemy archaeologist teaming up with Allied group in the interest of world knowledge during a major war."

Hancock sniffed. "She's hardly an enemy."

Josh covered his faux pas with a smile. "Sorry. Italian." She was the enemy to him, the wife of the man who had murdered his best friend and the rest of his crew, but he had to play his role with conviction.

He had to be more careful. If this was the attractive woman he saw in the photograph on Adamo's desk at Elmas, his plan would probably work. If she was some frumpy little woman with a horse face— the usual scientific type—the whole trip could be a waste of time.

He tapped on the door of Dr. Cunningham's quarters at precisely seven o'clock, feeling fresher after the shower and a stiff drink from one of the bottles of Scotch whisky Sabatini had "requisitioned" for him in Cairo. Hassan had done wonders with his other short-sleeved khaki uniform shirt and the one pair of long trousers he had brought along. Since the British were always impressed with medals, he wore his ribbons over the silver pilot's wings: the DSC, followed by the Distinguished Flying Cross with an oak leaf cluster, the Air Medal with four clusters, and the Purple Heart. His collar was, of course, open, and he carried an unopened bottle of Scotch as a gift for his host.

A man of about his own height opened the door. He was totally bald, with bushy gray eyebrows over piercing black eyes that frowned through thick eyeglasses. His prominent nose protruded above a huge walrus mustache. A smile touched his wide mouth as his deep voice boomed, "Come in, Captain Rawlins, come in." He stuck out his hand. "I'm Justin Cunningham."

Josh knew from the file he had read on the noted archaeologist that he was sixty-one years old, held several degrees, both earned and honorary, and had been working in Egypt since 1911. He would have been knighted by now except that his unwavering faith in himself and contempt for bureaucracy had long been expounded in a brusque, irreverent and unbending attitude. He had simply stepped on too many toes both directly and in the press for too many years.

Josh shook hands and gave him the Scotch. Cunningham held up the bottle to examine the label. "Ahh, some Black Guards. Are you sure it's the real thing, young man? You know, there's a way to cut the bottom out of a bottle with a hot wire and remove the original contents so a cheap imitation can be substituted."

"I have no idea, sir. I assume it's real."

"You've met Dr. Hancock." The man in the steel-rimmed glasses smiled back, holding up his wine glass in salute. "And this is my wife, Rebecca Cunningham." She was no more than five feet tall, slender, and most pleasant-looking. Her hair was copper colored and she had a splash of freckles over her nose. She was surprisingly young to be Cunningham's wife, probably less than thirty. She greeted him with a broad smile.

Josh shook hands and turned to the fourth person in the room. He wasn't ready for the sharp impact of beauty that greeted him. The young woman was tall, perhaps five feet eight inches in her flat shoes, her dark blonde hair drawn severely into a bun at the back of her head. Her eyes were large and a luminous sea green, with thick dark lashes. High classical cheekbones and a wide, full mouth accented by sparkling white teeth set off her tanned, olive complexion. She wore a short-sleeved military shirt, open at the throat, and a pair of tan shorts that reached to just above her knees. But even the mannish clothes couldn't fully conceal her shapely figure. "I'm Sella Adamo," she said in a low voice with an intriguing touch of Italian accent to her British manner of speaking.

Josh exhaled slowly as he took her firm handshake. She was incredibly beautiful! "My pleasure," he managed. "I've heard much about you, Dr. Adamo."

She held his gaze. "Some of it good, I hope."

She had the most unbelievable eyes! "All of it, Doctor."

"Please call me Sella," she replied quietly.

"No, we don't stand on titles around here," Justin Cunningham said. "Very unBritish, of course." He pointed to Josh's ribbons and smiled. "Otherwise we'd have to say, Captain Rawlins, DSC, BME, Order of the Bath, and Chief Procurer for the King, and that sort of thing."

Everyone laughed. Josh glanced at Sella Adamo and liked her smile but noticed that it faded quickly, as if she had heard the line before. He noticed that her expression, while attentive and composed, seemed to mask something.

"If you don't mind, Captain," Dr. Cunningham said, "I'll save this fine whisky for another time. We have some average wine, somewhat like a Chablis, that's not bad for an Egyptian brand."

"That'll be fine." Josh took the glass proffered by Hancock.

The hut, with its thick adobe walls, was quite cool and was much more pleasant than the primitive hovel Josh had expected. The fluid clarinet work of Artie Shaw playing "Begin the Beguine" issued from a small hand-cranked phonograph. A large painting of a beautiful Egyptian girl in exquisite heavy gold jewelry hung on one wall. A large framed photograph of a man in a mustache had been placed near it. "That's Howard Carter," Cunningham offered. "I had the pleasure of working with him for a number of years before his death four years ago. Do you know anything about him?"

It seemed to Josh that all eyes were on him. The question was pivotal—did he have any knowledge of their work, or was he simply trying to hit and run on a story? "Yes, a little," he replied. "I know that he headed the Tut discovery and excavation."

A smile touched Justin Cunningham's lips. "That's a start. I may as well be direct, Captain. Precisely what do you want of us?"

Time for more evasion. Josh cleared his throat as he looked back into the famous archaeologist's level gaze. "I'm not exactly sure, Doctor. I told Dr. Hancock that the piece should focus on Dr. Adamo, but I'd like also to absorb a certain amount of texture from your work here and use it where it's appropriate."

"I like the idea of a woman archaeologist getting some credit," Rebecca Cunningham said. "As long as it isn't exploitive." She, too, was watching him closely.

"I don't write exploitive articles, Mrs. Cunnigham."

"Good!" her husband said heartily. "Now, tell us something about the war. Are you Americans winning it for us?"

"Sir," Josh replied, glad to get off the hook, "we are all winning it." He glanced at Sella Adamo. "At least on the Allied side."

"Don't make allowances for me, Captain," she said quietly. "I want this war over as soon as possible. The quicker Mussolini and his predators are defeated, the sooner Italy can clean its wounds and find a way to hold up its head among the family of nations again." There was brief fire in her eye, but her expression quickly changed, and Josh sensed a sadness, something tragic about her. Sella, Sella—he remembered doing some Old Testament research on Cain and Abel. A woman named Sella married Lamech, who slew Cain by accident, then angrily killed the youth who had led him into the error . . . or something like that. A good biblical name, Sella.

The song ended and Winfield Hancock quickly cranked the phonograph and turned the record over. Moments later, the strains of "Indian Love Call" filled the small house.

"I hear the invasion is about ready to pop off," Cunningham said.

"I don't know much about that," Josh replied. "They don't consult too many captains about such planning. Besides, I've been in the hospital for some time and all I've heard is rumor."

"Can you tell us the rumor?"

Josh smiled. He hated playing this game, this damned lying. "I suppose that can't hurt anything. The big guess is that the Allies will invade somewhere, Sicily or Sardinia, or Italy itself, early next month. And I'm sure Axis intelligence has known that for some time."

"We're so far removed from it here," Justin Cunningham said. "When one is dealing with life as it was three to four thousand years ago, and learning of the many wars these Egyptians endured, the current conflict seems very insignificant."

Josh wanted to say, Unless you're in it, but replied, "Yes, I suppose that in the grand scope of history four years are but a speck of time."

"That's true," Sella Adamo said. "Which is another reason why I want Italy out of it as soon as possible. Then you can concentrate on getting Hitler."

Josh noticed the particular venom in her tone as she mentioned the Fuehrer. "Yes, I agree," he replied quietly.

God, Sella Adamo was beautiful! His plan would work like a million bucks!

The dinner was decidedly un-English. Hassan had broiled a large fish of a species Josh didn't recognize and surrounded it with a spicy rice and fruit combination. The fish had been deboned and tasted quite good to Josh. An Egyptian wine much like a Burgundy was served with it. He spent most of the meal listening quietly to the animated discussion, which seldom strayed beyond the work of the team.

"The painting of the girl on that wall," Dr. Cunningham explained, "is an artist's concept of Queen Ankhesenamun, the young wife of Tutankhamen. As you may know, Tut was only eighteen or nineteen when he died. It is assumed that Ankhesenamun was a bit younger. It's her tomb that we're seeking."

Josh nodded his head. "I believe I read something about the Valley of the Queens. Is that where you're looking?"

"No, we believe her tomb is right here, close to her husband's."

"Did she rule after Tut died?" Josh asked.

"We believe so, but no one is certain how long," Hancock replied. "That's why we think her tomb can be so valuable. It may tell us a great deal more about what happened in the royal family in the period following his death."

More American popular music was played throughout the meal and Josh decided that would be his entrée to start the game. When Sella came back from winding the machine and replaying "Begin the Beguine," he said, "You seem to like our music a great deal."

"Yes," she replied with a touch of a smile, "I have a husband who is quite enthusiastic about it—a result of his American youth, I'm sure."

Josh feigned surprise. "American youth?"

"Yes, he spent most of his first seventeen years there."

"And where is he now?"

"Somewhere in Italy. I haven't heard from him in a long time."

"What is he, an archaeologist or a musician?" Josh asked, hoping it didn't sound too casual.

She sighed. "Neither. He's in the great killing game like you, a pilot."

Her eyes grew serious. "But he's a fighter pilot, one of Italy's greatest, if he's still alive. I gave up worrying a long time ago."

Josh couldn't resist. "Maybe he and I have met in the air at some point. Wouldn't that be interesting?"

She gave a little shudder. "I don't even want to think about it. The war and my husband are completely remote to me, as are its brutalities. What is here has been and is real for me. Searching for the body of a girl queen who lived in about 1350 B.C. has far more meaning."

Josh nodded, deciding not to pursue the subject of his enemy, and asked, "May I see you at work? At the dig?"

She shrugged. "Tomorrow is Sunday, but suppose I introduce you to King Tut?" She glanced at Dr. Cunningham. "That is, if you have no objection."

"Of course not," he replied.

Turning back to Josh, she said, "Tomorrow is the first day in your life as an Egyptologist."

After breakfast the next morning, Sella Adamo began her orientation. Josh thought she was incredibly beautiful in a pair of wrinkled khaki shorts and a somewhat ragged matching shirt. Over her head she wore a conical straw coolie hat; her feet were covered by stained white canvas shoes. He admired her shapely legs as he followed her out of the Cunningham hut and had to force himself to pay attention because she spoke quickly, mixing the touch of Italian accent with her British English. On her personal turf, the gentle reticence of the night before disappeared. Her touch of tragedy was replaced by enthusiasm:

"One archaeologist explained this business thus: 'For many years European and American millionaires, bored with life's mild adventures, obtained excavating concessions in Egypt and dallied with the relics of bygone ages in the hope of receiving some thrill to stimulate their sluggard imaginations. They called it treasure hunting and their hope was to find a king lying in state with his jewelled crown upon his head.' An American by the name of Theodore Davis personified this description. Lord Carnarvon did not. When the well-trained British archaeologist, Howard Carter, teamed up with Carnarvon in 1907, their goal was information, not art.

"According to Carter, the perfectionist, Davis was lucky. Without precise scientific process, the American discovered several tombs, including that of Queen Hatshepsut. While these tombs were empty—

gutted by robbers centuries earlier—they held wall paintings that gave us a great deal of information, which in turn added to that derived from various artifacts the robbers had lost or deemed unworthy of taking. Several of these pointed to the presence of a King Tutankhamen, or Tutankha*mun* as he was known in the last few years of his life, and convinced Carter that this king's undiscovered tomb was a fact. In 1915, after Davis gave up and declared the Valley void of more tombs, Carter and Lord Carnarvon got their long-coveted concession to dig."

"But the Great War interrupted them," Josh injected. "I remember reading that somewhere." He didn't want to appear completely ignorant, not in front of this remarkable woman.

"Correct." Sella went on, "But in 1917 their efforts resumed. It was Carter's plan to dig down through the deep layers of rubbish and sand to bedrock. He was convinced that Tutankhamen's burial site was located within a triangular plot of land defined by the tombs of Ramses II, Ramses VI, and another pharaoh named Merenptah. He designed a search grid system similar to those used for artillery barrages so he wouldn't miss anything."

They reached the entrance to Ramses II's empty tomb and descended into its cool interior. Sella briefly described the remarkable wall paintings and recited a short biography of the great king who had reigned far longer than any other. Soon they reentered the bright sunlight. Pointing to the entrance to another tomb, she said, "That's Merenptah's, but we won't bother with it. The third corner of Carter's triangle is over there—the tomb of Ramses VI. While digging about a dozen yards from that tomb Carter suddenly burst onto the ancient foundations of several workmen's huts, a sure sign that a tomb had been built nearby.

"This made him even more certain that the tomb he sought was at hand. But five long years of frustration dogged him. In 1922 Lord Carnarvon, ill and weary of the lack of accomplishment, agreed to finance one final season of excavation, an extremely expensive endeavor that would cost a quarter of a million dollars these days."

They approached the entrance to the tomb of King Tut and Sella's sea green eyes took on the shine of enthusiasm. "And now the exciting part starts. The dig began on November 1, 1922, and two nights later Carter decided to remove the old workers' huts. Once that was done only a few feet of debris and sand remained above the bedrock. When Carter returned the next morning he was greeted by a strange silence among his normally noisy workers. Something unusual had happened! In moments, his foreman told him excitedly that a step cut in the rock had been discovered!"

Sella's eyes were even brighter. "Captain—Josh—let me explain what that meant. All tombs are reached by stone steps—sunken stairways."

Josh could feel the excitement.

Sella hurried on. "They dug feverishly, the frenzy of the find seizing them, and by the next afternoon the upper part of what turned out to be sixteen steps told everyone that the tomb of a king of the Eighteenth Dynasty, the time of Tutankhamen, was at their feet! Imagine how Carter must have felt watching the tedious uncovering of step after step, remembering his disappointments in the past, knowing full well that finding a finished, intact tomb that robbers had not sacked was a million-to-one shot!"

Sella took his hand and drew him down the first three steps of the stairway. Stopping, she turned back to him, her face aglow. "Just picture him standing here, forcing his patience, wanting to shout at the diggers to hurry, yet all the time nagged by feelings of doubt. And then the upper part of a door appeared, plastered over and stamped with hieroglyphs and several royal figurative sealings! Imagine how he must have felt, realizing this might be the most thrilling moment of his life!"

Josh touched the now smooth side of the steps and felt goose bumps.

"And then doubt once more set in because there was no name. The tomb could be that of some person of noble standing, not necessarily that of a king, or it could be a cache, a storage place. But one thing was certain. Since the sealings were intact, no human being, robber, worker or official, had entered this structure in over three thousand years!"

Josh shook his head. "But he couldn't even go in, could he?"

"No, he owed it to his patron to wait until he could arrive from England. He telegraphed Lord Carnarvon at once, and then covered up the steps to wait."

"That must have been hard to do."

Sella shook her head. "I don't know if I could have waited even a day, let alone three weeks! Carnarvon arrived with his lovely daughter, Evelyn, on the twenty-third, and the next day these steps were again cleared. But this time, they dug deeper and, finally, finally, Carter's dreams were confirmed: a lower sealing on the doorway held the name of Tutankhamen!

"They forced the door open and entered a long passageway that had been filled with sand and debris to protect whatever was beyond it."

Sella led Josh through the entrance and into a long, cool hallway. "And here we are, just as they were twenty-one years ago, Captain Rawlins." She smiled, looking around. "Oh, there were indications that robbers had been here, but what happened to them, whether they were caught in the act and killed, has never been determined. The sealings had to have been put on later. Anyway, Carter's party entered this passageway and cleared away tons of debris, slowly, carefully, until thirty feet beyond the first entry they found a second door."

Josh looked around and up at the faded yellow ceiling, picturing sweaty Arab workers and a couple of black Nubians standing quietly behind the archaeologists, caught up in the great moment, waiting.

They moved on to the second doorway.

"Imagine," Sella went on, "Carter's hands trembling as he took an iron rod and made a hole in the corner of this door. Holding a burning candle to the hole to test for foul gases, he stuck the rod back in the hole and widened it. Looking inside, he drew in a sharp breath. What followed was one of the most dramatic and surely the most famous exchange of words in the history of archaeology. From the flickering light of the candle, Carter said, 'I saw from the mist, strange animals, statues and gold—everywhere the glint of gold. I was struck dumb with amazement, and when Lord Carnarvon, unable to stand the suspense any longer, inquired anxiously, "Can you see anything?" It was all I could do to get out the words, "Yes, wonderful things." ' "

Josh looked through the doorway to where a guide was explaining much the same story to a handful of sunburned tourists who had managed to beat the wartime transportation problems: *"And Carter replied, 'Yes, wonderful things.' "*

He shook his head. How amazing it was to relive something this dramatic! He asked, "But he had to wait for the authorities before he could go farther, didn't he?"

"That's what he said in his book," Sella replied. "But recent evidence indicates that he, the earl and his daughter, and one other assistant went inside and roamed around in utter awe for the entire night. Carter later painstakingly took ten years to catalogue, describe, draw, or photograph every item, but for one solitary night he was like a child oohing and aahing on his first visit to a candy store. As an archaeologist, I can assure you his wonderment had to have exceeded anything he'd ever known.

"I won't go into what was there, except to say that there were some five thousand objects in four rooms—the antechamber, which we are entering now, an annex, the spectacular burial chamber, and the treasury. Magnificent alabaster, precious and semiprecious stones, enlightening paintings, and a rich plethora of gold—everywhere beautifully designed gold—filled the rooms."

"What about the mummy?" Josh asked softly as they strolled on into the burial chamber. He knew nothing about mummification. "Can a body actually survive all those centuries?"

Sella smiled. "The ancient Egyptians were experts at preserving the human body. They used various ointments, unguents, and the mineral natron, with many wrappings of linen. In the case of King Tut, his toes, fingers, and penis were wrapped in gold sheaths and survived quite well."

"Huh, and all of this, this vast collection of earthly goods, was meant to make him comfortable in his afterlife, is that right?"

"Yes, it was believed that the kings moved about freely in the underworld at night. Actually, wherever and whenever they wished. But back to the opening of the casket, it was over a year before Carter got to the body of the now world famous Tut. The great quartzite sarcophagus you see before you held four shrines or caskets of gilded wood, and inside them were three coffins, two of gilded wood and one of solid gold!"

Again Sella's eyes glowed. "Think of this: Carter invited about forty people, from royalty to world press, to observe the final opening of the coffin. Imagine the awe, the immense thrill, when he opened that magnificent final casket and found the preserved body, its face enclosed in a gold mask—possibly one of the most beautiful portraits in the history of mankind. Carter looked into the features of a young pharaoh who had been dead for thirty-two hundred years!"

Josh's eyes were wide as he stared at the sarcophagus and pictured the remarkable scene. "Where's the mummy now?"

"In the Egyptian Museum in Cairo, but it will be brought back here to forever lie in state some day."

Josh just shook his head.

"And that, my friend," Sella said triumphantly, "is the story of the discovery of the tomb of King Tut."

To keep up his pretense of the magazine story—and for his own interest—Josh took several pictures with a 35mm folding camera before Sella took him back to the Land Rover and drove him on a tour of the other tomb sites in the Valley of the Kings. Upon their return she drove to a point about six hundred yards north of the Tut site. There, it appeared that a major area had been dug up. "This is where we are seeking Queen Ankhesenamun's tomb," she explained.

"But why wouldn't she be buried in the Valley of the Queens?" Josh asked, wiping the back of his moist neck with a handkerchief.

"Because there is a great mystery around that young girl, and we think she could have decreed that she be buried near Tut. We've spent four long years digging around the site of her king's tomb, but to no avail. Now, after a faience cup inscribed with her name has been found in the center of our current dig area, we are encouraged that we'll find her resting place, hoping to clear up much of the mystery about what took place following Tut's burial."

Josh was intrigued. "What happened to her?"

Sella parked the Land Rover and turned off the engine. "That's the mystery. The most popular belief goes this way: Tut's powerful political advisor and the man who was possibly his father was Ay. He probably ran the country for the perhaps frivolous and youthful king. But another powerful figure was on the scene, General Horemheb, an aggressive officer who kept Egypt strong. It is accepted that Ay may have ruled jointly with the queen for a short time following Tut's death, or he may have threatened her position. Now, Ankhesenamun was no little lily, Josh. She had a forceful mind and knew she had to do something to keep her throne. So she wrote a letter to Suppiluliuma, the king of the Hittites, in which she said,

My husband is dead and I'm told you have grown-up sons. Send me one of them and I will make him my husband, and he shall be king over Egypt.

The king of the Hittites stalled for a time and then wrote,

Where is the son of the late king and what has become of him?

To which Ankhesenamun in despair replied,

Why should I deceive you? I have no son and my husband is dead. Send me a son of yours and I will make him king.

Now there are two stories about what happened next. Carter writes that too much time had passed and Suppiluliuma did not send a son. But further information tells us that the Hittite king did send an heir and that he was ambushed and killed by some of General Horemheb's cavalry. Since it's believed that Horemheb desired to marry Ankhesenamun to gain the throne, this seems quite logical."

"And then what happened to her?" Josh asked.

"That's all we know, which is why we want so very much to find her tomb."

"Are you sure there is one?"

"Not positive, but that faience cup is a strong prod to keep digging."

"What a remarkable story."

Sella smiled. "Yes, and just think, if her plot had succeeded, we never would have had a Ramses the Great."

The unrelenting heat was still increasing when they returned to the Cunningham house, where the thick mud walls—Josh called them adobe—provided the only respite. All four of the professionals on the dig used it as headquarters during the day and early evening. Sella Adamo slept there, while Winfield Hancock usually slept in a pyramidal tent equipped with a large electric fan. When they parked the Land Rover and entered, Dr. Cunningham handed Josh a message and said, "This came in from Cairo at ten o'clock."

Josh read quickly:

Capt. Rawlins is to bring Dr. Adamo to Cairo. An aircraft will pick them up at the same airfield at 1400 Sunday, 6,23. Transport will meet them at the Cairo airfield and take them to the Anglo-Egyptian Union, where they will meet Mr. Sabatini. Dr. Adamo should plan to remain in Cairo for a minimum of one week.
          —Macgruder, Wing Commander

He handed the message to Sella. "Looks like we're wanted back in the modern world."

"Do you know why?"

"Not exactly. This Mr. Sabatini is a big editor from New York," he lied. "*Time* Magazine, or something like that. Has some kind of connection with the brass. I was told he might want this story after the army gets through with it."

Sella absently pushed back a wisp of hair. "I haven't been any farther than Luxor in three years." Turning to Dr. Cunningham, she asked, "Do you have any objections to this, Justin?"

He shrugged. "I don't like this cavalier approach from Macgruder, but I've been asked to cooperate, so there isn't much sense in quibbling. Besides, my dear, a holiday in Cairo will be good for you."

Sella smiled. "Very well, it certainly won't take me long to pack."

Suddenly Josh was brought back to reality. This remarkably breathtaking creature with whom he was definitely infatuated was the wife of Franco Adamo, and he had to use her. He had to get all of his wits about him and manipulate her as coldly as her husband had gunned down his men.

And he didn't like the idea at all.

CHAPTER 18

✛

Major Rudolfo Sabatini made his way slowly along the busy street in Misr al-Qadimah, or Old Cairo. He was wearing a pale blue seersucker suit and a white panama hat. He was taking his time, pausing here and there to look at the goods in various little streetside booths. The continuous ringing of the tram bells chimed in with the cries of beggars as he entered the Qasabah, medieval Cairo's main street. Following this congested and historic thoroughfare for some three hundred yards, he came to the Mosque of Ibn Tulun, then moved on until he reached a small hotel with a faded sign announcing its name, the Haramlik. He took a table in a small garden at its front and ordered a glass of Cypress sherry. Lighting a Lucky Strike, he inhaled and began to watch the passing parade.

Just after the waiter, a grubby little man in an oily red fez, brought his drink, another man entered the garden and eyed him carefully. He was thin, about fifty, and was wearing a shabby white linen suit. Coming up to Sabatini's table he said, "I'm looking for Sidney Greenstreet," in a decidedly Yorkshire accent.

"I'm Greenstreet," Sabatini said. "Join me for a drink?"

"Don't mind if I do. Name's Lorre, Peter."

"Bogart send you?" The man Sabatini was expecting, the arrival who called himself Peter Lorre, was a retired sergeant from a Royal Artillery battalion that had long been stationed in Cairo. He was also a man of many talents, mostly destructive, with connections in the vast Cairo underworld. He had been sent by a sergeant-major in the British Special Air Service whom Sabatini had gotten to know while training back in Britain and had contacted the day after arriving in the city.

"Naturally."

They passed the time of day over the wine and finally Sabatini said directly, "How much will it cost me to have an enemy alien removed from sunny Cairo?"

The man who called himself Peter Lorre replied, "That would depend upon whom it is, sor."

"An Italian woman."

"Known by anyone?"

"Some archaeologists out in the Valley of the Kings."

"The police?"

"Possibly, but more probably the British military police."

"And Intelligence?"

"Yes."

"Will her disappearance create a problem?"

"The archaeologists might squawk. Intelligence won't care."

"Will she be difficult to reach?"

"Not very."

"Are there any special requirements?"

"Yes, I'll need a lock of her hair."

The retired sergeant stroked his chin. "I would say such a chore could be handled for about five hundred quid."

Two thousand dollars! Sabatini's eyes narrowed. "That's a lot of money for this part of the world. I can get someone off the street for far less."

Lorre shrugged. "But will it be done professionally?"

"Maybe."

"Quality work costs money."

This was the Middle East; one had to haggle. Sabatini said, "No more than two hundred."

Lorre shook his head. "Impossible. Four hundred and fifty."

They settled on three-fifty.

The twin-engined RAF Avro Anson that picked them up arrived at the Cairo airport at shortly before five. The same driver in the black Austin sedan from Wing Commander Macgruder's office met them, took their bags, and drove them into the city. Sella Adamo watched through the open window like a fascinated child. "I never get used to this exciting city," she said with a soft smile. "Other Middle Eastern cities are much the same, but Cairo has a flavor of its own, a distinct uniqueness, a continuity from the past. Some of its architecture breathes the Orient, while the touch of its pharaohs is never ignored. I think it is saying, "I am Misr, the jewel of a great past. When the peoples of the world were learning to make crude cloth my artisans were weaving it with gold; when others across the earth were wandering in nomadic tribes or still living in caves my people were building palaces and remarkable structures that would last unknown millennia. For in the beginning my children were superior to all."

Josh liked to listen to her almost as much as he enjoyed watching her. Her two accents and unique modulation gave her voice not only cultured appeal, but a powerfully sensual charm. At moments her sadness, her touch of tragedy, slipped back into her eyes, but mostly she had it stored away in whatever private niche she had picked for its hiding spot.

She chuckled, "And now I hope the descendents of those superior forbears have some lip rouge for sale."

"We call it lipstick."

"Yes, I haven't worn any down there in the Valley for years. In fact, I have only one dress with me, so I hope the limits of my arrest will not include any social life."

"Arrest?"

Her sea-green eyes widened. "Had you forgotten, my Captain, that I am an enemy alien, interred, actually in house arrest with Dr. Cunningham?"

"Yes, actually I had. It makes no sense. I mean you are so far detached from the war, you belong to an international community of scholars."

"Well, I am. In fact, after I received a letter from my husband a year and a half ago, you would have thought I was in command of the entire Italian Army! Just the idea that a single ruddy letter from an Italian officer could reach me in my incarceration made the Intelligence blokes think I had a whole network of spies working for me, that I was getting vital information directly to Rommel!"

That's what he was having so much trouble remembering—that she was a goddamned enemy! "What happened?" he asked.

She shrugged. "Oh, they hounded me for a few months, and then Dr. Cunningham went to the commanding general of all the British forces, and I believe he had some harsh words for the old man. At any rate, they left me alone after that, although I suspect they still keep an eye on me." She feigned an apprehensive look. "In fact, this arrangement with you may even be some kind of a plot, Captain Rawlins."

He had to force a chuckle. "Sure, and the whole U.S. Army Air Corps is in on it."

Sabatini sipped from his martini and decided it wasn't bad. It was hard to ruin good English gin unless you put too much vermouth in it, or a bad olive. He looked again at the pretty Arab waitress—light-skinned, far from Nubian, probably some European blood, built like a brick shithouse. Better than that little whore two nights ago at Madame Faruk's. Victoria, her name was. Yeah, the little queen.

Maybe he'd go back to Madame Faruk's again tonight. If he could find it. Probably ought to call Hooker, meet him later. After he got Rawlins and the Adamo broad squared away at the villa. Four days, that's how much time he'd allotted for the deal. Make it look good. Give Rawlins a chance to pick her brains. If she looked halfway decent they could adopt Rawlins' plan. That's why he had been particular about renting a villa with a swimming pool. There weren't many in Cairo. Macgruder had balked at the price, but had found money in some special fund. Probably bill the U.S. Army anyway. Had to put up the front.

He thought about the little whore again. Probably the hashish, but what an experience! Maybe someday, when things were set up after the war, maybe the hashish whorehouse idea might go in the States. Start with a few in New York, a couple over in Jersey, maybe a couple in Boston . . . D.C.—now that's where one ought to go, with all those goddamned congressmen. Yeah, might be worth looking into.

There they were, coming through the lobby to the bar, escorted by the bellman he'd paid to wait for them. Tall broad, about the same size as—in fact, she looked a lot like her. Same blonde hair. The eyes, what about the eyes? Heavy dark lashes, no makeup. Same long legs, the hint of a full bosom—she was a spitting image!

He got to his feet, staring. Rawlins was holding out his hand, but he didn't even notice. He was staring into her eyes, the same sea-green eyes that had captured him once across a smoky cabaret room. It was Teresa, his Teresa! Incredibly. She smiled as Rawlins made the introductions and then spoke. The accent was there, but her voice was the same—

He managed to tear his eyes away and get into the scenario. "Nice to meet you, Captain Rawlins. Heard a lot about you. Yeah, General Buell told me you were a hell of a pilot, hell of a fighting man. Yeah."

He went back to her cool green gaze. Incredible.

"We have our bags outside in the staff car. What should we do—"

Sabatini got hold of himself. He turned to the waiting bellman, handing him a bill. "Tell the driver of that staff car to wait. We'll be out in a few minutes." Turning back to Josh, he said, "Sit down and have a quick drink before we go to my villa." To keep from staring at her, he quickly held a chair as Sella Adamo sat down. He brushed against her as he did so. She even felt like Teresa!

The villa was surprisingly large once you were behind the wall. It was so elaborate that its builder must have had an ancient Egyptian palace in mind when he designed it. The entire bottom floor was white marble that flowed from one area to another. Everything blended without a wall from the great room that dropped over a series of steps to an inside marble swimming pool with sliding glass doors that could be opened in the proper weather. Several mature palm trees grew through holes in the stone near the pool. The color of gold dominated all of the wall art. To provide a comfortable setting, soft oriental music from strings that at times included a zither drifted continuously through the structure.

The area where they were eating from a heavy white table was on a ledge off to the left of the pool. The slender houseboy, Abdul, served lamb and rice as Sabatini poured more white wine. He didn't have any idea where Abdul, who was one of Macgruder's most prized local operatives, got the fine wine, and he didn't care.

All he cared about was Dr. Sella Adamo.

She was wearing her one dress, an out-of-style white cotton frock that did nothing for her bustline but provided a striking contrast for her deep tan. Her blonde hair was still back in a severe bun, but the large white loops she wore in her ears added a stylish accent. She was exceptionally lovely. Sitting at the head of the table between them, she was saying, "You should both go to the Egyptian Museum here in the city. Much of what Carter took from Tut's tomb is here, including the pharaoh himself."

"I never did ask you," Josh said, "What's the story of the curse?"

She shook her head. "It all started because there were so many journalists there after the discovery of the tomb. They came from all over the world and they wrote anything that bore even a faint resemblance to the truth. Since Carter's pet canary was supposedly killed by a cobra, and since Lord Carnarvon died shortly after the discovery from a supposed infection, the rumor of the curse began. It was pure nonsense. One story had the electricity going out back in Carnarvon's mansion in England at the moment he died. Other stories were made up and expanded. 'King Tut's Curse.' A sort of madness took over. Convinced that any Egyptian artifact was cursed, owners tried to turn in the most inconsequential stuff before it hurt them."

"Then it's all nonsense?"

"There isn't a shred of reality to it."

Josh grinned. "Good. Now I can quit worrying."

Sabatini watched them. As soon as dinner was finished, he had to get out. The woman was bewitching him, and Josh had to get on with his plan. If he stuck around there was no way he could stay away from her. "You two want to go out and see the town tonight?" he asked.

Josh tossed a glance at Sella, then replied, "I hadn't thought about it. I mean . . . would you like to go somewhere and dance, Sella?"

"Oh, I don't know," she said. "I haven't been out in so long, I don't think I'd know what to do."

"Nonsense," Sabatini said brusquely. "It'll be on my publishing company. Do you good. I'll even recommend a couple of places."

Josh thought of holding her close on a dance floor. "Let's do it!"

"I look so tacky," Sella protested.

"You'll be the most beautiful woman on any dance floor in Cairo!"

Slowly she nodded her head. "Very well."

Forty minutes later Sabatini was in a bazaar that specialized in European dresses. As the reddening sun cast its last assault for the day several merchants were trying to milk their final profits. He had brought the swarthy Abdul along to interpret and bargain for him. He'd already bought a swimming suit for Sella, a one-piece strapped red affair that would set off her tan and Mediterranean blondeness. Now Abdul was describing how tall and well-formed she was to a fat merchant with thick glasses and a broad smile. Sabatini liked a pale green dress that would go perfectly with her lovely eyes. He had once bought Teresa a dress the same color. It was even sort of the same style: high shoulders, a keyhole neck, and a peplum at the waist. But styles hadn't changed much and these models were probably prewar anyway.

God, how lovely Teresa had been in it.

This whole damned thing was stupid!

The Adamo woman would be dead in a few days, why buy her clothes? He told himself it was to help Josh with his plan, but that was bullshit. He knew what it was.

Teresa.

His beautiful Teresa had been thrust back into his life.

"You want this for five pounds twenty, sir?" Abdul asked. "I've gotten him down from twelve pounds and I don't think he'll budge another pence."

"You sure it'll fit her?"

Abdul shrugged. "He says if it doesn't you can return it."

Sabatini pulled out some British money. "I'll take it. And that bright yellow one, as well. And you can go on back to the house with the purchases. I have some things to do."

He had some things to do, all right.

Like recover his logic.

A woman had to be killed.

Don Nizzi had ordered it.

Sella felt a certain wildness about being out in Cairo with Josh Rawlins. It was like being on a date years earlier, during the period when she was attending university in Berlin. Actually it had been 1937, and she had met a handsome young Regia Aeronautica fighter pilot in Rome while on holiday. He was more American than Italian, which, added to his devil-may-care attitude, made him highly attractive. They had slipped away from the party where they'd met and he had talked her into going dancing, something she seldom did in the no-nonsense pursuit of her education. She had been in university, in Rome, Berlin, and Cambridge since she was seventeen, seldom breaking out of the rigid mold of study to do anything frivolous. She had had two brief love affairs before she met Franco Adamo, one with an older professor and one with a fellow student. Both had been unfulfilling and had ended abruptly.

The time in Rome with the reckless pilot had been fun.

She had taken the boat to Egypt the next day, and had been totally surprised to find Lt. Franco Adamo waiting on the dock when she arrived in Cairo ten days later. He had grinned that infectious grin of his and said, "So they wanted a plane ferried down to Ethiopia and I volunteered. Can I help it if I have to spend a couple of days here?"

They had fallen in love in those two days and on the last night he had asked her to marry him. She had laughed away the proposal, telling him, "My school must come first. One can always marry. Besides, you have Mussolini's stupid wars to fight."

To which he replied, "And one can always finish one's schooling while married. Just as one can fight a war while married. It's simply a matter of not making excuses, but accepting responsibility." Franco Adamo had always been a stickler about responsibility.

But she hadn't wavered. That was the night like this one, with a certain wildness, when they'd kicked over the traces and had a great time. Instead of pouting over the rejection of his marriage proposal Franco had ordered Champagne and had hired a car to take them to the best clubs in the city. And when it was over, she had consented to an engagement.

But tonight just held a certain abandonment for her. An unchaining. Josh Rawlins was a handsome young American with a certain boyishness and yet a touch of tragedy about him. She sensed a harshness, but guessed that it merely covered an undefined vulnerability. She could see it in his blue eyes, both in their expressions and in the fine squint or worry lines around them. And Justin Cunningham had told her that he was a hero, which, since she abhorred the war, was unimportant. Still, that quality added to his character, possibly to whatever it was that was tragic about him.

Now, as they danced quietly to the music of a four-piece combo in a small nightclub called the Sphinx, she felt his firm body against hers and liked it. The dance floor was tiny and crowded with British officers and their dates. At one time, during her stay at Cambridge, she had had a few dates with a young British Army lieutenant, or leftenant, as they pronounced the word. But she couldn't even remember what he looked liked. Too many ancient Egyptain faces, she guessed. The song was "Sentimental Journey," and Josh was singing parts of it in her ear: "to renew old me-em-or-ies."

Yes, she liked this captain. There was something about him, something like Franco, but without as much bravado, more, as she said, vulnerability. Her hand found the back of his neck. She had known him only for two nights and a day, but already she sensed she could hold him close and feel good with him. He was trusting, searching, as in the tombs, a boy wishing to learn about the world.

The music stopped and they went back to their small corner table. "For a girl who hasn't been out in ages, you dance very well," Josh said. "I just kind of move my feet."

She touched his hand. "No, you do very well, for a pilot." She laughed. He was so easy to laugh with.

He shrugged. "Be careful, pilots do lots of things well."

"Like making love?" She didn't know why she said it; it just popped out of her slightly giddy mood. Probably all the drinks.

"I can't vouch for that," he replied quietly.

"Of course not, silly. I was being a nosy Italian." Before they danced the previous set she had been telling him about her schooling, a safe retreat after her risqué remark. She smiled. "Besides, you asked me about Berlin before we got distracted. At first I liked it, even though the Nazis were making things difficult for the Jews. Being Italian and not political, I managed to ignore what was going on, until that terrible Kristelnacht, that grotesque night in November 1938 when they broke all the windows of Jewish shops and looted and burned. That was when I knew that Jewry all over Europe was going to suffer severely. And I also knew, even then, that Mussolini would kiss Hitler's feet. If the Fuehrer wanted Italian Jews to suffer like those in Germany, Il Duce would comply. I left Berlin two days after that terrible night and continued my doctoral studies at Cambridge."

This time he touched her hand. "That must have been terrible for you. Did you worry that you might get swept up in the net?"

"No—well, yes, somewhat. But I had my Italian passport and all, and I look more Aryan than Jewish, so I had no problem."

He looked at her somberly. "Were you married then?"

"No, but when I came back home for Christmas that year, Franco and I were wed." She thought back to the small ceremony. As she was a nonpracticing Jew and he was a nonpracticing Catholic, they were married in Rome by a judge. She had insisted, however, on a white lace dress and he had taken her to an RA officers' club where several of his squadron pilots held a zestful reception and tried to get him drunk, an endeavor in which they succeeded to a certain extent before she whisked him away in their rented Fiat. They drove to the small seaside city of Lido de Ostia for a short vacation.

"Did you ever live together?"

"Yes, for two months after I finished my university work in late 1939. Then, with Hitler overrunning northern Europe, Franco insisted that I contact my British archaeological friends to get on with them here in Egypt. He said it was the only way I could be safe. By this time both of my parents were dead, so it made sense. I left Italy eight months before Mussolini declared war on France and England in the summer of 1940."

"And you've only heard from him once since?"

She thought Josh seemed suddenly tense. "Only once since Italy came into the war. And that was when the British Intelligence blokes tried to make me out a Mata Hari."

The question was almost cold. "Do you think he has survived? Flying fighters, actually flying anything for a long period in combat can be quite dangerous."

She shook her head and drank deeply from her wine glass. "I don't even think about it, Josh. If he's dead, so be it. It's out of my control, has been for years. I live somewhere between hope and fatalism, with the latter ruling. I'm a scientist and I deal with the dead. Again, when one thinks about Egyptian dynasties, this time is but a moment, and as someone said, 'Our time on the stage is so brief,' or something like that." She took his hand and got to her feet. "C'mon, Yank, dance with me and hold me close. And make me laugh."

Sabatini had consumed a heroic amount of Scotch whisky in his wanderings since leaving the bazaar, but somehow he felt completely sober. He had missed contact with Joe Hooker at the different establishments, and when a British Army nurse encouraged him at the Union, he had ignored her. Only one person could lessen his trouble this night, and she worked for Madame Faruk.

He inhaled from the narghile and felt the hashish smoke go all the way down into his belly and relax him. Leaning back on the pile of pillows, he opened his eyes and observed the beautiful girl for whom he had paid double tonight, so he could keep her as long as he wished.

Victoria sat cross-legged beside him, totally nude except for a string of multicolored beads around her neck. She had puffed on the hashish, so her eyes were dreamy, dark, and moist, like shiny marbles. With one hand she stroked his penis, with the other she caressed her nipple. She sang a native song, low and unintelligible to him, but it reminded him of Teresa. Since his first glimpse of that Franco woman everything reminded him of Teresa. They had smoked some marijuana together a couple of times on their honeymoon in the Catskills, and she had sat like that, singing to him in her low voice, so soft, so satiny. In the moonlight, her eyes had grown dark and shiny, wet, like Victoria's, as she slid up to nuzzle his neck and fondle his erection.

He took Victoria's hand and gently drew her into his arms. But all he saw was that stranger with her hair in a bun.

He had to kill that stranger with her hair in a bun, and end all this confusion, this irrationality.

Rudy Lotions was always in control.

He kissed Victoria softly, then urgently, and moved between her legs.

When Sella and Josh arrived back at the villa it was shortly after one. She laughed as she recalled the funny comedian at the last club they had visited. He'd done a Cockney routine in which he came home from the war and found his girlfriend pregnant, and she tried to convince him that she didn't have a "bun in the oven," but a "loaf that had got stuck." Josh laughed aloud at her Italian cockney accent. He was spinning with pleasure from her delightful company, and keyed up with desire. Never had he known a woman such as this. She was earthy, stunningly beautiful, warm, and witty. Every time he touched her he wanted to crush her in his arms. And how she aroused him! When she moved close while they danced and he felt her hand on his neck, he had hardly been able to move his feet. Even though he had pulled back, she surely must have felt his erection.

Now, as they stood in the open area outside their bedrooms, she sobered and looked at him quietly. Holding his gaze, she moved closer and brought her hand up to his chin. Her kiss was sweet, lingering but controlled, her tongue touching his, lightly searching. He took her in his arms, pulling her close, kissing her more insistently. But she soon pulled back and opened her eyes. "Thank you, Josh," she said softly. "Thank you for reminding me that I'm still a woman who has emotions."

He tried to kiss her again, but she turned her face into his shoulder.

"No, that's enough for tonight. Remember, I haven't even been kissed in years." She stepped out of his arms and smiled. "You are a lovely man, Josh Rawlins, American writer and airman. Good night."

Moments later, as he closed the door to his room, he heard her shout, "Josh!" Hurrying to her door, he saw her holding up a red bathing suit.

"Look at this!" she exclaimed. "And this!" She held up two dresses. "Where did these come from?"

Sabatini had picked up on his plan—the villa with the pool, now a bathing suit. It was perfect for him to get pictures of Sella Adamo, bathing-suit pictures to have copied large-scale on a YB-40 to suck in her husband!

"I guess Mr. Sabatini had someone get them for you."

She danced around, first with one dress, then the other, finally picking up the bathing suit. "I haven't been swimming since I was last in Italy," she said with wide eyes. "Can we go in tonight, can we, Josh?"

He shrugged. Anything to be with her longer. "Of course. I'll go put some shorts on."

Five minutes later, after pulling himself from the pool and sitting on its edge, he watched her approach. Her hair was down, long, nearly to her waist. The strapped red bathing suit looked as if it had been made for her. Her figure was superb: full-busted, tiny at the waist, with lovely hips and shapely, slender legs. At first he stared, then he shook his head and let out a low whistle. "That's an American expression of approval," he said with a grin.

"I don't mind it. Italian men whistle too, but they also pinch."

She dove into the pool, entering cleanly, knifing in with her feet together, barely making a splash. With sure strokes she made three trips up and down the small pool, stopping in front of him, blowing out a deep breath and taking his hand. Moonlight poured over the pool through the sliding doors that Abdul had apparently left open, creating reflections like tiny diamonds where it struck the water droplets on her skin and hair. "Won't you come in and swim with me?" she asked, teasingly.

Sliding in the water, he said, "You're the mermaid. I'm a frog."

She laughed, swimming away from him. He followed her, and after two laps he caught her by the arm and pulled her close. Their kiss was more urgent this time, as her tongue met his and returned its vigor. Her hands went to the back of his head as she climbed up around him in the water, then down around his shoulders, holding him tightly, then stroking. Her lips found his ears, "Oh, *a caro,* my beautiful one."

His mouth moved down her neck to the swell of her breasts, kissing both as he massaged her nipple. Her legs came fully around him as they floated, going partially under, bobbing up, finding each other's mouths. She rocked against his erection as they went under the surface again, still kissing. Finding a step with his foot, he picked her up and carried her, dripping, out of the pool. With her arms around his neck and her lips nibbling on his ear, he took her to his bedroom and lowered her to the bed. "We're too wet," she whispered, pulling her suit down to her waist.

"Who cares?" he replied huskily, kissing a nipple and tugging at his dripping shorts. He didn't care about anything but her.

Moments later she helped him enter her, letting out a tiny cry as his glans stroked firmly up inside her.

CHAPTER 19

✛

Lt. Col. Franco Adamo worked over the charts in the Lightning revetment at the satellite field near San Vito, Sardinia. According to his calculations, it was 1,031 statute miles to the RAF airfield at Cairo. And as the Lockheed twin-engined fighter plane supposedly had a ferry range of over 2,200 statute miles he had over twice as much as he needed. Far more reserve than required. He could cruise at 370 m.p.h. at 30,000 and true out at a healthy ground speed if he didn't run into some hellacious winds. He should make it to Cairo in something like two hours and forty minutes, counting the climb and all. Nothing to it.

"I'll want a light load of ammo for both the fifties and the cannon, Diego," he said to his chief mechanic. Never knew what he might run into, and as he had so much range to spare, why not?

The sergeant, who had the cowling of the right engine up and was putting the spark plugs he had cleaned back into their cylinders, nodded. "Yes, colonel. Want to take along a couple of bottles of our best Sardinian wine? Those stupid Arabs probably don't know how to use the grape."

Franco nodded. He knew his promotion pleased Diego, that the mechanic liked to brag about working directly and privately for a high-ranking officer. He had already requested promotions for both Diego and Corporal Mazzei directly from General Manzella in Rome. A small reward for what they had done over the last couple of months. The higher ranks might help them in whatever position they might find themselves in after the enemy came. When it was all over.

"In here," Mazzei said from the front of the revetment.

It was the sergeant from Intelligence with the American uniforms. Franco had insisted that the man tell no one of his need for them. "I have two, sir," he said. "The flying suit you asked for, and a khaki uniform. Both are without identification and both have matching insignia, that of a major. And since I'm your size, sir, I tried them on. Should fit."

"You've done well," Franco said, nodding his head in approval. "When this secret mission is finished, I'll send a letter of appreciation to your commander."

The sergeant saluted and departed.

Franco slipped into the one-piece flying suit. It was tan cotton with several zippered pockets. Wouldn't be too warm at thirty thousand feet, he thought with a frown. A leather patch over the left breast was adorned with etched pilot's wings and a name: George E. Pickett, major, USAAF. Sounded like the name of the Confederate general who made a charge at Gettysburg, if he remembered his history right. Good name for him to use. And it did fit well. He'd wear a wool civilian jacket to keep warm in case that goddamned P-38 heater let him down again.

The khaki uniform had been laundered and pressed. Short-sleeved shirt with the appropriate insignia, wings and a gold oak leaf on the right collar. Long pants. Fine. He had decided to leave at 9:30 A.M. That would get him into Cairo right at lunch time. There should be nothing more than a skeleton crew on the flight line at mealtime, and they should ask fewer questions.

If all went well, he should be seeing Sella by the following morning.

Josh found Sella already up and swimming when he finally came out of his room at nine-thirty. She looked even lovlier in the glistening red suit in the daylight. He tossed his towel on the marble floor by the pool's edge and quietly said, "Good morning." He wasn't sure how she would greet him. They'd made love eagerly, almost hungrily at first, and then more competently as they got to know each other's moves and reactions, each other's gratifications. And it had lasted until they finally fell asleep about four. At times she had used endearing words, now and then in Italian. Sometime around five or six, he guessed, she must have gone to her own room.

Her long, wet hair hung straight down over her full breasts. Whoever had bought that bathing suit, he decided, had gotten the lowest cut in Cairo. He wondered if Sabatini had picked it out.

She smiled. "Physically, I feel marvelous—oh, a bit tired and my head reminds me of how much I sampled the grape last night, but relaxed." She had the candor of a mature Italian woman. "A woman needs a cleansing like that once in a while."

He relaxed, found a smile. "Is that what you think I am, the cleaning man?"

She chuckled. "Maybe."

"Have you had coffee?"

"Yes, but I'm ready for more." She pulled herself out of the water and reached for her towel.

As she dried herself, Josh watched in admiration. She was one of the most beautiful women he had ever known. And without a single doubt, he was madly in love with her. It was crazy, even ridiculous, but that was the way it was. He had never felt anything this powerful in his life.

The everpresent Abdul brought them fresh coffee at the dining table. Josh had no idea where one acquired real coffee in wartime Cairo, but he was sure the flourishing black market had everything. He watched her as she sipped: incredible.

Her green eyes lifted over the cup. "Why are you watching me so?"

"Because I simply can't help it."

She smiled. "That's nice."

"I think last night was, well, probably the most important night of my life."

She watched him quietly under those long dark lashes.

He didn't know how to go on. It was all so sudden, so direct, and he was totally out of his depth. He managed, "I think I'm in love with you."

She continued to watch him, creating an awkward silence.

He looked away, out the glass doors. "I know, you're married, and it's wartime, and we drank a lot, and I shouldn't say something like that after such a short time. I know all those things, Sella, but I have to tell you how I feel."

She touched his hand, her eyes wide with a touch of pain. "Please don't, Josh. What I did last night was wrong. Oh, I know, there's a good chance my Franco is dead, but I don't *know* that—"

"It didn't mean anything to you?"

"I didn't say that. But we can't make it into something *importante*—

there, now I'm using Italian words—we must think of it as something that shouldn't have happened, but did. And is past. A cleansing, remember?"

He didn't blink as he looked into her eyes. "It means more to me than that."

She finished her coffee and got to her feet. "I'm going back to sleep for a time. If Mr. Sabatini wishes to talk, he can join us later during your interview."

Josh had completely forgotten his role as a writer!

And he'd damned well forgotten why he was here. Somehow, he had to get organized and get off this love bullshit. She had just told him all she had wanted was a one-night fling, and here he was making an ass out of himself. He was sitting here, practically begging for her favors like a moonstruck schoolboy. Yeah, he had to get off it. But he knew it would be very hard to do.

Sabatini had watched their exchange from a slit in the blinds of his bedroom. He had returned to the villa shortly after daybreak, and he, too, felt the ravages of his night's dissipation. He sipped his coffee and saw Josh staring into the swimming pool. The kid was overboard, he knew it. He could see it in his eyes the night before at dinner. Hook, line, and sinker. Every time he looked at her it showed. Puppy love, maybe more. It didn't take long with a woman like her—an instant. In Sicily they called it the *rombo di tuono*, the thunderclap.

He knew. It had happened in that smoky nightclub in New York when Teresa looked at him. A sultry blonde with eyes as green as seaweed in a black satin gown that clung to her remarkable figure like moonlight.

He knew all about falling hook, line, and sinker.

She was from Jersey, twenty-four years old when he met her. She had fallen hard and fast as well. They were married three months later in a little parish church in Morristown to please her mother. He'd bought the house in Brooklyn Heights just for her, a row house, three stories and spacious. He let her buy the best of furniture and put a colored maid in the place three days a week. Even Vito liked to go there.

And then Vito left for Italy.

And Teresa wanted the big house over in Jersey to be closer to her mother.

When everything was still rosy.

Before—

God had made this remarkable Adamo woman her twin.
Why? Was it a sign?
If so, what did it mean?

The RAF ground crewman finished putting a wooden chock under the right main landing gear of the Lightning and smiled up into the bright sunlight as Franco climbed out of the cockpit. "Hello," he said in English. "I'm down from Constantine on a liaison visit. Should be here three to four days. Please have her topped off in all the tanks and check the engine lubricants, if you don't mind. I'd sure appreciate it." It was so easy to speak American again.

The crewman nodded and brought his hand up in a casual salute. "No problem, sor. She'll be ready."

Franco looked around at the hodgepodge of Allied aircraft parked on the visitors' ramp. The P-38 was in between a Hurricane and a de Havilland Mosquito. It felt strange to be so close to the blue-white-and-red roundels of the RAF. The only time he'd seen them in the last four years was in his gun sights. God, it would be so simple to have brought along some thermite bombs, something the demolitions boys could have perhaps rigged with small timing devices. He could probably have slipped them inside a few aircraft without getting caught, maybe destroyed a handful of enemy planes as he flew merrily on his way. "Where can I get transportation?" he asked casually.

"Operations should fix you up just fine, sor. Over there." He pointed to a building about two hundred yards away.

"Thanks." Franco slung the khaki uniform over his shoulder, picked up the small valise, and headed for Operations.

The operations duty officer, a flight lieutenant, told him a bus would be leaving within ten minutes and would take him into the city. He didn't dare ask many questions, nor did he want to answer any. He waited by the door until the bus arrived a few minutes later. Possibly because it was just after noon, the vehicle was empty except for the driver, a young Egyptian civilian. Franco told him he had to go to Bulaq, the port district, and gave him the address of a small hotel there.

Fifty-five minutes later the bus driver turned into the less crowded riverfront area. Franco looked around; here and there through the jammed buildings he could see the high triangular sail of a felluca. A large gunboat hove into view, and smaller fishing boats. "Here, Major," the driver said as he parked in front of a hotel with large crooked sign that had just been repainted. It announced The Babylon, the hotel his instructions

directed him to. It had a small, surprisingly clean lobby, complete with
a painting of an ancient British man-of-war on one wall. "Major Pickett,"
he told the desk clerk, who handed him a pen and asked him in excellent English to register.

After taking his belongings to the large room, he found a change
of clothing hanging in the small closet. He quickly washed and put
on the Arab sailor's apparel. He had no more than tied his shoelaces
when a knock sounded at the door. "Who is it?" he asked in English,
not wishing to ruin his cover in the event it wasn't a friend.

It was a friend. *"Viva Il Duce,"* a man's deep voice replied.

He opened the door to find a man in native Egyptian attire. "I am
Ismael Gardono," the visitor said in Italian.

There was no one else in the hallway, which explained why Gardono
didn't use any precaution. "And I am Colonel Adamo," Franco replied.
"Come in." He'd been told by Edda Ciano's special messenger from
Rome that Gardono was half-Italian, on his father's side, and half-Egyptian.
He was also a trusted agent of Count Ciano.

Gardono took a chair and went directly to the point. "Your wife is
still on a dig in the Valley of the Kings, as you probably know. She's
a member of the Justin Cunningham group that is searching near the
tomb of King Tut, not far from Luxor. And she is healthy. I have arranged a swift boat that will leave in thirty minutes and take us there.
I, of course, speak fluent Arabic and Nubian, and will be what the British
call a 'minder.' In short, I will take care of all logistical needs and
whatever interpretation you might need—sir."

"Very well, let's get started," Franco replied. "Will I need the American
uniform?"

"No. My plan does not include your meeting the Englishmen, only
her."

The boat was small, with a tiny galley and a crowded cabin with
two bunks. It was more accurately known as a *sandal*. But, while it
was badly in need of a paint job it seemed to be in good shape. It had
one large triangular sail and one smaller one, a balancer, both of soiled,
once-white canvas. Its engine was inboard and Gardono told him it
could give the craft a speed of seventeen knots, quite fast for a river
boat, even better if a wind assisted. Its captain was a swarthy man of
uncertain age named Faroz. The only other crew member was a boy
of about twelve by the name of Ibrahim. But Franco didn't care about

who was on this damned boat. All he was interested in was getting down, or actually up, the mighty and mystic Nile.

It would take nearly twenty-four hours, all of which would be dragging for him. It had been four long years since he'd seen her. Surely she wasn't under guard or confined. When he had met Dr. Cunningham in early 1939 the archaeologist had seemed a decent man, quite fair, in fact. Now he hoped the man would listen to reason. Sella's life had to be safeguarded from those murderers in Sicily. Oh, he knew who they were all right: the most powerful don on the island and his cohorts.

He didn't know how the bastards could reach all the way to the Valley of the Kings, but then if an RA officer could get there it would be no problem for the Friends.

Anything was possible.

"And when did you live with your husband in Rome?" Josh hated to ask these questions, but he had to keep going through the motions of interviewing Sella for his cover. He also hated to ask anything that would give him a mental picture of her with the man he so hated. He sipped from a glass of beer Abdul had just delivered to the table overlooking the pool.

"In 1939 after he returned from the Spanish Civil War."

Josh scribbled, knowing his notes were meaningless. "Did you ever meet Mussolini?"

"Yes, once. It was at a reception at Count Ciano's formal residence—the foreign minister's house, not the apartment where he and Edda lived."

"Edda—that's the dictator's daughter?"

"Yes, his oldest child and favorite."

"What was she like?"

"Quite lovely, and most pleasant to me. Although I later heard her referred to as the most dangerous woman in Europe."

"Why is that?"

"Supposedly she has strong influence over both her father and her husband. And Ciano, as foreign minister, is one of the most powerful men in the country. Possibly even second to Il Duce."

"How old was she then?" He was just plucking questions out of the air.

"Late thirties or close to forty, I think."

"How did you get to know her?"

"My husband served as the Ciano's private pilot for a time. I think she liked Franco a little too much."

"You mean they had an affair?"

"Maybe, but I doubt it. It was rumored that she was trying to get even with Count Ciano for having so many other women. There was even a funny story making the rounds that she went to Il Duce to ask him if she should leave Ciano for his infidelities. But Mussolini was busy making love to one of *his* women on a couch in his office!"

Josh scribbled more. "That's a good story," he chuckled. He looked into her eyes and knew he couldn't ask any more inane questions at this point. He touched her hand. "But the only story that's important to me right now is us."

"Don't, Josh," she replied softly. But she didn't move her hand.

"I'm not very experienced with this sort of thing, you know. But I do know that for two days I've been lost in the most wonderful dream, in the most beautiful pair of eyes I've ever seen."

She squeezed his hand. "You're a dear young man. Can you tell me about the hurt that I sense is deep inside you?"

Why not tell her, at least part of it? "I lost a crew of men when my bomber was shot down, including my best friend." He haltingly told her about Joe Orosco, uncovering the wound again.

She brought his hand to her lips and kissed it as he went on. "It was a treacherous act. An Italian pilot in an American fighter plane. . . ." He didn't, of course, tell her that he knew who the killer was, or his vow.

Her eyes were wide. "What a terrible thing. It makes me feel badly about being an Italian. It also makes me hate Mussolini all the more."

"Good afternoon," Sabatini said, walking up to the table. "How is the interview going?"

"Not bad," Josh murmured. He could pick the damnedest times to interrupt.

Sabatini picked up his camera. "Why don't I take some pictures of you two? You know, something that might work in the article."

"In my bathing suit?" Sella asked.

"Yeah, you never know. Maybe we could use one with a caption saying, 'Noted archaeologist finds an oasis after years in the desert,' something like that."

She smiled. "All right. Where do you want me?"

"Over by the pool. We'll take several—standing, sitting, lying down."

Josh watched him. It was a good ploy, but he saw something else in Sabatini's eyes, something that aroused his instant jealousy.

"It Happened One Night" wasn't exactly a new movie, but it was wartime Cairo and there was no direct mail service from Hollywood. As the lights came on in the theater area of the Egyptian Officers Club, Sella smiled. "I loved it!" she exclaimed. "I haven't seen a good movie in a long time. Claudette Colbert was so much fun!"

"And I suppose you're going to tell me you didn't notice Clark Gable," Josh laughed. "I saw you watching him all ga-ga."

"What is 'ga-ga'?" she asked soberly.

"Wide-eyed, holding your breath."

"Ah! You Americans and your silly slang."

"Don't they have movies in Luxor?"

"I think I've seen maybe five or six in all the time I've been down there."

They went out the front door and walked across the grass to the nearby Anglo-Egyptian Union, where they ordered a drink in the crowded bar. She was wearing the yellow dress, with its rather low bodice, and most of the men stared as they found a small table. A three-piece combo was playing beside a tiny dance floor at the end of the bar. After two quick drinks they danced cheek to cheek to "It's Been a Long, Long Time."

"They should have played this last night," she said softly into his ear.

"I thought you didn't want to talk about it," he replied.

"I guess I can blame my loose tongue on the wine again."

"I don't care what you blame it on as long as you stay this close to me."

Her hand ran up the back of his neck as her body moved even closer to his. She hummed the melody lightly in his ear for a few bars before she suddenly pulled back and said, "You aren't married, are you?"

He shook his head. "Of course not. Why do you ask?"

She chuckled. "Oh, I was thinking about our situation. All of this talk about my being married, all this guilt about Franco and all, and I was, what do you call it, daydreaming about us. You know, if something lasting were to come of this, and, well, suddenly I thought wouldn't that be a fine thing if you have a wife back in America!"

"Nope. Never even been engaged. But I feel like I am now."

She looked into his eyes quizzically. "Why?"

"Because someday I'm going to marry you."

Her eyes clouded. "Don't, darling. I don't even want to talk about the future. I've thought about this until my head ached. There's no logical or moral solution, so I've thrown those words away. Let's take what we can from the moment and when it ends we'll go back to our real worlds."

"But you just mentioned a *lasting* love."

She shook her head. "You don't understand Italian women. We don't always mean what we say. And we don't always say exactly what we mean."

Before he could make any kind of an intelligent reply she had moved firmly against his body and had begun nuzzling his ear. Moments later, she whispered, "I like the feel of your excited manhood. It arouses me, darling."

"Then let's go back to the villa," he replied, running his hand down over her shapely buttocks.

"Yes, but kiss me first."

Sabatini arrived back at the villa at shortly after two. No hashish and no Victoria tonight, just booze. He couldn't get Sella out of his mind, and no dark Egyptian girl, no matter how pretty or how satin-skinned she was, would do. No, he couldn't get Teresa—or was it Sella— out of his head. He had never been so fucked up in his entire life!

He had run into Captain Hooker and they'd gone back to catch Nefertiti's late act at the Royal Opus, but he'd declined when the British officer wanted to go light up a narghile. No dice, no fucking dice. One thing was driving at him, driving him out of his fucking mind, and that was this blonde Italian broad.

He went to the liquor cabinet and pulled out a bottle of Scotch. Opening it and taking a swig that ran down over his chin, he walked to the edge of the pool and stared out through the glass doors at the sky. Lotsa bright stars tonight, or this morning, or whenever the fuck it was. And the moon was hanging in there . . . maybe three-quarters or more . . . showering silver light over this goddamned worthless city. . . .

He lit a Lucky Strike and blew out a cloud of smoke.

No, that wasn't true—he liked Cairo. It was the kind of a place that a Rudy Lotions might set up. Yeah, set up the whole underworld. Hire a bunch of Abduls who knew how the place ticked, inside and out, and package the whole thing from dope and booze to gambling and broads. Yeah, and he'd get some of the action from the night clubs, like Tom Fauntleroy's Royal Opus, maybe have a finger in all the entertainment. Line up the Peter Lorres and keep them under control. Yeah, it could be done. Get the right top Abdul to be his Arab *consiglière*.

Peter Lorre! Or whatever the fuck his real name was. The hit on Sella was set up for the day after, sometime. He was to get Josh out of the way by taking him to RAF headquarters to see Macgruder, or something like that.

He took another wet swig of the Scotch.

But Sella wasn't really an Italian stranger.

No, she was Teresa, and by God, she was his!

He looked toward the bedrooms. He'd go in there right now, spread her goddamned legs and claim his conjugal rights! He ground out the cigarette, took one more swig from the bottle, and strode toward the room. Outside her door he paused momentarily, then turned the knob. It was open. Moving through the dim light to the bed, he felt a wild exhilaration. She was going to be his again!

But she wasn't there—the goddamned bed was empty!

He knew they were back; Josh's cap was on the table.

He stared at the empty bed.

They were over in his bedroom—fucking!

He swung around and lurched from the room and down the hall to Josh's room. By God, he'd set this fucking deal straight! He'd charge right in there and—no, what the hell was he doing? Was this Rudy Lotions, the guy who was always in charge? Was this Rudy Lotions about to lose his fucking head and do something crazy he'd never be able to walk away from?

Christ, she was going to disappear in a day and a half.

He couldn't get in a brawl and—

It would be rape. And when she came up missing, the war wouldn't be big enough to get him off the hook.

Slowly he took a long, final drink from the bottle, dropped it to the floor, and headed for his own bedroom.

CHAPTER 20

✣

Franco decided once and for all that he was not cut out to be a sailor. He could bounce all over the sky in the roughest of air, but the tiny rocking and swaying of the boat made him feel uncomfortable. He had grown used to the shudder of the propeller shaft as it danced to the dervish act of the ancient blades, and the aged engine's groaning discourse barely entered his mind. But he still couldn't wait to get off the damned thing. He had barely slept all night in the crowded berth, and although he'd tried to pay attention to Ismael Gardono's running commentary on the scenery as they proceeded up the Nile, the morning had dragged seemingly interminably.

Furthermore, the fumes and the odor of the unwashed crew members in such a confined area did nothing for his appetite, not that there was anything interesting to eat. Ismael Gardono had gotten him two bottles of Scotch whisky in Cairo, and that had helped. He had put away half a bottle during the night. Now he finished a warm glass of the Sardinian wine Sergeant Diego had stowed in the airplane. He checked the valise. Along with the other bottle of Scotch, it held her gift, an emerald brooch he'd found in a Palermo shop a year earlier. It would bring out the color of her beautiful eyes.

Now, as the *sandal* glided up to an anchorage on the west bank, he looked toward the pink Theban hills and felt a burst of anticipation.

That's where she was, just a few miles away!

Across the river to the east, Luxor's corniche and pastel buildings beckoned in the bright sunlight. He would dearly like to go into the city and rent a hotel room just to bathe, but he had no American identification. It was one thing to run around bustling Cairo in an American major's uniform, but the city that was once known as Thebes was much smaller, and someone might get curious.

After asking around Gardono finally found an old Ford lorry to rent and they set off for the Valley of the Kings. Their ruse was to go to King Tut's tomb and pretend to be tourists. From there, Gardono would ask questions.

Franco could hardly contain himself.

The workman's name was Hajj. He was a very black Nubian and he had been employed on the Cunningham dig for two years. Today he had a finger with a badly infected nail and was not working. He spoke some English.

"Tell the *effendi* what you told me," Ismael Gardono said.

He spoke haltingly, staring into Franco's eyes. "Doctor Adamo no here."

Franco couldn't believe those few words. "Where is she?" he asked, recovering his composure.

"Doctor go Cairo in bird."

"When?"

"Two days gone."

"Do you know why?"

The Nubian turned to Gardono with a shrug.

"The *effendi* wants to know why she went to Cairo," Gardono said in Nubian.

Hajj shrugged, replying, "I don't know. American come, she go." Ciano's agent translated.

Franco blinked. "What American?"

The Nubian shrugged, explained that the visitor was a soldier who came from Cairo. But he hadn't seen him close, nor did he know anything else about him. He had overheard someone say she would be back here in a week.

Franco blew out a deep breath. He couldn't believe it. He was all ready to sweep his beloved Sella up in his arms and she was gone off to—what American in a uniform would come here and take her away to Cairo? Suddenly the memory of an identification tag sitting on his desk at Elmas flashed through his memory. No, couldn't be—too far-fetched. "Ask Hajj if this American had silver wings on his chest, a badge over his left pocket that flashed in the sun."

Gardono translated and the Nubian nodded.

Franco stared at him in disbelief. "Ask him if this American had two shiny silver bars on his right collar," he said quietly, knowing what the answer would be.

Hajj screwed up his face and closed his eyes, then nodded his head. "Yes," he said. "They shine like sun."

No, it couldn't be this Rawlins. Too coincidental. No, something completely unrelated had come up. Had to be. Besides, Rawlins was only a specter, a pilot who had tried to steal the P-38. Still, the bastard had left his goddamned identification tag like a gauntlet thrown on the ground! That was no coincidence. And what U.S. Army captain wearing pilot's wings would have reason to come see his Sella and then whisk her away?

"What are you thinking, Colonel?" Gardono asked in Italian.

"It's too improbable to explain." He couldn't go to Dr. Cunningham or anyone else in his party. No matter how he cut it, he was an enemy officer. Regardless of his relationship, the Brits would blow the whistle on him as certainly as the sun came up in the east. Cairo—God, how could he find her in Cairo?

"I'll ask some more, Colonel," Gardono said.

"No, that might be bad. The only ones who would know anything would be the British. No, I'll leave her a letter and we'll start on back to Cairo. Will this man give her the letter for sure?"

Gardono spoke rapidly to Hajj for a moment, then replied, "Yes, I believe he's dependable. And I'll pay him well."

"Very well. Let me go to the truck to write it."

It wasn't what he wanted to say. How could one jam years of thoughts and feeling of love and longing into a note? But it would have to do, because he had to get on back to Cairo as soon as possible.

My dearest Sella,

I managed to fly to Cairo disguised as an American pilot. I had to see you for two big reasons. One: I love you with every iota of my life, and I had to see you, hold you. Two: I wanted to warn you that your life may be in danger. Remember the Friends who killed my father? For some crazy reason they have made a threat against us as well. Don't be alarmed, but be careful of any contacts by Sicilians or any other Italians. I have a responsibility to honor, so I must get back to Italy. But the war will be over for us soon, my darling, and we'll be reunited forever. I love you dearly forever,

Franco.

He folded the letter, withdrew a rubber band from the valise, and wrapped it around the gift box. Moments later he handed it to Gardono. "Tell the man, Hajj, that if Doctor Adamo gets this, I'll reward him later."

Yes, it would have to do.

Sabatini arose at noon and showered for over fifteen minutes before diving into the pool and swimming several laps. When he came out and finished drying himself with a huge terry cloth towel, he drank two cups of the strong black coffee that Abdul served him. Then he went back to the shower, where he stood in cold water for another twenty minutes. Next he dressed in the seersucker suit that Abdul had cleaned and pressed. An off-white necktie that closely matched his panama hat set it off. Two more cups of back coffee, a six-egg breakfast, and he was ready to face the world.

And take the worst step in his professional life.

He was about to break trust with one of the most powerful men in his world.

But he couldn't help it, the decision had been reached during his first shower, and confirmed during the second.

Abdul brought him a telephone on a long cord, and after trying for several minutes he reached the British Special Air Service sergeant-major referred to as Bogart.

"This is Greenstreet," Sabatini said. "I must get in touch with Mr. Lorre."

"That may be difficult," the sergeant-major replied.

"It's vital. A change in plan."

"I'll do my best. He'll probably want some kind of remuneration. Where should he meet you?"

"The same place. I'll be there at three."

"Very well. Cheerio."

*   *   *

Sabatini looked at his watch: 3:35. What if Lorre had been out of reach? He sipped from his glass of Cypress sherry in the garden of the Haramlik Hotel of the Qasabah, the same formula as when he met Lorre the first time.

Maybe Lorre was out of the city. Indisposed. Totally out of reach.

That would get him off the hook and the plan could be carried out as scheduled.

No, he couldn't let it go that way.

No matter what, the chances of him ever becoming the rackets czar of Cairo were about to be wiped out. Or maybe anywhere—

"Mr. Greenstreet?"

He looked up from his drink to see the thin retired gunner in the shabby white linen suit "Yes, Mr. Lorre. Nice to see you again. Will you have a drink with me?"

The man called Lorre took a chair and ordered a local beer from the waiter in the red fez. They talked about the weather until the beer was delivered, then Sabatini got to the point. "There has been a change of plans. I want to cancel our arrangement on the Italian woman."

The Britisher scowled. "Ummm, that may be a bit difficult at this late stage."

"It must be done."

"The people I've made the arrangement with are not easy to reach."

Sabatini looked coolly into the man's watery eyes. "It must be done at all costs. You can even keep the fifty percent of the agreed fee that I paid you."

Lorre sipped his beer, still frowning. "I'll do my bloody damnedest."

"Is it set for tomorrow as originally planned?"

"Yes, but I don't ask them for details."

Sabatini didn't even scowl; his cold black eyes did it. "It's all off. If they come, they'll have to fight me."

The retired sergeant shrugged. "I'll do the best I bloody can."

Sabatini tossed a bill on the table as he got to his feet. "Thank you," he said coolly as he turned to go. He knew he couldn't count on Lorre reaching his hit people. And he had to see Macgruder.

Josh looked at Sabatini in shock. "What do you mean she has to go back first thing in the morning? What the hell's the hurry?"

"Your airplane, that YB-something, has arrived at Constantine and the general wants you back immediately. Macgruder passed the word to me. We gotta pull up these fancy stakes and turn back into soldiers, sonny."

Josh frowned. It was the first time Sabatini had called him that since Sicily. "Is something going on I don't know about?"

"No, we just gotta get back to the war."

"A couple more days here won't hurt."

Sabatini pushed a magazine back into the .45 pistol he had been cleaning. They were in his bedroom. "They will if a general who has been ready to lock you up and throw away the key gets pissed off again."

Josh blew out a deep breath. "Yeah, I suppose you're right."

"It'll give you one more night with your lovebird."

"It's that noticeable, huh?"

"Like a sick calf."

Josh shook his head. "What am I going to do, Sabatini? This bullshit I'm giving her is eating my guts out."

"You want my advice, kid? Let it ride. Wartime quickie romance. Happens all the time. You'll get over it."

"But I'm lying to her."

"She's been lied to before, I'm sure."

"That's not the point. This whole thing is wrong. I'm taking her for a fucking ride so I can kill her goddamned husband—that's what it boils down to."

The New Yorker's eyes hardened. "Get off the shit, Rawlins. Adamo killed your whole crew, including your best friend, Orosco. You've been almost nuts about getting him, and now you're talking like a fucking boy scout. Screw the broad blind tonight, kiss her goodbye, and get on with it. We've got the photos."

Josh's expression hardened. "You know, Sabatini, you're a natural born asshole."

"So? Okay, look at it another way: you knock off her old man and then come back after the war and sweep up the widow. You can't lose."

"And that idea makes me feel like a total shit also. I've got to tell her."

"No way. God only knows who she's tapped into. You could blow the whole thing."

Josh shook his head and blew out a deep breath. "What's the plan on getting her back?"

"The RAF will fly her up to Luxor. Takeoff is at 0530."

"Can I ride up with her?"

"No, our flight to Constantine is laid on for 1200 hours. A gooney bird is coming down to get us."

Josh shook his head again and walked away.

Josh simply couldn't sleep. He finally swung his legs over the side of the bed and stared out the glass door to the courtyard. It was still, bathed in silvery moonlight. And it offered no solutions to his problem. He got to his feet and walked, naked, to where he could look out. He couldn't see them, but he knew the three great Pyramids were only a few miles away. In fact he could somehow *feel* them out there. And they, in all of their historical power, could offer no help. The dilemma was all his.

He turned to her form, ghostly gray on the other side of the bed. Her breathing was regular, gentle, trusting—he thought. She had fallen asleep in his arms, spent from their lovemaking, whispering that she loved him.

But it was all make-believe.

Tomorrow she would return to her quest in the Valley, and he would go back to the great flying engines of war. She would contribute to the knowledge of mankind, he would assist God in His greatest game. How strange—here, one reached back for thousands of years to an incredible culture, yet in today's far advanced, technologically superior culture, the goddamned common denominator hadn't changed: war. Nearly all of the Egyptian kings had conducted war, some of them many wars.

The common denominator that defied time.

Would it ever end?

Could he go back to Gen. Barney Buell, put that big airplane in the air, shoot down a killer, go on through whatever bombing and killing it would take to end this great struggle, and then spend the rest of his life in a peaceful world? Or would another modern pharaoh, or maybe more than one, begin another feast of death? Didn't they always bury a king's weapons with him, and tell stories on the walls of his tomb about his great wartime exploits and conquests?

No, it wouldn't end, not as long as men coveted what they did not own or control. It was that simple.

He remembered a passage from Shakespeare's *Antony and Cleopatra*:

O, wither'd is the garland of the war.
The soldier's pole is fall'n: young boys and girls

Are level now with men; the odds is gone,
And there is nothing left remarkable
Beneath the visiting moon.

But it wasn't really war that was bothering him, it was the duplicity of his actions. For the first time in his life he was truly in love, and it was all based on a sham.

She stirred and he knew her eyes were open in the inky shadow of the pillow.

"What are you doing?" she asked drowsily.

"Thinking."

"About what?"

"About deceit."

After a moment she asked, "Whose, mine?"

"No." He sat on the edge of the bed and turned on the electric lamp. He had thought about this from every angle and it had to be done. "Sella, there's something I must tell you."

She sat up, bunching a pillow behind her back. Her eyes looked wide, cautious. "Is this something that will hurt us?"

"Yes. I've lied to you."

She put her hand to his mouth. "Don't. I know you aren't a writer. I sensed it in the beginning down in the Valley. You came to me for some other reason, probably military intelligence, and I don't care. You have been a wonderful interlude. You are something very special to me, Josh Rawlins, and I don't want any sad confessions to spoil it. I don't want your truth."

"But—"

Her hand stilled his lips again. "No, Josh. I won't listen. I'm going back to my work while the two men I love—assuming Franco is still alive—violate themselves in this atrocity called war. I won't let anything spoil my memories." She pulled his head down and softly kissed his mouth. "And now, hold me, my darling, one more time before the real world returns."

Wearing the American major's flight suit, Franco walked confidently into RAF base operations to file his departure flight plan. He was filled with mixed satisfaction; he'd missed seeing his beloved Sella, but he knew she was well, where she was working, and he'd gotten a message to her. As far as the threat to her life was concerned, it could be hollow. At least she could be on the lookout.

He simply had to get back. He had promised General Manzella an all-out effort with the Lightning in the coming days of the invasion and that was a commitment. Also, he felt a certain responsibility to Edda Ciano for helping him. The war was a wretched, tired yoke on his shoulders, but he had to see it through. He'd taken an oath a long time ago.

He put down Chateaudun du Rhumel as his destination on the flight plan. Good as any. He would, of course, head straight for Sardinia and use his special call sign when he approached Italian airspace to alert the gunners that he was a friend in wolf's clothing—

"Captain Rawlins? He's right over there, Leftenant," an RAF sergeant at the counter said crisply to an American pilot in a flight suit.

It took a second to sink in. *Rawlins?* He turned. The lieutenant was striding toward a young blond American captain and a bulky American major—an Italian-looking type. But he locked on the captain. Could it be—

"I'm Josh Rawlins," the captain said. "You here to take us back home to Constantine?"

"Yeah, you ready?"

"Let's do it."

Franco stared. It was him! It was that fucking Rawlins! He watched as Rawlins and the major picked up their bags and followed the lieutenant toward the door. He ought to go after them, spin the bastard around, and get it over with right here and now! But then it would be curtains for him. He would be slapped in irons and shot for posing as an American officer.

Clenching his fists helplessly, he watched the back of the blond head disappear through the door. Then he got the idea! Shoot the bastard down! His pulse raced. Take it easy, make a plan. Yeah.

He went back to the counter and spoke to the same sergeant, "Hey, I overheard you say something about a Captain Rawlins, Sergeant. I think I know him up in Algeria. Is that *Joshua* Rawlins?"

"Yes, it is, Major. That C-47 pilot came in to pick him and Major Sabatini up."

"Where are they going?"

"Same place as you, Chateaudun."

Franco grinned. "Good, I'll see him there—uh, what's the fin number of that C-47? I might say hello up there."

"Six-four-nine-oh."

"Thanks. Cheerio." As he headed for the door, his grin faded: the bastard would never get to Chateaudun!

The number on the tail was 6490.

Franco nodded in grim satisfaction. It hadn't been difficult to pick up the twin-engined transport in the air. Its departure course was the same as his. The C-47 had lumbered through three thousand in its climb by the time he brought the P-38 down in a sweeping arc across its nose. He could almost see the startled expression on the pilot's face and guess what was going through his mind: What the hell is that asshole fighter pilot doing? He came around again, this time doing a big barrel roll around the American aircraft. At the completion of the maneuver he throttled back and pulled up beside the C-47, close enough to nearly overlap its left wing. He could see the pilot staring out at him from the pilot's compartment, and he could make out faces at the fuselage windows. He wondered which one was Josh Rawlins and what could be going through his mind.

Josh Rawlins' thoughts were clear. He knew exactly what P-38 was playing games with them. He would never forget that number, ES-41. And there wasn't a doubt in the world about who was flying it. How had that bastard found them in the middle of this vast, hot Egyptian sky?

"What the hell's that asshole doing?" Sabatini shouted from the next window.

"Don't you know?" Josh hollered back.

"That couldn't be—no, tell me I've been drinking too much!"

"None other."

"What's the son of a bitch doing *here*?"

"Right now he's sending us a message. He's telling us he can do anything he fucking well pleases with us."

"Do you think he really knows we're on this bucket?"

"Absolutely. He must have been right there in Operations."

"You think he's gonna shoot us down?"

"Who knows?"

Yeah, he must have been right there in Ops, Josh thought. But what was he doing in Cairo? Had the bastard been following him? No, too improbable. If he had known about him and Sella, he would have come in shooting.

Okay—why?

He stared at the face in the cockpit. It was just like that day when Adamo pulled up on the *Bitch*. Seemed like eons ago. What was he doing? Pointing a finger at him, like a little kid playing cowboy and shooting an Indian with his finger. Toying with him.

Now he knew: Adamo was letting him know there would be another time and place. The bastard had a sense of honor!

Franco hadn't yet made his decision when he pulled up on the gooney's wing. But in seconds he was telling himself, not here, not now. Not this way.

This son of a bitch Rawlins, whoever he was, was some kind of a knight. He'd had the balls to leave his gauntlet at Elmas. In all of this goddamned fucking idiocy of a war, this man had come to him like a knight of old, dressed in armor and wielding a lance. Or maybe a great Zulu warrior, sent out by his regiment to do battle with the best warrior from the enemy regiment, a bloodless solution, except for the warriors. Too bad he and Rawlins couldn't end this grotesque conflict that way. Or maybe they could. Maybe Rawlins was some kind of an omen for him, a sign that there was sanity somewhere.

Somewhere other than where Sella was.

What the fuck had this Rawlins been doing with Sella?

And what if Sella were on board this lumbering goose? God, he hadn't thought of that! No, he'd have seen her in Operations. But they might have boarded her secretly! God, what if she was actually in there, one of those faces glued to a window?

They could be taking her somewhere to get information from her. Maybe that was why they'd taken her from the Valley of the Kings.

No, they didn't have her on that plane!

Still—

He pulled in closer, but couldn't make out any features on the faces.

Okay, Rawlins, you noble bastard, another time, another place.

He pulled away a trifle to get space and then rolled the Lightning right over the transport, fired a stream of tracers across the C-47's nose, and headed for Sardinia.

CHAPTER 21

✜

Barney Buell had done as Josh requested and pulled the Eighth Air Force copilot from the crew of the YB-40. The others had gone back to England on the next plane. The copilot was a slender, freckle-faced country boy from Lodi, Ohio. His name was Jim Summerton and he had been quite a basketball star in high school a couple of years earlier. He had flown two missions on a regular Flying Fort before being detached to the YB-40, and had exactly one combat mission under his belt in this airplane. Not too much experience—although just one mission of the right kind could make a newcomer a veteran. Josh didn't want to judge him too hastily.

Jim Summerton, who had just made first lieutenant, had an infectious smile and Josh liked him at once. He briefed the Ohioan about their mission right after they met, leaving out the more intimate details of his vendetta. "Since you're the old hand with this bird, meaning you have *some* time in it, you're the expert, Jim. I want you to dredge up anything and everything you've ever heard about it, its idiosyncrasies, weaknesses, strengths, and so on. We'll have a new crew, so they'll need every single tidbit of information you can provide."

Jim Summerton shrugged and grinned. "Well, sir, I can tell you right off, with all those extra guns and ammo she's as heavy coming back as a normal B-17 is going out. Which makes her a hell of a poor escort. It's fine going to the target because all of the other birds are loaded down with bombs, but she'll automatically become a straggler on the way home."

Josh nodded his head. "I hadn't thought of that."

"You don't ever want to make much of a run for it."

"I don't want to run, I want to hit the bastard!"

"You got some good mechanics?"

"Tops, both the crew chief and the flight engineer."

Josh turned to the other two officers sitting in the Raghead Ritz. "As you can tell by these remarks, gentlemen, you know as much as I do about this bird. We'll all learn how to use it together."

"We ever going to bomb anything, Captain?" Second Lieutenant Freddy Smith asked. A round-faced former bartender from Maine, he had been pulled from the 99th Group. He was a brand new replacement from the States. Group personnel officers had a way of filling quotas dealt out by higher headquarters with the unwanted or untrained.

"I don't know," Josh replied. "I think our bomb bay will be filled mostly with fifty caliber ammo most of the time. Are you any good on the fifty?"

"It's the new Bendix chin turret, Captain. I've never fired it."

"Oh, yeah, I forgot."

"How about you, Owen, you any kind of a marksman?" Clyde Owen was from Fort Pierre, a cattle town across the Missouri from the capital of South Dakota. He was a first lieutenant who had been plucked from the 301st Group.

"Yeah, Cap'n, I've shot a few thousand pheasants in my time. I oughta be able to handle a machine gun."

Josh's eyebrows shot up. "You don't know how?"

"I've been an instructor ever since I graduated from navigation school. I just got to Africa four days ago."

Shit! No experience. Actually, the other officers of his new crew had a combined three missions under their belt. Oh, well, at least his navigator should be pretty good—instructor and all.

"Okay," Josh said. "We're all going to sleep with copies of the operating manual. We haven't got much time so I expect you officers to know everything there is to know about this bird in a couple of days. I'll conduct a little quiz day after tomorrow." He gave each of them a level look. "And I don't think I have to tell you that I won't put up with any ignorance. In fact, gentlemen, I won't put up with any shit at all."

*   *   *

Tech Sgt. David M. Gregg had the enlisted men of the crew lined up and standing at ease in the shade of the 97th Group maintenance tent when Josh walked up. Tech Sgt. Ambrose Tarbell's ground crew stood in a group nearby. Tarbell got a bit flowery as he said, "Boys, there's only one B-17 aircraft commander in this whole goddamned group with the Distinguished Service Cross. They don't hand that medal out for just driving an airplane. No siree. So each of us oughta be just plain proud to serve for a captain like the one you see before you. This here is Captain Josh Rawlins."

Josh nodded as he looked them over, meeting a couple of direct stares. After a few moments he said, "You've been assigned to a very important mission, gentlemen. Several of you have probably heard about the renegade Italian pilot who's flying a P-38 and shooting our planes down." He paused, eyeing them, and then added flatly, "Were gonna get the bastard." Then he told them a little bit about the YB-40, finishing with, "Since a bomber crew must be one of the most intimate of teams, I'll speak with each one of you crew members in the next couple of days. The same goes for you guys on the ground crew. I want to meet all of you because you're the ones who'll keep this big bird in the air. And I want maximum flying time out of it."

That was it. They were his new men. They would win or lose with him; some might even die with him. He gave them one more glance. This was one of the remarkable things about command in a war. In one broad brushstroke a man suddenly acquired a whole new batch of lives, of young men whose destiny he would control to some degree for at last a short while, some of whom were still boys rapidly becoming men, who would look to him for leadership of varying degrees. Some would be dependent, others—just a few—pure individualists, most of them far closer to the senior sergeants. But an air crew on a bomber was normally closely knit. This crew might not have time for that.

He looked up to see Col. Gideon Pillow storming toward him with Maj. Pat Cleburne striding along a couple of paces behind. God, he'd forgotten all about Pillow having such a hard-on for him. He hadn't even seen the bastard in weeks.

"What the hell's this all about Rawlins?" the group commander snapped. "And just where in Hell have you been lately?"

"I've been on special duty with General Buell, sir," Josh replied quietly.

A dark scowl clouded Pillow's handsome features. "If I recall, I put you in arrest the last time I saw you."

"The general countermanded that order," Pat Cleburne said softly. "Don't you think we ought to discuss this away from the men, sir?"

The colonel glanced at the group of enlisted men and nodded his head. "Yes, of course. Follow me, Rawlins!"

Pillow led them about twenty-five yards away from the tent before turning on Josh. "Now, what the hell's this all about, Captain?"

Josh wanted to shrug and tell him to go ask the fucking general, but that wouldn't solve anything—and the YB-40 operation had been attached to the 97th Bomb Group for logistical and administrative support. He explained briefly.

When Pillow looked at Pat Cleburne with a puzzled look, the squadron commander replied, "You must have missed the orders, sir. Possibly because the officers and men are all attached to my squadron. It's no big problem—just one airplane and its men."

The colonel's eyes narrowed. "Sounds like some more of your prima donna bullshit to me, Rawlins. Let me give you fair warning: you step out of line just one inch, and that goes for this bunch of losers you've got for a crew, and I'll have your ass. You got that, Captain?"

Josh controlled himself. In fact, he came to attention and brought his hand up in a salute. "Yes, sir!"

As the two field grade officers departed, Pat Cleburne turned and tossed him a shrug.

Josh dismissed the problem with an under-his-breath "Asshole," and turned back to the maintenance tent. The crew list Tech Sgt. Gregg had given him had five names on it:

> Radio Operator: Jack O'Brien
> Left Waist Gunner: Bill Cochise
> Right Waist Gunner: Bobby Cochise
> Tail Gunner: Alfred Price
> Belly Gunner: Tommy Keith

Price and Keith were practically rubber-stamped. Both were nineteen, both had just six missions under their belts, both were blond football players from Alabama, and both had been in trouble for fighting. One still had his buck sergeant's stripes, the other, Keith, having just been busted, was slick-sleeved. Although they were from different towns and different squadrons they were close friends. When they had heard

about the YB-40 they had agreed to volunteer. He talked to them together, giving them the stock "let's direct your fight toward the enemy,
not your buddies" routine. He ended the short interview with, "Gregg tells
me you can both shoot a fifty, which is all that counts with me."

Next he spoke to Jack O'Brien, an Irish kid of twenty from Boston
who had just gotten out of the stockade for going AWOL. He was the
radio operator who would man one of the YB-40's top ball turrets. Josh
went directly to the problem. "Why'd you go AWOL, O'Brien?"

A slight scowl touched the private's Irish features. "A girl, sor. The
prettiest little French girl in Constantine. I love her more than me own
mother, and she was sick. I just had to go see her, and I stayed five
days to take care of her. Missed two missions, I did. And they threw
the fucking book at me—excusin' the captain's pardon, sor."

Josh pursed his lips. "Supposing she gets sick again, and we've got
a mission, will you go over the hill again?"

O'Brien scowled again. "No, sor. I want to marry her and I need
the money my sergeant's stripes will bring in. You can count on me."

Josh stroked his chin, trying to read the radio operator's blue eyes
and finding that he believed him. "Okay," he said after a moment. "I'm
going to take a chance on you, O'Brien. Go get some corporal's stripes
and sew them on. I can't have a goddamned private for a radio
operator."

"Yes, sor!" O'Brien whipped his hand up in salute.

As he turned to go, Josh said, "Oh, and O'Brien, the bastard we're
trying to get up there is from Boston. I may need for you to interpret."

"Yes, *sor!*" the radio operator replied with a big grin.

The last two crew members were the brothers Cochise, buck sergeants Billy and Bobby. Twins, they were from Whiteriver, on the Fort
Apache reservation in Arizona. They were twenty years of age, short
and stocky with black eyes and hair and the stoicism of the Apache
in their calm expressions. "I hear you two can hit a buffalo in the eye
with a fifty caliber at five hundred yards," Josh said. "How come they
let you out of your last squadron?"

Billy spoke quietly, "White Eye, Indian-hating major from Montana
said it was plenty okay after I showed him the doll with the big needles
in it."

Josh's eyes widened. "The what?"

It was Bobby's turn to speak. At the position of attention like his
brother, he said softly, "We made a voodoo doll of the major."

Josh blew out a breath. He had read a little bit about the Apaches. "But Apaches don't have voodoo, do they?"

A bare hint of a smile touched the corners of their mouths. "The major doesn't know that."

Josh shook his head and also found a smile. "You going to make a doll of me?"

Billy answered, "No, you're too smart, Captain. Besides, Gregg told us you're okay, like Child of the Water."

"Child of the Water?"

"Yeah," Bobby replied. "He's sorta the old-fashioned Jesus."

"Me—Jesus?"

"Uh huh," Billy said, "Gregg said this was the way it was."

Josh frowned incredulously. "Sergeant Gregg put you up to all of this?"

"Only the voodoo doll."

"And the Jesus part?"

The touch of a smile returned to both their faces. Bobby said, "Our idea, Great Chief."

Josh shook his head again and waved them away.

Child of the Water?

The ground orientation lasted three days. Also in that time everyone took extensive practice on the range, as Josh had requested. Buell had gone along, and several dozen blow-ups of a P-38 were available to be tacked up at the sandbagged pits to be ripped apart by .50 slugs. Even Josh took his turn on the air-cooled machine gun. At shortly after nine on the morning of the second day Ambrose Tarbell brought a staff sergeant to where Josh was rehearsing procedures in the cockpit of the modified bomber.

His name was Elmer Zarney and he was supposed to be the best portrait artist in the theater.

Josh climbed out of the left seat, where he had been getting pointers from Lt. Jim Summerton, and shook hands with Zarney. Picking up the briefcase where he kept the pictures, he pulled out the black-and-white eight-by-ten-inch prints of Sella in the red bathing suit. There were six of them that would provide a good variety of her in different positions. Two were in repose and two were good close-ups with sharp detail. It moved him to just look at Sella's picture, but he shook it off. "I need a big portrait of this lady painted on each side of our airplane," he said. "Not the usual tiny nose art. I want this to run from below the cockpit windows back almost to the waist turret. And I want the name S-E-L-L-A to be readable from three hundred years away."

Sergeant Zarney whistled as he looked at the prints. "Quite a gal!"

That was an understatement. "Yeah, do you think you can do her justice?"

"Don't see why not. How big a rush you in, Captain?"

"Can you do it in two days?"

"Both sides? No, more like four."

"How about splitting the difference? I'm after a guy who's killing our men every day."

"You got it, Captain."

"Are you as good as Tarbell says you are, Sergeant?"

Elmer Zarney grinned. "He drinks too much. Let's just say the lady on your airplane here will look like the one in the photos. Okay?"

Josh shook his hand again. "Okay!"

The unveiling was on July 2nd.

Not only was Staff Sgt. Elmer Zarney as good as Tarbell had said, he was better. There, on the side of the YB-40, wearing a bright red bathing suit, Sella Adamo smiled pleasantly back at all who viewed her. The likeness was superb, her figure not only tantalizing enough to draw whistles from the crew members, but appealing enough to create even more longing in Josh.

God, he missed her!

The YB-40, with guns bristling in every direction, was a clean olive drab mixed with camouflage gray in its lower portions. The painting of Sella on each side seemed to pop out, lifelike. Tech Sgt. Ambrose Tarbell had acquired a bottle of local wine somewhere and cracked the bottle so it would break with any kind of impact. He handed it to Josh, who smiled at the little crowd of mechanics and crew members. But just as he was about to go into a short launching routine, a U.S. Army Ford staff car with red license plates that held a single white star skidded to a halt in front of the bomber.

"Doesn't a dignitary of some sort usually do this sort of thing?" Brig. Gen. Barney Buell shouted as he climbed out of the back seat of the sedan. The bulky figure of Sabatini followed him.

Josh turned back to the men and yelled, "Ten*shun!*"

He saluted as General Buell stopped in front of the wing, touched his cap with a swagger stick, and told the men to stand at ease. Surveying Zarney's handiwork with a smile, he said so all the men could hear, "That lady's too goddamned pretty to be flying with. Gal like her oughta be kept in bed day and night!"

The men laughed. Nothing like hearing a real general talk about fucking.

Buell turned to Josh. "Now let me have that damned champagne, Captain."

With a strong swing he smacked the bottle into a strut of the landing gear, breaking it and spraying bubbling wine everywhere. "I christen thee the *Sella!*" he said loudly, then shoved the broken neck of the bottle into his mouth and tipped it back for a big swig. When he finished he wiped off his mouth and handed the bottle to Josh. "To your brave aircraft commander!" he added.

"Hear! Hear!" Sabatini shouted.

Josh took the broken bottle and tipped it back. As the wine ran down his chin, everyone yelled, "Hear! Hear!"

When the noise settled down and the formation broke up, Barney Buell said, "I know you're about to go out on your maiden flight in this bird, Josh. You mind if an old, retreaded flyboy tags along?"

Josh shrugged. "I don't know how she'll handle."

"I know, but you're the best B-17 pilot in the command. What the hell's the difference?"

"I own a piece of this contraption," Sabatini said. "I want to come along too."

Josh shook his head, finding a smile. "Well, I guess you can simulate a five-hundred-pound bomb."

The *Sella* broke ground and climbed out just like any sluggish Flying Fort with a full load of gas and a belly full of bombs. Josh had had the tanks topped off and a double load of ammunition put aboard. No easing into this bird, he had decided—load her up and start simulating combat conditions right from the start. Her gear came up with a comfortable thud as he banked eastward toward the sea and continued a normal climb on his outbound clearance heading. Once he had given the tower the Code Seven of a brigadier general on board there had been no holdup in takeoff.

She felt solid, another good Flying Fort wanting to serve the people who trusted in her. He spoke over the intercom to each crew member individually, asking them questions about their position and their weapons.

General Buell stood behind and between the two pilot seats listening on an extra headset; Sabatini was below, behind the bombardier.

In a short while they approached the coast and picked up a heading of 050 out over the Mediterranean. After another twenty miles Josh spoke into his throat mike, "Pilot to crew. Okay, guys, I want everyone at his gun position. Pick out something, a bird or an imaginary enemy plane, and start shooting at it in sustained bursts. I want to see how this machine reacts to sixteen fifties at once."

A minute later he gave the order to fire and a furious racket rose above the drone of the four Wright Cyclone engines. He noticed a slight shudder in the wheel, but control of the airplane remained about the same. "Cease fire," he said into the mike, and three seconds later, he said, "Fire from all positions."

The result was the same. He turned back to General Buell, pulling aside his headset and shouting, "She's fine, General. You want a little stick time?"

"Yeah!" Barney Buell replied, removing his walk-around headset and handing it to Josh. He grinned. "Mind if I loop her?"

"They say a B-17 will take anything, but I'd just as soon take their word for it."

Barney Buell settled into the pilot's seat and fastened the safety harness. Nodding his head at the copilot, he took the wheel and said, "I've got it."

Actually Josh didn't mind a bit; it gave him an opportunity to wander around and talk to the other crew members. He started in the nose and found Sabatini pushing his thick body into the controls of the Bendix chin turret. "What the hell do you think you're doing?" he asked.

The New Yorker shrugged. "Who knows? These may be a big seller after the war. Just the thing for a heavy-duty hit man. I might as well know how to demonstrate one."

Josh turned and started back to the rear, running directly into the flight engineer. "Everybody's got a goddamned gun to shoot but me," he said to Gregg. "When we get back, I want you to scrounge a fifty caliber and mount it right beside the cockpit on my side. Find a way to put in an ammo bin and rig it so I can fire it from the pilot's seat. Can you do that?"

The little NCO shrugged. "Me and Tarbell oughta be able to work it out, skipper."

"Good." He couldn't shoot Adamo down personally, but it would be nice to contribute to the firepower. In fact, it was a great idea! If he never hit *anything*, it was a way to burn off a lot of steam.

When they landed forty minutes later Josh walked with the general and Sabatini to the staff car. "I plan on making three more orientation flights tomorrow, which should certainly be enough to qualify everyone in the aircraft. I'd like to start missions the following day, sir."

"That's the Fourth of July. The whole command'll be standing down," Buell replied. "But you can get going the next day. There oughta be some pretty heavy Jerry action due to the invasion buildup. I'll notify the 97th Group that you'll be tagging along with its last element on the way to the target. Okay?"

"Yes, sir!"

It won't be long now, Adamo.

Josh didn't like the idea of a stand-down, Fourth of July or not. He had a good new airplane and a green but promising crew. And they needed to be worked. But he also wanted to begin the hunt. Adamo was out there, the killer who had murdered his best friend and countless other American crewmen in treacherous and dishonorable attacks. Was immoral an appropriate term? No, he'd better not get into that area. It didn't matter, the bastard was out there flying that goddamned P-38, and he was going to find him!

And the sooner the better.

He hadn't really wanted to come into Constantine tonight, but the idea of joining his officers when they let a little hair down was sound. With a hot and heavy flying schedule about to start, it might be a while before they could do it again. With the whole command standing down Constantine was jammed. The bar at the Cirta was crammed with officers, all trying to get as much alcohol down as possible. He swirled the native beer around in the tall glass and thought back to Cairo. How lovely Sella had looked in that yellow dress. Yes, yellow was her color, at least in a dress. Red was her color in a bathing suit, that was for damned sure.

He would write to her tonight and tell her about the YB-40.

Wing Comdr. Harry Macgruder had told him he could get a letter down to her at Luxor now and then, as long as it wasn't a frequent thing. He had made that quite clear. He had even said he might be able to get a letter back to him, if she was inclined to write.

If she was inclined to write. God, she'd better!

"Hey, skip! I want you to meet someone!" It was Lt. Freddy Smith, his bombardier.

Josh turned to look into the beautiful dark eyes of Hermelinda Prospero.

"Hello, Josh," she said with a warm smile. "I heard you were back."

"Oh, hi, Linda. How did you hear?"

"I went out with Rudy Sabatini last night."

How could he still have an unsettling feeling over her going out with that man? Friend or not, it wasn't right for Sabatini to be sullying this fine young woman, Joe Orosco's almost widow. He said, "I can see your taste in men hasn't improved."

"Oh, I don't know. Do you want to dance with me?" She smiled at Freddy Smith. "I'm sure your new bombardier won't mind."

He couldn't refuse her, not with any degree of courtesy. He shrugged his shoulders and said, "Lieutenant, it would be my distinct privilege."

The group of local musicians were doing a passable job on "Don't Get Around Much Anymore." They danced quietly on the jammed little floor for a couple of minutes before she said, "You're awfully quiet."

He cleared his throat. "Yeah, well, I guess I was just thinking."

"About what? Sabatini told me you've got a new plane and crew."

"Uh-huh. We're going to start looking for Joe's killer tomorrow."

She didn't reply.

"By the way, anything Sabatini may have told you about that aircraft is classified. We don't want anything to leak out."

She pulled back, her eyes getting even darker in her sudden pique. "Who do you think I am, Josh Rawlins, Tokyo Rose?"

"No, I'm sorry. I shouldn't have said that."

She relaxed, came closer to him. "I've missed you," she said at length.

Why was she saying this? he asked himself. He ought to tell her about Sella, maybe get a woman's side. God knows, he wanted to tell *somebody* about his wonderful love, his beautiful Sella. But he couldn't. How would it sound to tell her he was madly in love with the wife of the man he'd sworn to kill? She'd wonder if he'd been smoking some of that hashish Sabatini mentioned sampling over in Cairo.

"Did you hear what I said?" she asked softly.

"Yes, well, that's nice. I've thought of you too," he replied lamely.

She pulled back and looked up into his eyes. "Is something wrong, Josh?"

"No, why?"

"You sound so strange, as if something is bothering you."

"No, just worried about putting this thing together, I guess. I didn't know it showed." The music ended. "Well, I guess I'd better get you back to Smith. How come you always wind up with bombardiers?"

As they left the little floor, she replied, "I don't always wind up with bombardiers, Josh Rawlins. Sometimes I like to be with pilots, at least pilots who can talk to me like I'm a trustworthy woman and not act like my father or my *confessor*!"

"Sorry. I'm concerned about you."

"Are you going to turn into a hermit down there once the missions start, or will I see you once in a while?"

He just couldn't tell her the truth. "I'll be staying in most of the time, Linda. But when I get Adamo, there'll be the biggest damn party this town ever saw. You can count on that."

She shrugged and managed a bright smile. "And that takes care of that. Okay, flyboy, if you get in the mood, I'll be around. As the Brits say, ta-ta." She turned to Freddy Smith. "I don't think we finished our dance, did we, Lieutenant?"

As they moved away, Josh hunkered down over his beer in the tiny bit of room his other two crew members had reserved for him on the corner of the bar. As he ordered another one Jim Summerton said, "That's some little chick you got there, skipper. If there are any more like her around, keep me in mind."

Josh just shrugged.

He couldn't tell anyone how it really was.

CHAPTER 22

✜

"I wonder what the invaders will do to a magnificent historical structure such as this?" Lieutenant General Manzella said as he gazed down into the delightful courtyard.

Lt. Col. Franco Adamo had just followed him up the monumental staircase to the loggia where they were standing. They were in the remarkable Palazzo dei Normanni, where the rulers of Sicily had lived since the Arabs built it many centuries earlier. Improved by the Normans and later the Spaniards, the palace had held the splendid courts of Roger II and Frederick II. From here they had ruled much of Europe. There would be no way for Allied gunners and bombardiers to miss it, for it stood on the highest ground in old Palermo. Franco shrugged, replying, "It has withstood dozens of invaders and survived in splendid fashion, General. I'm sure the British will want to preserve a structure as illustrious as this that relates to their own history."

"And the crude Americans?"

"I don't think they're as crude as some think."

The deputy chief of staff of fighters led the way back down the staircase. "I love this great building," he said. "My father first brought me here when I was ten years old. He was a naval officer, you know, an admiral. And he always enjoyed coming to Palermo."

Reaching the eastern part of the adjoining church, the Cappella Palatina, the general said, "One should visit this place at different times of the day because the light is always changing." He pointed to the ceiling of the nave. "This is one of the finest examples of Islamic art in the world. It could never be replaced if enemy bombs or artillery fire should hit it."

After a few moments of taking in the beauty of other parts of the church, Franco asked, "Do you think it will be destroyed, General? You talk as if there might be house-to-house fighting."

"No, I believe Palermo will be shielded from such destruction."

"Then you are positive the invasion will hit Sicily?"

"Absolutely."

"I've heard the general staff isn't positive."

"Ha! They aren't positive about which hand to piss with."

"Can you tell me when?"

"Personally, Adamo, I believe it will be within a week—which is, of course, why I'm here now. I want to visit several of our fighter squadrons and motivate our young pilots. The Allies will throw everything at us that flies, and our boys will need strong esprit to meet them."

"What is the approach, sir? I mean is it all-out, suicide, sacrifice anything for Il Duce? Or do we hit and run, live to fight when they some to the mainland?"

"Actually, some of both. Our brave pilots are to acquit themselves well in attacking the invaders, but they are also to use discretion. We can't lose our air force against hopeless odds."

Which translates to token resistance when the chips are down and all the bullshit is over, Franco said to himself. "What about Operation Outlaw?" he asked. "Am I to continue the plan with the P-38?"

"Absolutely. Your mission, Colonel, will be even more vital now in creating confusion and fear from within. I've even considered giving you another pilot to get maximum use out of the aircraft."

Franco shook his head. "Wouldn't work, General. We're already stretching our maintenance to the limit to keep her in the air as much as we do now."

"I guessed that might be the case," Manzella replied. "Very well, just get as many of them as you can. I trust your judgement, Adamo."

"What about our friends in the Luftwaffe, what are they going to do?"

"Same as us. Galland told me they'll fight hard but pull back as necessary. Sicily is expendable to our German friends because they plan on a dogged campaign in Italy itself." The general smiled as he pointed to some extraordinary mosaics in the cupola. "But let's not talk any more about dreary matters. This wonderful mosaic is of Christ, surrounded by angels and the archangels. Of course you recognize the Nativity there to the right of the apse, and on the upper part of that wall, Joseph's Dream and the Flight into Egypt."

Flight into Egypt. Franco immediately thought of Sella, wondered if she had returned to the Valley of the Kings, and if she had gotten his note. Mussolini's Arab agent, Ismael Gardono, had promised to follow up, but that could mean nothing.

Would he ever see her again?

He barely heard what the general was saying as they walked out of the church. It didn't matter anyway, very little did.

As soon as the general departed for the airfield, Franco went to see his mother's uncle. Giuseppe Lorda was seventy-nine years old and lived in an old house close to the Piazza Scaffa. He had once been active in the Friends, but when Mussolini curtailed their activities several years earlier he had ceased to take part. Now he was confined to a wheelchair.

With a generous mane of white hair and alert dark eyes under heavy black eyebrows, Giuseppe Lorda was still a handsome man. He greeted Franco warmly from his place in the shade of the small courtyard the old house provided. "Ah, Franco, I don't believe all of the wonderful things I've heard about you—a colonel, no less. And such a hero! Your mother would have been so proud!"

Giuseppe Lorda's housekeeper, an attractive woman of about forty, brought a bottle of wine, opened it, and served them. The host praised the wine extensively, then made a toast to Franco's mother. "She was such a beautiful girl," he said. "I was several years older, but I think I loved her from the time she was twelve years old."

Franco let him talk on, reminiscing, carrying the conversation with facts and memories from his world. When at last the old man asked him why he was in Palermo, he replied, "I had to meet an important general here today, Uncle. And I need some information."

Lorda spread his palms. "Anything, my son."

Franco had to play it carefully, even with his great-uncle. This was still Sicily. "I've been told that Il Duce has not stopped the Friends from their traditional business. Is that correct?"

The old man pursed his lips. "Yes, to some extent. More so, now that the war has come to the island and they expect the Americans to arrive."

"Who is the most important don in this area now, my uncle?" He knew who the bastard was, but he didn't want to sound knowledgeable and raise any kind of suspicion in his great uncle's mind.

Giuseppe Lorda pursed his lips again. "One doesn't mention such names in public, my son. It's the way."

"I know, but I'm thinking ahead to a time when the guns are silent. And I haven't the time for the old ways."

"There are several on the island."

"I could go to Count Ciano and find out, I suppose."

The old man looked at him with widened eyes. "You know Ciano?"

"Yes, I was his private pilot for a time."

"Hmmm, then I suppose . . . well, you *are* a colonel."

Franco waited patiently. C'mon, old man, spit it out!

"Don Nizzi Gaetano Calgogeri is an honorable man with many friends."

"Yes, I've heard the name."

"You won't get me in any trouble with the don, will you?"

"No, Uncle. Where does he reside, here in Palermo?"

"No, in an old Norman castle out by the village of Mistano. About four or five kilometers outside of the city. I believe it's called Castello Carmelo."

"Thank you, Uncle. Now tell me, where do you find such good wine during a war?"

One hour and forty minutes later Franco drove the old rented Fiat into the village of Mistano. Stopping where two boys of about ten were playing with a large tan mongrel, he asked, "Can you please tell me where I might find Castello Carmelo?"

They looked at each other, then approached his car. "Are you a general?" the taller one asked.

"No, not quite. I'm a lieutenant colonel."

"Is that like a general?" the other boy asked.

"Somewhat," Franco replied with a smile. "But generals are fatter. Do you know where the castle is?"

The taller boy pointed to a hill above the town to the south. Near its peak, overlooking Mistano and everything else, stood a tall gray stone structure right out of the Middle Ages. Although it had to be at least a half kilometer away, it stood out distinctly against the hot blue sky. He gave each boy a coin and thanked them, then drove on.

Two minutes later he parked in front of the gate that led to the castle. A mustached man in a black suit and flat cap stepped out of a small gatehouse and challenged him as he got out of the Fiat. He was carrying a *lupara*. "I have a letter for Don Nizzi," Franco said, pulling a white envelope from his inner pocket. The guard eyed him suspiciously for a moment, then took the envelope. "Do you wish to wait?"

"No, I just came to deliver the letter."

"What is your name?"

"The don will know when he reads the letter." Franco turned and got back into the Fiat. Moments later he was on his way to the airfield.

Don Nizzi Gaetano Calgogeri looked up from his afternoon coffee and chocolate. The hot sun's rays reached only part of the garden, above the table where he was seated, so it was quite comfortable there. "A letter," Signora Calgogeri said quietly as she walked into the garden from the great room. "Luigi said an officer with many medals delivered it just now."

Don Nizzi frowned, taking the white envelope. "Huh," he grunted. The envelope was plain, with only his name on the front. He looked up at his wife with a raised eyebrow. "An officer with many medals?"

"That's what he said."

"Is he still here?"

"No, he drove away."

He took a knife from the table and slit the top of the envelope. Withdrawing a single page, he looked at it and slowly his face blanched, then began to turn red.

Isabella Calgogeri took the letter from his drooping hand and read it:

> In simple Boston English, Don Nizzi, fuck you.
> —Franco Adamo Accurso
> Lt. Col., Regia Aeronautica

Josh brought the *Sella* in a little hot. With the extra weight, the YB-40 needed a few more miles per hour to be on the safe side, a little more landing space. He didn't want any kind of a stall on low final. They had just returned from a big raid on Messina on the eastern tip of Sicily. That was the funnel through which the rats would try to flee to the mainland once the invasion force had begun to sweep the island.

On the return leg he had dropped back and left the formation, even feathering an engine and flying directly over Elmas. But no Adamo. But then he didn't think he would get an immediate contact. There could be a dozen reasons why the renegade Lightning wouldn't be available: there was a hell of a lot of sky out there, other Allied formations for Adamo to pick on, and the fighter could have all kinds of maintenance problems that would ground her from time to time.

But he would keep plugging along.

Fifty miles west of Sardinia he started the feathered engine, set up high cruise, and headed directly for home.

"I think our ghost got Major Cleburne," Tech Sgt. Ambrose Tarbell said excitedly just after Josh swung down from the bomb bay of the *Sella*.

Josh stared at him. "What do you mean?"

"I just heard it a few minutes ago. Captain Buford's crew heard some radio chatter that ended with the major saying something about a P-38 shooting them down. That's all I know."

No, not Pat! Josh swung into a trot for the squadron debriefing tent, bursting in moments later and running directly into Capt. John Buford. "I just heard about Pat!" he said. "You picked it up on the radio?"

"Yeah," Buford, a gray-eyed Kentuckian, said wearily. "He got hit by flak over Messina and was limping back. I don't know where he was—I guess just west of Palermo somewhere. His transmissions were weak. But he was talking to a fighter jock about getting some escort home. And all at once he shouted something like, "What the hell are you doing—"

Josh stared at Buford, picturing the scene in the air, knowing exactly what was coming.

Buford went on, "Then I heard something in Italian, and after that Pat shouted, 'The bastard's shooting me down! It's Rawlins' P-38!' And that was the last I heard."

"Anything from Air-Sea Rescue yet?"

Buford shrugged. "I don't know."

God, Pat had been such a friend.

"I can't believe it, Josh. That bastard is real, isn't he?"

"What the hell did you think this was all about?" Josh snapped back.

Buford shrugged again. "I guess I just—"

"Yeah, I know, too weird to be true until it happens to you."

"Did you hear about Pat, Josh?" Capt. Wilbur Scragg, the flight surgeon, shouted, running up.

"Yeah."

"I just came from Group and they got a call five minutes ago from Air-Sea Rescue. They had a PBY close to where Pat went down and when he switched to the emergency channel they got enough of his location to spot the wreckage before it sank. They picked up five survivors. No names."

"Yeah, I heard the bastard quit strafing the rafts," Josh said absently, reliving the terrible scene when the *Bitch* was sinking: the Lightning roaring in at wavetop level, its nose ablaze with gunfire, bullets ripping into men, tearing the life from them, screams, blood, treachery.

"The bastard!" Doc Scragg snapped, slamming a fist into his palm.

Josh thought about Pat Cleburne, the freckle-faced Cleveland history teacher caught up in this madness. Down to earth, a thoughtful, caring commander. Warm friend. Maybe he was one of the five who'd made it—

"C'mon," Scragg said. "Let's go over to my tent. I've got some nearly drinkable stuff I cooked up. We'll drink a toast to Pat and hope he's one of the survivors."

He wasn't.

Maj. Pat Cleburne was shot to death strapped in the pilot's seat when the enemy P-38 made its shooting run. According to his copilot a .50-caliber slug got him in the left temple and he died instantly. The copilot landed the crippled B-17 in the water and, of course, was one of the survivors. Another, a waist gunner, died two hours after the rescue by the PBY crew.

Six more victims.

Josh Rawlins took it hard and personal. This was the first time since the *Bitch* that Adamo had struck close to home—right in his own squadron, in fact. When he and Doc Scragg left the copilot in the Constantine hospital late that afternoon they decided to walk through the Place des Martyrs and have a drink at the Cirta. They went to the bar and ordered the strongest drink possible, a local brandy that Wilbur Scragg swore tasted worse than any of the medicinal alcohol concoctions he had ever dreamed up. They chugalugged the first two and ordered another, which they sipped. "You know," Scragg said softly, "he was the best friend I ever had. There were a couple of guys in medical school

I liked, but Pat Cleburne was a gentleman, the warmest man I've ever known. I—"

"Afternoon, gentlemen."

They looked up to see Gen. Barney Buell walking toward them.

"I figured you might be here. I'm sorry about Major Cleburne. We lost some other fine people today, but his being shot down by your nemesis, Josh, made him special. Mind if I join you for some of this shit they call booze?" The general's tone was soft.

As soon as he had a drink in his hand he said, "I wanted to tell you in person. A P-40 pilot from the 325th reported seeing a P-38 landing at a small airfield a few miles up the southeast coast of Sardinia in the middle of the morning. It was shortly after the time Cleburne reported contact with the Lightning."

Josh's attention perked. "Does he know exactly where this field is?"

"Yes, I have the coordinates he reported."

"I'll blast the son of a bitch off the map first thing in the morning!"

"I've already listed it as one of tomorrow's targets. And I'll tell Pillow to let the 414th have it."

"No, General, I want it all to myself."

Buell narrowed his eyes over the glass. "And if Adamo isn't there?"

"I'll blow his fucking nest sky high."

The general thought a moment, then said, "I think the 99th is hitting Sardinia tomorrow early. I'll have you attached to them as a tail-end-Charlie."

Josh gulped the rest of his drink. "C'mon, we gotta get back to the airfield. I want to talk to this P-40 jock and get a description of that airfield to make damned sure I know what I'm hitting in the morning."

The flight surgeon turned on a pained expression. "And leave all of this wonderful brandy?"

Barney Buell gripped Josh's arm. "You get that bastard tomorrow and we'll have Scotch in my quarters tomorrow night."

The next morning was clear and already warm at takeoff time. Fifteen miles from the Sardinian coast the German fighters came down out of the sun to meet them, swarming, snarling, tracer-marked death flashing from their guns. This morning they were all 109s in their normal camouflage paint, marked with the black-and-white cross that the Luftwaffe had adapted from the old Maltese Cross of the previous world war. Josh's gunners had a field day, knocking down two of the little fighters before, like wasps with some sixth sense that told them to evade a mysterious enemy force, they backed off. The *Sella*, in turn, took a few minor hits from the enemy machine guns, but nothing serious. As soon as the fighters broke off their initial attack, Josh put the YB-40 into a slow descent for the small airfield that the P-40 pilot had described as, "tucked in beside the steep hills on a beach guarded by tall trees, no buildings or revetments discernible. Didn't see any other airplanes, didn't even see the P-38 on the ground." The fighter pilot hadn't been able to take a closer look because he had to stay in the low-level formation of his squadron as it hurried on to its assignment.

Probably had revetments in nearby trees, covered by camouflage nets, Josh had decided.

His navigator, Clyde Owen, called up from the plexiglass nose, "Steer another five degrees left, Skipper. It oughta be coming up in about two, three minutes. Stay right over the shore line. That's it."

Josh eased the throttles back slightly and checked the airspeed indicator: 165, 160, 155. Altitude: 400 indicated, then 350, 300, 250, 200 feet. "Okay, crew, all eyes on the ground when we go by." They had been briefed to look for fighter aircraft in sandbagged revetments, or empty revetments, vehicles such as a gas truck, anything else a temporary or forward, unimproved airstrip might contain.

"There it is, skip!" Owen said crisply over the intercom. "See the little wind sock by the trees?"

"I see it!" Josh replied, banking slightly right then left to give them a bit more room to see. "Half flaps," he ordered and eased the throttle back a bit more to get them down to 140. "You've got it, Jim," he said to the copilot, then strained his eyes left. Sure enough, there they were: one, two, three, several revetments. One held what looked like a Macchi. A couple of trucks. They were right on the money!

There was no antiaircraft fire of any kind.

And then they were past. Josh took over the controls again and began a climbing turn. They had four five-hundred-pound bombs in the bay. "You got a good fix on it, Freddy?" he asked the bombardier.

"Yeah, skipper. From five hundred feet I can make mincemeat out of that revetment area."

"Good! Let's do it!" The plan was to make four bomb runs if there was no ack-ack, so the bombardier could practically hand-place each bomb for maximum effect.

Josh brought the heavy aircraft around and set up a low approach. Two thousand yards from the target Freddy Smith took control and steered directly for it. Josh checked his watch, mentally guessing the time to release. Moments later, Smith called out, "Bomb away!" and Josh stared back at the huge explosion in the trees behind them.

On the second run a huge, roiling, gold-and-black flame shot skyward, and they knew they had gotten the fuel supply. Another blast probably meant they had hit the ammo.

On the third and fourth runs Smith placed the big bombs directly in the middle of the runway twelve hundred feet apart. No fighters would take off from that strip for a while.

Then Josh brought the *Sella* around for a strafing run. "All right, you guys," he said into the intercom, "I want to see that place pulverized by fifty caliber slugs." Shortly every gun that could be brought to bear on the left side came into play, firing furiously during the pass. After returning from the other direction so they could get the left waist gunner, Billy Cochise, into the gunplay, Josh swung the aircraft around for a frontal attack.

He had never before flown a big bomber like this. Keeping in mind that her extra weight was a hazard, he was still maneuvering her like a huge fighter plane. And now, with the special .50 machine gun his sergeants had mounted on the left side of the cockpit, he was going to blow out some of the hate that had consumed him. At one thousand yards he fired his first burst. Three seconds later he pushed the firing button hard and held it. His tracers mixed with those of the nose turret, and once more a small pillar of flame shot up from the target. At the last minute he hauled back on the wheel, and the big Boeing bomber lumbered up over the nearest hill in a climbing turn.

That's for Joe and Pat!

The last firing he heard came from Sgt. Alfred Price in the tail turret. Everyone had gotten in the act! And Adamo's lair had been devastated, he was sure.

Okay, you bastard, he said under his breath, I'm closing in on you.

Franco Adamo's lair had been devastated, but his crew had been unharmed. Sergeant-major Diego and Sergeant Mazzei, both newly promoted, had run through the trees to the nearby cave at the first sound of the YB-40's approach. In compliance with Lieutenant Colonel Adamo's specific orders, that was their routine. Take no chances: unless an approaching aircraft was positively a friendly, go direct to the cave. The cave was their temporary home and supply room, and had a large boulder guarding its entrance. Now, as the two mechanics listened to the four-engined enemy bomber fade away into the distance, they were extremely glad the boulder was there. On the last pass the bomber's guns had fired right into it.

"I think someone knew we were here," Mazzei said softly.

"How long did it take you to figure that out?" Diego asked sarcastically. He lit a cigarette and stared across the two hundred feet at what remained of the burning fuel truck and what had been the ammo revetment. The Macchi C-202 was a burning hulk as well. In fact, he guessed there was virtually nothing salvageable anywhere outside the cave. Diego walked out to the landing strip and soon determined that it would take local workers several days to repair the huge craters the enemy bombs had created.

But it wouldn't matter; if the enemy knew they were there, they'd be back.

Diego went inside the cave and pulled out the pennant. Red and green, it was the prearranged message Colonel Adamo had set up to be flown if the airstrip had been put out of business. He returned to the runway and hung it under the wind sock. By the time he began packing things for the move to a new strip Mazzei was back with the cargo truck that had been hidden a thousand yards away under good cover.

They would move to the next field in the evacuation chain.

Franco spotted the red and green pennant on his high pass over the field. Thank God they hadn't been hurt, or a least incapacitated, he told himself. He had seen the thin remnants of smoke during his letdown and had known at once that the field had been hit. But with all of the Allied aircraft in the sky, it figured that someone would have detected him landing or taking off.

He banked around and headed straight north up the Sardinian coast. The next airstrip was twenty-nine miles away. It was similar to the last one, but with an unmarked runway of hard, packed sand right beside the water. It, too, had nearby trees, but no cave and only one revetment. There was a number of five-gallon gas cans with aviation petrol stashed there, but if he were to continue operations they would have to find a tanker trunk somewhere.

He called the new strip Scully Square.

Seven minutes later he greased the P-38 in over the hard sand, turning back to a break in the trees near the center of the landing area. Diego was out in front, directing him with hand signals to a parking place under the high limbs. After shutting down the engines Franco slid the canopy back and crawled out on the wing. Stretching his cramped muscles, he said, "Looks like you had a little cooking party back there."

"Yes, sir," Diego replied. "Everything got cooked."

Franco jumped down from the rear of the cockpit. "What hit us?"

"A B-17."

"A B-17?"

"Yes, sir. One, with a big painting of a woman on its side. He made four passes from low level, dropping bombs, then strafed in both directions and finally machine-gunned straight into our cave. It was amazing, Colonel, just as if he knew exactly where we were and didn't want to let anything or anyone escape."

Franco's eyes narrowed. "A B-17 *strafed*?"

"That's right."

The big Fortresses didn't strafe. Somebody had to have a special interest to go to all that trouble with a big bomber. "He flew right into you?"

Diego nodded his head. "On the last pass."

It had to be him!

All along he'd pictured this Rawlins as a fighter pilot.

He was a goddamned B-17 pilot!

CHAPTER 23

✛

SUMMARY OF THE INVASION OF ITALY (SICILY) JULY 1943:

The code name for the invasion of Sicily was HUSKY. Although it was obvious that the Allies would invade the island, a certain amount of misleading information was believed by Italian and German intelligence, and opposition to the landings on July 10th was not as stiff as it might have been. While the British force under General Montgomery landed on the southeast corner of the island, Patton's Seventh Army forces under Generals Bradley and Truscott executed successful landings on the southwest beaches by 0600 on D-Day. Allied air support was extensive. Of the 4,900 operational aircraft, 146 squadrons were American, 113 British. Landing areas and primary objectives were well saturated by Allied bombing as well as naval gunfire, and in general, excellent fighter cover over the beaches was made available. Mishandling of the paratroop and glider operations was a glaring package of errors, but overall the entire invasion was highly successful and Allied troops pushed inland to succeeding objectives during the next few days. From July 10 on, the underbelly of Axis Europe was open.

Josh Rawlins's quest for Franco Adamo was secondary during the July 10–12 period. The *Sella* flew six sorties—two per day—of straight escort duty for the heavies of North African Air Forces. Once the returning bombers began to creep away from the slower *Sella* on the way home Josh reverted to his decoy role. But not even a friendly P-38 came close to him. In the three days the gunners of the YB-40 shot down three enemy fighters, one each being credited to the Cochise brothers and Cpl. Jack O'Brien, the radio operator.

Franco Adamo flew seven sorties during those three days, shooting down two bombers, an American B-24 and an RAF Wellington. He also shot down a P-38 from the U.S. 14th Fighter Group when he slipped into a ground attack on an airfield near Gela. He nailed a Spitfire from the 31st Fighter Group with a similar tactic. It was his fifty-fifth kill and it gave him no satisfaction whatsoever. In fact it depressed him, and he drank himself into a stupor that night. His only pleasure lay ahead.

Rudy Sabatini, held in limbo at Constantine until the military government phase of the occupation of Sicily could be placed in effect following the capitulation of Axis forces on the island, went AWOL. He talked his way into an infantry battalion headquarters C-47 in the drop of the 504th Airborne Regimental Combat Team, telling them he was a secret observer for Eisenhower. On the ground, he took off his major's leaves and fought happily with a parachute infantry company for five days, personally wiping out a German machine-gun nest. He was subsequently put in for the DSC. On D-plus-6 he hitch-hiked a ride back to Constantine in a gooney bird. The pilot was newly promoted Captain Bltner. Rudy Lotions was looking for another adventure; he asked Josh to let him go along on a raid, but was refused.

On the evening of July 15, Josh went to dinner at Gen. Barney Buell's quarters in Constantine. Buell lived in a comfortable apartment on the top floor of the Massinissa Hotel, a seven-story hostelry close to NAAF headquarters. The table was set with white linen, a brigadier's china, and polished silver, complete with fresh flowers and two red candles. The general's cook had managed to purchase some choice lamb chops and some fresh vegetables, and an RAF group captain had brought him two bottles of Scotch whisky from London two days earlier. So Josh was in for the best meal he had eaten in a long time. As the general had wanted this to be an intimate meal such as an uncle might have with a favorite nephew, he and Josh were the only two at the table.

Through the long meal they talked about the old days, of the Thompson Trophy Race, flying the Gee Bee, Josh's father, and the acrobatic characteristics of various planes. The subject then shifted to the *Sella* and

Josh's pursuit of Adamo. Josh nearly broke down and told him about his love for Sella Adamo, but once more he felt it too absurd to talk about and resisted the urge.

Over real coffee and some more Scotch Buell launched into a new subject: "Have you heard about the upcoming raid on Rome?"

"Just a rumor. I don't think the 414th is involved, is it?"

"Not yet, but I think this will be an all-out effort, so they should get the word soon. This will be quite a raid. We're going to hit them right in the very heart of Italy. Rome, the Eternal City. It will be one of the most significant operations of this entire war."

"Because the Vatican is there?"

"That's a big part of it. Mussolini was smart—he built many of his warmaking factories right next to religious and art shrines, assuming we'd never take the chance of hitting something that would shake up the whole Catholic world. So all through this war Rome has been fat, dumb, and happy. Now, with huge amounts of Axis war materials funnelling through the city's two large marshalling yards, it's time to think militarily and get off the bullshit. Rome is the heart of the Italian rail system. Its two major marshalling yards control most of the country's traffic and rolling stock. Yet there has never been one single raid on the city. The decision was so critical it had to be made by Eisenhower himself, with British concurrence of course. Touchy. We'll even drop leaflets to tell them we're coming."

Josh shook his head. "If our boys hit anything important of an artistic or religious nature there'll be hell to pay."

"That's why we've trained the crews so carefully. Our bombardiers should know the exact location of every single architectural treasure or holy place, as well as their specific targets. If we get the kind of daylight visibility we expect, there should be no problem." Buell's eyes shone. "It'll be the most important mission in the war to this point."

"Isn't there more to it than those railyards, General?"

Barney Buell smiled. "Of course. The Italian populace is already a little shaky. Hit Rome hard and they may start thinking seriously about dumping Mussolini and calling it quits. We're going to put five hundred bombers in the air and drop three-quarters of a million pounds of bombs!"

Josh pursed his lips. "Sounds just like the kind of an operation that would attract Adamo."

"Exactly! That's why you're taking that flying machine-gun nest to Rome. If everything works out, our formations will remain tight and encounter little damage. You might stick out like a sore thumb if he's in your part of the sky."

Josh downed the rest of his Scotch. "Christ I hope so. He's beginning to haunt my dreams."

Franco Adamo's dreams were very much haunted. His sleep had been fitful ever since his return from Egypt. Now, with Sicily being chopped up and the apparent defeat of Italy becoming a reality, the faces that had long plagued him were more insistent than ever. Only now one of them was that of a young American captain he had seen just once in an RAF operations building at Cairo. Another was that of an old man with white hair whom the Friends treated with great reverence, an old man who ruled a shadowy kingdom with ritual and death. That face had no features, but he knew whose it was.

It hounded him most of all.

Even more than Sella's.

He had driven all the way to Poetto to see Baroness Angelina Ricardi two nights before, but when he got there he had turned around and gone to a small inn he knew and tried to drown in its terrible wine. He couldn't even be a lover.

The airplane had been sick for three days and he hadn't cared. He didn't want to fly and he didn't want to kill any more than he had to. When the aircraft was down for repairs it was out of his hands. He didn't think the Lightning would last much longer anyway. It had a pound of Diego's baling wire holding it together now. Next it would be string.

He waded barefoot in the shallow surf as it slid up on the sand and just as quickly retreated, its bubbly remains sinking instantly. The water was warm, and he thought about how nice it would be to just lie down in it and forget everything—commitments, death, sorrow, debts—forget it all.

So easy.

He got down on his knees and then sat, waiting for the next wave to roll in. This one was a little larger and came up to his ribs.

So easy.

He looked off to the east, where the dawn was breaking quiet and peach-pink over the reflective water. There had to be a place and time of no torment.

Somewhere.

But first there was something he had to do.
He got slowly to his feet and walked back toward the trees.

Franco approached Palermo at shortly before eight, wanting to get there after the first Allied air attack of the morning. He could have found it without a compass. The smoke from the fires on the city's docks could be seen from many miles away. Dropping down from fifteen thousand, he kept his eyes moving around the sky to detect any kind of Italian or German fighter plane that might come after him. That was one of the bad parts of this sneak flying—everyone could be your enemy. But the chance of any trouble along that line was slim. Nearly all Regia Aeronautica aircraft had evacuated the island, as well as most of the Luftwaffe fighter squadrons.

The Allied ground and air juggernaut was simply too powerful.

It would be just a matter of days before Palermo fell to the American or English ground force, and then it would be all over. At least he figured it that way. According to the previous night's report on shortwave radio from Tunis, the Italian army was being routed and the Wehrmacht couldn't hold out long without air support—not in today's warfare.

That's why he had to do it today, the eighteenth.

It had to look good.

An American plane on a combat mission.

Wrong target?

Wrong intelligence?

The fortunes of war.

Diego had rigged four one hundred-kilo high-explosive bombs to the Lightning. That was enough to destroy any kind of structure.

He levelled off at a thousand feet, surveying the smoking dock area. The railyards had been hit again, as well. He wondered if anything would roll again. Turning southwest, he was over the village of Mistano in what seemed only moments. He throttled back to slow cruise and banked around to come in low over the castle. It stood gray and stark, its battlements missing only pennants to put it back a few centuries, its courtyard wanting a helmeted knight in shining armor astride a magnificent black horse.

Black, the horse would have to be black, for this was the evil knight.

He saw a dark-suited guard come out of the gate house with his *lupara* and look up, shielding his eyes with his hand.

He hoped everyone else was awake, particularly the don.

Swinging the P-38 wide so he would come in east to west, approaching the most exposed side of the ancient structure, he checked the bomb toggle switches. One at a time, that was the plan. One right in the middle of the east wall as a starter. He was an expert at close air support and dropping bombs from fighters; this should be a snap.

Maybe it would be the last and most important bombing mission of his life.

He lined up on the center of the castle and headed in.

Steady, wait . . . *Now!*

Pulling up sharply and banking steeply, he stared down at the target.

Smoke obscured the wall, but he knew the hundred-kilo bomb had blasted a huge hole in it. Now for the reverse: lay it right into the west side through the courtyard.

Don Nizzi Gaetano Calgogeri hadn't come close to jumping anywhere in over a decade. But when the first bomb hit it threw him out of the huge bed in his south wall bedroom. When the second bomb blasted into the west wall he jumped to the window and searched the landscape frantically. What was happening? Lightning? There wasn't a cloud in the sky! Dynamite—who would dare? Artillery? That must be it! How? The Americans were supposed to be many miles away yet. Why—?

"*Isabella!*" he screamed.

His wife came running out of the bathroom, naked and dripping, her dark hair hanging down stringy over her ponderous breasts. "Under the bed, Nizzi!" she shouted. "Hurry!"

At that moment he spotted the American aeroplane swinging around to the south. It looked like some kind of small gray hawk. He watched it, transfixed, unblinking, as it turned toward him and began to grow rapidly in size. What was it doing? Could it be bombing him—Don Nizzi? He had no enemies who had aeroplanes!

"Get under the bed, Nizzi!" Isabella shrieked from where her head stuck out from below the huge four-poster.

He continued to stare at the aeroplane. Who?

And all at once he knew.

God, did he know—

It was the last realization he ever had, because when the bomb exploded in a blast of incredible color a shard of glass tore off the top of his head.

Franco looked around as he swung in low over the castle after dropping the last bomb. Slow flying with flaps down, he was able to get a good look at the crumbled castle. Only one portion stood erect, the northeast corner. Almost every other part of the small fortress had either been blown apart or otherwise devastated. Smoke from a dozen rapidly developing fires licked from its ruins. It was quite possible that there could be survivors, he decided, but they would have had to be deep in the castle's dungeons, if it had any. Or in some other well-protected spot.

He blew out a deep breath. So be it.

If others died, that was too bad.

He felt no remorse whatsoever—they were his personal enemies.

The bastard had killed his father, hurrying the death of his mother. And he had threatened to kill Sella—

To say nothing of himself.

Did this make him, Lt. Col. Franco Adamo Accurso, a cold-blooded killer?

If so, so be it.

It was the end. The Friends would forget his case and he could go on with his life. It also had a certain Sicilian beauty to it. Their don had been killed by an inexplicable bombing by some disoriented American pilot, or one who possibly had been ordered to hit a castle that might be some kind of an enemy headquarters.

Who knows such things in war?

Don Nizzi would probably have the largest funeral this part of the island had seen in a long time.

A great man. What a pity.

He pulled the Lightning up and headed for Sardinia. There was only one great adventure left for him in this grotesque war, if he could somehow find the other man who wanted to kill him.

CHAPTER 24

✣

"You got a hot date or something, skip?"

Josh turned from the small mirror he had propped up on the wash stand outside of the Raghead Ritz and looked at First Lt. Clyde Owen in the early morning light. "No, why?"

"You seem to be taking more time than usual shaving."

Josh shrugged. "Yeah, I guess I am." He finished the job, wiping away the remains of the shaving soap with a towel. In fact, he seemed to be taking greater pains with everything this morning: brushing his teeth, setting up his uniform, he didn't usually care as much about getting the collar brass on too accurately. He was wearing khakis with long pants today because it might be pretty cool high up in that Roman sky, or maybe it was because he just wanted to be dressed right. The Roman sky. Sounded almost poetic. He had a funny feeling about that Roman sky this morning, and it didn't have anything to do with poetry. It had something to do with fate or whatever it was that was hovering over him.

Maybe it was because this was the day of the great strike on Rome, maybe he was caught up in some kind of special enthusiasm or something. Regardless of the reason, he just knew something different was going to happen this fine July day. Barney Buell had started him thinking about today by saying that Adamo would surely want to get into the act on such a raid. Was this strange feeling that seemed to possess him this morning a premonition? Was this the day? That had to be what was going on—today was the day!

Or was he just wanting it to be the day? Hell, he wanted every day to be the one. No, he felt different. He'd noticed a keen sense of anticipation when he got up to relieve himself at three o'clock, and it hadn't left him. He hadn't even gotten back to sleep.

So was Adamo going to find him up there in the violent sky?

Finally?

Maybe so. Why else all of this bullshit this morning?

He went inside the Ritz and put on his shirt. It was still warm in the damned shack, always was. Didn't cool off at night like it did down in the Valley of the Kings. He thought about Sella, his beautiful Sella. Well, she wasn't exactly his, but that was how he pictured her. She loved him, didn't she? Didn't that make her his?

He tied his right shoelace. If that goddamned Adamo would just be up there today, by God she'd be *all* his.

"You ready to get some breakfast, skip?" his copilot asked from the doorway.

"Yeah, be right there." He looked at a snapshot of Sella that he had had blown up and framed, and the doubt that had been haunting him ever since his return from Cairo returned. Was he going to kill Adamo because he truly had to, or was it now a way to free Sella to be his wife? The damned thought had picked away at him every now and then since his return. Dumb. Besides, he'd vowed to get Adamo long before he met her. Adamo was a murderer. He was an enemy ace with the blood of hundreds of brave Americans and Brits on his hands, not to mention that of other Allied airmen, probably a number of Spanish pilots, and possibly even some Russians who were over there in Spain. After all, you didn't just count the planes a man shot down—no, you had to consider all that strafing, and the numbers of crewmen who perished directly under his guns or as a development from them. All of those lives were in the goddamned box score.

But they said he had stopped strafing survivors.

Fine, but what about the ones he *had* strafed?

What about Joe Orosco? And the rest of the guys from the *Bitch*? No, he had to quit this kind of thinking.

Franco had gone out to the surf again to get a fresh start on the day. After a vigorous swim and a few minutes of contemplative thought he felt good, the punishment from his previous night's bout with the grape gone or at least subdued. Walking back to where Diego and Mazzei were adding last-minute touches to the aircraft, he felt a certain elation.

Something was different about this day, this nineteenth day of July 1943.

He knew about the raid on Rome; everyone did. And he was definitely going to get involved. But why did he have this odd feeling? Did it have anything to do with Rawlins? Surely Rawlins would be in on this raid because Doolittle was going to throw a maximum effort at the Eternal City. Somewhere in that vast aerial armada his enemy would be boring along in a B-17 to drop a load of eggs on one of the world's greatest cities. Could this be the day of their encounter? Was Rawlins's lance sharpened, his armor burnished?

He went inside the tent that served as their sleeping quarters. Its sides were pulled up to permit air and light inside, but it smelled of oil. In the corner, by his cot, he drew out the fresh summer uniform and decided he should go forth into today's joust properly attired. He withdrew the box that held his insignia of rank and medals. It was only fitting that he be properly accoutered.

The ribbons would do. He pinned the lower bar over the left breast pocket of the short-sleeved shirt, then the second row, topping it all with the red-striped blue ribbon of the Medaglia al Valore Aeronautica, Oro.

Somehow he thought back to a sunny day at an airfield outside of Rome. He was standing in a formation of graduating flying cadets and a colonel was pinning gold wings on his dress jacket. They were the only adornment, for he had been nowhere and had accomplished nothing as a brand new officer in the RA.

The chest of his uniform had been as bare as a recruit's sleeve.

And now he could load it with a whole handful of, of what? The baubles of war. But this was a special occasion and he should wear his honors, dubious as they might be. The more he thought about this strange feeling that possessed him, the more he was convinced that this day would bring Rawlins to him.

The *Sella* cruised along comfortably in the azure sky. She was tail-end-Charlie with the 97th. Including the forming up and climb, the estimated time en route to Rome was two hours and forty minutes. They had been airborne just over two hours now and hadn't had a smell of an enemy fighter. Up ahead, in the lead plane, the group commander was probably wondering where in Hell their opposition was. But so far nothing, not even when they flew past the southwest corner of Sardinia, Adamo's old lair. Josh thought briefly about how much he disliked the group commander. Col. Gideon Pillow had walked by the YB-40 prior to takeoff and given it a contemptuous look, but Josh had ignored him completely. Pillow simply didn't enter into his scheme of life any more. When this episode was over one or both of them would probably be gone and he would forget the bastard completely. Just as someday he would try to forget this ugly war.

He thought back to Egypt and the Valley of the Kings. The idea of becoming an archaeologist someday was quite appealing. History had a way of putting things in the right perspective.

"Pilot from crew chief."

"Yeah, Gregg, what's up?" Josh replied.

"I think we've got a slight oil leak in number four."

Josh looked off to the right, past the copilot. A thin dark stream of fluid was running back from the engine over the wing and flap. "Yeah, I see it." He glanced back at the number four engine oil pressure gauge on the instrument panel. It still showed a normal reading. "What do you think, a seal?"

"Yes, sir. I'll keep my eye on it."

"Roger."

The fighters showed up six minutes later, flashing down out of the sun to pick off the outside bombers. They were Me-109s, tiny blazes of yellow-orange light sparkling from the front of their wings, spewing tracers like long searching rays of pink sunlight. But they weren't bothering the 97th for some reason. And there weren't too many of them. "Stay alert," he warned the crew.

The fighter attack was short-lived. Ten minutes later, another flurry from enemy fighters was more of an annoyance than a danger. Apparently the Luftwaffe commanders didn't want to waste their machines and pilots on such a heavily armed air fleet. But they could be waiting to hit them closer to the target.

The next five minutes were uneventful, and Josh's thoughts turned back to Adamo. Where would he be, hiding in the sun somewhere off the east coast of Sardinia? Probably. The *Sella* could dally, fly a big racetrack pattern waiting to be attacked. Try some different altitudes. There was plenty of fuel.

He looked down at the coast. Depressing the mike button, he said,

"Pilot to crew. Sunny Italy is coming up below us, so Rome isn't far away. We'll make the bombing run with the formation, then break away after the turn."

Flak! The black puffs ahead were aimed at the lead group.

Gideon Pillow's voice came in over the command channel, "This is Reno Leader. All right, the flak has begun ahead and it looks like they've got our altitude pretty well figured out. Keep it closed up and you bombardiers use a sharp eye. We want to hit *nothing* but our targets."

Josh swept the sky; still no more fighters. The flak got closer, those abrupt explosions with the white-hot or molten-gold centers. The outskirts of Rome were coming up. The Eternal City. He felt pumped up, as he always did on a bombing run, even though he had no eggs to lay. But there was more today: Rome, the feeling that Adamo could be around somewhere. All they had to do was get through this damned flak. Looking over at Jim Summerton, his copilot, he slowly nodded his head and smiled.

He glanced down again, seeing smoke from the lead groups' eggs. By God, today's Romans were finding out that war could come to them! It was sort of the Christians and the lions from an abstract view. He wondered suddenly if Barney Buell was right—would the Italians depose Mussolini, sue for peace? And if so, how soon would that end the war?

Yeah, he was pumped up.

A cake walk.

Colonel Pillow had turned the bomb run over to his lead bombardier and now the big eggs were beginning to fall like a sheaf of giant bludgeons.

BLANGGG!! The explosion rocked the *Sella,* forcing him to practically stand on the controls. Son of a bitch!

Slowing forcing the heavy ship back to straight and level, he heard Summerton shout, "They got number three!"

Josh stared out at the left wing. The number three engine, the second one over, was a twisted, smoking tangle of metal! The big prop was somehow continuing to turn lazily, though one of its blades was gone. He hit the feathering button. A jagged hole the size of two footballs had been ripped out of the front leading edge of the wing between number three and number one engines. "Pilot to crew," Josh said as calmly as he could, "We've suffered flak damage on number three, but we're okay."

The *Sella* bounced as another antiaircraft burst exploded just ahead and to her right. "We'll be through this in nothing flat," Josh said reassuringly into the mike. But the nearest Fort was beginning to pull away, and he knew the *Sella*'s airspeed was falling off. So much for formation, he said to himself. We were going home alone anyway. He started a slow turn to the left, into the dead engine, and headed gradually north, quickly diving to a lower altitude to get out of the enemy gunners' flak level.

"Skip, Freddy's been hit!" Clyde Owen barked through the intercom.

"Give me our outbound course and see what you can do for him," Josh replied to the navigator.

"Roger, skip. Three-oh-eight for four minutes, then turn to one-nine-five."

Franco didn't want any part of the big formations returning from Rome. General Manzella had told him resistance over the capital would be token. The Italian fighter squadrons were practically out of the war and the Germans weren't interested in sacrificing their veterans for a foreign city, even if it did involve the strategically vital railyards. And they were right; the Allied planes would only come back in wave after wave.

But the stragglers would be along soon.

And maybe one of them would be Rawlins.

He opened a bottle of rather good wine at 0930 and poured each of the mechanics a glass. Holding his at shoulder height, he said, "I want to toast you, my friends. Without your dedication, I wouldn't be alive."

Diego sipped his wine quietly, eyeing his commander. "Is there something special we are celebrating, Colonel?" he asked softly.

Franco smiled. "No, I just feel quite good today and thought I should say what has been on my mind for some time. You, Diego, and you, Mazzei, deserve more than I've provided. The flyers get the medals and the glory, but it's men like you who keep them in the air. I wish the reward system were more equal."

Again Diego spoke softly. "Why do I feel that you are saying goodbye to us, sir?"

Franco smiled. "I'm not. It's just—how shall we call it—appreciation day. I greatly appreciate the way you two have disregarded hardship and found the means to keep this tired airplane flyable time after time, when it has been ready for the junkyard." He poured more wine in all three glasses. "I think this war will soon be over for us, and it can't happen too soon for me."

He raised his glass again. "I hope in the years ahead that both of you will find your personal happiness."

They both drank and thanked him.

Franco threw his glass against a nearby rock, shattering it, and handed the nearly empty bottle to Diego. "And now I must attack the Anglo-Saxon invaders."

Swinging deftly up the small ladder at the rear of the cockpit, he was soon in the low seat. Diego followed him and handed him the shoulder harness. Shortly, after starting both engines, Franco nodded pleasantly when the sergeant-major waved him forward from the parking area and saluted stiffly.

Five minutes later Franco hit the handle that retracted the landing gear as he banked up into the bright sky.

Josh had decided to use a lower elevation for the return to Constantine. With number three engine out and oil still leaking from number four he had to abandon any ideas of finding Adamo. He didn't have to feather an engine to look crippled, he was! His crew came first, or at least what was left of it. Lt. Freddy Smith was dead, a victim of a ragged piece of flak the size of a wad of bubble gum. The mangled engine, along with the hole in the front of the left wing, made it difficult for the *Sella* to fly smoothly. She couldn't be trimmed properly, so Josh and Jim Summerton took turns flying her. And she vibrated badly.

He had levelled off at eighteen thousand feet, which would give him plenty of glide room in case there was any need to make a forced landing or ditch.

Josh kept his right eye on the number four oil pressure gauge, which was beginning to fluctuate. He knew it wouldn't be long now, and he didn't relish the thought. He had feathered an engine on each side during one of their shakedown flights, and the heavy YB-40 had been sick as hell. In fact she had stalled on him.

The *Sella* could be in serious trouble, and he felt a new level of awareness.

God, he'd barely gotten to know Freddy Smith. Nice kid.

Fucking war!

He looked down at the big island of Sardinia off to his left and remembered Elmas. Maybe he could make it to that airfield if worse came to worse. No, he'd get this big-assed bird back to Africa if he had to carry it. "Pilot to crew," he said into the mike. "I want all of the extra ammo in the bomb bay thrown overboard as quickly as possible once the doors are opened. The same goes for any extra shells you have at your gun positions. Keep only what you have in your guns at the present."

As each crew member rogered he turned his attention back to the worrisome oil gauge. Leaning over to Summerton, he indicated that the copilot should lift an earphone so he could hear what he was about to say. "Go back and check to make sure everything's okay."

Summerton nodded and slipped out of his harness.

Now Josh's eyes were glued to the number four oil gauge. With one final bounce the needle dropped to the bottom and remained perfectly still. Josh stared out at the right wing, waiting for it to happen. No engine ran very long when its lubrication was gone. At least it would be easier to trim he told himself ruefully, with one out on each side.

The vibration increased even more.

Summerton slid back into his seat and gave him a thumbs-up to indicate that everything was okay. At that moment the number four engine shuddered and ground to a halt. Immediately Josh felt the airspeed begin to fall off. He trimmed for a shallow descent before feathering. The airspeed continued to decrease. This airplane was simply too heavy for any sustained flight on two engines—at least with the kind of drag that damaged wing and engine created.

"Pilot to crew," he said briskly. "Remove and ditch all the guns you can get loose! Gregg, you supervise personally. Over."

Everyone rogered.

In a few minutes, Sergeant Gregg tapped Josh on the right elbow and leaned into his ear. "I think number one got some of that flak. Look at it."

Josh jerked his head around. *The closer engine had fluid running from it, some of it dark like oil!*

That would be all he needed.

Franco spotted the lumbering B-17 moments later. All alone and making no better than 160 knots, the bomber would be all his, a piece of cake, as the Brits supposedly said. He had already passed up one straggler. There was only one B-17 for him, one with the big picture of a woman on it, and he had decided not to attack any other aircraft. If he found Rawlins, fine, if not, so be it. But something told him this was not just another sick airplane with a big tail. Diego had thought the woman in the painting was naked or maybe in a bathing suit. Didn't make any difference, he'd know if it was Rawlins.

The Flying Fort was about four thousand feet below him, so he throttled back and began a banking descent that would bring him alongside the pilot's compartment. If this was the enemy knight, he wanted to see him.

He *had* to see him.

He switched to the 14th's escort frequency and cleared his machine guns.

This aircraft would have a big woman on its fuselage, he knew it.

He could feel it!

He feathered number two to play the game. Pretend he had an engine problem.

He picked up the painting when he was a thousand yards away. Big, like Diego said, it took up much of the fuselage above the wing. Looked like a woman reclining in a bathing suit. Rawlins, you bastard, here I am!

Drawing closer, he could see the B-17 had an engine out, no two! The one on the left wing had apparently been hit. So he couldn't be playing possum. Something was different about this B-17—it seemed to have more gun turrets than he could ever remember seeing, the painting was really something, what a beauty, she looked like, no, she looked like Sella! And then he made out the letters: *Sella!* The son of a bitch had his wife's picture painted on his fucking airplane!

"P-38 with one engine out coming in on our left, skipper!" Bobby Cochise announced over the intercom.

Josh snapped his head around. God! Not now! But there it was, moving in close. He tried to make out the letters on its tail, but couldn't read them. "How many guns we got left, Gregg?" he barked into the intercom.

The crew chief was wearing a walk-around headset. "Not many, skipper," he replied from the back of the aircraft. "The tail turret guns, those in the nose, that Mickey Mouse job of yours."

Josh shot another look at the closing fighter plane, then back at his airspeed indicator. The *Sella* was down to 145, the needle fluctuating. With this drag she could stall any time. "Give me minimum flaps," he said to Summerton, then switched to the fighter channel.

"—is Outlaw One, over." He could almost remember the goddamned voice!

"This is Reno Six-niner, Outlaw One. What are you doing here?"

The transmission was perfectly clear. "You know damned well what I'm doing here, Rawlins."

It was him! And the son of a bitch knew who he was! Josh could feel his skin tingle. No pretense. "It's about time, Adamo. I've been looking for your yellow ass for weeks."

"What's your big fucking problem, Rawlins?"

"Do you remember shooting down a B-17 and strafing the crew on June the third about fifty miles south of Sardinia? You let one man on a raft survive."

After a pause, Adamo replied, "Maybe . . . yes, one idiot shooting back at me with a pistol."

"That was me, you murdering son of a bitch, and you butchered my entire crew!"

Josh felt a tap on his shoulder. It was Gregg, who shouted, "I don't think this thing's gonna fly much longer, Cap'n. There's a big crack in the fuselage near the tail. Must've gotten some shrapnel back in that goddam flak!"

Josh glanced sharply over at the P-38, frowning. "Okay, we'll have to ditch."

"I don't know if she'll take a ditch."

Josh nodded, making an instant decision and hitting the intercom, "Pilot to crew. We've got some serious problems, so get ready to bail out. I'll call Air-Sea Rescue and give them our position. You all know what to do. I say again, bail out!" He turned back to Gregg. "Everybody goes, Sarge. See to it."

Gregg nodded and hurried away.

Jim Summerton said briskly, "I'll stick around, skip."

"No dice—out you go!"

"But—"

"That's an order!"

Josh quickly called Air-Sea Rescue and got an immediate reply from a PBY. After he gave his position he switched back to the fighter channel and looked out at the P-38 that now had two engines going. It was almost lapping over his wing tip. He could see the pilot quite clearly, almost make out his features. "You still there, Adamo?"

"Yeah, I guess I've been talking to nobody. What the hell's the idea of the painting?"

"I wanted to suck your gutless ass in. I figured a picture of my lover might do it." Josh had planned this kind of talk from the day he first set foot in the YB-40. And he detested doing it, absolutely loathed the thought of talking cheaply about Sella, but only one thing mattered now.

*   *   *

Franco could see Rawlins quite clearly when the American leaned close to the window. And he could guess what was going on in that cockpit. Unknown damage, crippled airplane, some kind of emergency procedures—

But this!

"Don't give me that crap, Rawlins! I know you were in Egypt, but Sella wouldn't let you near her."

Rawlins's voice came back, loud and clear, "She's a great piece of ass, Adamo. Did you teach her some of those tricks she knows?"

Franco knew what Rawlins was doing, but it didn't make any difference. He felt his hands tighten around the wheel. At that moment he saw the first figure drop out of the bomb bay, then another, and another. Parachutes blossomed like tiny white mushrooms behind and below.

"Do you read me, Adamo? I fucked Sella silly and she loved every stroke of it. Cried for more. She told me she'd never had anything like that before—"

Franco's knuckles were turning white. There wasn't anything chivalrous or knightly about this. This Rawlins was a common piece of shit!

"—and what a blow job she gives, Adamo. I'll bet she's back there in Cairo right now, taking on whole crews. I mean that gal has to *have* it! No one man can satisfy that bitch!"

"You're a goddamned liar!" Franco blurted into the mike.

"How come they let you play the sneak, Adamo? Couldn't you face a fair fight anymore? Did they need someone without balls to skulk up on a crippled enemy and knife him in the back? Is that the way it is with you wop cowards? Is it, Adamo?"

Franco knew better than to listen—this Rawlins was a pig! He broke in, "You're a stupid ass, Rawlins. I can blow you out of the sky in a minute."

Rawlins came right back, "How—from behind?"

On the intercom Tech Sergeant Gregg radioed: "Our passenger refuses to jump, skipper, so I'm the last of the crew to go. Good luck!"

Passenger? Now what the fuck was going on?

As if to answer, Rudy Sabatini slapped Josh on the shoulder. "Hello, sonny."

"What the hell are *you* doing here?" Josh shouted, staring at the big major.

The New Yorker grinned. "I stowed away and told your crew I'd shoot the first son of a bitch who told you. No, I told them I was your best friend and I was coming along as a surprise."

This was all he needed. Josh snapped, "Get the fuck off this airplane, Sabatini. That's an order! Bail out!"

Sabatini grinned again. "I'm a major, you can't give me an order."

"On this plane I can."

"Look, sonny, you can't shoot that asshole down all by yourself, so I'm going down to the nose to fire those fifties. I gathered up a couple of belts of ammo before they tossed everything overboard, and I'm an ace on a machine gun, so I'll see you later."

Before Josh could say another word he was gone.

The aircraft was getting harder to handle by the moment, so he had to get Adamo as fast as possible. Sabatini or no Sabatini, he'd ram the son of a bitch if he had to. Switching to the fighter channel he punched the mike button again. "All right you gutless bastard, do you have the balls for a head-on shootout?" Even without Sabatini, he still had his single .50 on the side of the fuselage. Maybe with a little more guile he could suck the bastard in close. Otherwise the Lightning's cannon and four machine guns would end it all in a hurry.

Adamo's angry retort was immediate. "Rawlins, you're stupid. You're about to become my last kill in this stupid fucking war!"

Franco tried to shake off the violent anger that now possessed him, but he couldn't. Imagining Rawlins rutting with Sella was too much. There had to be something to what he said, otherwise why had she gone to Cairo with him? Or how did he get this painting to be so accurate?

He'd get him, blow him out of the sky!

Now he knew for sure that this was his final combat, but instead of an encounter of quality, it was nothing more than the others, even worse. This damned Rawlins was nothing more than a revenge-crazed fanatic, an asshole who was lying about his beloved wife! This whole mad, stupid war had finally come down to one final gasp of lunacy. He heaved a deep breath as he brought the P-38 around to make a head-on attack. Rawlins had to be crazy—the weakest point on a B-17 was its nose, everyone knew that. Suddenly he knew—Rawlins, in his fanaticism, was going to ram him! Never, he'd never give him a chance. There was absolutely no way a big bomber could outmaneuver a fighter.

Rawlins's voice crackled in his headphones, "Okay, Adamo, that's it. Show me your yellow Italian balls."

Franco levelled off and headed directly for the Fortress.

"Can you hear me Sabatini?"

"Yeah," the New Yorker replied. "I been listening."

"Those guns okay?"

"We'll find out—here he comes!"

Fighting the big bomber, Josh stared ahead, aiming it at the rapidly growing fighter. "Now!" he shouted, hitting the firing button of his private gun. The *Sella* vibrated even more as the chin guns joined in, tracers streaking straight at the gray Lightning. There—an explosion as the P-38 pulled up over them!

He snapped around, looking for Adamo. Where was he?

There, slightly above and off to the right, smoking, flying slower.

"We got the bastard, Sabatini!" he shouted. "We got him!"

Franco shook off the disbelief. How in the hell did those rounds come out of the nose of that B-17? They had hit him before he even fired. A couple had smashed through the plexiglas of the cockpit, but some others had hit the right engine and caused something to blow up. It was already burning. The bastard! He shut off the fuel to that engine and hit the feather button. It could blow the damned wing right off—

His experience took over. Having been shot down three times over the years, he knew there was no sense in trying to get it down. And there was no valor in staying with a crippled airplane too damned long. He reached up to the right and jerked the hatch lock handle, then ripped open the canopy. Releasing his straps, he pulled himself up and stepped out on the wing.

Now!

One thousand, two thousand, three thousand—jerk!

The chute blossomed over his head as he headed for the water below.

"He bailed out!" Josh barked into the mike.

Moments later Sabatini stuck his nose in the cockpit. His Italian face was creased in a grin. "So, we got him, right?"

Josh nodded. "But the job isn't over yet. Get in that copilot seat and fasten the harness. If this tub holds together, I'm going to finish it."

"You mean—"

Josh started the *Sella* around in a steep descending turn toward the tiny parachute far below. "Yeah, I'm going to give him the same thing he gave my crew. This one's for Joe Orosco and for Pat Cleburne, and for the rest of my crew members and all those other poor bastards he's killed."

Sabatini shrugged and asked, "You sure it isn't for you and Sella?"

Goddamn it, there it was again—why did the son of a bitch have to say it?

"Whose damn conscience are you, all at once?" Josh blazed back.

Sabatini gave him his best imitation of a Sicilian shrug. "Forget I said it."

Josh continued to dive the shaking *Sella*, hoping the tail and bad engines would hang on until he finished what he had to do. He looked at the altimeter—they were going through a thousand feet. He cleared the .50 again. Oughta be plenty of ammo left in that drum. He'd never be able to handle this brute and get the bastard in midair—have to get him in the water—send Sabatini back to the chin guns.

Hang on, baby—

Any man's death diminishes me.

Now, why in the hell did he have to think of that?

What did a poet like Donne have to do with anything like this?

I do nothing upon myself, yet I am my own executioner.

No, I don't want to hear it!

He hauled back on the control column and pulled the *Sella* out of its slow dive just as Adamo's chute dropped into the nearby water. He would have his Mae West inflated by now, still be right there floating when they came back around.

Giving both engines full power to keep from stalling out in the turn, he banked the big Fort around to make a low-level run on the man in the water, the man he'd sworn to kill. He'd have to ditch this big bird anyway. Might as well get the bastard with the airplane—smash right into him with twenty tons of destruction. "Go back and get ready to get out in a hurry. "We're going to ditch!" he snapped at Sabatini.

"No, I'll stay right here and follow you out," the major replied.

Franco finished unsnapping the parachute harness just as he spotted the bomber levelling out and heading straight for him at wavetop level. No, no, he wouldn't! In a flash, he knew what Rawlins was going to do.

He stared, transfixed, at the nose of that big, crippled, still roaring airplane that was boring in on him. Its guns weren't even blazing. No, the bastard was going to crash right into him! He was crazy!

He should dive deep, but he couldn't, not with the Mae West.

Suddenly he knew what he had to do—the only proper thing for this final moment. The only element of quality remaining. He jerked the pistol from its holster and pointed it at the onrushing B-17.

To hell with Sabatini, Josh thought. All that matters now is that white parachute ahead. Just pancake. Piece of cake—into the wind, calm sea, no sweat—twenty tons right on the bastard—

He could see him bobbing around, looking toward them, knowing.

Dead ahead, chop the power in a few seconds, kill him, kill him—

Any man's death diminishes me!

Any man's death.

NO! GODDAMNIT, NO! He poured on full power and climbed right over his target.

Sabatini turned to him with narrowed eyes. "What are you doing?"

"You're supposed to land between waves when you ditch."

"But there aren't any waves."

"You just can't see them," Josh replied softly.

EPILOGUE

✥

United States Air Force Museum,
Wright Patterson AFB, Ohio

The man stood in front of a painting by Wilson Hurley and remembered that the famous artist was also an Air Force pilot who had flown in three wars. He turned to another painting. The strains of Glenn Miller's "Little Brown Jug" drifted in from the other side of the museum.

"Josh!"

The man turned at the male voice. Coming toward him were five people. The one in the lead, the man with the gray hair and deep lines around his eyes, was wearing a black American Airlines captain's uniform. A broad grin creased his face as he stuck out his hand. "Hello, Josh," he said warmly in a Boston accent. "Damned weather had me holding over Columbus for an hour."

Josh Rawlins hadn't seen his old friend in five years—this reunion in Dayton was his idea. He smiled as he said, "You look pretty good for an enemy pilot, Franco."

The man beside Accurso stuck out his hand. What was left of the hair around his bald pate was white. He walked with a cane, but his carriage was erect and powerful. He was wearing a black chesterfield over an expensive dark suit. A tall, blonde woman was on his arm. Rudy Sabatini flashed his big grin and said, "Those bastards at the door wouldn't let my bodyguards bring their guns in, so I told them to wait at the limo. How are you, sonny? Say hello to my lovely Teresa. Still digging around for old bones?"

"Yeah," Josh replied. "I'm working on a new Athapaskan dig out in New Mexico." He spoke warmly to Sabatini's wife, the one-time singer.

"Hello, Josh," the other tall, graying blonde woman said, kissing him on the cheek. Her luminous green eyes looked at him fondly as she added, "I want to hear all about your Athapaskans as soon as we get a chance to get away from these mortals."

"Oh, no, you're not going off alone with my wife again. I know what happens when you do that," Franco said with a laugh.

Josh hadn't seen Sella in over six years. Slim and tanned, her face slightly lined from all the years in the sun, she still looked great. She was currently working for the Metropolitan in New York on a special Egyptian project. It gave her a way to be near Franco, who was based at La Guardia.

He turned as the last lady put her arm around him and kissed him warmly on the lips. Her black, Hispanic eyes flashed as she said, "If anyone's going to be alone with this man, it'll be me." Her black hair was gray at the temples and she was a bit thick in the waist, but her face was that of the same young woman he'd married, Josh always thought when he looked at her.

Sabatini interrupted. "Now, let's not start that crap, Hermelinda. You and me've still got some dancing to do. Your husband can just twiddle his thumbs, or whatever else it is that he can still twiddle."

Everyone laughed.

Josh took a deep, enjoyable breath.

This was going to be a fun weekend for everyone.

They might even talk about the war before it was over.

Author's Note

✜

The true story: During the preinvasion bombing of the Italian islands in early June 1943, an American fighter pilot made an emergency landing with a P-38 on Elmas airdrome outside of Cagliari, Sardinia. Before the pilot could set fire to the aircraft, Italian troops dragged him from the twin-engined Lightning. A colorful Italian fighter ace stared at the P-38 and came up with an idea: leave the markings intact and shoot down straggling Allied bombers. Mussolini himself quickly approved the plan, and the story on which this novel is based swung into action with incredible success. An American B-17 pilot who survived one such kill reported the incident and was selected to seek out and destroy the unknown enemy. A YB-40 was brought in from England, but the select crew was unable to find the renegade P-38 until intelligence discovered the Italian pilot's identity and the fact that he had a wife living in North Africa. The American pilot got a picture of her, and an air corps artist actually painted a sexy picture of her on the YB-40. *High Noon* over Sardinia was the final scene as the two pilots met head-on one day.

Dr. Ferdie Pacheco, the "Fight Doctor" of TV fame, encountered the story sometime in the early seventies and wrote a film treatment. A Civil War buff, he was fascinated by Robert Skimin's novel *Gray*

285

Victory, the alternative history in which the South has won the war. One night he called Skimin from his home in Miami, and a friendship was begun. In El Paso to broadcast a fight, he convinced Skimin that the P-38 story would make a compelling novel and that he could sell the story to Hollywood for a movie.

Among the many coincidences involved in writing this story, one stands out. During the research of U.S. Air Corps units in North Africa, Skimin arbitrarily picked the 97th Bomb Group as the American pilot's organization. Little did he realize it was the same bomb group that was the basis for one of his all-time favorite movies: *Twelve O'Clock High.*

About the author

Robert Skimin, a former army aviator and bestselling novelist, is the author of the award-winning *Chikara!* and the critically acclaimed *Gray Victory*. Residing in El Paso, Texas, for many years, he is a native Ohioan whom the *San Diego Union* has described as "a masterful storyteller."

About the author

Dr. Ferdie Pacheco is the famous "Fight Doctor" of TV boxing. He is also a TV movie critic and book critic who has become a successful artist as well. An entertaining storyteller, he has written movie scripts as well as books. He resides in Miami.